SPEED
OF LIGHT

other books about meridian

MERIDIAN

WILDCAT FIRELFLIES

SPEED OF LIGHT

AMBER KIZER

delacorte press

Text copyright © 2012 by Amber Kizer
Jacket art copyright © 2012 by Chad Michael Ward

All rights reserved. Published in the United States by Delacorte Press, an imprint of Random House Children's Books, a division of Random House, Inc., New York.

Delacorte Press is a registered trademark and the colophon is a trademark of Random House, Inc.

Visit us on the Web! randomhouse.com/teens

Educators and librarians, for a variety of teaching tools, visit us at RHTeachersLibrarians.com

Library of Congress Cataloging-in-Publication Data
Kizer, Amber.
Speed of light. / Amber Kizer. — 1st ed.
p. cm.
Sequel to: Wildcat fireflies.
Summary: Meridian and Tens continue to grow closer and explore their relationship of Protector and Fenestra, while sixteen-year-old Juliet Ambrose, grasping at any hope of finding her parents, considers accepting the help of Ms. Asura, a proven Nocti.
ISBN 978-0-385-74114-9 (hc) — ISBN 978-0-375-98428-0 (ebook) —
ISBN 978-0-375-98987-2 (glb)
[1. Angels—Fiction.   2. Supernatural—Fiction.   3. Death—Fiction.
4. Good and evil—Fiction.]
I. Title.
PZ7.K6745Spe   2012
[Fic]—dc23
2011044331

The text of this book is set in 12.5-point Apollo MT.

Book design by Angela Carlino

Printed in the United States of America

10 9 8 7 6 5 4 3 2 1

First Edition

To Barney Wick:

GODFATHER
UNCLE
FRIEND
RACE FAN
HAND-HOLDER
CHEERLEADER
CONFIDANT
BELIEVER.

I love you.
Semper Fi.

If I die it is but a part of some vast Life which does not cease with the last breath.

—Keith Green

I cannot say, and I will not say
That he is dead.—He is just away!
With a cheery smile, and a wave of the hand,
He has wandered into an unknown land. . . .
Think of him still as the same, I say:
He is not dead—he is just away!

—James Whitcomb Riley, "Away"

Every morning lean thine arms awhile on the window sill of Heaven and gaze upon the Lord. Then, with that vision in thy heart, turn strong to meet the day.

—Unknown

SPEED
OF LIGHT

PROLOGUE

What if a young woman was both a girl to the living and a portal to the dying? I know the answer because I am. Look at me. If you see a girl on the edge of womanhood with shoulder-length curly brown hair and features tilting more classic than trendy, then congratulations—you are *alive*. If you see light, as if I am standing in front of the sun, then say your goodbyes—your time is coming. If all you see is light, you're moving on, dead, and probably not coming back.

We are Fenestra, human beings made angel Light by those of the many names and faces. Just as recessive genes emerge unexpectedly, bringing forth red hair and green eyes to a brown-haired, brown-eyed couple, the angel genes that constitute a Fenestra stay hidden until the right baby, the right family, and the right generation. We appear human to the living; to the dying we are Light. We are windows to the afterlife, shepherds of all life's energy.

Before there were presidents and kings, before there were religions and sciences, before history books were written and the dinosaurs roared, there was Light and her companion, Dark. Day and night. Positive and negative. Beginning and end. Neither existed without the other.

We call this source-light the Creators. You may call it God, Allah, Buddha, Fate, science, Yahweh, or the Way. It answers to many names and has many forms and followers.

I answer to Meridian Sozu. My first name belonged to my great-aunt Meridian Laine Fulbright. Auntie taught me all she could in the few sunrises between my sixteenth birthday and her death. And my last name, Sozu, belonged to my father, who is out there somewhere, hiding with my mother and little brother. Hiding from me and from the Aternocti who hunt me. The Aternocti are the Dark who extinguish the Light. My light. Your light. Any and all energy can be hijacked by them. They kill innocents easily, without remorse.

My destiny was set in stone at my birth, on December twenty-first, at midnight, on the winter solstice when I entered this world, carrying forth my family's lineage. I was not just a girl born into a family who carried Fenestra genes, but I was also a girl who could change the course of death, a girl who could shelter a soul and pass it back to the Creators, back to the Light.

I found Juliet Ambrose, a sister of the Light, with the help of my soul mate, Tens Valdez. Aided by a fledgling coalition of humans who chose to follow good and thwart evil, we pushed back against the Nocti with a small victory. Juliet's destiny began on March twenty-first, the spring equinox. We survived Juliet's transition from a Fenestra girl to full Window on her sixteenth birthday. Much like Auntie did with me, I taught her what little I knew in the hopes she wouldn't be pulled across. She made it through. Barely. But her already wounded heart continues to bleed for the family she doesn't know and for the children of Dunklebarger who she was unable to protect from the Nocti. I lose more sleep over her future than I do over my own. I have Tens. She seems lost and unwilling to trust. Angry beyond reason.

Hard to imagine that only five months before this, the Nocti wanted me dead and Juliet's light turned into darkness. Preying upon greedy, entitled humans, the Nocti built a machine of oiled precision that tested children for Fenestra genes and forced their obedience. The torture and sacrifice of children without families was hidden from the world by a "charitable" institution by the name of Dunklebarger Rehabilitation Center. Here the children were housed until the Nocti were able to ascertain whether they were only human or part angel as well. We are still trying to find all the generations of children who were killed or who disappeared, in the hopes of finding more of us alive. Auntie told me Fenestras who aren't transitioned by other Fenestras are lost to the world. We need to find them all, any souls the Nocti didn't drag down into the void. Each person who lives needs love. In a world where love is harder and harder to find, this new mission layers upon our duties to the dead.

Throughout, the one thing the Nocti didn't count on, that they couldn't begin to understand, was the bond formed between good people. The radiation of heart-lights united in common purpose reflects greater in the darkness than anything man-made ever can. Together we'd proven formidable. We'd broken the Nocti reign at Dunklebarger, DG, and a Creator's tornado did the rest of the demolition. We'd held off Ms. Asura and wounded her. *But we all know she's still out there.*

Tens is my Protector and was described by Auntie as a rare gift, a soul mate who has always known my feelings, even when miles separated us. I don't have to lie to him about being a Fenestra. At some point we're supposed to be able to communicate without words, but so far that hasn't happened. Human in all other regards, he's got my back; we're each other's sidekicks, not halves of one soul but amplifiers of each other.

We're joined by creatures of the Creators. A wolf-dog named Custos, her name meaning "guardian," is Tens's best friend. She's been with him since he trekked from Seattle to Revelation to find Auntie. Custos comes and goes as she pleases, doesn't eat much, and seems to give her opinion in tail wags and tongue licks. It's clear I'm lower on the ladder than she is, at least in her mind. On the journey as well is a long-haired, short-tempered Maine coon named Minerva, or Mini. Minerva is named for the goddess of knowledge, and her expression says it all.

Mini arrived at Dunklebarger months before we did. She kept Juliet going, easing the ache of souls using Juliet's window without her knowledge. Mini saved Juliet's sanity, and maybe her life, more times than I care to count. She is the Fenestras' creature and favors Juliet over me. I'm waiting. She'll like me. Eventually.

But since our battle at Wildcat Creek, the Nocti are quiet and invisible. *Evil never gives up.*

Auntie gave me a journal in which each generation of my family's Fenestra had written their experiences and pieces of our puzzle down for the next. Its cover is made of thick, cracking leather, embossed with all things alive. The penmanship is tiny and cramped. But I read it. Tens read it. We decipher more daily. Looking for ways to fully defeat the Nocti. To free Juliet's mother, Roshana, who seems trapped at the window. To help ourselves.

If the writings of my ancestors are any indication, Ms. Asura, a Nocti and Juliet's bogus social worker, will be back. Stronger. Determined. And bringing her own contingent of soldiers. It is only a matter of when, where, and what they'll exploit.

How many innocents will die before we stop them?
If we stop them.

CHAPTER I

A carpet of violets rose beneath our feet, dancing to the tune the May winds strummed. Cherry trees lifted pink petals in offering. Paved paths wide enough for cars wound around the grassy hills, linking one section to another. Stone guardians and perpetual mourners of all sizes populated each plot. Benches made of granite but fashioned like tree limbs invited the weary to rest awhile. Whole tree trunks of limestone towered above, twined with ivy, calla lilies, and anchors. Up on a hill, sturdy stone monuments belonging to prominent families overlooked the best view of the Indianapolis skyline. Below us, an angel with unfurled wings held her hands out in invitation, her eyes closed as if she, too, saw beyond this life and into the next.

Cemeteries were my universal comfort place. I'd learned over the last five months that any burial place felt safe. In Colorado or here in Indiana. Wherever we went next, I knew I'd find the same peace at burial grounds. Their irrefutably homey feeling filled my heart with quiet contentment. Standing in Riverside Cemetery picking out two lots in section forty-six, one for Auntie's grave marker and one for Juliet's mother, Roshana, I wasn't sure if I felt this safe because of all the dead or because the living worked so hard not to forget them. There, surrounded by monuments of draped obelisks and marble lambs, my grip relaxed. Maybe it was because the only souls coming to me were long since deceased and knew exactly what they were doing. Or maybe any earth dedicated to memories and the past was my temple, my church, my sacred ground—I didn't know, didn't question.

"Earth to Merry?" Tens brushed my hand with a half smile and a teasing glint in his eyes. "You okay?" His lips, too full and pink to be masculine, added to the beauty of his face and contrasted with his rugged, razor-sharp cheekbones and strong jaw.

I knew what those lips were capable of and my stomach knotted a silent answer. I'd like to lock us in a room, simply the two of us, pause the world so I could stop worrying, stop thinking, stop being a Fenestra and just be a girl in love with a boy. Just for a moment or two.

"Here comes Rumi," I said as our giant friend, whose

heart was larger than his frame, marched toward us beside the cemetery's sexton. Rumi blew glass, acted like a self-appointed human watchdog, and threw around rare, antiquated words the way most of us said stupid things like *cool* and *sick*. His bald head was offset by a multicolored and intricately braided beard, his eyes sparkling with ever-ready laughter and capable of seeing the world painted in vivid colors.

"Merry?" Tens frowned at my half answer. He took his job of Protector seriously, even when I didn't need him to. Was it possible to balance being entwined without being smothered? If only we could share thoughts without words, like we were supposed to. Protectors didn't seem to have angel genes, but when paired with the right Fenestra, they shared memories and experiences from a very early age. In the beginning, Tens's uncanny ability to feel what I felt unnerved me. Now I found comfort in not being alone. However, that didn't mean I needed him to take care of me. I might not have superpowers, but I wasn't helpless. I wouldn't diminish myself to placate his sometimes overbearing sense of duty.

I snorted. In short, we were still working out the kinks in our relationship. "I'm fine. Just breathing." Rumi brought me to this cemetery on a whim before the Feast of the Fireflies to visit his mother's grave. We'd found grave markers chiseled with windows, like ones I saw shifting souls to the other side. They were also reiterated in the artwork Rumi's ancestors passed down.

I hadn't noticed the trees in February, but now the

leaves unfurled like sails in late-spring breezes heading toward summer; it was as if the trees, too, had stories to share. The gentle wind whispered over us, raining petals and rustling the violets.

I glanced over at Tens. To think we were connected, entwined, destined to be together blew my mind. He was taller than most men, and his shoulders used to be straight planks and right angles but now subtly curved and rounded. His legs ate up the ground beneath him with the grace of rushing water—purposeful, intense, impossible to refuse. His deep black hair was shot through with shades of blue and purple and rust as the sun struck it. Forever too long, it fell over his ears and winged eyebrows, into his eyes. Eyes that appeared black, too, but flecked with a rich coffee brown, his pupils and irises blended. And it was as if he saw things most people missed. Maybe he did, not because he was a Protector, but because he was awake and aware of the world around him. He listened with every cell, every breath, knew the intention of every word of the people around us.

Rumi's booming voice carried on the breeze. His odd accents and vocabulary made watching conversations with him a spectator sport. No one knew half of his words; I figured out the context and tried to look them up later. "Lass, this is Thomas. Are you sure this be the spot for your cenotaphs, your empty graves?"

"Merry, you're sure you want to do this?" Tens leaned down into my face, cupping my cheeks. His breath was flavored by the cinnamon gum he preferred.

"Yes, they need stones and we need earth to visit." Auntie's remains had been in her house in Revelation when Perimo and the Nocti burned it down. If there was anything left, we had no idea when, or if, it would ever be safe enough to return there. She taught me that Fenestras are finite—if a Fenestra dies and isn't transitioned by another Fenestra, then they are lost to the world. Which is a very good reason for the Nocti to hunt us to change or kill us. I'd helped Auntie over the window, but she couldn't go to the Light beyond. She seemed stuck and the only thing we'd been able to figure out was her bodily remains weren't marked, weren't rested.

So although I could only mark ground for Auntie, we hoped to find Juliet's mother, Roshana, somewhere nearby. *Please be where we can find you.* I feared Juliet would never relinquish the tight hold on her grief if we were unable to bury Roshana's remains. It was as if Juliet couldn't hold on to her actual mother, so instead she clung to the pain of not having a mom. Roshana had been taken by the Nocti, probably by Ms. Asura, years ago, and we had no idea where she might be buried, or if she was at all. "I won't be back to Revelation soon to bury Auntie near Charles, and Juliet's mother was a local, right? It makes sense to mark this ground, where Rumi's family rests, before more time passes."

We knew Rumi ordered plain stones for his family; mysteriously, the suspected Fenestras and Protectors had been re-marked with much more elaborate stones. We hoped to lure whoever was responsible for changing the grave markers into the open. *Who are they? Can they help us find more Fenestra? Assist us in uncovering Juliet's father's identity? Why change the stones? Did it keep the Nocti from desecrating the remains of Fenestra, or were they mere decoration?*

I rubbed my aching forehead. *Too much thinking. Not enough knowing.*

"This is only a tittle away from where my family's plots are." Rumi stroked his massive beard, today decorated with blue glass beads, and wiped his head free from sweat with an embroidered handkerchief. The late May weather was proving hot, unpredictable, and fickle.

I followed Rumi's finger toward the gravestones of his generations. Granite window casings, swords, and foreign markings we didn't recognize graced the ground. When they'd arrived and who carved them remained unknown. If they were Fenestra, or Nocti, or simply tied to us was part of the mystery. *It would be easier to list the few things we know about us, rather than keep track of all the questions.*

"I agree," Tens offered, tipping his head to the right in a movement so slight neither Rumi nor the sexton saw it.

Custos, with her honey-and-molasses-tipped hair, hid her bulk behind an oak tree heavy with cascading flowers and poked her snout around to stare at us. Part wolf, part dog, and part divine-something-or-other, her lips curved and tail wagged. She seemed unusually pleased with herself.

I chuckled, slipping my hand into Tens's. My finger-tips tingled with the heat and strength he provided my soul like air for my lungs. *If cemeteries are a safe place for me, Tens is my home.*

"It's done, then. If you'll sign here?" Thomas held the paperwork out to Rumi for his signature and marked the two plots with wooden stakes and laminated numbers.

Today wasn't only about closure; this might aid in solving the mystery. Calculating the risk, we'd decided to order plain stones, similar to the ones Rumi picked out originally. I hoped that by ordering plain headstones we might flush out whoever, or whatever, knew to put the special Fenestra headstones and footstones on the graves. Was it some sort of heavenly magic, or were there humans behind it? We needed knowledge, information, anything to add to our collective. The headstones delivered anonymously matched the drawings in his mother's belongings and many of my visions at the window.

"Would you please be punctilious and let me know exactly when the stones'll be delivered?" Rumi asked Thomas.

"Sure. I'm on it, Mr. Rumi. Not a problem. Let me just note it here." The sexton wandered off alone back toward his golf cart.

Rumi turned to me. "I'd like to take a rubbing of the words, send it to a friend at the university to give a dekko, a look, at 'em. See if she can tell us what language is carved into them."

"Is it worth the risk?" Tens questioned.

"I trust her. Besides, whatever is written here is on stones for all the world to see, not in an abditory, a secret place."

"That's a good point," I agreed, tucking my shoulder-length curls behind my ears. They no longer wilted when I transitioned the dead, and I'd given up hiding behind wild hair colors.

"Rumi, we're going to be late to your own meeting." Tens checked his watch. "You willing to tell us what it's all about now?"

"No." Rumi grinned.

CHAPTER 2
Juliet

I popped the pits out of cherries like squashing beetles.
Pop! Pop! Pop!

Is it possible to burn up and freeze over at the same time? I alternated between stoking the fires of rage and revenge and wishing for the pure oblivion of cold. *Here's your mother's book, but you can't read it. Here's your long-lost father figure, but he still sees you as a five-year-old with pigtails and a sweet tooth for butterscotches. Here's a new life, but it's not normal. No, it's nothing like the stories you imagined, but what is? Here's the boy who loved you come back to take you away, but he died trying to save you. Here are new friends who want you to be fine. FINE. And the dead don't go away. Oh, no, who wants the dead to go away?*

I grabbed a peeler and started on the rhubarb strings. I felt each tug and pull as if they were a part of me, as if I were flaying skin. But I kept peeling.

Here's a happy ending for your littlies, for Bodie and Sema. Here's a perfect family, but they have to go far away for the summer. Away from me? Because of me? I couldn't see them. Couldn't protect them. Didn't know if they were being watched or threatened. Who would protect them from *her*?

Who will protect me from *her*? Because she's back. *I feel her.* The way Meridian talked about feeling that reverend, the way Tens said he knew Ms. Asura wasn't just my social worker but also evil.

I yanked a knife out of the chopping block and diced the rhubarb so fine it would melt into the custard and mix with the sugary egg.

I'm FINE.

Here's a disk of music to a movie that was important to your mother. But why? Nah, you don't need to know that.

Here's your mother at the Window, but she can't speak. Can't hardly move with her dimpled skin and scars, but don't worry about her—she's fine.

Here's a pretty pink room tied up with a bow and a dazzle of chocolate sauce, but you don't get to feel safe in it unless you sleep in the closet. You're fine.

I sifted flour into a ceramic bowl so big and heavy

that babies could use it as a bathtub. Using two paring knives, I cut the icy butter into the flour so fine it formed tiny pearls. Dunking ice cubes into a bowl of water, I stirred then dribbled it into the butter and flour until dough formed.

Breathe, Juliet, breathe. I wanted to hit the ball of dough on the counter until it flattened, submitting itself. But piecrust never worked well with anger; it preferred a cool head and a steady, firm hand. These wouldn't be the best crusts of my life. I'd be happy if no one noticed at dinner tonight.

"Anything else?" Tony marched in laden with bags of ingredients I'd asked him for. "You sure you don't want to go yourself?" he'd asked.

"No." I paused. "No." If I began listing all the things I'd never done in my life, it would sound as if I were three hours old and still blinking at the bright lights. *Only babies aren't afraid of every little thing.*

"Can I help?" Tony hesitated, staring at me, wanting something from me.

If I knew, if I could give him what he needed, I would, but he simply stood there unblinking.

Without waiting for me to answer, he poured himself coffee. "Have you seen Mini lately? She hasn't been around much. Maybe if we could have stayed home, she'd be in the kitchen with us."

No, I don't know where my cat is. She's gone most of the time. I shook my head. We couldn't stay there. I felt eyes there. And here, at Rumi's studio, I could look for clues.

He nodded. "So is there something I can—"

"I need garlic," I interrupted, hoping he'd stop talking.

He set the mug down. "But I just came from the store and—"

"And Saigon cinnamon."

"Don't you have cinnamon there?" He pointed toward the overflowing spice rack Rumi kept adding to.

"Not the right kind." I shook my head, pressing the dough into the tin, pinching the sides up so the juice stayed in.

"Oh." He looked so disappointed I almost relented. Almost shrugged it off. But she'd be back and she'd want to know what I'd found. And if I didn't give her something, she'd hurt him. So much worse than my words ever could.

I slid a pie onto the oven rack. With my back toward Tony I frantically blinked back tears. He couldn't see me cry. He'd want to know why. He'd want to help. *He can't help; no one can help me.*

"You need these for this meal? Now?" Tony crossed his arms. I could tell by the way he worked the rosary beads that I tried his patience. I didn't know why he stayed around. He didn't deserve this, but I couldn't stop it, couldn't take it back. *If only he'd never found me, he'd be okay. They'd all be okay.*

"Why don't you come with me? Show me what you want?" he asked.

"No. You know. There's a pie in the oven."

"You have to go someday."

"Meridian's going to take me."

He brightened at the idea that Meridian might spend more time with me. I knew he wished he'd inherited her instead of me. "I'll return in a few. They'll be back in a few hours."

Meridian decided my mother needed a grave marker. Meridian decided to ask Rumi to help her. Meridian decided. Meridian decided. Meridian decided.

I waited until Tony was gone and wiped my hands on the towel. I started in the studio itself. The colors of the glass sparkled like candies and rock sugars. The Spirit Stones glowed, happy to see me, unaware they shouldn't be, because everything around me shattered, spoiled. I touched one globe threaded with rays of pomegranate and concord, bits of blueberry and currants spun around the tree trapped inside. *This one is mine.* I tucked it in my bag and headed for Rumi's desk.

Breathe, Juliet, breathe. Like the pie dough, snooping required cool hands and a calm mind. I chewed my lip until I tasted blood. *Rumi's forgetful. He'll never even notice anything is gone.* A few notes, nothing I could read easily. Piles of books covered by sheets. Sheets of numbers. *Nothing.*

Heading down the hallway, I pinched myself on the wrist for wavering above the trunk he kept in his bedroom. A treasure chest from all his trips around the world. That's what he'd called it when I'd asked about it last month. Like he had no secrets. Nothing to hide. *Unlike me.*

I lifted the lid. The top was filled with snapshots. People I recognized from Valentine's Day, St. Patrick's Day, Easter, and Passover. Any excuse for a party. For a meal together. Meridian was outlined and barely visible. I was a pure blob of washed-out white. A Fenestra thing. *We control our ability and we get to be immortalized on film.* Or so they say. Meridian swears she saw photos of her Auntie—the only other Fenestra we knew about, except maybe my mother. *Maybe I have an Auntie somewhere, too? If I do, all the more reason to find something to give HER.*

More photographs of Rumi's friends, elders like him who dished out stories the way I added salt to mashed potatoes.

I shifted through until my hands felt the old scaly leather of a portfolio. I lifted it out; tears ran down my cheeks. How do I betray my friends to save them? Or refuse and let her mete out punishment. *They are innocent. I have to protect the innocent.*

CHAPTER 3

The car ride back to Rumi's glassblowing studio and living space in Carmel's Art and Design district was quiet, save for Custos. Her butterscotch haunches took up most of the backseat, while her tongue and jowls painted drool pictures on the glass. She was a two-hundred-pound goofball, and I wondered if we were wrong and she simply was an odd dog and not a creature of the Creators. *Given a choice, wouldn't they pick a more stately and elegant messenger?*

Rumi's industrial warehouse, on the corner of Meridian and Main Streets, was divided into a studio for his whimsical rainbow of glass creations and a monastic living area behind it. The Nocti attack during the Feast of the Fireflies shattered and ruined much of his inventory. He'd built his stock back up with the usual tchotchkes and pretties, the practical dinnerware, and the giftware of platters and frames. To us, his most important work was the Spirit Stones. An ancient indicator often called Witch Balls, they lit up in the presence of Fenestra and darkened around Nocti.

If the constant stream of customers was any indication, the busy summer season, which typically began on Memorial Day weekend, started two weeks early this year. I often manned the counter at Rumi's shop, watching him work. His hands gracefully spun, expertly crafting the glass, seemingly without his head and heart giving input.

When we arrived, Custos disappeared into the trees and brush along the paved Monon Trail. The Spirit Stones, hanging from the rafters and hooks under the eaves, glowed brightly as I walked under them. Rumi's had become our main gathering place.

"Thank you for coming early, Tony, Juliet," Rumi greeted us as he swept in from checking on the front. I think he felt as if he could make Juliet trust him by immersion. He shouldn't take it personally. I wasn't sure she trusted any of us. *Not really.*

"Did they have a choice? You insisted." I grinned.

In the kitchen, Juliet chopped vegetables. She was tall, and her frame was sturdy, which gave an insanely capable and responsible air to her sixteen years. However, in many ways, I felt like she was a middle-aged toddler—so burdened by life's hardships and yet completely clueless about the current world. Her blond hair bleached more each day as she spent time outside, secretly, at her creek. She thought we didn't know where she disappeared to, but DG and the Wildcat Creek drew her back. Whether she found comfort there or was doing a weird kind of penance, I didn't know. We made progress and lost ground at almost the same rate.

The air was fragranced with sautéing onions and garlic, baking bread, and cooling pies. I wondered which souls' memories were on the menu tonight. Auntie quilted the soul dust off; Juliet's talent was food. When a soul transitioned through her, Juliet picked up a highlight reel of tastes and recipes from the soul's life. I hadn't yet figured out my own way to deal with the soul dust—quilting made me bleed, and I was barely capable of nuking leftovers in the microwave. I'd taken to carrying a notebook in my pocket to jot down words and reflections. I continued to doubt what my talent for soul dust might be. The best I could do were words and stories.

Tony, a former priest and Juliet's legal guardian, washed dishes piled around the sink. He'd known Juliet's mother, Roshana, and given her sanctuary before the Nocti kidnapped them both and placed Juliet at DG. He carried the guilt of those years in his whitened hair and the lines around his eyes.

"Have you been here long?" I asked, hugging hellos.

"She woke early this morning needing to make six kinds of pie." Tony smiled toward Juliet and pointed at a stack of old books on the table. "I brought reading." The soft strains of Irish folk ballads floated in the background. Pies of cherry, peach, sugar cream, and pecan lined the counter. The crusts were flaky and perfect. I knew she'd done it all by hand, even the tiny pastry birds on the top of the cherry pies and branches on the peach.

"Are you going to tell us why Rumi insisted we meet early?" I asked.

"Nope." Tony grinned. "His show."

I shrugged and snagged an extra piece of dough Juliet covered in butter and sprinkled with cinnamon and sugar before baking. *Heaven in a bite.*

We'd settled into a rhythm of weekly dinners together, mostly on Sunday afternoons and evenings.

"Can I help?" I asked Juliet gently. I might very well cut off a finger, but I would do anything to get her to open up to me. Anything at all.

Juliet shook her head no, her braid swishing down her back. "I've got it." Unfortunately, she continued to skitter like a shy wild animal around us. Occasionally, I glimpsed strength and reasoning in her that Auntie would be proud of. However, her anger simmered below the surface, ready to boil again. She needed time and routine. And her Protector. *Does she have one?* I grinned at Tens, who listened intently to Rumi's meandering story. *What would I do without Tens?* Before Tens, I had been as lost and angry as Juliet.

I grabbed a specialty Stewart's grape soda out of the

fridge, holding one out to Juliet as well. We loved grape anything. Rumi preferred his food in glass containers, so I didn't have the heart to tell him cans of grape Faygo were easier to stock and were tastier. *Artificial grape goodness, the more purple the better.*

I know Rumi and Tony believed they were educating us, but mainly they entertained us with their antics. We counted on these family dinners to continue building our relationships and to share news. They'd grown into recitation times of stories and poems, each of us trying to outdo the others with our theatrics and selections. Tony and Rumi took their job as self-appointed mentors to new levels. The two now leaned toward each other over a flattened map.

"Juliet, can you come out of the kitchen? Join us? We need to chin-wag, talk," Rumi called, his voice serious.

About what? I glanced at Tens. His expression was as confused as mine.

Juliet's comfort level visibly dipped as she dropped next to me on the couch. When Custos brushed the swinging door open and Minerva marched in beside her, I knew we were embarking on a potentially scary conversation. *They only show up for serious business.*

At Tony's nod, Rumi said, "We've been expatiating about your futures. We think you children need to have a perdurable, an everlasting, education."

"We are not going to high school." Horrified, I shrank back at the thought. "You can't possibly think—"

"You can't make me." Tens crossed his arms.

Juliet simply paled further, withdrawing against the sofa.

Tony held up his hands. "No rioting. Just hear us out." He motioned for us to relax.

I wasn't the only one perched on the edge of my seat ready to bolt. *High school? They've cracked up. The pressure is too much and they've lost their minds. I remember the uniform, the name-calling, the pinches and shoves.* Not a single pleasant memory of school lingered.

"We're not enrolling any of you at Carmel High School," Tony said, but his glance at Juliet seemed to say it wouldn't be a bad idea.

At least I'd had some school; she'd been ostracized her entire life, hidden away until she became a viable Fenestra. Her eyes flashed what seemed like a warning to me. *What?*

Rumi unrolled a long white parchment scroll and started tacking it up on his wall. Written in cursive and blocked with different colors of ink were names, dates, and acronyms. It was a timeline of sorts. "We don't mean you need to evolve into mathletes or cheerleaders."

I laughed. I couldn't help it. "Tens would make an awesome cheerman. Bottom of the pyramid?" *That's a picture!*

Tens sent me a scathing glance and replied, "I think quarterback, or striker, is more my style."

"In your delusional dreams, emo-wannabe-delinquent!" I teased him.

He nodded his agreement with a red face that had us

all laughing. Rumi stood back, quite pleased with himself. Tens's curiosity was both his strongest trait and his weakness. "What's that?" Tens walked over to the scroll, peering at the writing.

Rumi traced the chart with his finger, thrilled he'd snagged the interest of one of us. "This marks dates and any information we have on the girls and your kind. We had to be covert, in case anyone else saw it, so there is a text that matches the notations. We only used knowledge that's proven as truth, a priori."

Tony held up one of his old books; inside it hid a spiral notebook.

"Clever." The fake book was a dictionary from the nineteenth century. *Not gonna be stumbled over there. Unless Rumi needs more archaic words.*

Rumi continued. "But these are the Fenestras, Protectors, and Nocti we think we know about. The underlines are the for-certains. That's four."

"Four?"

"Meridian, Tens, Juliet, and your Auntie," Rumi answered. "We don't have confirmation yet that Roshana, Juliet's mom, was a Fenestra, right? Anything substantial?"

I shook my head. "I think she was, but I haven't figured out how, or why, she's disfigured or aging on that side of the window." *Big questions. Without easy answers.*

Tony smoothed Juliet's hair as if trying to reassure her with his touch. "What your Sangre Josiah told me has resonated in the months since." Josiah had visited Tony with messages and medicine that helped us temporarily defeat Ms. Asura. The Sangre were warrior angels higher up the chain than Fenestras, but Josiah wasn't forthcoming, so my understanding was frustratingly limited. "When I approached Rumi, he'd been thinking the same thing."

"Which part of Josiah's edicts are you referring to?" Tens asked before I could.

"Josiah said that united we're stronger," Tony answered.

Rumi agreed. "Part of uniting, of accreting together, is having as much knowledge as possible. It will help us stay resolute, be pertinacious."

"I've read Auntie's journal. It's like a jigsaw puzzle with a million pieces." My ancestors wrote cryptic bits and seemed to think they'd get around to writing the full stories later. They never did. Irritated, I continued. "We don't know anything concrete."

Rumi's eyes lit up with excitement. "But that's not true. We're assuming a lot of lack here. And we do know pieces. Don't you see? We don't know what we don't know. We need Cognoscenti."

Confusing much? I rubbed my temples.

"A who?" Tens asked, as if he followed Rumi.

Tony took over. "Rumi's right. We haven't examined what we know with fresh eyes and with people who bring more knowledge to the conversation. Even without Auntie's journal, there's plenty to study. Religions. History. People. Anthropology. Myth. Cultures. Dying practices around the world. We don't know which paths might lead us to more of you. Cognoscenti are experts. We need more in our coalition. To build strength with knowledge."

I shook my head. "I don't want to tell random people." *Besides, who would believe us?*

"I don't either." Juliet spoke up; her voice wavered until Mini jumped into her lap and rubbed on her face. Mini, the enormous cat who'd shown up at Dunklebarger, came and went as she pleased, but she soothed Juliet. She scratched me.

Rumi grabbed a pen and started writing topics, people's names. He'd introduced us to many of our current group. Joi owned the cottage we rented and Helios Tea Room in Carmel. She'd adopted two of Juliet's littlies from DG—Bodie and Sema—and taken them north to Wolf Lake for the summer. They needed to be kids. I knew it was hard on Juliet not having them around. She defined herself by shielding them. *Without the kids, she may feel useless.*

"We don't have to expand too far. Think about it. Of each of us who already know the truth, we have mavens. Tony understands many of the religions in the world. Nelli's fluent in law, psychology, and the social programs exploited by the Nocti. Joi knows the gossip and happenings of Carmel long before they're public. I know art and cultural customs."

Nelli worked for the state's attorney general investigating abuses in the child services division. She'd taken it upon herself to uncover the truth of Dunklebarger and find all the missing kids, dead and alive, who had gone through there over the years. She was also the niece of Gus, Rumi's best friend and retired history professor from Butler.

Rumi continued. "Faye knows music. She plays and teaches many instruments. Gus knows Indiana and world history from teaching it for years at the university. Each of us has a talent, an expertise that will benefit the cause if we utilize ourselves fully." He finished listing the people he'd introduced us to months ago.

"And there's your Auntie's journal, which Tens began transcribing and sharing with us. There are generations of experts."

I swiveled my head toward Tens.

He kissed my cheek.

"That's what we mean by education. The curiosity of this life takes on a more relevant importance to us, to your safety, your duty. We wouldn't be doing our best as elders if we didn't suggest this. You don't have to study the usual things, only the parts of knowledge that may lend you an advantage." Tony appealed to me, then turned to Juliet and asked, "Why didn't any child at DG go to regular school?"

"To keep us away from people." She shrugged, her eyes cast down.

He nodded. "But maybe more importantly to control the flow of information?"

"Don't you know that old ditty that 'information equals power'?" Rumi asked me.

"We want to empower you." Tony leaned in.

"By making us do homework?" I asked.

"In part. Maybe. But we need you to buy in. You have to believe in knowledge as power, too, or us digging up resources is a waste of time."

"There will come a time when you'll know as much as we do."

"Sooner rather than later?" Tens asked Rumi with a wicked grin.

"Ah now, boy, careful there, don't be full of hubris!" Rumi chortled.

"But until then, we've set up a list of texts and resources. Then we'll come together and discuss our findings and what questions they lead us to—which will carry us on in the quest and so on."

Juliet raised her head from Mini's neck. "What if the Nocti start making trouble?"

"What about our duty to help souls?" I added.

"That won't get in the way. We're not trying to tie you to a chair and give you busy work. This will ebb and flow around the rest."

I squinted at the scroll. "I am so tired of not knowing what's next. Maybe even more tired of not knowing what I don't know." My brain twisted. "I'm in. If there aren't pop quizzes or tests." My mind wandered back to December and that final day of my old life, of real school with silly subjects and useless rules. *Who knew so much would change so fast?*

"The tests will be seeing if anything is applicable to

our fight, yes? Do we learn anything that uncovers Nocti? Gives us an advantage? Answers the questions about Roshana and the missing? Leads us to more Fenestra?"

"I'm in. I have pieces of my history, but not enough," Tens answered. "I'd love to meet another Protector."

We turned to Juliet, who'd grown quieter and more still the longer we'd talked.

"So?" I asked.

"I can't." Her eyes wide and filled with fear, Juliet practically vibrated where she sat.

CHAPTER 4

Now what?

"Why not? What's wrong?" I asked.

Agitated, she seemed to shrivel. "I can't . . . um . . . read."

"But you said Kirian taught you." Confused, I glanced at Tony. No way would he put her on the spot and embarrass her. Not intentionally. *He doesn't know. What else don't we know about Juliet?*

Tony prodded gently, "Juliet?" He reached out but she flinched away.

She inhaled and lifted her head. "He did. Basic stuff like labels, food, medicines for the littlies, but not books.

Not more than a word or two at a time. The words jumble and flip."

Tony and Rumi shared a look.

"What?" she demanded.

"Yeah, what?" I added at their hesitation.

Tony answered, "The words move around? You can't follow a line of text?"

Juliet shrugged.

"Maybe dyslexia. I wondered when you didn't touch the cookbooks I bought. And when you flipped through your mother's book of sonnets but didn't stay on a page long enough to read it all. We can conquer this," Tony said.

"We'll help you." No wonder she still seemed isolated and lonely. Roshana wrote in the margins of a book of sonnets she left with Tony to give to Juliet. *I wish I'd known sooner. I could have read Roshana's entries to her.*

Rumi patted her head. "That only makes weeting, knowing, all the more important."

Tony brushed his hand over hers. "There are lots of tricks we can try. But don't you see, kiddo? You get proficient at reading, with whatever tools it takes, and you grab back a piece of you that they took away. Claim your right to read anything and everything. Don't stay in the dark."

She sat straighter, uncomfortable with our scrutiny. I tried to take the focus of the conversation back. "I know I'm always bitching about not knowing what's coming. You really think studying will help?"

"Can it truly hurt, lass?" Rumi answered.

"Point goes to the old folks." Comically, Tens made an imaginary notation on the wall and broke the tension.

Rumi's guffaws filled the room, while Tony's laughter rocked his shoulders and whistled out his nose. Tens's face lit beautifully with his smile and warmed my heart. Juliet's giggles surprised her expression every time. My laughter hurt my cheeks and crinkled my eyes until they teared.

"Where do we start?" I asked after catching a breath.

"Since you're the only ones who've read the entire thing"—Tony passed out packets—"we start with Auntie's journal, Meridian's ancestors, and branch out from there. Anything new that jumps out at us we write up on this scroll; then we go in that direction."

Like a magician unveiling a rabbit, Rumi yanked a crisp white sheet off stacks of books piled against the wall. Minerva leapt to the top of them and cleaned her paws.

"Where did you get all of those?" I asked. So many new, old, and ancient spines jumbled together that it was like the contents of a library had been robbed and dumped here. *That is a lot of reading. What in the world did I agree to?*

"Retro, preread, bookstores in town."

I gaped at the sheer volume. "You expect us to read this much in a week?"

"Nah, I figure it'll take a month or two." He smiled, the beads on his braids clicking like crickets.

I was fairly certain there were more words there than

I'd read in my lifetime. *A month? He has to be kidding. A decade, maybe.*

We studied printouts of Auntie's journal—only fifty pages but the font and size made it a hell of a lot easier to read than the original, which was fading, spidery ink on onionskin parchment. I let Auntie's words wash over me.

> I met a man today. With one look, he seemed to know my heart was bursting with the pain around me. He plied me with spirits until I was too drunk to hold the tears in check. I ruined his uniform shirt and several hankies, but he never doubted me and what I do for the dying.
>
> Meridian Laine, 1943

> None of us operates alone. In a void of human relationships we lose our strength. Love is our power, our greatest gift. We must use that gift in all ways, at sickbeds, at workhouses, among the lowest of the humanity and among our extended families. Light burns brighter when shared in the darkness of fear.
>
> Linea M. Wynn, October 7, 1962

"We need to add all the writers in Auntie's journal to our scroll." There were generations of Fenestra dating back two centuries. Cassie Ailey, Lucinda Myer, Jocelyn Wynn, Luca Lenci, Melynda Laine, and so many more.

Rumi grabbed a pail of markers and handed it to me. "Please."

Tens and I began to make notes based on what we'd both read. "Do you know how you're related to these women?"

"We're going to have to sort it out." My mother never talked about her family, and Auntie focused on keeping me alive, not on genealogy.

When Juliet moved to the kitchen to finish preparing dinner, Tens called out to her, "Whose memories are we eating tonight?"

Juliet paused and nodded at an unseen audience. "Enid." She offered us Enid's favorites of roast bone marrow on toast, deviled eggs, beef and barley soup, broccoli strudel, Hoppin' John, creamed lemon chicken, and fresh sweet peas. Rumi's rustic wood table seemed to bow under the weight of its offerings.

Enid and her sister Glee were the last elderly patients at DG. Glee was killed by the headmistress, and Enid struggled to recover in the months following. Her death two weeks ago spawned Joi's decision to take the kids north and give them a summer vacation in a new place.

All of Juliet's meals felt more like life menus to me—as if each course of a person's life contained a certain flavor combination. What might have tasted like a hodgepodge of oddities blended seamlessly on our plates and in our stomachs.

Juliet and Tony laid platters of food on the table. The wisps of fragrance tickled my taste buds. I remembered a time when food hurt in my body and nausea was my closest companion. *So much change in so short a time.*

Tens mounded his plate and dug in as if it were his last meal for the season. His metabolism burned at nuclear levels; in an hour he'd eat another plateful.

"Tens's trenching with the right spirit. I'm eximiously esurient tonight myself!" Rumi spread a huge pat of butter on his bread and took a bite. Melting butter dripped down his chin. "Fantastical meal, Juliet me lassy!"

"Sorry I'm late." Nelli arrived carrying a cardboard box of files. Ever since she'd taken it upon herself to clear DG's storm cellar of its boxes of patient and kid files, I didn't think I'd seen her without some of it in her arms. Most files were moldy and water damaged and incomplete, with records dating back to the sixties. Her apartment became the sorting warehouse.

As a social worker and investigator for the state attorney general's office, Nelli seemed to feel a profound responsibility, as if she herself had failed these kids. We had told her the whole story soon after the destruction of DG. Partly because we knew she'd immediately begin searching for the missing kids and partly to enlist her help making sure the Nocti weren't doing this anywhere else in the state. It made sense to all of us to trust her. I can't say it was the easiest conversation, but it wasn't the hardest either.

"Rumi, may I speak with you?" Nelli disappeared back into the studio space. They returned a few minutes later looking ashen.

Rumi's expression heartbroken, he and Nelli whispered back and forth.

"What's going on?" I asked.

Rumi's brow furrowed and he didn't answer, so I turned to Nelli. *What's going on? Do they know something about Juliet's parents? The other missing children? The Nocti?* "No secrets, right? That's how this works." I sat down in a chair next to her. Tens pressed my shoulder. I knew he wanted me to back off, and politeness begged me to let it go.

"Share," I demanded.

Dinner over, Tony and Juliet began clearing up.

Tears brimmed along both Rumi's and Nelli's eyelids. I handed Nelli a box of tissues but pressed again, "What's going on? Is it Roshana?"

Nelli cleared her throat. "I request permission to inform Faye and Gus of your abilities." She sniffled as if holding back more than tears. "About your angelness."

I heard Tony and Juliet stop clanking around in the kitchen and join us.

Angelness? That's a new one. I nodded, keeping my face blank but open. *But that shouldn't make them look like their dog had been kicked.* "Okay, why?"

They seemed to freeze and shrink. Tens leaned in behind me, wrapping his arms around my waist and propping his chin against the top of my head. I motioned Tony and Juliet out of the kitchen and toward us.

"I'm sorry. I should have waited. You weren't even finished eating." Nelli's tears spilled over.

"It's okay—it'll reheat." Juliet tried to make it okay for Nelli. "Besides, I need to cook it, not eat it!" She gave Nelli a small smile. Once Juliet made a recipe, she could move on. Tony took many of her creations to the homeless shelter.

Tony sat down on the couch and gathered Nelli toward him in comfort. Juliet paused, poised to flee on the edge of the circle.

Nelli tried to pull herself together enough to get the words out but stumbled over the sounds, sobbing. Her freckles bled together in red splotches and her shoulders hunched low as if she were waiting to be kicked.

Rumi drenched his handkerchief, then used his sleeve. "Faye is sick. She has the malison malebolge, cursed hell pit, of cancer." He looked as though he might vomit.

Nelli heaved a breath and added, "It's terminal. It's everywhere inside her."

"Oh." I squeezed Tens's arms around me.

Nelli continued. "She doesn't believe in any god. Any after. Uncle Gus is going crazy to convince her to have hope and fight, but she won't. She thinks it's lights out and nothing more. She won't believe me when I tell her there's more to come; she's not enjoying anything!" Nelli's last words took on a tinge of hysteria.

"And you think if she knew about us that might help?" I quickly swallowed around my own grief. Faye was smart, funny, and quirky. I learned so much about being a woman when she was around. Another reason to do what Rumi and Tony wanted with their Cognoscenti schooling. *Expand the circle for ourselves but also to bring comfort to our friends.*

"I had nothing to do with this." Rumi held his hands out to me in supplication.

"I know." I quieted, searching my brain to make sure I wasn't missing a future ass-biter. *Telling another human is always a risk. A huge risk.*

Misconstruing my silence, Nelli knelt in front of me, pleading, "I'd like you to be there to aid her. If you can? I wouldn't ask for myself, but—"

I tugged her back up; the expression on her face made me very uncomfortable. *Where is the line? Will I know it when I see it? Is this my choice alone to make or is it a group decision?*

Rumi wiped his eyes. "If it's possible to be a Paraclete, a comforter, to Faye with this truth? No refusal from me. But I know Faye. And Gus. For years. They're rara avis, rare souls, and only good for our esprit de corps, our group spirit."

Tony and Tens nodded their agreement.

Juliet simply waited, looking to me for my approval or disapproval. When had I become the final say? "I—"

Nelli turned to me again. "When you explained Fenestras to me, you spoke of a duty to assist a soul's transition. Right? Don't you think peace beforehand is as much that duty as being the Window?"

She was right. Not only was I born to do this, but also I was called. Duty to the Light, to souls. If I'm to shepherd the world's souls who come to me, why not deliberately be available to people I know? *Isn't that what I did for Auntie? For Charles's spirit?* My duty extended to my friends. "I do. I actually do." But what if telling two more people backfired? How was I supposed to know who to tell and who to shield from us? I scanned the faces around me and knew they wanted this too.

Relief chased the shadows from Nelli's face. "Good, I'll go call them. I'm sure they can be here in time for dessert." She leapt to her feet.

"Now?" I gaped at the dizzying speed.

"We can't wait." Nelli paused, shredding tissues in her hands. "I don't think we can wait."

I hugged Tens's arms. He knew how hard it was for me to trust. Anyone. Even him. In a few short months, I'd gone from feeling alone and adrift with only conditional, judgmental anchors to being here with people who not only knew me, but also loved me. All of me. Even the hard parts. The parts that piled animal carcasses at our doors and windows.

I followed Juliet into the kitchen. "Are you okay telling Faye?"

She shrugged as she whipped fluffy clouds of cream in a bowl with a whisk. *Aren't there gadgets for that?*

I tried again. "You have a say."

"I don't." Her voice quivered.

"What do you mean?"

"It's you and Tens and your Auntie's words. Who am I?" Defeat saturated her words.

Surprised, I reached out. "Hey, where is this coming

from? You're my friend, my sister. You are important and I want to know what you think."

Her expression tortured and tired, she lifted her eyes. "Have you been around the dying? Not those ready to die, but those whose bodies are being eaten, ravished, by disease? People who can't let go?"

I swallowed. The pain in her eyes slashed at my heart. "No," I answered in a tremulous voice.

"It's the most powerless place in the world." Tears glistened in her eyes. "I would do anything, anything at all, to keep my family from that."

"Should we not tell her?"

"I'm not saying that."

"Then what are you saying?"

"I—" She broke off, shaking her head as Nelli walked into the kitchen and peered out the window.

CHAPTER 5

"Juliet . . ." I didn't want to end the conversation. *Talk to me!*

Gus drove the car into the alley as close to Rumi's glass doors as possible. I watched Tony and Tens help unload a wheelchair from the trunk.

"Is there hope?" Nelli asked me, standing at Rumi's back window, watching them unload and get situated. Gus lifted Faye out of the car and into the chair.

"I'm not clairvoyant, Nelli. I don't know," I said, trying to sound gentle and patient.

"But you see things."

"Only when the soul leaves the body. Only when it

tugs me toward the curtain between this and the next world." What I didn't say aloud was that my very human eyes saw a sallow, yellowing skin tone, white roots at the base of Faye's very fake red hair, and a stooped, crushed frame. *I don't need to see the future to predict this one.*

Rumi was our connection to Faye and Gus. We'd met them at a dinner party Rumi had held last February, partly to help us find Juliet and partly because that was what Rumi did—connecting the dots of the people around him.

This past year, Faye's headaches had kept Gus at her side and well away from the Nocti bombardment of the Feast of the Fireflies. The terrorist attack took many lives and sent ripples of fear through Carmel. I shuddered, remembering the carnage and chaos of that night.

We all exchanged embraces. I'd learned this group was demonstrative. I no longer flinched and even tried to awkwardly initiate the affection.

"Rumi, be a love and turn down the lights. I can't hardly make out the girls it's so bright." Faye's voice trembled over the words.

We stopped midmotion, deliberately avoiding eye contact. If she was seeing light instead of, or around, me, she was dying. It wasn't the sun or a lamp. *And it isn't her eyes that are the problem.*

Tens swiped his sunglasses from the table and gently placed them on her face. "That help?"

"I can see you fine. The girls are standing in front of the sun. Tell them to move." She patted Tens's cheek. "Let's just get this announcement over with. My lucky headache turned out to be cancer." Faye's graceful poise didn't allow her to slouch in the wheelchair, though she held her right hand down with her left to stop the tremors. Her brave face didn't betray any fear or wallowing. Gus took over, interjecting a false optimism that I called denial. "It's not as bad as it sounds. There's all sorts of things they can do. There's a leading medical research center right here in town. You have to listen to them and do what they tell you."

The *them* were doctors. Doctors who delayed death as long as possible but hadn't quite learned how to prolong life.

With a sigh, Faye argued with him. "Honey, I can't hold my violin. I can't see to read music. I can't even write my name. I'm not letting them poke me or poison me."

"But you enjoy watching your shows."

"Game shows and soap operas aren't enough." She whispered these last words.

Gus seemed kicked in the stomach. Gutted. He thought she was giving up. I understood the only thing Faye controlled here was how she handled dying, not whether she was.

"Marry me and I'll make sure they do what you want."

"Oh, Gussy, I don't need you to bear that responsibility." She shook her head. Her eyes gleamed while Gus, frustrated, sighed heavily.

I searched the faces around me. Juliet lifted her head and made eye contact. When she nodded yes to my unspoken question, Tony followed, then Rumi and Nelli. Tens leaned down and kissed the hollow between my neck and shoulder. His breath whispered over my skin and I nodded.

"Would you like tea or anything? We need to tell you something," I said to Faye.

"I'm not hungry. And I haven't seen you this serious since we first met. What's going on?"

"Gus, would you sit, please?" I asked.

Tens wheeled Faye toward the sitting area.

I perched next to her. "Faye, can you please close your eyes?"

"What?"

"Close them, please."

They drooped shut behind the dark lenses.

I needed to understand if she was seeing our light with something other than her eyes. Maybe her soul? If we darkened the room and she continued seeing light where no one else did, she might believe us. *Worth a shot to demonstrate.*

I held my hand out to Juliet, beckoning her over to me. Her hands were cool and damp and I felt her shiver a little as she extricated herself from my grasp quickly.

"Now what?" Faye asked.

"I'd like you to tell me when Rumi shuts off the lights. Okay? Tell me when he flips the switch."

"I'm confused. Why are we doing this?" Gus questioned.

"Bear with me," I answered.

Rumi cut the electricity and the lavender of twilight filtered through the curtains. There wasn't enough ambient light left to make out more than shapes.

"I'm not sure I'll know with the sunglasses on." Faye lifted a hand and pulled them down. "Okay, I'm ready. Is it those new fluorescent bulbs, Rumi? Why do you need it blazing like the sun in here?"

I counted to twenty-five.

"It's the cancer, isn't it? It's in her eyes? Her brain?" Gus's voice quaked.

I brushed my free hand across Faye's cheek, then tugged Juliet away from them. "Keep them closed until Tens tells you to open them, okay?"

Faye nodded.

I gripped Juliet's hand and headed for the long hallway toward the bedrooms and bathroom.

When we were behind Faye and had closed the first door, we heard her say, "Oh my, that's better. But you're sneaky—that's not all of them yet."

"Open your eyes, Faye," Tens mumbled.

"What's going on?" Gus sounded perplexed. "I don't understand."

Juliet stayed close to me as we reentered the room hand in hand.

Faye snapped the sunglasses back on. "Can we leave them off? I don't know why my eyes are so bad tonight."

Gus's voice dipped as he leaned down in front of her. "Sweet Tea, Rumi hasn't touched the light switches." He turned toward me. "Why does the light seem to belong to you? And why can't I see it?"

"Because Juliet and I are Fenestra. Angel-infused

humans who shift souls to the afterlife. We are the light for the dying," I explained.

"No, she's not dying!" Gus's chin wobbled and his voice, though a shout, cracked at the end.

"Yes, I am. What did you call yourself?" Faye asked when she could find her voice.

I could almost see her trying to digest this as truth. "Fenestra."

"Interesting. In many languages, a variation of that is the word for window," Faye said with her head cocked thoughtfully.

I nodded. "We came first, but yes."

"Do that go-away-and-come-back thing again." Faye waved her hand at us.

Juliet and I repeated the process several times, each time witnessing Gus and Faye's disbelief and confusion fade a little more.

"Like a sorority? A newfangled club? Why aren't you invited?" Gus asked Nelli.

"They're born this way, Uncle Gus. They're special." Nelli smiled through tears.

"You're special." He patted her knee. "You could do this too."

That's what families say to each other. Juliet's face was full of longing before she covered it with a bland expression.

Nelli giggled.

Faye said, "I have questions. Rumi, you know about this?"

"Yes."

"You've never lied to me. Never." She wagged her finger at him.

"No. I'm telling you straight."

"Angels appear in literature dating back millennia. We've talked about the nonfiction research about an afterlife before," Gus inserted.

"I never believed it." Faye's expression was considerate as she held out a hand to me. "And you're saying there's something beyond this life?"

"I know there is. I help people, and animals, find their way there every day. I know it's a lot to take in, but we have nothing to gain in telling you." *And maybe a lot to lose.*

"They be speakin' truth, my friends," Rumi said.

"I asked them to tell you," Nelli added.

"You knew?" Gus swiveled his head to meet her gaze.

"I did, but only after the tornado took down that terrible Dunklebarger place. I've been looking for more children like them."

"Meridian and Tens came here to rescue me. Us," Juliet said.

"And Tens? Are you a Fenster too?"

"I'm a Protector. I try to keep Meridian safe from—" Tens broke off. *How much to tell?*

"Don't stop now. Keep speaking your noumenon, your truth," Rumi insisted. "They can handle it."

"There are others called Nocti, Aternocti, who steal

souls from the Light. They're the ones who blew up the Feast."

"Not terrorists from a sandy land far away?" Gus gave a half smile. Unlike the public, he'd never thought the Feast of the Fireflies offered a big enough target to make any jihadist hit list.

"No, just evil."

Faye sniffed the air. "Do I smell rhubarb pie, or is that you too?"

We all laughed.

"And sugar cream." Juliet ran for the kitchen. Food was her language, her gift.

Faye wiped her eyes with a tissue and pronounced, "I think we should have dessert now and you should start at the very beginning. Suddenly I'm craving sugar."

Tony served tea and coffee while Juliet piled dessert plates with slices of oozing dark cream, slick glistening fruit, and marbled custard wrapped in flaky crusts.

I cleared my throat and began.

* * *

Late that night, tucked into the guest cottage behind the Helios Tea Room, Tens and I curled up together on the couch listening to his new favorite music. He said it reminded him of me. I lay on his lap, heart to heart. I measured my breaths to his. Inhaled with the rise of his chest and exhaled with the fall. Open windows welcomed the cool breeze. Crickets filled the night air with fiddles and clicks. The occasional car putted by and owls told knock-knock jokes up in the trees.

I wrapped my fingers around Tens's silky hair, tucked my head deeper beneath his chin, and kissed the pulse at the base of his throat.

He tightened his arms around my back, flexing. "Can't sleep?" he asked me in a throaty rumble I felt everywhere.

I shook my head. "Did we do the right thing telling them about us?"

"Faye and Gus? I think so." He smoothed my cotton tank top and tucked his fingers under the bottom hem, rubbing circles on my bare flesh. Goose bumps broke out along my arms. I held my breath, willing his hands to continue. We'd promised each other months ago we wouldn't stop when we were both ready to make love. I was ready. He kept stopping.

I leaned up, my lips touching his, melting indulgently together. He tasted of minty forest shadows. I shifted my position on his lap. He lifted his head; his lips placed a soft comma on our kiss.

"What are you thinking about?" I asked when he frowned.

"Juliet is unraveling. She's keeping secrets and spending too much time on her own."

I nodded. "Where's her Protector?"

"I don't know. I think if she has one, he'd have shown up by now, right? Especially in March for her transition?"

That is the worry. Sure, Fenestras through time made

54

do without Protectors. We didn't always have a match. Charles and Auntie were a good case—he wasn't a Protector but was simply a human who loved her and became her husband. They didn't communicate telepathically and he didn't know any of her feelings or experiences before they met. Auntie told us Tens and I were special. Us finding each other, sharing the destined bond we did— that was rare. Maybe it was selfish, but I wanted Juliet to have the same.

"Let's practice again," I demanded. *You will read my thoughts this time.*

"Again? I'm tired, if you're not."

"Please?" We'd started practicing telepathy. There were several journal entries that spoke of Fenestras and Protectors who managed to share thoughts and feelings. Since being together, Tens could only occasionally pick up on my feelings, and the random thoughts he grabbed were total coincidence. In his mind, all of my childhood seemed to have happened to him as simultaneously as reality.

I had to base my knowledge of him on the very human basics like words and body language. Even those I managed to muck up more often than not.

"Now, what am I thinking?" I asked.

He scrunched his eyes. "You're picturing a pink hippopotamus doing pliés on top of a giant pumpkin pie."

"Gee," I giggled. "How'd you guess?"

"I'm good."

"Full of it anyway." I ran my hand along his ribs,

finding his Eureka tickle spot. He bucked at me as our laughter spilled out around us. He flipped me over and straddled me, trying to pin my hands above my head. The lead singer belted out an impossibly high note that made my ears ring.

Ignoring us, Custos lay on the double bed, chewing on a piece of old tire she'd drug in from somewhere nasty. She insisted on gnawing the thing near my pillow.

A pounding at the door could have been anything but had Custos leaping to her feet with a low growl. Tens reached for the stereo remote and clicked off the music. Eerie silence invaded spaces left by the fading notes.

I rolled to my feet. "It's probably Juliet." I opened the door and glanced around before Tens had a chance to push me aside, to protect me from nothing. He'd stuffed his feet hurriedly into his boots, but I'd stayed barefoot.

Custos threw out a nasty, rumbling growl and brushed past me to march outside. She laid her ears back, lifting her guard hairs like she'd stuck her paw in an electrical socket. Behind her, Tens stepped in front of me.

My heart accelerated; my mouth cottoned. I huffed a breath. "I can't see anything. Probably Minerva messing with Custos's mind." *And mine.*

We'd been here since January. With each passing day, Tens became less a lanky young man and more a full-on muscled man. In another year, his body wouldn't be the same as the boy I met. It was like his frame finally figured out he needed to be built like a bodyguard rather than a swimmer on a restricted caloric intake. It didn't hurt that he ran and worked out as if he were training for the Olympics. *Actually, it aches a lot.* He was under the impression I needed to join him. I wasn't born an athlete and hated every minute of prepping. That was what he called it. *Prepping.*

He grunted in answer, his head on a full swivel. I half expected him to sniff the air.

"Tens?" I tried to shove him to the side, as my short stature made it nearly impossible to see around him. A piece of rope, or cable, on the doorsill caught my attention. I leaned down. "Tens!"

"Merry, be patient." As he stepped farther out, his soles crunched on something. *What?*

"You're standing on something." Quickly, I flipped on all the front lights.

"They broke Rumi's Spirit Stones." Colors of shattered glass littered the porch. Not a single orb we'd hung survived.

None of the pieces glowed, even as I picked them up. Their magic was gone. Some were slick with dark blood. "What's that?" I pointed to a piece of rope where he stood.

Memories of Perimo's followers flooded me. Perimo's Believers trashed Auntie's porch and left mutilated animals as warnings.

Tens moved off it as I bent down. "Don't pick it up—"

It was still warm, and I quickly realized it wasn't a piece of trash.

The roughly haired tail was pink as I held it up to the porch light. "It's a tail." Where the tail once attached to a body was jagged and bloody. "Someone yanked it off."

Dead rats often appeared at my doorstep, along with possum, bats, and feral cats. They, too, sought out my window to the Light. But none knocked, vandalized, or left bloody tails behind. My thoughts turned immediately to the Nocti. *Is this a warning like the desecrated animals Perimo left for Auntie in Revelation? Is it starting again?*

Tens reached for his knife. "Stay here."

Custos yapped and took off galloping down the street. In the distance, a cat's howl was abruptly silenced.

CHAPTER 6
Juliet

"Kirian, I can't understand you. What did you say? No, wait! Come back!" I awoke soaking wet with stinking sweat, repeating the same phrases over and over. "Come back. Come back." *Please come back. Let me save you.* My voice hoarse, my throat parched. Tangled in a nightshirt and sheets, I noticed the streetlights from Main shone brighter than a night-light. Tony's condo was within walking distance of Meridian and Tens in one direction and the littlies from DG, Bodie and Sema, in the other. He'd picked the location for me without my asking him to. *I wish he'd ask me what I want instead of assuming. Maybe I want to move to Sydney or Honolulu, nearer the turquoise water of my good dreams. Everything and everywhere here extends my nightmares.*

This bedroom (calling it "mine" tasted foreign) was much bigger than the closet, with its toilet paper and cleaning supplies, under the stairs at Dunklebarger. But while that felt like a cave, a den I escaped into, this one felt almost too abundant, too much, with its high ceilings and bright colors. *Who is the girl who lives here? She's not me.* Its saving grace, though, was all the food aromas drifting up from the restaurants on street level. The charred, grilling meat and the greasy coating of waffle-cut fries from the burger shop across the street. Or garlic and tomato, mixed with the baking crusts, of the pizza parlor downstairs. A doughnut and frozen custard place opened recently and woke me in the wee hours with the scent of hot coffee and frying dough. I knew hours, every day, based on the food whiffs in my room. There was a rhythm, a pattern. *By four a.m. I should be inhaling java and sugary glazes.* Food brought me comfort and did more to make me feel normal than any of Tony's reassurances and soft words. *Doesn't he realize that every time I look at him I am reminded of my dead parents? My unknown history?*

Tonight I woke confused and unsure of my surroundings. Kirian was in my dreams. *Again.* He was back, confiding secrets in this bedroom. A room starved of the usual smells of foodstuffs. Instead, clouds of cloying sandalwood and patchouli choked out any oxygen. Only its sickly spicy scent clogged my throat, making breathing nearly impossible.

Air. I need air. Clawing at the covers and tossing pretty pillows aside, I rolled to my feet and stumbled to the window. I threw it open with such force I expected the glass to shatter. My lungs and stomach heaved as I gasped, leaning out over Main Street. *Empty. Not a single soul. Deserted.* Even the last of the bar patrons were tucked in at home and sleeping. Not me. Sleep came hard and in spurts of exhaustion.

I threw a leg across the sill and braced my back against the wall, much like I sat in my tree in the middle of the creek. *I'm fine.* I'd adapted to this new place and the new people. *Or not.* Slanting much of my body into the night air, I inhaled greedily, trying to recognize and orient. My eyes tried to focus on the merciful glow from the windows of art galleries below, illuminating colors from paintings and sculptures displayed behind clear panes. Even the clothing boutiques lit their windows, with textures and rainbows of real life, at all hours. Sweat dried on my chest and broke goose bumps along my arms.

The air was thick and tugged at me. Muggy. Heavy. *What are you doing, Juliet? Pretending to be normal? To have moved on? What a joke. Wait till they see who you really are.*

Where is Mini? She'd come to me less and less since my sixteenth birthday. As if she didn't have a use for me anymore. As if I was supposed to figure this out myself. *How? How do I keep going? Betray to protect? Save them to lose them forever?* Panic gripped at my heart. At least they'd be alive to hate me.

My mind whirled in a million different directions. *Breathe. Walk. Breathe. Think. DG is gone.* Nothing worked to stave off anxiety. Eyes closed or open, I saw Kirian's face tangled up in the ivy tendrils peering down at me. Haunting me. Why couldn't he love me like he promised? *What is wrong with me?*

She was back. I sniffed the air, hoping for a scent of the familiar. No scents filled the air around me. Not a clove of garlic or a leaf of basil. Nothing. I swallowed bile as it crept up the back of my throat. I glanced at the clock. A few hours from dawn. I climbed back into my room. Dare I open the door to the rest of the condo? What if Ms. Asura's out there? An irrational fear, maybe. *Or not. She is everywhere I go.*

I leaned my head against the slick white door; my hand hovered above the door handle. It moved. *No, it didn't.* I gagged, tears slashing down my cheeks. *Nono-nonononono!*

Tony was helping at a shelter downtown. He'd told me to call him anytime. I'd said I was fine. A hollow laugh bubbled up. *Fine? This is fine?*

I picked up the phone. Started punching in the numbers to call him, confide my fears. I forced myself to press the first few: 3-1-7—

She'll hurt him. She'll hurt all of them. I can't. I tossed the phone onto the bed and tugged on shorts over panties so new they didn't feel like mine. A jacket went over my sleep shirt. I slipped into flip-flops. The messy bun on my head slipped low like it was trying to break free. *I know the feeling.* I yanked open my bedroom door and sprinted down the hallway, never slowing, flying down two flights of stairs. Grabbing the front door, I bounded down the outside steps without looking back. Made it. Now what? *Run.*

Main Street was quiet, except on weekends near the restaurants and bars. Tonight it was easy to slip between cars and duck onto the Monon Trail. I ran. My sandals slapped the pavement, sliding on my toes. I stopped to kick them off and ran barefoot. *Go. Go. Go.* Breaking out into a neighborhood, I cut between cars and driveways, across a road, then went the wrong way around a roundabout. Something sharp sliced my foot. *Shit. Ouch!* I didn't stop moving. Pain equaled life. Mistress taught me many lessons at DG, but as long as I'd hurt, I'd known I was alive.

I galloped toward Rumi's studio, the hanging Spirit Stones lighting up as if on a motion sensor. *I'm a Fenestra. Special.* I paused. *Why me? Take it back. I don't want it.* Winded, I gasped to breathe past the sharp pain in my side. Rumi would pour me grape soda and tell me not to worry. Then he'll die too. Leaves rustled and footsteps slithered in the darkness.

Someone's behind me. Gaining on me. Rumi will get hurt too.

Move. Go! Go!

I stumbled back into a full run. Saw the twinkling

lights of Helios and sped up. Skirting the empty tearoom and parking lot, I stumbled toward the guest cottage, where Meridian and Tens lived. The windows were dark. *Where are the Spirit Stones?* They were sleeping, but I didn't care. I couldn't care.

I heard Custos rumble a greeting as I tumbled against the front door. My throat burned; my muscles screamed in protest. Sweat from exertion and from fear dripped down my neck, my shins. I shivered. "It's me, Custos. It's me," I whispered against the wood.

Tens opened the door, catching me as I fell against him. "Juliet?"

"Sorry. Sorry." I sank to the floor, boneless, Tens unable to catch me completely.

Meridian grabbed my hand. "You're okay now. You're okay. Catch your breath."

Tens picked up a gun and moved toward the door. "Were you followed?"

"I don't know where Mini is. I had a dream." I puffed and tried to catch my breath. "I don't know. I heard steps." *An army chased me.*

Tens stepped away from the door and opened it farther. "Mini's coming."

Meridian pointed and I turned. Racing along the path toward the cottage was Mini, her long hair trailing behind her like wisps of moonlight. She sped past us into the house and leapt up on the kitchen table to sprawl. Her sides worked like a bellows as if she'd run a million miles to catch up to me.

"I didn't know where else to go," I whispered as Meridian pulled me into her arms. My Wildcat Creek felt too far.

"It's okay. It's okay." Meridian tried to soothe me, but I couldn't relax.

Nothing's okay.

Tens popped the tab of a soda and handed me an icy can. Without checking, I knew it was grape, which always tasted better than water and seemed as necessary to us. I sipped, then gulped the sugary fizz.

"Where's Tony?" Tens asked.

"Downtown at the shelter." I straightened, away from Meridian's arms. It was too tempting to let her hug me.

Tens swore and I felt the need to defend Tony. "He doesn't know about the nightmares. I don't need a babysitter."

"This has happened before?" Meridian asked, her expression concerned and confused.

I nodded. I could almost hear her thinking that I should have told them sooner. *They want me to tell them everything.* They didn't understand that Kirian and Nicole were my only confidantes. And now I had neither. Easier to say nothing than risk saying too much.

"These dreams, are they always the same? Do they change?" Tens knelt down on the floor with us.

Mini meowed and rubbed her head along my shins.

I shook my head. I didn't want to think about them. About Kirian's death. Of the look in Ms. Asura's eyes as she fled into the forest. The calculation in her voice yesterday. *Cunning. Rage. Revenge.*

"I'll let Tony know where you are." Tens moved away quickly, flipping on more lights. He picked up his cell phone.

"Do you want to talk about it? It might help?" Meridian pressed, leaning into me.

"No." I dropped the empty soda can and wrapped my arms around my middle.

Meridian paused. "Juliet? What happened to your foot? Where are your shoes?" She gasped.

I saw bloody footprints on the porch, and my foot was smeared with drying red. "Sorry."

Tens brought out a first-aid kit. He started wiping the jagged wound with a wet cloth. "We should go to the hospital. This might need stitches."

I stiffened. "No hospital."

He nodded. "I'll do my best, but this is going to sting."

Meridian reached for my hand and pressed her fingers tightly into mine. "Want to hear a story about a potential Fenestra Rumi found in Indiana's history?" She held eye contact.

She is trying. So hard.

Anything. I nodded. I didn't tell them the pain felt like a release. A relaxation of sorts. A reminder of who I was and where I came from. Mini draped across my lap as if trying to accept a part of my burden.

Meridian shifted so she blocked the view of Tens and my foot. "There once was a woman named Polly Barnett who owned a farm on the western side of Indianapolis. She had a daughter who disappeared the night before her sixteenth birthday. The town searched but nothing was found. People speculated she ran off with a beau. Others say she headed east to pursue her dream of being famous. Although personally, it was around 1854, so it's not like there were reality shows or Broadway, so I don't buy this explanation."

I smiled on cue, knowing Meridian was trying to change my focus and leaven the mood.

"Anyway, no one knows what happened to her daughter, but Polly took to the dirt roads and fields of central and southern Indiana. She walked them, calling for her daughter, asking people if they'd seen her. She walked the rest of her life, searching—fifty-four thousand miles." Meridian paused. "That's a lot of walking."

I nodded. "She's a Fenestra?"

"We think so because at some point a black cat walked beside her. And when people would get her to stop and rest, to eat or cool off, all Polly could talk about was windows and light and an evil darkness that took her daughter. I guess it didn't take much of this talk to get people to stay the hell away from her. Eventually, only a few people would leave food out for her, but they all watched her walk the roads thinking she was possessed or broken by grief."

Intrigued, I asked, "What happened?"

"One day, when she was an old lady, they found her dead, sleeping under a tree in the local cemetery. The black cat was right there with her until they buried her. Then the cat disappeared too. They put a stone on her grave with a cat on the top of it. We think we should check it out. Rumi's trying to find out exactly where her farm was. Because if there's any truth to it, then there were Fenestra and Nocti battling in the state before the Civil War. Maybe there are more of us."

I nodded. All the story made me think of was my mother. *Where is she buried? Why is she disfigured and wounded when I see her on the other side? What is her connection to Ms. Asura? Was she a Fenestra? Where's my father? Is he even alive?* I gagged again over the knot in my throat.

"I need to know my mother's story," I whispered. "Do you think Nelli would let me help go through the DG papers? Maybe there's a clue there?"

"I don't see why not. I'm sure she'd love the help. But we don't know for sure your mother was at DG, do we?"

I shook my head. *No, all we know is that she's dead and stuck at the window.*

"We'll keep looking. I promise. We'll figure it out." Meridian sounded so sure.

"Done." Tens finished wrapping gauze and a bandage around my foot and ankle.

"Thanks," I said.

"No problem. Why don't you sleep with Meridian tonight? I'll take the couch," Tens suggested.

Jealousy bit my cheek. "Where's my Protector?" The words slipped out before I could stop them. I didn't want Tens; if anything, he was an annoying older brother. But I wanted my own person for the middle of the night. Meridian didn't face waking up from nightmares five times a night, alone. I slumped forward, dropping her hand and bending my leg back toward me.

Tens frowned. "I don't know. I wish I did. I'm trying to remember everything I can that my grandfather told me."

Meridian touched my back. "Auntie said not everyone has—"

"Do you smell that?" I asked. The sickly cloying perfume came in on the wind.

"What?" Meridian frowned.

Tens shook his head. "Meridian had a candle burning earlier."

"Vanilla." She nodded.

Nothing as nice as vanilla. I didn't smell a candle. "I need to use the bathroom." *You're not good enough for a Protector. That's what they're not saying.* I couldn't hear that I'd be alone. Alone for a lifetime? I simply couldn't handle that tonight. Not with Kirian's face hovering in my peripheral vision and my nose not working. *Even here I smell nothing edible.* Only that familiar perfume that stuck to everything in my past.

Meridian lifted her hand. "Okay, through there."

They helped me to my feet and I limped over. I stopped at the door. "Thank you." The words tasted of sawdust. I didn't have words beyond *thank you*, which felt both awkward to say and inadequate. I wondered what my life would be like if they'd never found me.

"We know." Meridian's concern was blatant.

I tried to close the bathroom door, but Mini and

Custos barged in. I splashed water on my face and drank mouthfuls, trying to rehydrate my throat. Not even the grape soda had slaked my thirst. Tears dripped down my cheeks. I didn't bother to check them. I merely crawled into the bathtub; I yanked a towel from the rack to use as a pillow. I left the lights on. *Nowhere is safe. She's still watching. Waiting.*

Custos carefully climbed in and lay down half at my back and half on top of me. Her breath whispered along my neck. Her weight and warmth loosened my muscles. Mini positioned herself like she used to, under my chin and between my arms, as if she were a living teddy bear snuggling me to sleep.

Someone cracked the door. "Juliet?" Meridian whispered.

I pretended I was already sleeping. She turned on a night-light and crept back out, flicking off the main fixture.

I opened my eyes and stared at the ceiling, thinking about DG. About my task, my choices. *Are there more kids out there?* Anyone who escaped and made it out of her grasp? Can I shield those around me? No matter what I do, nothing good comes to people who spend time with me. My parents. The patients at DG. Kirian. No one and nothing. *I don't know what to do.* "Tell me what to do," I whispered against Mini's throat, but she stayed silent.

CHAPTER 7

I watched Juliet and Tony pull away. Worry gnawed. She and I connected as Fenestra, but we kept missing each other's hearts. "I don't know what she needs," I said to Tens. *She slept in the bathtub instead of with me. Does she not trust me, even in sleep?* It was hard not to take that rejection personally.

He shook his head. "She keeps everything so close I don't know either. I wish her Protector would show up." He smacked his fist on his palm.

I frowned. "You know that might not happen. If they weren't together when she opened fully . . ." I let it hang. I'd hoped and prayed, beseeching Auntie, the Creators.

Yet we'd been on our own during her birthday. I lifted up on tiptoe and kissed Tens lightly. His lips tasted of chocolate and peanut butter. He'd been with me for my change, and I wasn't sure I'd have survived without him.

"What was that for?" he asked.

"For being here. For being you." I smiled and traced his jaw as his face reddened. I'd learned he blushed with any mushy talk. Every time. *Like the tickling, I will exploit those points at every opportunity.*

He said huskily, "I know you want to make this easier for her. But there are years of abuse she's trying to overcome, in addition to being a Fenestra." Juliet was routinely beaten, bruised and bled at the hands of DG's headmistress. The woman who worked with Ms. Asura and, though wholly human, lacked a soul.

I frowned. "Being angelic might be the least of her problems, you mean?"

He nodded agreement. "She won't talk about Kirian's betrayal or Nicole's disappearance, will she?"

"No." Kirian befriended her when she'd arrived at age six. Three years older, he'd left at sixteen to travel the world. Only we learned later, his allegiance was turned to the Nocti and everything she thought she'd known about his travels were lies. He'd been bait to get to Juliet by her sixteenth birthday. "She has to be overwhelmed. Even with Tony around."

Tony met Roshana when she was pregnant with Juliet. He'd been an uncle, father, and grandfather figure for them both. Until the Nocti managed to track Roshana, trick Tony, and kidnap Juliet. They'd been separated for a decade that Juliet didn't remember well. Sadly, the fists and blood of Juliet's DG years seemed easier for her to grasp than hugs and kisses from Tony and her mom.

Nelli's car shrieked up the driveway to the cottage with reckless speed. The expression on her face had me swallowing past a lump in my throat. *Uh-oh.* "What's wrong?" I asked, walking quickly toward her.

Nelli called out her window. "Grab whatever you need quickly. We might already be too late. Bales found bones north of here that could belong to one of the DG kids."

The Nocti used Dunklebarger to raise kids who might be Fenestra until they were sixteen. On their sixteenth birthday the teens disappeared; we were still trying to account for all the missing. If they died, they were sacrificed to force Fenestras to turn Dark. I didn't begin to hope that any were alive, well, and Light. We needed to collect their souls and remains—to bring justice and peace to the victims. Each encounter gave us more information on the Nocti and, we hoped, their future plans.

Tens grabbed a duffel bag from the van and folded into the backseat of Nelli's compact. Custos ran to the car door and barked until he slid over and made room for her. I frowned and took the front next to Nelli. I swept my hair into a ponytail that danced between my shoulders.

Nelli drove the back roads at a clip that lost me immediately when we left Carmel proper. The open windows let the sun-warmed air fill the car with the pleasant scent of earth and fresh-cut grass.

"Who's Bales?" Tens asked Nelli, the wind whipping his heavy black curtain of hair into his face.

He needs another haircut.

Nelli's hands tightened on the wheel but she never took her eyes from the road. "A friend." She hesitated. "I think we're dating. I'm not sure." She shrugged. "We were in college together. He used to be a cop, then became a PI after he got shot two years ago. He doesn't know anything about you. Just that I'm trying to solve a bunch of cold cases of missing kids. He's been hunting up locations for me. He used to work homicide, so he knows what he's looking for."

"What did he find?" I asked.

"He called last night, said there was a report about finding skeletal remains and artifacts. He poked around today. Called in favors. Found out that the timeline might work for us to get there. We need to get in and out, without disturbing anything, before they remove the bones."

We turned onto an old Indiana two-lane highway lined with grasses and copses of cottonwood and willow trees. To my right, a Cooper's hawk pounced onto an unlucky rodent—its brown and white feathers blended in perfectly with the skeletal remains of last winter's corn crop. Even though the calendar read May, the fields had been too wet, too cold, for planting yet. Many were filled with the mustard-yellow, tiny-faced goldenrod and broad swaths of white yarrows. Purple thistles poked up through the grasses. Red-winged blackbirds and goldfinches picked their way between the tops of vegetation and tree branches.

Round, silvery metallic buildings dotted the land-scape like shiny buttons on a camouflaged uniform. Brick ramblers not far from the traffic of the road were flanked with lilacs and peonies. Old farmhouses and red barns were set farther back down drives lined with tractors and combines.

"Where are we going?" Tens asked.

Nelli sighed. "An old converted milk factory in Lebanon."

What? Where? "Lebanon? How are we supposed to get to Lebanon?" I asked.

"It's a rural town northeast of here. We're not talking about the country." Nelli twisted her lips and smiled.

I had begun to tumble onto the fact that a person could travel the entire world and never leave Indiana: Paris, Moscow, Peru, Brazil, Edinburgh, and now Lebanon. *Is it any wonder I get confused?*

Nelli chewed on her lip. "I've thought about this a lot. I need to run something past you."

"What?" I waited.

"I've been assigned an intern, who started volunteer-ing after DG hit the news. He's a foster kid himself who's going to Butler University."

"Okay . . . ?" *Where is she going with this?*

"He's a really nice kid, very earnest. I think he would be good for Juliet. Give her someone to talk to."

"You mean set her up with him?" Tens asked.

Nelli shrugged. "I don't know. Maybe. At least put them together to see if they hit it off? Maybe I'm wrong, but I think he'd understand where she's coming from. Maybe get through to her, where we can't?"

"I don't know that she needs a boyfriend, but she could definitely use a friend," I said.

"Have you told him anything?" Tens asked.

"About her being a Fenestra? No, of course not. He's very kind. Last week, he made me pull over to rescue roadkill."

"Did it live?"

"We were too late, but he took it home to bury it properly. He says he wants to change the world by using computers to improve the poverty divide. I think he will. He's very focused on technology and he's a wiz. I thought I'd ask him to help with the investigations—the organizing, getting all the information uploaded into a database we can reference, doing the legwork, nothing dangerous to you. Then he and Juliet can spend time together. No pressure. That's where we're headed." Nelli pointed out the window, toward a tall brick smokestack towering far above the buildings around it. Cracks ran down the stack, making it appear as if the decrepit brick might topple at any moment. Painted down the side, emphasized by large cracks, was the word *MILK*.

Interesting. Kinda creepy, kinda hick.

"Are you sure this is the place?" Tens asked.

Railroad tracks and crossing signs cut the earth and roads. Buildings clustered together in what served as suburban sprawl around lesser cities and towns in the country.

"That's where we're going. Not into downtown." Nelli pointed. "It's an odd and rare collectibles store now with a seasonal theater troupe. It used to be a milk production and distribution plant."

My heart sped up as we neared. "Where'd they . . ."

"Find the remains?"

"Yeah." *Please help us send you home.*

"Bales says the owners of the building are expanding the theater sections and were going to refloor the dressing rooms. There were stones out of place. Crews noticed a bone fragment. When they lifted a tile, there was more. This is a skeleton, not a person."

"Do they know when it was placed there?" Tens asked.

"Based on the clothing, they're thinking the remains were buried there in the early seventies. It'll take time to pinpoint completely. I haven't seen anything yet either."

Puzzled, I asked, "How did it take so long to find?"

"The building was abandoned for years, and even when it was used, not all the cubbied offices and storage spaces were occupied." She shrugged, her expression clouded. "There are lots of gloomy crevices in the world."

We turned into a parking lot in the rear of a large brick building painted to look like a collection of row houses.

"There he is." Nelli pointed at Bales standing across the street.

Tallish and burly in a way that leaned toward either intimidating or teddy bear based on facial expressions, Bales pushed off the tree and sauntered toward us. His sun-darkened complexion clearly delineated a farmer's tan and crow's-feet. He wore industrial overalls, steel-toed work boots, and a crew cut so short it merely hinted at brown hair. Except that he wasn't much older than Nelli, he could have fit in at any diner, drinking a cup of coffee, talking about the good ol' days.

His face softened and lit up when Nelli hugged him.

We shook hands. His were the size of baseball mitts and he loomed over both Nelli and me. With beefy shoulders that appeared used to lifting hay, Bales made Tens look like a skinny praying mantis.

"How do you want to do this?" He directed the question at Nelli. "The coroner will be here soon and it's technically a crime scene."

"Can we get within sight of where they found the remains?"

"Yeah, there's a walkway above they use for lights and props now. People built walls but didn't lower the ceilings. Looks like a maze from up there." His voice was deep and gravelly as he led the way with his hand planted firmly on Nelli's back.

"We could be charged with tampering—you're all aware of that?" Bales asked, no censure in his voice, simply curiosity.

"We know," Tens answered for us.

"It's important." Nelli squeezed Bales's hand.

"Must be since you're not a rule breaker, darlin'." He gave her a private smile, making her blush.

As we walked closer to the building, my thoughts

turned to whoever's remains we were here to find. *I hope these bones let us close a chapter for one soul.* And lead us to answers instead of more questions.

"Want to see if you can get within sight? I don't know that he's related yet." Nelli let her question hang.

Related as in a Fenestra? "Yeah, let's go." Tension lifted my voice up an octave and I rubbed my hands on my denim shorts.

Tens's shoulders were tight and he walked on the balls of his feet, as if ambush might come from any direction.

The ladders swayed and rusty hinges creaked. A pigeon studied us and cooed.

"They say the birds keep coming in, but they don't know why or where," Bales informed us. Dust motes hung in the air and it took a moment for my eyes to adjust. I heard and smelled cows from the not-too-distant past.

Heading in the direction Bales pointed, Nelli took over the lead. Her sensible pumps clipped and slipped on the rungs.

Exasperated, Bales asked, "Woman, why didn't you wear sneakers like I told you to?"

"I don't wear sneakers." Nelli didn't hesitate to answer.

"I'll buy you a pair. If we keep working together, I don't want to worry about your ankles turning."

I shared a glance with Tens and a smile. They sounded like an old married couple.

The brick walls were worn and stained. What few

new windows there were didn't feel quite right in the industrial design of the space.

"Just down this catwalk. You'll see the crime tape." Bales motioned ahead of us.

I whispered to Tens, "Do you see that?"

"What?"

"The light."

He shook his head.

"Grab me." I'd gotten better at being on my feet, but I didn't trust myself yet not to fall off a ladder. Especially when my Fenestra self went to the window and left my human body behind.

I felt his hands slide around my waist.

"What's wrong?" Nelli turned her head, but her body was wedged ahead on the catwalk.

CHAPTER 8

"I don't know." I said the words to Nelli as I found myself standing at the window to the next world. When Auntie taught me how to be a Fenestra, we started with a curtained summer window. According to her, I should be able to control the window itself, but either I was a slow learner or there was a difference in my window's operation. For the most part, the dying seemed to conjure scenes reflecting their lives, their history, and their loved ones. The view to the other side could be anything from meadows among snow-capped mountains to movie theaters showing black-and-white classics. Usually, smaller family groups to large crowds showed up to welcome and embrace the newly departed. At some point, they all moved beyond the window to the Light on the horizon.

But this was eerie. This window was a blank void. A nothing. Neither dark, nor light. No life, no animals, no people. An emptiness hung heavily as if it sucked the air out of the space. No one stood next to me. I shivered, unsure why I waited at a colorless, featureless rectangle.

"Hello? Is someone here?" I heard a tearful voice call from behind me.

I turned and saw a teen, in torn and dirty brown corduroy pants and an orange striped shirt, bare feet muddy and scraped, huddled in a corner. Long hair streaked with dried gook made it impossible for me to tell the gender or the age. Fear radiated toward me. *Don't cry, Meridian. Be strong.*

"I'm Meridian," I said, startling the person. I lowered my voice. "I'm a friend. What's your name?" I carefully picked my way closer, crouching with each movement because every noise begat a startled reaction. Closer inspection made me think this was a boy my age, or a bit younger. Pale and too thin.

"I'm— Oh no, oh no, oh no." He started to hyperventilate, each syllable growing in panic and volume.

I held my hands up and out. "Slow down, slow down. I'm not going to hurt you."

"I don't remember my name. Who am I?" He lifted his head toward me.

A gasp broke from my lips—his eyes were melted

shut. As if someone played with the skin and smashed it together like a sand castle under a heel.

I knelt and scooted closer. "I'm a friend. I'm not going to hurt you." My pulse quickened. He couldn't see me and the wounds didn't appear accidental. *Who could wound another person like this?*

"Are they coming back? Did they hurt you too? What do they want?" He clenched his knees, drawing himself farther back into the corner.

"No, no one's hurt me." My heart ached for him.

"It's so bright. Is it summer? Why can't I see your face? How long have I been here? What's my name?"

"I can try—"

He interrupted, as if he hadn't talked to anyone in decades. *He hasn't.* "Can you take me home? What's my name?"

"You'll remember it, I promise."

"Can you take me home? Where's Uriah? Aileen?"

I shook my head, fighting back sympathetic tears. "It's going to be okay. Can I take your hand?"

He held out a shaking hand blotched with grime and muck. His ragged, bloody fingernails were painful to see, as if chewing on them had been the only way to pass the time. "Have you seen Lucille? I heard her scream, but she hasn't answered me. Can you take me home? I want to go home."

I gripped his icy fingers, trying to move us closer to the window. No one still alive ever met me here. He wasn't alive but didn't know he was dead. *This has to be the soul belonging to the skeleton Nelli brought us to investigate.*

"Can you walk with me? Just a few steps?" I felt the sill to my right. It was Auntie's summer window; I finally sensed the breeze through the curtains. I didn't understand why the window wasn't of this boy's making and choice. I'd had to manifest it, call for it. *How did I do that?*

"Where are you taking me?" he asked, trembling.

"Out of here. Okay?"

Someone, Nelli or Tens maybe, clinked on the catwalk above me and whispered apologies. The living plane rarely infiltrated my space here. Neither did this world appear to the living. They couldn't hear me speak or see me move. Auntie could be in both planes at once—that was my goal. I wasn't there yet. I appeared catatonic now that I wasn't passing out each time.

The noise frightened the boy and he shrank away, trying to let go of my hand. "Are they coming back? You have to leave me here. Go now. Can you escape? They'll hurt you."

"I'm not leaving. You're okay. It'll be okay. Do you know Juliet?" I tried to distract him while we inched closer. *Is he a kid from the recent past or the long past?* His clothes were so outdated that I couldn't imagine he'd know her.

He cocked his head and stopped. "Who?"

Not Juliet. Older than her? On a long shot, I asked about Juliet's mom. "How about Roshana?"

He nodded. "She's Argy's girl."

"Were you friends?" Excitement tinged my voice.

"No, they're part of the brat pack. New arrivals."

"How old are they?" I tried to calculate which decade this boy came from. If he was older than Roshana and she was sixteen when she had Juliet, I'd figure it out later.

I took mincing, shuffling steps toward the window, gently bringing him with me.

"Seven, maybe." He shrugged. "I'm sixteen. I think."

I was trying to do the math but it wasn't working right. My back hit the windowsill.

"You need to climb through here. It's a window. Can you feel it?" I faced him and helped him feel the casement with his hands and lean against it with his hip.

He dragged his hands around the opening. "Can you take the blindfold off? It hurts."

Tears stung my eyes. "I can't. I'm sorry."

"I don't want to go by myself. Can you take me home?"

"I promise you'll get home if you go through the window."

"Is it a way out?"

"Yes. Please?" I begged.

"If I stay, they'll come back and hurt me more, won't they? I don't want to leave my friends." He seemed torn between fleeing and wanting to help the other kids he thought were still around here.

"They can't hurt you once you're through the window. I promise I'll look for your friends. Maybe they already got out?" I didn't take my eyes off of him, willing him to acquiesce.

He hesitated, his hand barely passing the sill, reaching beyond. "You think maybe they escaped?"

"I haven't seen anyone else." *An honest statement, if not completely truthful.*

He reached a hand completely through, then pulled it back.

I bit back frustration. I heard activity around us: cars in the parking lot, voices. We were running out of time before the police and the coroner arrived and we had to leave. I didn't want to abandon this soul here. Not after all he'd been through. With all of my heart, I pleaded, *Auntie, please come. We need you!*

"Will you go first?" he asked.

"I can't go with you yet." I thought fast. "Not if I need to look for your friends. Right?"

I felt light hit my face, warm like a sun ray. I smelled apple blossoms and roses. I glanced back at the window and saw hands reaching for his. As he passed into the plain, they grabbed him and gently tugged him through. I recognized Juliet's Kirian. Roshana. Others I couldn't name. More with disfigurements, scars, and wounds, in apparel that would be tagged vintage in a flea market. *More DG victims?*

Auntie waited in the distance, nodding at me, her expression fiercely serious and filled with overwhelming compassion. *Is this how she experienced the war? Souls whose bodies were so wounded it affected their insides? This deep, abiding grief and helplessness to stop evil in its tracks?*

After he swung his legs over and slid through, he turned back to me. "I know my name now! I'm Howie.

What is this place? It's warm here." He smiled, as if the fear was left behind on this side and he had nothing to worry about beyond.

"It's home," I whispered as the voices of his greeting committee started chirping like a flock of sparrows.

"Aileen? Uriah?" He sank against friendly hands.

Kirian regarded me and shook his head. Worry seemed to pour from that side of the window into this one.

I blinked as the window faded and I fell back into my body, drained. Tens held me up, braced against his body.

The top of a skull and several other bones below us glowed. *Who is making them glow? Me? Something other? Howie?*

"I'm okay."

Somewhere Custos whined, urgently.

"His name is Howie. About late seventies?" I said to Nelli, hoping she'd recognize his name or the era.

Nelli nodded agreement but glanced at Bales, who was holding a list he'd dug out of his pocket. "On the list. She's probably right. Dates work." Bales shrugged. "Medium?"

I waited for him to freak out, but he didn't seem to even blink. *If you only knew.*

"Something like that," Tens answered for me. "You okay with it?" His tone was hard, as if he expected to defend my honor.

"Sure, had a bit of good luck with the help. Take any-thing I can get to crack a cold case." Bales shrugged him off. We heard clomping footsteps and calling voices. The police drew closer. "We need to scram. Through here."

Bales led us out a back crawl space. He asked me gently, "They need to look for any more?"

"A boy and girl maybe," I answered. I didn't think Uriah or Aileen were accounted for yet.

Without looking at me but pointing at the crumbling smoke stack, Nelli added, "Seems like a good place to dump and run."

"There's rubble in the stack but it's got a door. I'll tell 'em." Bales kissed her forehead and headed around toward the front of the building.

"Are you okay?" Nelli asked me, her eyes filled with apprehension. "Was this too much?"

"I'm okay. He knew Roshana when she was a kid—maybe seven. He mentioned a boy connected to her named Argy. I'll write down everything Howie said. He was hurt like Roshana."

Nelli's phone rang. "It's my boss." She moved away to take the phone call.

"Can we head back now?" Tens didn't loosen his grip.

He's worried. It had been a while since I was this shaky with a soul.

"You need to rest. That one took a lot out of you."

I needed to figure out why Howie didn't call his own window and how I managed to do it for him. That was a new development and not one I was entirely comfortable with. "I promised Juliet a trip to the chichi grocery store. She hasn't been there yet and it might cheer her up."

Tens opened his mouth to argue.

I stopped him with a hand on his chest. "She's finally

agreed to go—that's huge. We need time together. There's a great big something eating her."

Nelli fluttered back to us. "I missed a meeting. I don't know how I forgot about it. My boss is furious. Do you mind if I drop you off and run? We can talk after work?"

"That's perfect."

We piled back into her car. Custos continually sniffed me like I'd rolled around in bacon. Tens kept handing me peanut buttery cookies from Helios and telling me to drink more milk. He equated appetite with strength.

By the time we got back to the cottage, Juliet was waiting for us on the stoop, looking fiercely aggressive like she was waiting to battle a dragon. *This is gonna be fun.*

"Are you really up for this?" Tens asked me under his breath.

I nodded.

"I'll get the keys."

* * *

Juliet wandered bug-eyed through the aisles and among the racks of the high-end artisanal grocery store. She wore the look of a thirsty nomad sighting a verdant oasis. She twisted like a top and ran from ingredient to ingredient. Touching packages, lifting them to test the weight and hear the shake, rattles, or sloshes. She held everything to her nose, inhaling like an addict trying to get a fix.

The breads she poked and squeezed, watching them rerise. The samples of cookies and Danishes disappeared into her mouth by the twos, leaving the platters empty. She opened all the doors of the frozen food cases, exclaiming with delight over all the exotic flavors of ice creams.

In the canned goods, she puzzled over foreign words on labels that neither of us could pronounce. "You're sure you can't read that either?" she asked repeatedly.

"I'm sure. It's French. It's Japanese. It's squiggly something," I assured her each time. I tried to spark conversations, but she turned her back or interrupted me with questions about products and what dishes an ingredient might be used for. I mostly shrugged my shoulders, unable to answer, and wished I'd paid more attention when my mother turned the channel to the Food Network.

Juliet's experience at DG was sheltered to the point of prison. The headmistress received food deliveries weekly, generic packages of industrial calories. Juliet never visited a supermarket, a mall, or a movie theater. She was slowly letting us expose her to these. *One down, two million to go.* Then Nicole appeared at DG and mysteriously produced the ingredients Juliet needed to cook off the soul dust. When we got to the fresh fruits, I paled when her fondling became so enthusiastic we drew the attention of a clerk. He eyed us like we were going to shoplift the cherries and melons.

At the mangoes, I had to stop her from simply taking a bite. I wasn't sure how we'd be charged by the pound when they'd disappeared into her stomach.

I gave her room to explore and added a few more exotic

greens to the cart to appease the weary stocker. When the radio station stopped playing light jazz and broke in with a special news bulletin, it drew my attention.

"Practice sessions this week at the Indianapolis Motor Speedway, but things have heated up and not in a good way. Reports are a large fire under the stands was finally noticed when the smoke drifted into the pit lane. Officials are saying they spotted the camping site of a squatter under the bleachers in Turn Four. Looks like a simple garbage fire was abandoned when it got out of control. Officials say no one was hurt. If the flames had been another fifty feet to the right, they could have touched off highly flammable storage tanks, and then we'd be talking about a whole different incident. Again, no one was hurt. Let's hope the rest of the month proves as lucky. I'm Jessica Martin for Eyewitness News Channel Six."

"Excuse me. Excuse me?"

It took a minute for me to realize the woman was speaking to me. "Yes?"

Juliet froze. She seemed ready to run out of the store.

The stranger continued. "I'm sorry to interrupt. I don't normally talk to teenagers in stores, but this is so odd—I can see your light. Both of you. Like I'm dying again. Why can I see it?" Her voice quivered and her intense grip on the shopping cart was noticeable.

"Huh? What?" I tried to evade, buying time. *Can she really see Light through us?*

Juliet ducked behind an aisle header and I lost sight of her. *Thanks for the backup.*

The woman continued pressing. "The light of Heaven. I can see it through you. Why?"

We drew interested, eavesdropping glances.

Middle-aged with a rich espresso complexion and a short cropped Afro, there was nothing sinister about this woman. Her question was polite, if baffled. She began to get louder as she spoke.

I grabbed her hand and pulled her over toward the relative privacy of the cheese section.

"Could you lower your voice, please?"

She nodded. "Did you die too?" she whispered with wide eyes.

"Excuse me?" I tried to motion Juliet over, but she completely evaded my gaze and kept half hiding, half staring at the food around her. It was as if the allure of the tastes overrode her fear. I glanced around for Tens, who'd gone off to grab coffee to give us space. *Too much space.*

"I thought maybe you'd understand . . ." The lady frowned. "Maybe I'm wrong. I'm sorry. Never mind."

"Wait." *Crap, can I trust her? Is she Nocti? Is this a trap?* "Do you have time for coffee?" I asked, looking deeply into her eyes and seeing no void, no darkness. *Not Nocti.* "I'm Meridian."

"Delia." She relaxed. "Please. Coffee would be great."

We shook hands. I saw Tens heading toward me, frowning.

"I'll meet you at the coffee bar. Just let me pass off my groceries, okay?" I asked.

"Sure."

I pushed the cart over to Juliet and Tens. "She can see me. You." I waved toward Juliet. "I think I need to talk to her."

"I don't want to talk to her." Juliet pouted.

"I'm not asking you to. Buy anything you want." I shoved a wad of cash at her. "I'll talk to her, then come find you in line or at the van, okay?" I asked Tens.

"What if she takes you before I can get to you?" Tens shook his head.

"I'll risk it."

"But . . . are you sure you should talk to—" Juliet argued, on the verge of shaking.

"Of course not, but I have to investigate why she thinks she can see us—me. Maybe she's dying like Faye, or maybe having a near-death experience changes everything. I don't know. But I need to find out. This will help us with your mom." I finally said the magic word. Anything to do with Juliet's mother seemed to be the right thing. We didn't understand why Roshana was wounded and aging at the window. Her wounds kept her from speaking, so at best I got moments of pantomimed motion when I helped a soul through.

She nodded. "Fine."

"Stay within my sight," Tens commanded.

"Sure."

"Don't give anything away. She might be fishing," he warned.

I found Delia sipping on an iced latte when I sat down.

"Thanks for waiting." I didn't know where to start with small talk, so I dove straight in. "What did you mean about dying and light?"

Delia hesitated, then plunged ahead. "I don't talk about this very much. People don't understand. They think I lost my mind on April second, 2006."

"What happened that day?"

"I was giving birth to my second child and I hemorrhaged. I don't remember much, a few minutes, maybe seconds after that, I watched it unfold below me."

"Out of body? Like in the movies?" *I should take notes.*

"You think I'm nuts too." She lowered her gaze with chagrin.

"No, not at all. I promise. I'm only trying to understand. Please keep going."

She shrugged. "I died. They brought me back. But while I was dead, I went somewhere. There are no words—the best I can say is that my world became the most amazing light, brilliant but not blinding. Warm. Relaxed. Peaceful. I didn't want to come back. Only the thought of my children without a mother overcame my desire to stay there. It changed my life completely. I was a maternity nurse for years, but a few months ago I switched to hospice. I'm in my third month at the inpatient center."

"That's a huge shift. From babies to death?" *What*

does this mean for us? What are the ramifications? Can all near-death patients see us?

She smiled. "It's not as big as you might imagine. Both include labor and new beginnings. Everyone deserves a good death, don't you think?"

"Yes, I do. What do you see when you look at me?"

"Briefly, out of the corner of my eye, I saw that same dazzling, incredible light. Focusing on you, I can see your face, but if I don't really try, I don't know . . . I'm sorry. It's so hard to explain. I'm shaking. I'm sure I scared you. I don't normally accost strangers."

"I'm not scared of you." I shook my head.

"Did you also have a dying experience? Is that why there's light around you?" Delia asked.

"Of a sort. Why don't you tell me more about where you work?" I thought of Faye's upcoming battle.

She nodded. "Deal." And she settled into her story.

chapter 9

Tens closed his eyes thoughtfully. "You think because she's been on the other side, the veil is thinner? She can see Light even when she's not actively dying?"

"I don't know. That makes the most sense." I stretched out on the bed, shoving aside piles of our research. My eyes were sandpapery.

"Lucinda Myer has several journal entries that talk about mirror gazing and people being able to see the light when they're in a trance."

"That's the Abe Lincoln reference, right? That he saw himself dead?"

"Hmm, and Patton talked to his dead father before every battle."

"We know Señora Portalso could see my Light." She'd sat next to me on the bus from Portland to Revelation, then helped us when Tens almost died.

"Rumi can see a little of it."

"So there's a whole type of person, who isn't angelic, that is aware of us." We'd tacked up a scroll similar to Rumi's that we were adding to. I got off the bed and started a new list. "Near-death experiences—that's Delia. Señora is an unknown. Rumi has a familial connection to Fenestras too."

"We don't know for sure which of Rumi's family members are Fenestra, right?"

I shook my head. Rumi shared the heirloom writings with us like we shared Auntie's journal with him. "What about his uncle? Do you think he was just a black sheep or did he turn Nocti?"

Tens frowned. "It would kill Rumi if he finds out he's related to Dark."

I rolled my neck. *Ouch.*

"Knots?" He motioned me over to the edge of the bed.

I propped myself up and he started digging gently with his thumbs and then with more force. *Oh, yay.* I moaned.

"Maybe we need to add stretching or yoga to our daily routine? You can't function well if you're all twisted up."

Surprised, I gulped, "You know yoga?"

"I did a stint as an errand boy at a retreat center in eastern Oregon," he said matter-of-factly.

On his way to Auntie's? In the years he only had himself to rely on? He couldn't have been more than thirteen or fourteen. "And they didn't ask questions? Like where your parents were?" *How they could help you?*

"No speaking was allowed. They fed me, gave me a place to stay, and I ran all over taking written messages to people." He shrugged. "Watched a lot of contortions during group meditations."

"You meditated?" I blanched at the shock in my voice. *Why am I so surprised?*

"Nah, it wasn't bad."

"Why'd you leave?" I glanced over my shoulder.

"You weren't there." He lowered his eyelashes and concentrated on rubbing my shoulders.

My heart grieved for the little boy he was but also rejoiced in knowing this man would do anything, endure anything, confront anything, to protect me and keep me safe. *All of me—my soul, my spirit, my body.* "Is it possible to be really sad and really happy at the same time?"

"Every day, Supergirl."

I leaned back into his arms and he wrapped them around me. He dropped his lips to the curve of my neck and nibbled. I sighed, relaxing into his touch, inhaling the pine and earthy aromas belonging solely to him.

His fingers flirted with the skin along my midriff; his

calluses tickled and stroked until I shivered. I turned in his arms and fit my lips to his.

Our tongues met, promised, and danced. He shucked my T-shirt over my head and tossed his too.

The feel of his naked skin on my breasts thrilled. His nipples pebbled against mine. Waves of heat rolled off of him and I wrapped my legs around his hips.

He pressed me down into the mattress and I reveled in the weight of him against me. My hips arced toward him. Clothing rubbed and felt like an impediment, too heavy and thick between us. I reached toward his waistband, dipping my fingers under it when the "Hallelujah Chorus," digitized and electric, interrupted. *What in the world?*

We froze. The ringtone began again.

"It's Tony," Tens said against my mouth. Frustration at the disruption was evident in his growl.

I started laughing. "How apropos."

"Wanna know what your ringtone is?" Tens gave me a tender smile as he hit TALK. His fingers circled along my ribs, my breasts. I caught his hand. Stopped his exploration. As much as I wanted to continue, wanted to peel every layer of clothing and focus on the feeling, I couldn't. It felt like making out in front of my parents, even though Tony had no idea what we were doing.

My lips felt swollen and hot. I tugged on my shirt, not worrying about a bra.

"Sure. Yeah. We'll be there soon," Tens said as a single drop of sweat ran down his chest.

I reached for my bra. "We're going out?"

"Juliet's disappeared again. He's worried. Tony wants to talk to us."

I nodded.

* * *

Usually leading-man handsome, Tony was haggard and disheveled, as if he'd aged ten years in the last week. "What is she thinking?" he implored me about Juliet.

"I wish I knew," I answered honestly and with utter conviction.

"She has no idea how much I've tried to shield her from. She doesn't know who to trust. Who to talk to. Who to ask for help if she gets lost. It's worse than having her as a toddler because now she's angry and hurt and stubborn as hell. What am I doing wrong?" He wiped his mouth and took another long drought of coffee. "I thought it would get better with time, but it's like she keeps fading further and further away from me."

He's right. "I feel it too," I said.

"Should I have sent her north to Wolf Lake with Joi and the kids? She keeps asking about Bodie and Sema. She doesn't believe me that they're being kids swimming, building tree houses, and eating ice cream."

"She doesn't have a reference place for normal. It's like a foreign language," Tens said.

"How do I help her?" Tony repeated. His salt-and-pepper hair was uncombed and mussed.

"Have you talked to her?"

"Aside from letting me teach her tricks to read, she won't speak about her mother. When I couldn't tell her who her father was, it's like she decided we had nothing to talk about." He trembled and set down the mug. "She not only looks like her mother, but she's also as closed off as Roshana was, especially in the beginning."

"But Roshana learned to trust you?"

"Not enough, clearly, because if she had, I would know about Juliet's family. I might have been able to stop Roshana from getting in that car." His voice broke. "From dying."

"No, I'm sorry, but no." Tens's answer was harsh and direct. "You recognized Ms. Asura as the woman in the car that carried Roshana away, right?"

"Yes." Tony nodded. "She hasn't aged a day, so yes, I'm certain that it was her."

"These Nocti are organized, vicious, and don't hesitate to kill innocents to get what they want. If Roshana had told you who she was running from, assuming you'd believed her, you would have gone with her that day or brought in the police, correct?"

Tony sighed. "Probably."

"And you'd be dead, too, and no one would have protected Juliet until she was six." Tens made valid points.

"They got her anyway." Tears rolled down Tony's cheeks.

Tens shook his head. "You couldn't have predicted the church's wild-goose chase was a ploy to get you away from Juliet."

"If I'd taken Roshana and Juliet, we could have run somewhere safe."

"There is nowhere safe," I interjected. "Life everywhere means death is everywhere—it's unavoidable—and where there's death, there will be Nocti and Fenestra."

"You have to stop feeling guilty for things you are not responsible for," Tens said. "You have to be her parent as Roshana asked you to be."

"Roshana gave her life to protect Juliet and the Nocti got her anyway." Tony blew his nose.

"But they don't have her now," I whispered. *At least, I hope not.*

CHAPTER 10
Juliet

I knew no one understood what drew me back to DG's grounds. I couldn't explain it, even if I'd wanted to try. It nourished me in a way that transcended physical hunger. Even though it was, as Tens said, hell on earth, it was the only place in the world where I felt a connection to my mother. It didn't matter that Mistress was dead. That the stairwell I'd hidden under in that monstrous tornado was gone. The debris bulldozed into piles and hauled away. That the cement foundation and the old storm cellar were the only parts left. The trees that hadn't been plucked from the earth and blended to sawdust were stripped clean down to the bone beneath the bark.

With my eyes, I saw that DG was nothing like what I'd grown up in. The run-down mansion that hid unspeakable horror was reduced to a foundation slab—memories like spiderwebs drifted everywhere and clung to every bit of my heart. I couldn't inhale past the pain without focusing all my energy on my lungs, my ribs. Each motion happened in thick honey, deep in cold porridge.

I picked leaves to shreds as I stared at the land. When we'd fought her at the creek, Ms. Asura mentioned my mother. Tony thought she was connected to my mother's abduction from his church. That the Nocti had conspired to steal me from Tony too. *To raise me until they could use me on my sixteenth birthday. Tony is so sure, so convinced he knows what my life should be.*

Last February, Ms. Asura brought Kirian back here to seduce me into their company. Only thoughts, and love, for Nicole, Bodie, and Sema kept me from truly embracing what he'd offered. I'd only had them to lose. Now I had so many more people to lose. *How am I supposed to do it? How do I make sure no one else hurts because of me?*

Nicole, my best friend, my confidante at DG, hadn't been human after all; rather, she'd been an angel, a guardian to help me survive. I wrapped my fingers around the silver filigreed necklace she'd worn and mysteriously hung on my neck as she'd left. Engraved on it was a Bible quote promising guardian angels to guard and protect. She'd tried to spur me to hunt up my truth, but I'd brushed her off too many times. *Wasted opportunities.* But the little sips and nibbles of my history only made me hungrier to know more. *I need to know my blood, my family, whatever it takes.*

Seeing Tony again brought back much of my early childhood, but I'd been so little, still a baby when she'd disappeared, that my mother never shared any of our story with me. *Why is she so badly injured when I see her at the window? Who is my father? Where is he?*

I found solace by the water, along the shores of Wildcat Creek that ran through the woods behind DG. More than the house itself, I was pulled to the creek. Listening to the water roll and gurgle sounded like Mother Earth conversing with Papa Time. I pretended I could hear my mother and my father speaking in the distance as the water ran by.

The early evening sun beat down on my shoulders and even my long blond hair warmed to the touch. I'd left it long, continued to grow it. I wasn't strong like Meridian. I didn't want to cut my hair off to prove I'd moved on, the way she'd hacked hers off in Revelation. She told me her stories like they were mine. *We are so different. She doesn't understand the choices I make to keep the littlies safe, giving myself to hatred to spare others. She may never understand.*

I shucked off my leather sandals, unwrapping the dirty bandage from my foot. I stayed on my toes, rolled up the cuffs of my jean capris, and waded out. Murky ick gave way to perfect sand, then small pebbles. The trees with leaves like spinach danced and fluffy white seeds sprinkled through the air like sifting flour in slow motion.

The water sparkled and dipped in colors that ranged from the gray of moldy bread to the gold of olive oil to rich kale greens. Lime-colored grasses taller than Bodie grew in clumps along the side of the creek. Wildflowers the colors of blueberries, butter, and whipped cream helped themselves to sun and dirt and water. *This is my home.*

A pair of lemon and licorice butterflies played tag with each other among grapefruit-sized dragonflies and mosquitoes. *They are my family.*

A kestrel perched low above me, watching smaller birds. A blue jay and a brown squirrel fought over seeds. A family of mallard ducks swam along the edge of my vision, keeping their ducklings close and staying between us. *These are my friends.*

Going out farther, I enjoyed the cold rush of water along my calves and the textures underfoot. The cut on my sole ached. Tony will scold me for getting it wet.

This is my world. As welcoming as any kitchen. This is comfort food for my heart.

I worried about the littlies. There was so much change in their lives. Too much. Children were resilient until they broke. I'd seen it often enough in my time at DG. *They have the family I've always wanted.* Jealousy flared bitter on my tongue.

My gaze was drawn toward the hole of DG's storm cellar. I'd helped Nelli cart out boxes and storage tubs of files, some so old they were yellow and broke apart at the slightest touch. Some had mildewed and molded with the fuzz of being in an unfinished cellar for so many years.

There'd been rumors that two teens had used the cellar for secret romantic meetings. *At least that's the reason Mistress gave for never letting us go down there, when the sky turned green and the twisters came.* Not being in the cellar was why the tornado that destroyed DG almost killed me too. *Should have killed me.*

I jumped out of my skin when in the distance the tornado sirens blared their weekly test. "Tony reminded you they test the sirens today. *It's just a test,*" I said. Months passing hadn't dimmed the adrenaline shooting through me or the pulse flying at my throat. Each time they sounded, I was back in the house with Enid trying to make it downstairs to safety while the freight train made crushing impact. That we'd survived, and Meridian's Sangre Angel, Josiah, had saved us, didn't lessen the fear that gripped my insides.

I focused on breathing until once again the birds' chatter and traffic on the road behind me were the loudest sounds.

"Oh, isn't this lovely. Fancy meeting you here." Ms. Asura's voice came from a dense group of trees across from me. Her perfume snaked its fingers onto the breeze and wrapped around my nose, my mouth. I coughed. *Sweet, cloying, nauseating.*

I started to stand. Ready to what? Run? *No, not anymore.* Anger burned. "Where are you? I can't see you."

"You don't need to see me, sweetie. Someone burned

my face. You wouldn't know who I should punish for that, do you?"

Vines of poison ivy rustled, giving me a spot in the brush to focus on. "You did it to yourself." I tried to sound brave. *What would Meridian say?*

"Now, now, we both know that's not true."

"What do you want?" I demanded. *How does she find me? So easily. So often. Be brave, Juliet, be brave.*

"To see how you are, how you're faring."

"I'm fine." *Lie to her—you know how to lie.*

"Doesn't look that way to me. All mopey and teary, talking to ducks and frogs. It's a little pathetic. Has Meridian dumped you yet? Figured out you're useless and stupid?"

"I am not stupid." *Meridian thinks so.*

"Can't read yet, can you?"

How does she know that? "Of course I can."

"I had a job for you, Juliet."

That's what this is about. "What?" My heart sped up and thwacked against my ribs. *Can I disobey? Play dumb?*

"You were to find and bring me information I want. You know this."

"Why?" I asked. *What does she want?*

She didn't answer me. I glanced around as the seconds passed.

Did she leave? Where did she go?

"I don't have to remind you of the consequences of disobeying, do I?" She clucked her tongue. "How is Kirian?"

"Dead." *You killed him.*

"That's news to me. His body was never found."

Her words stabbed. My heart thumped. "What do you mean?" *Can he be alive? Were we wrong?*

She continued as if I hadn't spoken. "It would be a shame if Meridian disappeared. Or Tony. You have so many new friends. How is Bodie? Still wandering outside alone on adventures? That cat followed him around too."

Bodie? Meridian? Tony? Mini?

"Why would you threaten them? Why not take it out on me?"

"That's no fun. Besides, I've seen you suffer. You're quite talented at it. I wonder if you can make that into a career."

"What do you want from me?"

"There's a book that belongs to us. We want it back."

"A book?"

"Pages? Cover? Writing on the inside? Ring a bell?"

"But who has it?"

She huffed as if I was purposefully being obnoxious. Maybe I was.

"Do the living mean nothing to you?" Without waiting for my response, she asked, "How badly do you want to know where your parents were dumped? They were broken up about the whole thing." She laughed.

"If I give you something, will you tell me where to find them? And Kirian?"

"Hmm, the book, Juliet. If you'd rather know about the dead than keep your living friends safe, that can be arranged," she stated as if truly weighing the options.

I wanted to swear at the pathetic desire in my voice.

She'll use them. She uses everyone. "The living, they'll be safe too?"

"Your new friends haven't figured it out yet, have they? That you're playing them? How sad. Or maybe they know it all and think you won't be able to handle the truth. Maybe they're playing you. Hmm, has Tony touched you yet? You know he will, don't you? What else are you good for? How could he love you like a daughter and not look for you all those years? Maybe he gave you to us. Did you think of that?"

He's not capable of that, is he? I knew what girls who came through DG experienced. What some of the boys cried about. *I'd fight back, wouldn't I? I'm not fighting back now, though, am I?*

"Which book?" I hated thinking she might be right that I didn't know enough. Anything.

"You'll know it by this marking."

Talonlike nails the color of raw beef dropped a white piece of paper into the creek. As it floated toward me, it snagged on a rock. I leaned down. The black ink on the page was already spreading, melting off the sheet. *I can't read it! What is this?* Ink-dyed water dripped down my hands, my arms.

"But what is this?" *Wings? A stick? Nothing in the portfolio at Rumi's had these drawings on them. Did they?*

"Dig around, Juliet, and you might be surprised as to what you find."

"Where do you want me to bring it?"

"We'll find you."

"Y-you're . . ." I stuttered over my tongue, words fleeing like birds before buckshot.

"Get used to it." She laughed. "Ta-ta, we'll be in touch."

"Wait!" *Come back. Tell me what you know. Please!* I slogged through the water toward the opposite bank, but all I found was trampled grass and indents in the mud from stiletto heels. I collapsed, slamming my fists into the earth until my knuckles cracked and bled. *Can I give her what she wants without it killing me completely inside?*

* * *

I tiptoed past Tony's bedroom, listening for his snore and hearing nothing. *He must be out volunteering again. Saving another soul.*

I closed the bedroom door behind me, hoping I hadn't dripped creek water in a trail down the hallway.

"Juliet?" Tony sat in a pink velour armchair he'd pulled over near my door.

Startled, I jumped. "What are you doing in here?" I turned on the light, staring at him.

"I was afraid you'd come back through the window or I wouldn't hear you."

"I'm here now." *Caught.*

"And for a while that was good enough." Tony held his head.

The disappointment in his eyes was unbearable. *What do you want from me?* I didn't know how to answer, so I kept silent.

Tony continued. "We have to talk about your choices."

I felt my heart pick up rhythm. *You are not my father. Every time I look at you, I see my dead mother's scarred face.*

"I don't know how to help you unless you talk to me." Tony's voice was so quiet I strained to hear. "Your mother asked me to watch over you and I failed you. I know that, but I will not fail you again. I have suspended my volunteering schedule indefinitely so I will have more time with you."

"But . . ." If he didn't leave the apartment, he might figure out how much time I spent at the creek, or trying to find this book, or in the kitchen cooking, trying to rid myself of the faces and memories by mixing ingredients together.

"I would like you to give some thought to questions you have. I called Nelli to see if her boyfriend can help us track down your father, if that's something you'd like to do. If you want to go up to Wolf Lake to be with the kids, I'll drive you. Also, I know a very good family therapist if you'd like someone else to talk to."

He kept throwing out ideas and questions that made my head spin. Find my father? Go to another state? See a doctor? I desperately wished for my closet under the stairs, my jugs of treasures. I couldn't hold on to anyone. No one stayed put. Only things stayed where they were placed. People disappeared.

"Stop." I couldn't breathe. *Stop! Stop! Just let me be.* The pain scalded. *Why doesn't he know I'll never be the good little girl he wants? He should have let me stay at DG.*

"We'll talk more in the morning. You look tired." He stood, joints creaking. "Can I sleep knowing you're going to stay in the apartment for the rest of the night?"

I nodded and he moved toward me. I held myself stiff while he placed a light kiss on my forehead. He lifted his arms as if to hug me but dropped them without actually embracing me.

I closed my eyes. *Even this man doesn't find you loveable enough to hug.*

"Good night." Tony shut the door behind him.

I turned on the CD player Rumi gave me and hit RE-PEAT on the song that reminded me of my mother, "Juliet of the Spirits." I fit the headphones over my ears and twisted the volume as high as it would go. Then I took the whole thing into the closet with me, shutting the door tightly.

The first chords filled my head. They blocked out everything.

I tucked my head down onto my knees and let the tears flow.

How is this for screwed up?

Where is this book?

Who has it?

What's in it?

Who will die because of me this time?

CHAPTER II

I lay on my stomach next to Tens, enjoying the sun and the feel of him next to me. We were on a stakeout of sorts. Again.

Riverside Cemetery was one of the oldest, largest burial grounds east of the Mississippi. It never occurred to me to look for information, or more Fenestras, among the stones, monuments, and mausoleums until Rumi brought me here to visit his mother's grave last February.

Aside from the ones Rumi pointed out, we'd found seven more, plus three that were so old the marble had washed into bumps and grooves, making it impossible to read. The names and dates were similar in script; all had one of two epitaphs we were working to decipher.

The trees made the cemetery feel like a horticulture park, with winding bike paths large enough for cars, rather than a place where people decomposed. The best parts were the purple violets overtaking the grass, just below the surface of the mower blade. Tiny intricate buds opened into fairy slippers, so that between tendings, the earth appeared indigo from a distance, a carpet of plush purple. The air sugared with the fragrance of blooming lavender lilacs, blushed peonies, and blossomed tulip trees. *So beautiful. Peaceful.*

Tens and I lay on our stomachs on a beach towel in the grass among trees on a hill, quite a ways from the plots we'd purchased. We had a guitar case and backpacks near us to appear like teens ditching class to neck. Binoculars in hand, Tens took first shift watching all the traffic and people for anyone who looked untrustworthy.

A rusty pickup truck with door signs on it from the monument company pulled to a stop at the marked location for the grave markers. We watched four men pile out. Using ropes, pulleys, cables, and brute force, they moved the plain granite rectangles into place. From here I could see the names Roshana Ambrose and Meridian Laine Fulbright chiseled into the stones. *Anything?*

My attention was drawn to a wandering soul who'd spotted me. "I've got one coming toward me," I said to Tens.

A little old lady wearing a pink chiffon gown glided

over. Her feet, which were not quite touching the ground, were my only clue she was a spirit needing the window.

"I've got you covered," Tens answered as I felt the wave and let my eyes drift shut.

My window appeared. "Thank you," said the old lady as she quickly slipped across the threshold into a concert hall, where musicians played a big-band tune and the audience broke into wild applause as she walked onto the stage, growing straighter, taller, more solid as I watched.

Tens caressed my cheek. I smiled as I opened my eyes. *Shepherding souls really does become easier with practice.*

"You okay?" he asked.

"Did I pass out?" I remembered a time when the souls using me drained me so completely that I was forever sick. Now stronger, I was more able to do my job.

"No, I think you fell asleep. You snored." He grinned and leaned into my kiss.

We didn't get much sleep after Tony's worry-filled venting last night. We'd spent hours trying to untangle Juliet's mind-set and motivation. *What are we missing?*

I sighed, entwining my arms around his neck and weaving my fingers in his hair. He shifted closer, pressing his hips and thighs against me. He smelled of soap and pine forests and wet dog. I flashed to Custos and pictured her tongue in my mouth instead of Tens's. *Lordy! Not sexy!*

I giggled, unable to hold back.

"What's so funny?" Tens leaned back and gazed at me.

"I *really* didn't get enough sleep last night. I'm feeling a little nutso today."

"That has nothing to do with last night," he teased, rolling away.

"Oh, really?"

"Yeah, you're crazy about me. I addle the ladies." He puffed up his chest.

"Oh, you do, do you? Picking up on Rumi-isms?" Laughing, I threw a handful of grass in his direction. Violets landed in his hair like a haphazard crown that made me giggle harder.

I wished for the millionth time that I could make time freeze and Tens and I could simply be together without interruption. *Without the world of death dictating we steal moments to cobble a life together.* I didn't know how Auntie managed the window all those years and carried on with her life in this world without skipping a beat. I'd barely passed the point of blacking out for chunks of time. I had to figure out how she could walk around, nurse the ill, take care of her family, and let souls through at the same time.

As Rumi said, being a Fenestra was like walking, chewing gum, patting my head, and rubbing my tummy all at the same time. Only energetically. That was the best way to describe it.

I glanced at the plots. "So, they delivered the stones we ordered."

"Yep."

"Anything?" *No signs saying, "Talk to us, we know what you want to hear"?*

He shook his head. "And I didn't see anyone watching or loitering. They did their job and moved on to another section of the cemetery."

"So it's not the stonemasons." I wrote this in my notebook.

"Doesn't appear to be." Tens kept shifting.

"So we wait?" I asked. *I hate waiting.*

"Yep."

I pulled out a few books from the backpack. "For you." I handed Tens a copy of *Roman and Greek Mythology for Dummies.* "Homework."

"What are you reading?" he asked.

"*Women in Judeo-Christian Religions.*"

"I think I'd prefer to take gym and shop classes," he grouched.

I snorted. "Me too. Only I don't think we'll find our roots among jumping jacks or table saws." I tried to shake off the drowsy, cloudy brain that came from reading stale stories about long-dead, ballsy women. As if the men who wrote the stories cut out all the interesting parts.

"Why'd we let Rumi pick the assignments?" Tens asked.

"Tony helped."

He snorted as if that mattered. "Can we get cheater's notes?"

"Yours is the abbreviated version already."

Tens leaned back against a tree and I settled my head

in his lap. From there we had a view of the entire forty-sixth section.

"You'll tell me if you see anything?"

"Sure thing. Unless I'm too engrossed in the antics of Aphrodite to notice."

I knew his eyes were teasing behind his sunglasses even if he worked really hard to keep a straight face.

"You do that."

As the sun set, no one had come by the section except two joggers. We stretched and put our stuff away. The gates closed soon, and being locked inside wasn't exactly my idea of a hot date. "We need to head back. See if Nelli's heard anything more."

As we walked down the hill, a small black sedan with tinted windows roared around the corner.

"Way too fast for the cemetery." Tens ducked behind a tree, dragging me with him.

The driver threw it into park but didn't cut the engine. The latest summertime club jam pumped from speakers too large for the vehicle. *Auntie would say it's loud enough to wake the dead.*

Tens kept moving, skidding closer, behind a mausoleum the size of a storage shed. *It is a storage shed—cheery thought.*

We were close enough to see the driver of the sedan was not much older than us. He was built like an athlete, his jeans were faded and ripped, and his Bulldogs T-shirt memorialized the last basketball championship of a local university.

"Be careful," I whispered urgently. We didn't know if he was good or bad.

Tens dropped his backpack and slid down closer, around toward the back of the vehicle.

The driver dug into his pockets. It looked as though he hadn't shaved in days; bluish shadow accented his jaw. Shaggy brown hair was stuffed under a green baseball cap worn backward. He took out his phone and snapped a couple of quick photos of the headstones before turning back toward the car.

Tens wouldn't make it to the car in time.

I stood up from my hiding place. "Hello? Can you help me, please?" I waved and hurried down. "I'm so glad I spotted you. I was here for a school project and got lost." I tried to pout prettily while continuing. "Now, I don't know if I go that way for the main gate or that way?" I tried batting my lashes and sounding helpless.

He hesitated at the driver's side of the car, seemingly torn between getting out of there and answering me. "Uh, I don't know. Just follow the white or gold lines on the road."

"Which way are you going? Maybe I can get a ride back?" I loped down, trying to appear as carefree as a high school sophomore should.

"What school did you say you went to?" he asked.

"She didn't," Tens said from behind him.

The man jumped, yelling, "What the hell?"

"Why are you taking pictures of these graves?" Tens's face was harsh with angles and reflective sunglasses.

"Uh . . . uh . . . m-man . . . ," he stuttered.

"What's your name?" Tens sidled closer.

"Ah, shit." The driver slammed into his car and locked the doors. He hit the accelerator and took off.

I started to call out the license plate number so I could remember it: "W-I-2—"

"Holy hell, that went well." Tens went to collect our stuff with a frustrated stomp.

"He was nervous. Fidgety."

"Yep. Good thing he was wearing a Butler University shirt."

"Everyone's got those."

"Not ones that say they're from the student welcome home at Hinkle Fieldhouse. Did you see his hat too?"

"Grass green, but he wore it backward."

"Capital *W*, lowercase *o*, capital *W* under a tree."

"WoW trees? Like a student ecology group?" *Weird.*

"I've never seen one like it. Have you?"

"No. You think it's important?"

"I don't know. We can ask Gus, see if he recognizes it. Otherwise, I'll be looking college bound and hanging out on campus until I spot him."

"You really think you can find him again?"

"Do you doubt my abilities?" he asked with a twist of his lips.

I held my hands up, smiling. "Nope. You sure found me right quick," I teased.

"If only you'd flown, I would have been all over the airport to collect you!" With both backpacks slung over his shoulders, he hugged me to him. I'd been put on a bus across the country and arrived at the station with no one to meet me. Josiah, in the guise of a taxi service, made sure I got to Auntie's. It wasn't the finest hour for either Tens or me.

"That was the problem? Glad you tell me that now!" I laughed. "Where's my notebook?" I patted my pants.

"Don't know."

I ran back up the hill to where we'd planted ourselves. Sure enough, it lay there in the grass. I'd taken to having a notebook in my pocket at all times. I wrote down Rumi's astonishingly big words (or tried to). I wrote down ingredients and French cooking terms that Juliet seemed to cough out with each breath while she cooked. I wrote down bits and pieces of things I picked up when souls went through me. But mostly I wrote down questions. *Lots and lots of questions.*

I jotted down everything we could remember about the sedan, the driver, and the license plate number. Tens took the notebook from me and drew the artwork from the hat. A deeply hued almost black-green tree, like an oak, and a font that looked like scripted cursive. WoW. *Huh.*

"Why did we park so far away?" I asked.

"Need me to pick you up?"

"Nah." Actually, I did, but if I said that, Tens would increase the cardio that he seemed to think was a necessity to my well-being. I hated every step of the miles he made me run with him. But I loved him, so I did it.

Near the Gothic Chapel, we walked past an area with a newly dug grave, the green canopy and chairs set up for the morning service. "Tens, soul," I said, clueing him in that I was about to be pulled under to the window.

An African American man with a white beard and full three-piece suit seemed overjoyed to see us, waving and calling out greetings as he neared. I stopped walking so I wouldn't run into any stones. I couldn't help the smile on my lips as he brought me to his window.

This time the windowpanes were stained glass, filling this side with colorful lights and bright rays of joy. Without skipping a beat, the deceased danced over and into a full church sanctuary mid-service. A choir sang, the congregation clapped, and the preacher at the pulpit welcomed him home.

I was just about to turn back to my life when I saw Howie, his face still frozen in scar tissue, sitting in the back pew. He seemed a little older. His hair longer but still muddy, his clothes still dirty.

"Howie?" I leaned across the window, calling for him. Shocked, I felt my human legs give way. I hoped Tens was close enough to catch me.

"Hello?" His voice broke.

"It's Meridian. What are you doing here?"

"I can't go on. Not until. You said I was going home!" He turned toward me, falling over the back of a pew in his haste to get to me.

My heart broke. *Why isn't he better? Are his wounds the same as Roshana's?* The window faded before I could say anything else. I blinked my eyes open and saw Tens leaning over me, shading my face with his.

"Meridian?" Tens held bottled water to my lips.

"He's still there." *Howie's stuck at the window? How do we heal him?*

"I know. We're in the van. I carried you here. You were yelling for Howie." Tens tried to reassure me.

After the tornado dispensed with Jasper's truck, we'd bought a used van. It wasn't exactly great on mileage but it allowed us all to mostly travel together.

I nodded.

"Let's get you home." Tens touched my cheek.

We need to talk to everyone.

We drove through the gates as the security guard moved behind us to close them.

* * *

I watched neighborhoods flow past us, banners of black-and-white checkerboard and bunting draped across mailboxes and hung from porches. The entire city turned black and white, white and black in May. Forget patriotism on the Fourth of July; this was Indy 500 month, where race cars and racing were the topics of united celebration. It wasn't lost on me that our month was turning very black and white, too, only evil against good, Fenestra versus Nocti.

As I watched yet another street of decorated houses speed by along an old avenue of tree-lined turn-of-the-century mansions, I tried to assimilate all that I'd seen. Nothing else could possibly pack itself in. I jinxed myself.

The van slowed. "Tens? What are you doing?" I asked, sitting straighter.

"Didn't you see her?"

"Who?"

"The hitchhiker."

"Pretty?" I teased as he pulled to the shoulder. "Uh, no. We are not stopping." I didn't have to watch late-night cop shows to know picking up hitchhikers wasn't a smart thing. That there were baddies after us only added to that. Capital letter N-O.

"Already stopped." Tens shrugged.

"She could be Jack the Ripper's cousin," I debated.

"Merry." He rolled his eyes. Clearly, I'd begun to wear off on him. "Her sign. Did you see her sign?"

I guessed, "Will work for food?"

"Close, but no." He set the parking brake as cars continued whizzing past.

"What?" I asked as he snapped off the ignition.

As Tens opened the driver's side, a huge truck rumbled by, almost taking the door off with a honk and an obscene gesture.

"'Will Protect for Food,'" he yelled over the traffic sounds.

"Huh?" I scrambled to follow him.

The hitchhiker turned, grabbed a hobo bag, and headed toward us.

I turned my head and read the sign dangling from

her hand. In thick black marker, she'd written WILL PROTECT FOR FOOD. *Weird*. *Creepy*.

"She's one of us." Tens shook his head at my expression.

"Yeah, right. She's probably on drugs and creatively minded."

His certainty didn't extend to me.

Her hair was military short in the back and sides, but layers of punked out curls on the top were scrunched into waves like white-water rapids. It was hair that either took hours to appear so messy or she didn't bother to style it at all. Hard to tell.

A black leather jacket, three sizes too big and with rolled up sleeves, covered a layered skirt sewn of knockoff silk scarves. Fingerless black gloves with silver studs competed to reflect the sunlight with miles of chains draped around her neck and bracelets up her arms. Earrings of feathers and tinsel bracketed a face full of kohl and color.

I hung back, ready to flag down assistance, but Tens strode forward like they knew each other. As we faced off, she smiled at Tens, flicking her hair out of her eyes. "Took you long enough."

"Hello?" I said, wondering at her attitude.

"Tens and Meridian, I presume?" she answered in a heavy accent I didn't recognize.

Tens grinned big and goofy. *I'm missing a joke.*

"I'm Fara." She handed Tens one of her bags.

"Is that supposed to mean something?" I asked, perplexed by her confidence and swagger.

"She's Juliet's Protector," Tens said to me out of the corner of his mouth.

I turned to him. "How do you know?"

He shrugged. "I know it."

"I had no idea getting from New York to you would take this long. She's still alive, right? Made it okay without me?"

Barely. Thanks for caring.

"When did you arrive?" Tens took her other bag and started walking back toward the van. I trailed along like a third wheel.

"Supposed to be here before Nowruz."

Now-what?

To me, she clarified like I was a simpleton. "The Persian New Year. Zoroaster's birthday. Also Juliet's day of blossoming. I should be here for that."

Yeah, you should have been, but you weren't. "So what happened?" I asked. Thinking of the sleepless nights I spent worrying. Trying to remember everything and anything I thought Juliet needed to know before the clock struck midnight and souls knew her window was fully open. Get her through or she would die. *As in dead dead.* I could have used backup beyond Tens and Auntie's journal. Maybe that accounted for the bitch in my tone.

She ignored me. She didn't need to speak a word to break the silence. The jingles and jangles, twangs and tings of all the metal announced her every step.

I'd never seen anyone wear clothing covering so much

and yet showing more than it left to the imagination. She had on at least three pairs of tights—fishnets, sheer black, and sheer pink on the bottom—all ripped strategically to look like an advertisement for layering nylon.

Her body had the curves of 1940s pinups, with breasts and hips that made her seem way older than me. The entire makeup counter on her face didn't pin her age down either. She grabbed shotgun and left me to take a backseat. *Like Custos.* I tried to be pissed, but really it left me in a place where I could make sure she didn't pull a knife and slit my throat from behind. *Safety before ego.*

Yeah, okay, I'm not a fan. I envied her woman's body. Not the arrogance.

"Where are you staying?" Tens started the engine and merged back into traffic.

"Gotta floor?" she asked, carefree and casual.

Uh, no. "What are you plans?" I said.

She shrugged. "Find Juliet. You bring me to her."

It's that easy, is it?

That sounded familiar, but we all knew there was an after the introductions that needed to be factored into the equation. *How exactly do we prove she is who she says she is?* Just like we hadn't known quite how to tell who was a Fenestra like me, I wasn't sure we knew how to tell if a Protector crossed our paths. *Is this how Tens felt last winter when I barged into DG, riding to the rescue?*

"We're headed to meet up with our friends. We need to talk to them. You're not invited," I said.

Tens shot me a censuring glance. I didn't care. I wasn't

talking about Howie, Delia, and the college kid at the cemetery in front of someone I didn't know.

"No problem. There a coffee shop around here?"

"Sure." Tens turned down Old Meridian Street.

"I figured you'll want to check me out, talk about me. Ex-eter-a. Ex-ecter-ah."

Et cetera.

She was a force of nature. She took everything I dished in stride and with a contented twist of her lips. As if she'd traveled hard and could finally relax, and nothing I said could ruin that.

"Exactly," I answered her.

"Want proof?" She half turned toward me.

"Of?" I asked.

"I am her Protector. I've seen things. I've dreamed her forever." She looked at Tens, and he nodded. "Private things. Ask her about the treasures she keeps in plastic bottles."

I flashed to us crammed into Juliet's crawlspace at DG and the hollowed out bleach bottles full of birds' nests and pebbles. I hadn't asked her about them since the tornado.

"What about them?" Tens asked.

"She has more under her new bed. Just look."

I didn't say anything.

"I cannot prove me, but I am not going anywhere. I belong here. I fight to stay."

The fierceness in her expression chased away any sarcastic retort on my tongue. I nodded.

"We'll come back and get you when we're finished,"

Tens added as he pulled up in front of our favorite coffee shop in town.

"Can I leave my stuff in your car?"

"I don't have a problem with that," Tens said.

Fara turned around and winked at me. "Just put it all back in same place, okay? And if you can wash the dirty, awesome!" She pulled earbuds out of her backpack and tuned us out as she opened the door, got out, and slammed it behind her.

Are we done? I raised an eyebrow at Tens and he simply laughed.

As we neared Rumi's, lights and sirens blocked the street. News vans and crews with spotlights and sound equipment were set up on all corners. Rumi was standing with three uniforms, appearing to answer questions.

"What's going on?" Tens asked, turning left and heading instead for Tony's.

CHAPTER 12
Juliet

I walked toward Rumi's, each step weighing me deeper into the earth, as if the gravity of my deception buried me in an early grave. The portfolio of little window paintings and notes that might have been gibberish if I hadn't seen Rumi read them was tucked in my bag. I saw nothing like the symbol Ms. Asura wanted. *I need to put these back before he discovers they're missing.*

Can I do what Ms. Asura wants, manage to keep every-one safe, and still find my parents? I have to try. I may have to tell Rumi the truth. But he'd tell them all. They'll hate me. *They'll send me away. Give me to Ms. Asura with no regrets.* I staggered as the threads of dark ate my reasoning. *Fear is the most powerful emotion, isn't it?*

I froze as blaring sirens and flashing lights racing past me. Immediately, I was back at the aftermath of the Feast bombing. The smell of singed flesh and burned corn choked me. I ducked into an alley behind a bank of Dumpsters. *I'm too late. Too slow. Too stupid to find what she wanted.*

Had Ms. Asura made good on her threat to injure my people? Was I not moving fast enough?

I fished around in my backpack for the cell phone Tony pressed into my hand this morning. I'd missed three calls. All from him. I dialed him back without listening to the messages.

"Where are you?" he asked, sounding weary and upset with me.

My heart hammered; my tongue barely worked. "There are police at Rumi's. Is he okay?"

"You're at Rumi's? Get home, Juliet. They may still be watching."

Answer me! I wanted to scream. Instead I repeated, "Is he okay?"

Tony barked, "Yes, yes, get out of there. His studio was vandalized. I don't know details, but everyone's headed here to meet up. Why don't I come get you? Where are you?"

I'm not a child. "I'm fine. Everyone is all right?"

"Yes, come home now!"

His fury slapped at me. *Even he doesn't think you can walk around Carmel alone.*

"Okay," I whispered.

"Don't talk to anyone. Don't get into any cars."

My blood boiled. *I'm not incapable.* I stabbed my finger against the bricks until my nail broke, tearing with a crimson smile.

Tony continued. "Tens and Meridian just drove into the parking lot."

"I'm coming," I said, the phone already away from my ear. Uniformed policemen screeched to a halt outside the alley; they shouted instructions to each other.

"Why don't I send Merid—"

I hung up the phone and dropped it back into my pocket, sitting heavily in the trash and debris around me. I peeked around, trying to understand the chaos at Rumi's store.

Policemen scurried around taking photographs and studying the ground. There was so much broken glass on the sidewalk that they couldn't avoid cracking and popping more. *Like breakfast cereal.*

I waited until I saw Rumi. He appeared shocked and stricken. His eyes were glazed and gleaming as he tried to answer questions. He kept shaking his head as if he had no knowledge to share.

I put my hand down to push myself up and touched fur. *What?* I jerked my hand back, startled.

Under the Dumpster was the headless body of an orange tabby cat. Near her lay three dead kittens, as if they hadn't known what to do when their mama died. Eww. *Where's her head?* Spooked, I booked down the alley toward the condo, ignoring my throbbing foot wound.

I thrashed up the stairs and collapsed onto the couch, my bag clutched against my chest.

"Juliet? Are you okay?" Meridian asked. Concern crimped her forehead and narrowed her eyes. *She knows. She knows what's in my bag.*

I nodded, catching my breath. Avoiding her eyes, deliberately relaxing my fingers so they didn't show so white against the cabbage-green canvas. I hadn't taken two breaths before Tony and Tens swooped down on me as well.

"You're bleeding," Tony rebuked and chastised me. "What did you do now?"

The gash on my foot reopened in the run, leaving dollops of blood on the wood floors.

"Sorry." The word sounded hollow since I used it so often. *I'm always apologizing. I'm always making their lives harder.*

"You're going to get an infection if you don't take better care of yourself." Tony shook his head as he fetched the first-aid kit, and Meridian wiped up the blood. Tens simply watched me. When he reached for my bag, it took everything I had not to flinch away.

By the time Tony was done rebandaging my foot and lecturing me on being alone and vulnerable, Nelli and Rumi entered without knocking. "I'm sorry. I didn't mean to involve the police. The punctilious insurance salesman across the street came in late. Heard noises. Saw the broken windows. Went all Doolally crazy and called nine-one-one."

Rumi's size used to intimidate me, because his eyes saw too deeply into me. His presence reminded me of truffle risotto and cream-of-asparagus soup with crusty, steaming Parker House rolls.

"Where were you when this happened?" Tony asked, sounding upset at Rumi but looking at me.

How sorry do I have to be? His life would be so simple without me. I avoided Tony so often, too often. It wasn't his fault. *How can I tell him that seeing his face reminds me he couldn't save me from them before, so why should I believe he can now?*

"At Faye's trying to spell Gus a nap." Rumi rubbed his eyes. "If only her cold, froideur, daughter lived in town and was willing to help."

"But she's a drama queen you wouldn't want to have around," Nelli said. As Gus's niece, she probably knew more than the rest of us. "I'm heading there tonight for the same thing."

"What exactly happened to your shop?" Tens asked. He asked questions so quietly they shouted, like a spicy dish that starts out mild but follows with a scalding kick of heat.

Meridian wrote fast and furiously, as if her life depended on recording every word of our discussions. She'd done a lot of writing since I'd known her; it was as if stories were nourishing for her heart the way food was for mine.

"Bricks were thrown through the front windows; all

of the Spirit Stones were smashed. Most of my Nain's and family's writings were stolen."

"Say that again?" Meridian asked, her head snapping up.

"They obliterated the glass balls into smithereens. Took my family's archives." Rumi cocked his head.

"They stole Nain's collection?" I asked.

"Not all. I had a few in a safety bank box."

I felt as though I'd eaten a bushel of hot peppers. *They think the Nocti stole his papers. Not me. How can I return them now? How will I find what she needs?*

Meridian hummed.

"What is it, lass? What are you thinking?" Rumi asked Meridian.

"There was a possum tail and intestines smeared on the cottage porch two nights ago. Someone broke all of the Spirit Stones you'd hung from the rafters there. No one's touched Auntie's journal, but we were home, so maybe they couldn't get to it as expected," Tens answered for Meridian.

"It's like Revelation, like what happened at Auntie's," Meridian added.

"What about Revelation?" Tony asked.

I straightened, listening intently. Any time Meridian spoke of Auntie, I missed my mother more. *Where are my ancestors? Aunts? Cousins? Grandparents?*

Tens said, "Perimo and his followers began escalating their harassment of us in the months before Meridian arrived in Colorado. It's their way of warning."

"I think it's safe to assume the Nocti equate desecrating any living thing with a threat."

"They're afraid of the Spirit Stones," Rumi said, cradling a coffee mug full of cream and sugar with only a splash of dark brew. "And our knowledge."

"There were several churches graffitied and vandalized downtown two nights ago," Tony said.

"My store was the only place hit in Carmel that I'm aware of," said Rumi.

"It's possible it was kids who heard about the downtown incidents and thought to try it out here," Nelli said. She was built like a plump roasting hen, her hair the color of crisped browned skin. Freckles covered freckles like sprinkles of nutmeg over whipped cream. She wasn't far out of college, yet her presence felt motherly instead of only a few years older than us. She always looked at me with painful guilt and responsibility.

"It's possible but not probable," Tens disagreed. "Kids might break glass, but steal specific writings?"

"Do you have any extra Spirit Stones here?" Meridian asked Tony.

"I don't, no."

I cleared my throat. "I do." *Under my bed, because I stole it.*

Rumi raised his eyebrows. I knew he was wondering how I'd gotten ahold of one without paying him for it, but he didn't say anything. He would have given it to me if I'd asked.

"I can get it." I stood and the nerves in my foot

throbbed to life. I grimaced before I tamped down my reaction.

Catching my wince, Meridian shoved me back down. "Where is it? I'll get it."

"Under my bed, but wait—"

She was already sprinting down the hall. I didn't want her to see what I'd stashed under there. Rocks. A fossil I'd found near the creek. Arrowheads. Halves of hatched robin's eggs. A nest like the one Kirian gave me that blew away in the tornado. A brooch I'd pocketed at Helios last month in the shape of a hummingbird and covered in rhinestones. Meridian's green scarf.

Meridian came back out with the scarf draped over her neck and the Spirit Stone in her hand. It glowed like a million refracted rainbows, the tree inside spreading out, inviting us all to dive into its light. She didn't say anything to me about all the stolen goods. *She doesn't have to.*

"Why the escalation?" Nelli said. "If it is Nocti?"

"You found the remains of an old DG boy, right? Howie? Or maybe because Juliet survived her transition to full Fenestra?" Tony asked Nelli.

Why are they escalating? Because they can. They don't need a logical reason. There's more to it, Juliet. Figure it out.

"Are we being dumb not considering other options? Criminals without supernatural connections?" Nelli pointed out.

Tens shook his head. "It sounds like Nocti, but we

should keep our eyes peeled regardless. I don't know why humans would care about the Spirit Stones. They're just trinkets."

"I'll go make dinner." I tried to stand and flinched as the nerves in my foot woke again and pulsed.

"Sit!" Tony scolded me. "We'll order in pizza."

"But . . ." *I love the kitchen.* They coddled me rather than understood my need to escape there. The pity rolled over me like breaking waves and made me nauseous. *Poor Juliet. She's too fragile and useless.*

"Don't worry about it tonight, okay? We have lots to talk about." Meridian used the scarf to make a nest on the coffee table and set the sphere gently into its folds.

I wasn't used to being waited on. It rankled. *She's probably going to tell everyone I stole her scarf and hid it under my bed. At least the folio is in my bag. They don't know about that.*

"Thanks," I said, not meaning it.

Nelli told us about going to the Milk building and gathering the boy's remains. They couldn't identify the cause of death. "Too much time passed; there was no evidence of foul play." Nelli flushed. "My boss isn't being helpful. He's not even sure we have identified Howie correctly. There's no information about his past anywhere. It's as if he didn't exist except for the tiny bit in the DG papers. I've requested Howie's remains be given to me for burial."

"What happens to him if you don't get them?" Tens asked.

"There's a mass grave at Riverside Cemetery for the unclaimed, and there's a monument his name would be engraved on if we prove his identity."

"He mentioned meeting Roshana and Argy. I think maybe they were all at DG together—at least their time overlapped," Meridian said.

"How does something this horrid happen for decades without anyone noticing and stopping it?" Nelli hung her head.

"Because people turn away from truth. From seeing the dark sides of life. If it's not happening to them, it doesn't matter. Hiding in plain sight," Rumi said, voicing my thoughts perfectly. "They made the children anchorites, living in seclusion, and the murders were secretive murdrums. The general populace doesn't believe in things they don't see. Much of reality they turn away from so they don't have to see it or believe it."

I pressed my foot against the chair leg until I felt the edges of the cut break apart and bleed again. I'm still alive. *For the moment.*

"You'll never guess who we met today." Tens demanded everyone's attention.

My heart pounded. *Had Ms. Asura come to them as well?*

"Juliet's Protector."

The room erupted with questions and exclamations.

Who? I shook my head, not sure I'd heard correctly. "What did you say?"

"Her name is Fara, and she's been traveling from New

York, but I don't think she's American," Tens answered. "She claims to be your Protector."

"So she says," Meridian plugged.

How could Meridian gloss over such an important announcement? My Protector made contact? *Who is she? Where is she? Is it Nicole come back again?*

"Mirabile dictum! Precious good news!" Rumi exalted.

"We have to talk this through." Tony's face twisted in doubt and fear.

Tens leaned down to me and whispered as the decibel levels around us rose. "We'll introduce Fara to you as soon as we finish this discussion, okay?"

"But—" *No!* I didn't want to wait. *Why are we waiting? Where is she? Not a boy? A girl?*

Meridian tried to reassure me. "We can't bring her here with all of us. Everyone needs to understand the risk. What if she's a Nocti sympathizer?"

"You've looked in her eyes? She's not Nocti?" I asked.

"No, she's not. And Tens feels certain she is your Protector. But there are questions—"

"Then why didn't she get here in time for my birthday?"

"I don't know. I really don't. She's at the coffee shop on Main waiting to hear from us."

"Let's go now." I stood up.

"Not until we've all talked about it," Meridian said, and shook her head.

My opinion was dismissed as the pros and cons were battled around. I lost my appetite, counting the minutes until the pizza arrived. Until they'd eaten their fill and decisions were made. *Events with the Nocti are rising again. No one knows why.*

I wanted to meet Fara. Decide for myself. Make up my own mind.

Tens finally took pity on me and suggested he go get her.

"No. You can't bring her here," Tony objected. "Not until we know more about her. Juliet is just starting to get comfortable."

Really? News to me. "But—" I tried to argue.

"Juliet can't walk on that foot," Nelli pointed out.

"We do have her bags . . . ," Meridian suggested, and let it hang in the open space as everyone heard her and thought of the invasion, the line that going through her bags crossed.

I leapt to my feet, putting all of my weight on my wound, showing no weakness even though a light sweat broke out along my scalp. "I want to see her bags. Now."

Meridian winced as if she regretted suggesting it.

"Okay," Tens said. "I'll get them, but I think we're invading her privacy."

"She dared us to, Tens." Meridian shrugged.

He nodded, his expression closed and hard to read. "Fine." He headed out the front door and I sat back down.

"Don't get your hopes up," Meridian said to me.

What does she mean by that? Maybe Fara wasn't here sooner because she, too, knows I'm not worthy. She knows how damaged I am.

CHAPTER 13

"An extra pair of combat boots, enough metal jewelry to remold into a jumbo jet, and a wardrobe from Madonna's 1986 closet," I huffed. Nothing incriminating.

"I told you she's one of us," Tens scolded me.

I almost stuck my tongue out at him. "I didn't expect to find a Nocti membership badge." But maybe something, anything that lent a little suspicion. *There's nothing.* Just the bags of a girl who shopped at thrift stores and collected shiny objects like a magpie.

Juliet sniffed a sweater but abruptly stopped when she realized I was watching her. I raised an eyebrow but didn't say anything. She'd stolen my scarf, hidden merchandise from Helios, and stashed the flora and fauna of the creek under her bed. *What else is she hiding? Why?*

"How do we know we can trust Fara? You're sure you felt a connection?" Tony asked Tens, having a complete change of heart.

"On my grandfather Tyee, she's like me." Tens nodded.

Tony and Tyee served in Vietnam together. Tyee saved Tony's life, and it was this long-standing relationship that brought Tens and Tony together.

Tony crossed himself. "We must have faith. If you say she's worth trusting, that must be good enough for me. Why don't we put her bags in the guest room while you go get her from the coffee shop?"

"I'm sure she can stay at Joi's house while they're gone. I don't know how comfortable I am with her here." Nelli's anxiety notched up a level. "What if she's—"

"Does anyone care what I think?" Juliet's face flushed bright red. "If she's my Protector, then she should be near me. Unless Tens is going to go to Joi's too?" Her defiance felt overblown, but I understood her view. *Juliet has to fight everything. She knows no other way of life.*

"It's a risk," I pointed out.

Juliet simply stared me down.

"Okay, Juliet wants her here." I shrugged. I wasn't going to argue, and no way in hell was Tens leaving the cottage. *My man stays with me.*

Tens nodded. "She's just down at Book 'n' Bean. I'll be right back." He brushed a hand against mine as he left the condo.

"Why don't we hang the Spirit Stone in the front hall-way?" Nelli moved toward the living room. "That way everyone who enters must pass by it."

Bad people don't make the glass darken, nor do good people make it lighten. Only Nocti or Fenestra changed the light within. But whatever, Nelli was nervous.

"We'll unpack Fara's things." Juliet began taking stacks of clothes into the room across the hall from hers. "That way it won't be like we snooped."

"She won't have any idea," I muttered under my breath, grabbing boots and another scuffed leather jacket full of metal spikes. Juliet needed a Protector who was nurturing and cuddly. Someone who would give her confidence and teach her to navigate this world. I felt like Juliet lived most of her life in a very nasty bubble. The last thing she needed was arrogant, cocky, know-it-all Fara.

"Can Protectors be female?" I asked no one in particular.

"We've found evidence of male Fenestra," Rumi answered me from the hall. He didn't need a ladder to hang a hook in the high ceiling, only a footstool.

But is Fara Juliet's soul mate? Like Tens is mine? Or does that have to happen? Can you have a soul mate who isn't also a lover? Juliet loved Kirian, but he was human. A fallible manipulated innocent who hadn't stood a chance against Ms. Asura and her cohorts.

My thoughts tumbled over themselves, twisting, knotting, tangling, and giving me a headache. A very human throb at the base of my neck.

Juliet disappeared with her canvas satchel into her bedroom and shut the door. I thought about knocking but decided to give her a minute alone. Each change seemed to take a lot out of her.

Tens came back less than five minutes later, Fara in tow. She marched in, filling the spaces with bravado and conceit as if she belonged and we had no say in the matter.

"That was fast," I said by way of greeting.

"There's a GPS tracking bug in my bag. I was already outside." She shrugged.

My jaw dropped.

"Nah, I just like old spy movies they show late at night. But Dark could do that, so we'll have to be more careful." Fara straightened when she realized there were more people in the room. She considered each face, dismissing us quickly. Clearly she thought she knew what Juliet looked like.

I half expected her to crack her knuckles and pop her neck like she was preparing to go into a boxing ring.

"Welcome." Tony was the first to hold out his hand. "Juliet is like a daughter to me. You'll care for her to the utmost of your abilities?"

Fara nodded, taking his hand. "Fara Vishi. I will."

"Lass, I'm Rumi." Rumi engulfed her in a bear hug that made me giggle. Fara's stiff acceptance made me think she wasn't used to such displays of affection.

"Where is she?" Fara let herself be guided toward the couch.

Nelli answered, "We have a few questions for you first."

Juliet was still nowhere around. I excused myself to find her, and after knocking on her door, opened it.

She was in her bedroom, rocking back and forth with her arms around her knees. I knew Tony wanted her to feel at home, but he'd decorated the room as if a six-year-old had requested a theme of unicorns, princesses, and Laffy Taffy. But the interior decorating wasn't making her cry.

"Fara's in the living room," I said quietly, trying not to startle her.

Tears clung to her bottom lashes as she raised her head and wiped her eyes on her T-shirt.

"What's wrong?"

"Bad day," she said so quietly the words floated before drifting away.

"Are you worried about Fara being corrupt? Tens swears he knows she's one of the good guys. The Spirit Stone didn't do anything when she walked under it either." *Not like it would.*

"No, I . . . just . . ."

Don't interrupt her; let her speak. I slouched down, trying to give her more room to get the words out. Sometimes Juliet seemed like a wild animal.

"Never mind." Juliet shook her head.

"No, I want to know," I pushed. She couldn't keep shutting me out. It was as if we took one step forward and two steps back.

"I thought when my Protector got here I'd feel better. Like it would fix everything. And she didn't fix anything. Nothing!" Juliet raised her voice and tossed a pillow.

Not sure what to do with her anger, I shook my head. "Tens and I fought when we first met. It wasn't easy and it certainly didn't make everything better."

She nodded.

What is she really thinking? "I wish I *could* make this simpler for you. I do. Just talk to me, okay? Tell me what you need. Let me try to help?" *How do I prove I'm her sister?*

"Okay."

"Promise?" I asked, holding up my pinkie, mimicking Bodie and Sema's new swearing ritual.

She gave a tiny smile and hooked her finger. "Promise."

"Want to go meet her now?" I asked.

"No." Juliet stood and put all her weight on the toes of her foot. She stumbled, losing her balance, then righted herself with a frown and a shallow breath.

"We need to get you crutches, don't we?" I suggested, already knowing she'd shoot me down. Juliet didn't like relying on anyone, let alone anything.

"It's not that bad. Nothing a little chocolate frozen custard with red grapes can't fix." She offered a gentle smile that apologized for not trusting me more.

"I'll run down and get a pint from Auntie Em's." Taking a custard order seemed the least I could do.

After taking my hand, Juliet followed me down the hall toward the living room. It felt as though she were preparing herself for another blow, sinking deeper into her center away from the rough edges life kept brushing against her.

Fara stopped midsentence as we entered the room. I was struck by the sight of Mini sitting in Fara's lap and Custos licking her face. *Okay, I get it. She's good.*

I waited to move nearer to Tens until Juliet dropped my hand and stepped toward Fara.

Closing the distance, Fara reached into a pocket in her skirt and held out a cellophane baggy. "I brought you dark-chocolate-covered raisins. Sorry, they're a little melty."

Juliet relaxed. "These are my favorite."

Fara nodded and I think blushed. All the adults stared with smiles that spoke of relief, of resolution.

"Who else wants frozen custard?" I asked loudly, making a big display of taking orders, trying to give Juliet and Fara a moment to adjust to each other without an audience.

Tens followed my lead, tucking hair behind my ears as we walked down Main. "What do you think?"

"She's not what I wanted for Juliet," I answered honestly.

He guffawed. "Like I was what you wanted?"

"Good point." We'd danced and crackled around each other like a match put to kindling.

Tens and I returned with cold bags and individually dished custard from down the street.

Fara was finishing a story about her upbringing. "I've been trained my whole life for this job. I expected it to happen later, though, when I was older and my father finished teaching—" She broke off, glancing down at her hands.

I handed her a dish of chocolate.

She placed a dainty spoonful in her mouth and her eyes widened. "What is this? It's better than iced cream."

"Frozen custard—the secret is in the recipe," Rumi answered her. "Not the same thing as ice cream; it's our mana from heaven in the summers."

She nodded, digging deeper into the cup.

Juliet didn't touch hers but watched it melt.

"So it's your family's business? Being Protectors?" I asked.

"Yeah, a calling I think, in blood?"

"It's in your blood?" I clarified.

She nodded, smothering a yawn with a quick apology. *It is late.*

"How long have you been training? How will you protect Juliet?" Tony asked.

"Can you read her thoughts like Tens is supposed to do with Meridian?" Rumi asked.

"What about Nocti? Have you met any of them? Killed them?" Nelli added.

"How do we know we can trust you?" Tony added.

They all talked over each other.

Fara put her custard down and inhaled. "I cannot prove I am who I say I am. But I am here, and if you ask me to leave, I will sleep on that bench out there. I will be here every day. I will be respectful but I will know where Juliet is at all times. My father swore on Zoroaster, as did his father, and his father back forever. We give our lives to Dey, the Creator. Everything I am is here, in this life, to help Juliet be her full self. My life is Light's. I am Haji Firuz on Earth. I answer to no one but Light, and I will fight the Dark, with or without your blessings. But I would rather we be friends." She looked each one of us in the eyes as she spoke. Sincerity vibrated off each word. "I am sorry my father's Amordad is not here to introduce me to you and make right."

"Amordad?" I asked.

She glanced at me, her brow furrowed. "You say Fenestra."

I nodded. "Yes."

As if the discussion was over, Juliet stood. "I trust you. I put your things in the guest room. You must be tired."

With that, the conversation was truly over. Juliet took control and even when Tony opened his mouth, she limped past him, dismissing us.

Fara hesitated.

"If you are not who you say you are, my vows to God will not protect you from harm. I will not lose her again." Tony waved a hand in Juliet's direction.

"We understand each other," Fara said, and disappeared down the hallway.

We left the van in Tony's parking lot, preferring to walk home and make sure there was no one watching for us at Helios. No vandals, no news crews spilling over from the story at Rumi's studio following leads to us. No Nocti that we saw.

"You think they'll be okay?" I asked Tens, swinging our hands.

We passed a statue of a mother with a stroller and I swore her eyes followed us. As callous as it might sound, I preferred homeless people to the statues. At least the homeless smiled back occasionally when I handed them coffee and a hot dog. The statues seemed to watch everything and judge.

"Given enough time and space, she'll be fine. Juliet's wounded, Merry. It's going to take her a long time to heal."

"I know. I don't know how to help her." *I refuse to believe it's too late.*

"You can't. You have to let her ask. Maybe Fara will get through to her."

"Custos stayed at Tony's. Aren't you a little jealous?"

"Jealous?" He stopped and tipped his head in question.

"She's yours," I insisted.

"Oh no, I learned a long time ago that I was *hers*, and only when she wanted me. She's of the Creators, Supergirl. She comes and goes as she pleases. Makes sense she'd stay with Fara. Juliet knows her, trusts her. She's going to buffer as long as she needs to."

"That's very wise of you." I smiled up at him.

"Oh, I'm very wise. You should listen to me more often." He grinned, leaning down to kiss me.

"I should, should I?" I said against his lips before melting into his embrace.

"Mmm-hmm."

No one had staked out the cottage. The door was secure and Tens's special-ops double check of a single dog hair across the threshold was intact as well.

He flopped onto the bed and held up his feet. "Remove my boots?"

I snorted back a laugh. "Let me consider it . . . yeah, no."

"You wear me out," he sighed.

"That's cuz you're so old." I flopped down next to him. "Ouch."

"You'll be how old on your birthday?"

"Twenty, and you know it." Tens leaned over and unlaced his boots, toeing them off.

"Your feet stink." I wrinkled my nose playfully.

"Really?" His eyes twinkled.

I didn't like his expression. "No. No. No." I backpedaled. Hard. "Roses? I smell roses."

Tens grabbed me and tossed me down on the bed. "My feet stink, huh?"

"Kisses? I'll give you kisses?" I tried to pucker my lips and meet his.

Instead, he belched in my face.

I gagged. "Lordy, hell."

He rolled over onto his side, laughing so hard I thought he might hurt himself. "My feet don't smell so bad now, do they?"

Boys.

CHAPTER 14

Nelli's apartment was really the old carriage house to an estate in a very high-end part of town. The type of neighborhood that housed professional athletes, television personalities, and heiresses. The private drive was on the back side of the property, and I couldn't even see the main house from her living room.

Tens dropped me off on his way to speak with Gus and track down the student photographer.

I hadn't been to Nelli's in weeks and gawked at what used to be a neat and tidy living area. If the tornado that went through picked up all of the households in February, it deposited all their papers here. The smell of mildew and dust was overpowering. *What fresh disaster is this?*

"What happened in here?"

Nelli's eyes were red and swollen. "Here, take one of these allergy pills. They help." She held out a glass of water and a bottle of over-the-counter medication as I walked in. "I know it's not a very elegant offering, but trust me, you'd rather have that than crackers and cheese."

I swallowed a pill because my throat scratched immediately. Perfect.

Nelli opened windows. "Can you turn those air cleaners on? Bales dropped them by last night when he unloaded the rest of the boxes from the storage unit."

"Sure." I found the right switches and the cool rush of air ruffled file folders, notepaper, and sticky notes.

"It looks pretty bad, doesn't it," Nelli said. "When I got home last night, it clicked for me. I've been looking for a piece of paper I'm sure had Howie's name on it and several others, including Argy. There was a photograph attached. It's got to be here. Somewhere." Hysteria and exhaustion lifted her voice. "It's got to. I think it's a piece of Juliet's past."

She's one minute from a breakdown.

"We'll find it. Where should I start?"

She pointed to different sections of the room. "Decades are split up, then years between them. Anything that is patient files and not kid related goes to the dining room. Yes, it looks as bad as this. Why don't you start over by the fireplace?"

"Sure." I wasn't convinced the organizational system worked.

Nelli switched on the television. "Will it bother you if we watch race practice? Uncle Gus got me hooked when I was a kid."

"No, it's fine." I didn't realize that the world revolved around a left-turn axis until the calendar hit May and the semis hauled in cars. Snazzy buses brought in teams and drivers. Everything in town became about the Indianapolis 500 race. *Black and white.* With a teasing smile, I asked, "So, how is Bales?"

Nelli's blush started in blotchy red at her collarbones and moved north up to her plump cheeks. "He's amazing."

"I think he likes you. A lot." I picked up another pile. *Patient. Patient. Kid.*

"I like him. I think I love him." Nelli ducked her head and focused intently. "But I need to see this through. Make it right before I can move on." She waved her hand.

"Nelli, you know you can't make it right, don't you?" I looked around the room. "There's no logic to Nocti evil. They have no boundaries. You didn't do this."

"I know, but my office should have caught on sooner. Forty years, Meridian. Forty!"

"And you've worked there how long?"

"Four."

"Uh-huh. And you've known about us for three months? You didn't let kids go there, right? Didn't send the elderly there?"

She put down a stack and looked at me squarely, seriously. "I don't want to alarm you. But there is no other explanation for all of this." She spread her hands to encompass the room.

"For goodness' sake, what are you talking about?" I half expected the CIA to come storming in.

"There had to be someone in the children's services office who knew. Someone on the inside who helped. Maybe more than one person. This is a long line of cases."

I nodded. "It makes sense. Maybe several? This is a lot of years of no one noticing, which means they were really good at hiding."

"Or there were lots of people in on it and they didn't have to hide."

I shook my head. "I don't believe that most people would let this go on. Do you?" Watching how torn up Nelli was about this abuse of power, I couldn't imagine the majority of people feeling differently.

"You can't imagine the things I've seen. People in my job have to let a lot of things that bother us go. If we don't add up the little bits and take stock occasionally? Refocus our energies? I can see blind eyes being turned."

"That's sad."

"Sad is my job on a daily basis. It's not the cartoon channel."

I nodded. "But you make a difference, right?"

"Not to any of these kids." Nelli spread her arms wide and brushed the tops of the piles with her fingertips.

"You can't think of it that way." I shook my head.

"Hard not to."

"So who helped the Nocti? Do you have any theories?"

"I don't know. I need to dig, but I wanted to make sure you were okay with me pursuing it."

It could be dangerous. Tens's voice echoed in my head. He'd tell her no.

"That's standard too. Hard to take children away from a drug dealer and not see a gun or two."

I shuddered. "Delightful."

"Nah, mostly it's boring paperwork." She smiled.

I'm not sure I believed her, but maybe she needed me to. "Bales has your back, right?"

"Yes, but he doesn't know everything. Not the supernatural stuff, not about you or the Nocti."

"Does he love you?" *I see it in his eyes when he thinks you're not watching, but do you know?*

"Maybe."

"Then we'll need to tell him. So he knows what he's up against. It's not fair to keep him in the dark."

"You'd let me share?" Nelli's eyes watered.

"Of course." At this point, we needed all hands on deck. Especially if Ms. Asura had an alliance of her own and was moving toward us again. "You don't have to do this—to try to unravel who the Nocti are or figure out which children were Fenestra. You can give us the papers and we can take over."

"This is my job." She shook her head. "Besides, it's the

moral right. My department is there to rescue kids; someone failed them, so now it's my turn to see it through. But I don't know who to trust."

"Let's start with a list. Who's been in the office longest?"

For the next several hours, we made a list of everyone who was in Nelli's department that she knew and what she knew about them. We agreed she'd tell Bales, and if we needed to have more of a discussion, we would.

When her cell rang, it was her boss. "Okay, yes. A funeral? That's a good idea. Yes, okay, I'll let you know. I'll be down shortly."

While Nelli talked, I watched cars on the TV turn around the track at furious speeds. One at a time, the cars spun; then the screen filled with men and women wearing headsets and jumpsuits directing the action. There were bright colors, lots of sponsor names, and logos. But other than recognizing a few of those, I really had no idea what I was watching. *This is a sport?*

"Howie's cremains are ready for me to pick up. Since we aren't sure who he is, no one can find his relatives. Should we hold a funeral for him?"

"Something official?" The idea of standing in for a family that loved him and would remember him pleased me. "We could do it ourselves in Auntie's plot."

"That's not technically legal."

"Not like she's there. Who's going to know?" I asked.

I glanced at the clock as Tens drove down the

driveway. "Nelli, try not to worry so much, okay? We're going to do right by the kids—we will, but it might take us a while."

She hugged me goodbye, already on the phone with Tony to see if he could officiate Howie's burial.

CHAPTER 15
Juliet

With the portfolio safely stashed in my closet and Fara sleeping in the hall, I spent the predawn hours tossing and turning. I relived my reunion with Kirian over and over again, then watched him die at Ms. Asura's hands, unable to save him. When we'd returned to the glen from rescuing the littlies, his body was gone. *Could she be telling the truth? Was he not really dead? Can he be alive and still appear at the window?* Logic told me no, but my heart wanted to insist on the impossible.

The aromas of frying dough and percolating coffee

drifted through the cracks of my window and up through the floor. I stretched, my injured foot pinned down by a warm furry stomach, with Custos draped across the foot of my bed. Mini curled over the top of my head like a crown.

I gingerly placed my feet on the carpet and realized the cut was much better. Custos whined. *Magic?*

"Thanks, guys, it doesn't hurt so much." I petted her head and moved toward the window to inhale the fresh scents of early morning.

I checked out the street below. We were in the dawn time when the earth is lit with layers of maroon light like a red onion. I turned and saw the shadow of a man, a baseball cap pulled low over his eyes, his arms and legs crossed as he leaned against the brick building across the street. *Watching. Looking up at me.* It seemed as though he stared up at me for a moment before disappearing out of my sight. I hurried toward my bedroom door and flung it open.

Fara tumbled in. Wide awake, she bounced up, reaching inside her boot to pull a knife free while speaking a torrent. When I didn't understand her, she repeated her question in English. "What happening?"

"What are you doing?" I glanced down and saw the pallet she'd made with her bags and a knitted blanket.

"You okay? Where you going?" She moved around my bedroom, checking the corners, behind things.

Without thinking, I answered honestly, "There was a man across the street. He was staring up here."

She didn't wait for me to finish my thoughts; instead

she raced downstairs and outside the house, the chains off her neck and in her other hand. Custos bounded after her. I ran back to my window in time to see her run down the alley and into the shadows.

Don't get hurt. Please come back. I'm sorry. I shouldn't have said anything.

I don't know how long I waited for her to return, but Tony kept snoring in his bedroom. I hadn't heard his five a.m. alarm go off yet.

"Anything?" I asked as she came back inside. *Thank goodness you're okay. If anything happened to you because of me—*

She shook her head. "Tell me what you saw."

"A man, athletic frame, taller than me maybe. He had a baseball cap on, pulled low."

"Any writing, symbols, or anything?"

He leaned like he'd been there awhile. I squinted, trying to remember. "Maybe white squiggles, the letter z or something. I don't know." I blew out a frustrated breath. "Was it Nocti?"

"Maybe, but they don't usually watch; they kill. Unless there's a plan we don't know about. I'll have to think about it, speak with Tens."

My stomach flipped. "Do you have to talk to Tens? I really don't want Meridian to know I overreacted. Again."

"He'll keep quiet." She pursed her lips.

I scanned the pile by my door. "What were you doing sleeping in the hall?"

"My job."

I stared at her quizzically. "How is that?"

"They have to get past me to get to you. How are you going to sleep well wondering if you're . . . What's the word for *weakened*?"

"Vulnerable?"

"Yes, that's it." She nodded, repeating the word several more times.

"Oh." I'd never had anyone sleep between me and danger before. I was always the one sleeping at the dragon's mouth to protect the littlies from punishment at DG. I protected, not the other way around.

"You think you can go back to sleep now?"

"No." I shook my head. *I need to bake.* "You can tell me more about Iran and your family."

She shrugged and followed me into the kitchen. We spoke of everything and nothing and long minutes stretched when we didn't need to talk at all.

Several hours later, Tony joked, "I'm living with a couple of mice—you two are so quiet."

Fara and I didn't mention he'd slept through the excitement as he dug into his four-cheese omelet, cinnamon rolls, and hash browns.

"Sorry." I knew he wanted me to chatter incessantly like the girls I watched shopping in the streets below us, but keeping to myself was more than habit; it saved me beatings. *Hard to break that reinforcement.* I nibbled on sourdough toast and marmalade preserves.

"My English is no good." Fara smiled at him with a

teasing glint and popped a piece of melon into her mouth.

Tony kissed us both on our foreheads and held up the cell phone. "You call me anytime with anything, okay? Anything at all."

"We'll be fine. We're going to Nelli's to sort files." *And maybe find out more about my parents.* "Then we'll see you at the cemetery for the boy's funeral," I said.

"Still. Call," Tony said as he slipped out the door.

"He is very worry about you."

I didn't know how to reply, so I evaded with a question of my own. I ran soapy water in the sink. "What do you usually eat for breakfast?" I asked Fara. Whether someone picked leftover pizza, ice cream, or fruit, these choices told me everything. I knew people by what they put in their mouths. I needed to know her.

She shrugged. "What-even."

"Whatever?" I asked.

She dipped her hands into the water to wash with a noncommittal shrug.

Frustrated, I accused Fara. "I don't think your English is as bad as you want me to think it is. It's a convenient excuse so you can listen to me and not have to answer my questions or so you can change the conversation easily."

"Uh, maybe," she said, her eyes cast down.

"See. How can we be friends if you lie to me?" *Let alone have the intimate partnership Fenestra and Protectors need. That I watch Meridian and Tens have every single day.*

"I'm not lying. You speak fast and use words I don't always know." Fara blanched.

"All the time?" I wanted to splash water at her.

"No?" She stopped.

"How. Slow. Do. I. Need. To. Talk?" I asked sarcastically.

She glared at me, her skin shades of cinnamon and cocoa powder, her eyes bittersweet chocolate drops.

"That's a universal expression." I wiped the omelet pan until the towel grew hot in my hands under the friction.

"You're being silly," she said. "What I eat? How important is that?"

"You're being arrogant." Food was one way I knew how to categorize people.

"Why?" She stopped, frowning.

"Because you waltzed in like I was having a party and you're a few minutes late." My life was hell on earth and where was she?

She tossed a dish into the sink, throwing soapsuds up. "I don't—"

"Don't. Don't say you don't understand." I smacked the counter.

"I was going to say that I don't intend to be arrogant. Do you think I wanted to wait? Don't you think I asked about you? I knew where you lived, and I knew every lash of the belt and every casually thrown insult. I knew the moment they took you from the church, from Tony, the minute you were alone and scared. I came as fast as I could. No lie."

I stopped. The fire in her eyes drained the anger in mine. "So tell me. Please?" I asked, deflated.

Fara gazed out the window as if she saw something very different than the streets of Carmel. "My *baba*, he didn't care that I was a girl. I was supposed to be a boy. They think only boys can be one of them. But he believed my destiny was with you, with an Amordad. He knew to train me. To teach me. To be what I needed to be. His family hated this. They wouldn't speak to him. They wanted him to apologize to Ahura Mazda. He wouldn't. He said the Creators make no mistakes. And then he disappeared into the car of the secret police. Into the walls of a prison far from Qom."

"What happened?" My heart beat in my chest so loud I thought she might hear it. *Where is Qom and who is Ahura Mazda?* Sometimes it wasn't the wording Fara used; it was also the content that tripped me up.

She shivered. "They dumped his body in the dirt outside the prison. Called us traitors. Labeled our family unless we paid up and did what we were told. It wasn't always this way in Iran.

"My mother remarried my uncle. He didn't believe I could be one of the few. No *girl* is special! There was much discussion, negotiations behind closed doors. Everyone talked about me like I killed my father, like I brought this unholy upon us."

"Why?"

She shrugged. "I'm a girl. That was reason enough. I talked to my baba about you before my tenth birthday. But no one else. They wouldn't let me come to you. They wanted me to marry in my people. The boys . . . the boys are the Protectors, not the girls. We take care of them. We have more little babies to train. We do not go out and make war on Dark." She set a clean plate in the drainer so hard it broke, but she didn't notice.

"My soon-husband was twenty years older than me. He wasn't a Protector, but my family had strong blood-lines and he was willing to teach me how to be a proper wife. Plus he had friends in the police. He wanted many sons. I was the third wife. The first two died in child-birth. There was no place for me in my uncle's house. I had to marry at fourteen. Or . . ."

"Or?"

"Or run away and come to you myself." She paused, drawing a deep breath.

"You ran away across the world? From Iran to Indiana?" My eyes closed at her words. So often I'd thought of running but was never strong enough. *She did. For me.*

"I knew your name. I felt your pain. Your humiliation. Your terror. And I could do nothing for you but pray. I prayed and I prayed. All the times I was supposed to be kneeling to learn how to be a good girl, I prayed the Creators would send you an angel, to help you until I was strong enough to get away."

"How did you?" *Oh, Fara, I know this pain too.*

"I hid in a caravan of medical supplies. I walked across the sand and hid. I worked, doing bad things, un-til I could pay for the container space on a ship to Canada. I snuck here to New York. I thought you were there. I thought New York was all there was of this country. Two cities—New York and Los Angeles. I was wrong." She managed a smile.

I couldn't let her stop. *We're more alike than I realized.* I pressed, "And then what?"

"I found a homeless teen center. I stayed there. I walked streets. I learned there were other ways to make money than do what I did. I listened." The look on her face told me Fara's apparent arrogance was more a defensive façade than truth. *I know that too.*

"How old were you?" I asked, afraid to hear her answer. *Too young. We're always too young.*

"I was fourteen when I left home. It took me five years to get here." She whispered as if even saying the words broke her again.

"Five years?" So many days and hours of uncertainty, pain, and exploitation.

She'd arrived in a country alone and with nothing. *Like me, only she didn't have Tony looking for her.*

"Too much time in the city of New York." She shuddered. "It took many months to walk here. When I crossed into Indiana, I felt the presence of my father. I prayed for his help. I realized it wasn't him, but another like us. Tens. I knew his name and Meridian's as their van passed me on the road. I didn't know he knew me, until he came back. He feels of family, like Baba."

"Oh . . . I wondered how you'd known to come here." I began to understand Fara's journey and why it took her so long. My anger faded completely.

"In my dreams, I saw you near the sign of glass . . . Rumi's? With a little boy."

Bodie?

"I used the computer to see where this is. I tried to be here faster. I know you needed me." There was an apology in her tone.

I nodded. "Just don't act like you don't understand what I'm saying, unless you really don't, okay?"

"I'm sorry. I listen. Sometimes it's easier to let people think I do not understand. It gave me a way to defend myself. It's a habit. My English isn't perfect, but it's okay."

Her English was in many ways better than mine. *At least she speaks her truth.*

CHAPTER 16

Twilight dusted Riverside Cemetery in mauve. We gathered at Auntie's plot with the air humid and fragrant with early summer lushness. While we waited for Nelli, Tens dug a small hole at the base of the plain headstone.

"We have about half an hour until the gates close." Tony glanced at his watch.

Juliet stood apart from us, staring down at her mother's new headstone. I started toward her as Fara walked over and started whispering. I watched Juliet's shoulders relax.

Tens noticed and motioned me to stay put. *What did Fara say that made Juliet sigh away a little of her tension?*

Nelli drove up. In the car next to her sat a Kirian look-alike. All-American, wholesomely handsome with a nice-guy air, he unfolded from the car holding a gallon ziplock bag filled with ashes.

"They left Howie's cremains dropped on my desk." Nelli shook her head ruefully.

"It's really disrespectful. Hi, I'm Sergio Rafa." He nodded at us, but his hands were full and he made no move to relinquish the ashes.

"Sergio is my intern. He's going to be helping with the investigation, especially transferring all the files into a database," Nelli said. "He wanted to be part of this. And he has skills I badly need." She shrugged.

"I would want someone to remember me." His eyes seemed shiny with unshed tears.

"Welcome." Tony squeezed his shoulder.

I found it fascinating to watch Fara size up Sergio and place herself in front of Juliet, who looked as though she'd taken a blow to the stomach. I understood her reaction. He could be Kirian's cousin.

While the others made a bit of uncomfortable small talk, I walked over to Fara and whispered, "He looks like Kirian."

She nodded her acceptance of my explanation. I wasn't sure if that was because she trusted me or because she shared memories with Juliet and knew more about Kirian than I did.

Sergio moved closer to Juliet. "I'm sorry we're meeting like this, but I want you to know how brave I think you are."

She glanced down, stepping away. "Thank you."

"Maybe sometime we can talk about it? I was in a group home south of here that was similar. I don't really have friends who know what I'm talking about."

She started to say something but Rumi reached into his box. "I made a Spirit Stone special." Rumi's glass creations usually hung from ribbon and were closed like a sphere. This one he'd left open at the top. "I thought we might bury Howie in this as an ossuary, an ash container?" Rumi seemed hesitant and insecure.

"It's beautiful," I said. "Perfect." We all agreed.

Sergio and Nelli carefully emptied the bag of ashes until it filled the Spirit Stone, as if it was made for it specifically.

"Shall we?" Tony asked, commencing the brief burial service for Howie.

Rumi recited a poem called "Away" by James Whitcomb Riley, a local poet who was also buried here. Tony asked us to bow our heads while Rumi recited a prayer his *nain,* his grandmother, taught him to pray over the dead.

Nelli dropped candy and a model race car into the hole. The black-and-white race paint job was more about the time of year than Howie's unknown interests.

Juliet knelt and started burying him with a handful of dirt. Fara was next and the rest of us took turns, until

Tens replaced a patch of grass and violets over the top. It was as if we'd never been there. Out of his pocket, Tens pulled a whittled wood "Howie" and tucked it against the base of Auntie's stone. "Until we can get something more permanent."

A rush of love surged through me. *Tens thinks of everything.*

I hoped Howie was home. *Healed.*

"Rumi, what did you say?" Nelli asked.

"Nain's prayer for the dead. I don't know how to translate it exactly, but it's about wishing the soul wings and God's speed on its journey."

"It was beautiful," Sergio said. "I'd love a copy of it, if you can write it down sometime? I have a professor at the university who collects prayers like that."

"Sure." Rumi nodded.

"So you're new to town?" I asked Sergio.

"Yeah, pretty new. I came for school and stayed to work. I've volunteered at the racetrack the last five summers. This is a great time of year to be in Indy."

Nelli's cell phone rang and she moved away. Juliet and Fara went back to hovering by Roshana's plot. I tried to focus on Sergio. He seemed like a little puppy desperately wanting attention.

"Why?" I asked.

"Ah, it's May. The big race. All the events. The thrill of cars moving at two hundred thirty miles per hour. It gets addictive. You are going, right? To the Indianapolis 500? The 'Greatest Spectacle in Racing'?"

"Uh, hadn't planned on it."

"It's gonna make history this year. It's the centennial race. Biggest event to hit this country in years." He nodded his head as if keeping time to a drumbeat only he heard.

"Oh, okay, I guess we'll think about it." I backed up another step. I leaned up to Tens's ear. "Was that a weird conversation to have?"

"Not everyone is as connected to the unliving as you, Merry."

"I know, it's just—"

Nelli interrupted, "Can you guys come to Faye's? Gus wants to talk to us."

* * *

"I hope you can talk some sense into Faye, Meridian." Gus hugged me.

This didn't sound good. "About what?"

"He's mad I don't want to go on a cruise around the world or learn how to skydive before it's too late."

"That's not what I said, was it?" Gus's eyes were sunken and the fragile skin around them was bruised and puffy.

"Honey, the trick is to live until we die. To fill up those moments." Faye wrapped a knit shawl around her shoulders. "Do you know how many people don't breathe correctly? They take little mouthfuls, little dainty bites of air instead of filling their lungs to capacity. Not breathe, right? Can you imagine? Most people don't live right either. They take tiny nips and tastes, but they don't remember to inhale deeply and consciously live. We're going to live until—"

"Then marry me, woman." Gus threw his hands in the air.

Faye's chin wobbled. "You know Dolores won't be able to handle that."

"Your daughter is an adult; she will handle it if you let her."

"Regardless, we can't."

"Then aren't you a hypocrite with all your talk about living life?" Gus slammed out.

Whoa! I didn't know where to look. The emotion echoing around us was almost unbearable. I heard Auntie telling me that sometimes grief starts months before the death itself.

"He's right, isn't he?" Faye's eyes filled with tears.

Nelli knelt down and wiped her cheeks.

Rumi tsked. "He shouldn't be so adamantine, unyielding, to storm off like that."

"Why, because I'm dying? I don't want kid gloves, Rumi. I want life." Faye shook her head.

"Then you'd better storm after him and marry him," Nelli said quietly.

"Why don't I go get him?" I slid from the room while their murmurs continued.

I found Gus weeping into his hands on a bench behind the house. I dug into my pocket and held out wadded-up tissues. I was beginning to get the hang of the accessories of grief and never went anywhere without a few clean Kleenex.

"She won't break her daughter's heart, so she'll break mine," Gus said.

I stayed silent.

"I never married."

"How'd you meet Faye?" I asked, picking a pink blossom and burying my nose in its happy scent.

He smiled through his tears. "The first time I met Faye, she and her husband had just moved in next door. I was mowing my grass and noticed how long their lawn was. It was a scorching summer day, so I cut hers too. She came out onto her porch and offered me a tall glass of sweet tea to thank me. First sip of that tea I thought I was going to die." He gagged in memory. "It wasn't sweet but salty. She asked if it was okay, as she'd never made it before. I didn't have the heart to tell her. I drank that whole thing. Tasted worse than seawater. Years later, she confessed the sugar and salt got mixed up in the move."

"That's why you call her Sweet Tea?" I smiled.

"Mmm-hmm."

"When she sliced into a red velvet cake and cut me a piece the size of a house, I had no idea how I was going to choke it down. But it tasted rich and moist, with a hint of something unusual. Delicious. When I asked her, she confided that it was her secret and she could only tell me if I promised not to enter it into the state fair against her. I promised. Never baked a thing in my life. I found out later the tea took all the salt and she'd bought more sugar for the cake." He chuckled. "Looking back, I loved Faye even then."

"But she was married?"

"Yep, so we were friends. And after her husband died, I didn't know how to make her see me as the man who loved her. So I stayed her friend instead of risking her rejecting me. We could have had twenty years together instead of a few months." He paused as if waiting for me to berate him and agree. When I didn't, he continued. "And now she won't marry me because her daughter can't handle it. It's her mother's death she can't stomach. Not a wedding. All I want is to say those vows in front of God and friends. I know that's not the legal part, but that's the part that matters to this old man."

"So do it." Seems simple.

"What?"

"I'm not an expert or anything, but if you want to say wedding vows, you don't have to say them wearing a white dress," I said, trying to make him smile. The hopelessness of waiting for goodbye weighed heavily on him. How do people watch their loved ones die without losing their minds?

"That's good, 'cause white really isn't my color."

We laughed.

"You know what I mean. Say the words. Invite whoever you want to. We can do an officially unofficial wedding."

"I wouldn't know where to begin."

"Start with what you want to say. We can do the rest."

"I'll think on that. Thank you, kid." He patted my shoulder.

Rumi came out with Tens and Tony in tow. "Why don't we men get a squoosh of air? Deliquesce, disappear, and leave the ladies to primp for us?"

I didn't argue as the men dissolved into the night around us. I headed back into the house to see what I could do for Faye. I knew how to soothe the dying, the newly dead, but those days or weeks away from it? *Not so easy.*

Faye dozed and shifted.

"I can't get her comfortable." Nelli frowned.

I stooped at Faye's feet. Inhaling deeply, I gathered my courage to speak. "Faye, I met a woman. I'd like to call her. She's a friend. And she works at a hospice. Maybe she can help?"

"How?" Faye opened her eyes and then closed them. "I keep forgetting I can't see you but for the light. It's very disconcerting."

"How do you think she can help?" Nelli asked, repeating for Faye.

"I don't know, but I think she can get you comfortable and maybe help Gus understand your point of view?"

"You know I would like nothing more than to marry Gus, but it's too late. Too much has happened," Faye said.

"What do you mean? It's never too late." I glanced at Nelli, who frowned.

"My first husband and I got married by the justice of the peace. I got my daughter out of it. I'm not complaining."

"But you wish . . . ?" I let it hang. *Wait, let her speak.*

"I wish Gus and I *could* get married. A real wedding."

"When's your daughter coming?" I asked.

"Soon."

Behind Faye, Nelli shook her head and shrugged. Dying wasn't convenient; the dying didn't make an appointment on the calendar. It doesn't work that way.

"Why don't you tell me what you'd like, if anything were possible?" I asked.

Faye's expression got faraway and dreamy. She let herself wander through a vision of her wedding. I quietly took notes as she spoke.

Faye abruptly stopped her flow of words between flowers and vows. "Gus has a surprise planned for tomorrow. I used to say I wanted to drive the track, but now? I don't know how I'm going to do it; it's so important to him to make me happy."

"What's he got planned?" Nelli asked.

"Let him tell you himself. Yes, call your friend, Meridian. Maybe she knows how I can manage this." She slowly drifted into a slight sleep.

I used Faye's phone to dial Delia, who said she'd be right over.

Gus reentered, bolstered. I didn't know what the other men said to lift the weight he carried but it worked. "Faye, Sweet Tea, exactly like you wished years ago, we're going racing tomorrow. I've got you a car that's going to take you across the yard of bricks, faster than the speed of light."

She pretended surprise and delight.

Tens slipped his arms around me.

There is nothing easy about dying. Nothing at all.

CHAPTER 17

"Did you sleep at all last night?" Tens rolled over and nestled against me.

I sighed. "Not really."

"What was that boring documentary?"

"An in-depth report on the tornadoes this spring and how the city and state—"

"Stop! I don't care. How come you didn't fall asleep to that?" Tens sounded appalled.

"It was kinda interesting." I shrugged. Not really, but Gus's story about wasting time in fear reiterated so much of what I read in Auntie's journal and what she'd tried to teach me. Death without a life is meaningless. Whispering, I asked, "What's on your bucket list?"

"Thinking about Faye and Gus?" He glanced down at me.

I nodded.

"I'd like to see South America, run a marathon, eat my way through that ten-pound hamburger at Bub's, see you when you're Auntie's age . . ." His voice trailed off.

"You've really thought about this."

He nodded. His palm pressed me against his side with slow strokes along my back. "I have. What do you want in your lifetime?"

"I want it all." *And I do. I finally have some of it.*

"Thanks for narrowing that down for me." Tens poked at my ribs.

"Normal stuff." *Living up to my legacy, seeing my brother again, having a family with you someday, seeing you when you're Charles's age.* "Like waking up next to you every morning for the rest of my life."

"Does it count as waking up if you never slept?" He chuckled. "You have to come up with something outrageous to do for a bucket list. Not normal stuff."

"What, like skydiving?" *I'd probably get hit by dying birds.*

"Or running naked in the rain. Or raising a flock of emu."

I laughed as he continued spouting.

"Or camping in the Australian bush. Or—"

"Stop! I can't take it." I dove for his tickle spots and straddled him. He let me pin him for a kiss. "Do we have to get out of bed today?"

"I think someone might notice. Rain check?" He kissed me, then swung out of bed to pad toward the bathroom. I snuggled my face in his pillow, inhaling his sleepy warmth.

"Come on, Merry!" Tens shouted. "You lost your chance to sleep."

"Coming," I mumbled.

* * *

Unprepared for the sheer enormity of the Indianapolis Motor Speedway, we'd driven around the outside before I knew what it was. *So that's why this entire town is called Speedway.*

From the back, it looked like giant gray scaffolding and bleachers. The outside was fenced in chain link and sported paths with white-pebbled gravel. Golf carts flocked at every entrance.

"That's where we're going?" I asked. "That's a racetrack? Not an airport?" *Or a construction site? Or an alien colony?* A ten-story glass pagoda stood guard over it all, either as sentry or proud parent. *They call this place a finicky female.*

Juliet's eyes were as wide as mine felt.

"Wait until you see it from the inside. The infield alone can hold eight football stadiums." Tony grinned at me. "I'm not much for the cars, but the people watching . . . ah, that is most awesome."

We'd broken into two travel groups. Gus, Faye, and Rumi rode ahead. Tony, Juliet, Fara, and I rode in our van, with Tens at the wheel. Delia, the hospice nurse who'd descended on Faye last night upon angelic wings of mercy, was meeting us. She'd gone early to try to make miracles happen.

We drove up to the Hall of Fame museum with its flagpoles and imposing cement construction with architectural tire tracks running down the front.

Delia waved at me as we parked and unloaded. Faye was tucked deeply into her wheelchair with shawls and blankets, and she had a hat and scarf covering the rest of her.

Gus enfolded Delia in a bear hug that clung. When I could, I asked her, "How'd you pull off the rest of this? Gus said he'd only booked a ride in a car?"

"Help from friends I've made at Never Too Late. You can imagine how many locals wish for this particular final lap. We have to work between teams' practices, though."

In so many ways, the timing could be better. I knew Gus would cherish this memory, but I wasn't at all certain this was Faye's wish for an outing. She gazed up at Gus with all the love and understanding I hoped Tens and I had in fifty years.

An old converted school bus was our chariot. Its lift brought Faye inside and we gathered, listening to a hilarious tour guide rattle off race trivia. *Who knew there were faster things to watch than Indiana corn grow?* Not that I'd seen that yet either.

The tour guide began. "Now, sports fans, notice we have the Colts colors in the sky above us today. Between the blue of the heavens and the fluffy white clouds, it's clear that even heaven cheers for our local football team."

I'm not sure nature takes sides quite like that.

Tony and Gus laughed. I hadn't paid any attention to sports teams in the area, so I simply smiled.

The guide continued. "It's our centennial year here for the Indianapolis 500. A very important year. Only a World War has canceled the race, and we've proudly run the events in all weather and through all accidents. The world keeps spinning and so do the cars folks, always to the left, of course."

The bus took us down under the track and up into the garage area. Cars and trucks were parked around another fleet of quads, cats, and tractors.

"More than a century ago, this was farmland. It belonged to a family named Barnett. We don't know much about them, except that the last member died without heirs and the farm was made available about the time the automobile market exploded at the turn of the twentieth century. Investors bought the farm and made a track to test out the strange new contraptions called cars.

"And we're arriving at the pit area," the guide said. "This is where the cars get fuel and changed tires. Where the teams make adjustments during practice and at race time. Did you know that last year, the fastest lap in May was two hundred thirty-two miles per hour?"

I got queasy when Tens hit eighty-five miles per hour on the interstate. Four times that? Uh, no thank you.

"We get to go into the pits?" Gus asked, sounding like a kid as we piled off the bus.

Rumi quietly snapped photographs of Gus and Faye interacting. *Their smiles are priceless.* We all knew this was her last big outing.

Rallying, Faye stood, all but throwing off the blankets when they wheeled her near the two-seater.

"I hear we have a special guest driving today?" A salt-and-pepper-haired man with curly locks and larger-than-life charisma marched over holding two helmets.

"That's Mario," Tony whispered to us. Even he was awed.

Obviously, Mario is a local celebrity. I feel silly not knowing him on sight.

Fara stood farther back from the group looking like a metalhead without a mosh pit. Watching her, I realized she'd stationed herself on the periphery and was on constant alert. *She's guarding Juliet.*

I was so used to Tens doing the same for me and trying to for Juliet that I took his actions for granted. He'd taken the opposite side from Fara. Careful not to draw attention to the weapons under his arms. Fara, too, must carry. *The chains. Knives?*

Faye seemed like her old self, settling into the cockpit of the car as if she'd never been ill and frail. She yanked the helmet down like a pro and gave us a thumbs-up as she listened to Mario point out dials and controls.

Rumi handed out earplugs. *How loud can it really be?*

The track's announcer constantly updated weather information, track stats, even calling out names and numbers of drivers and their teams over the loudspeaker.

"Ready?" Mario called. "Wave as we go by!" They started the motor, and I felt the twang in my guts. The noise was so intense I pushed the earplugs deeper.

I was sure Mario carefully maneuvered the car down the lane and onto the track, but it seemed as if he peeled out and hit the accelerator in one motion.

"Are you sure this is a good idea?" I asked Delia.

"You know better than to ask that. Look at Gus's face. Did you see how she got into the car so easily? She's rallying, Meridian. This is common."

I nodded. I usually wasn't around the dying before they were within moments of transitioning. Auntie lay down to nap and didn't get back up. The people in hospitals I helped were so ill. Their souls hung on by mere threads.

Faye's teaching me.

Behind us, dozens of hot-air balloons lifted off. Baskets full of excited families and spectators rose into the bright blue sky. Their vivid colors and creative artwork from geometric designs to solid swaths of rainbows gave us slow-motion kaleidoscopes above.

When Mario came around the first time, he slowed so

Faye could wave, only a few fingers. I think I heard her squeal with glee.

They spun the track again and again, each time faster. Our crew cheered and shouted.

In between passes, I people-watched. The camera for the jumbo screen panned the airborne crowd. The people in the hot-air balloons waved at all of us below. One balloon's occupants caught my attention. Inside the basket, a figure wore a scarf wrapped over hair and face, with a big floppy hat in black. I squinted, my gut singing for my attention. *Is that a man or a woman? Why the subterfuge? Who are the suited men in long-sleeved button-down dress shirts?* They seemed to snap photographs from every angle. *Press?* I put my hand up to shield against the sun's glare. I needed Tens's binoculars. The balloon's design was all black and white, but the basket had an insignia with wings and something like a snuffed out candle. *Or a torch? What is that?*

The JumboTron panned again and changed views. Without the zoom, I couldn't see the group. *Can they be Nocti? Ms. Asura?* I didn't have proof, nothing more than a brief glimpse and a bad feeling to ponder as Faye and Mario came around again.

Word must have passed to race teams and mechanics working today that Faye was living out a last wish, because as her car came around the last time, everyone stopped what they were doing and walked to line the pits. Between the low cement walls, they formed a human tunnel, clapping and giving Faye high fives as Mario drove her slowly between them and back to us.

Her eyes danced with delight, and her lips stretched from one side of the infield to the other.

Tens joined me as we loaded back into the bus. I tried to find the weird balloon again but couldn't. "Did you see the balloon with the guys in suits and the person in the scarf and hat?" I asked under my breath.

He shook his head. "I was watching the stands and the traffic behind us. Why?"

"Thought it might be Nocti. Maybe Ms. Asura."

"In a hot-air balloon? Here?" He frowned.

Tony heard us and leaned in. "Probably press. Sounds like foreign journalists. We get a lot of them. Hot-air balloons give them a unique experience to write about. Should we ask someone?"

"No. *No*." I didn't know who we'd ask or how'd we explain who I thought I saw.

* * *

"I brought your favorites." Nelli laid a spread before us in Faye's kitchen that smelled of spice, seafood, and the bayou of Louisiana country.

I was glad no one assumed Juliet would be in charge of dinner for all of us. Though she was fierce in the kitchen, I worried Juliet might begin to feel used by us for her culinary skills if we counted on her cooking every time.

Juliet closed her eyes, inhaling. I think she'd probably

be able to name the ingredients for me in every dish, especially after Faye passed.

"Mudbugs?" Faye clapped, naming her favorite restaurant.

Fara grabbed a napkin and a hot hush puppy. She handed the bundle quietly to Juliet with a smile that seemed to understand.

"Best in town." Nelli kissed Faye's cheek.

Plates were piled high with cheesy crawfish casserole, shrimp étouffée, jambalaya, gumbo, red beans and dirty rice. Hush puppies, with bits of corn and a hint of sweet, cooled down my mouth along with pickle-full potato salad. The salty goodness of freshly fried potato chips added texture to the feast. There were even boiled crawfish that Gus took great delight in sucking the innards out of. *He can have those.*

Juliet tried everything. No one spoke as we all ate as fast as we could. Sighs of contentment were punctuated with Rumi's exclamations of, "The étouffée is sipid! This is kickshaw; you must taste! I've eaten so much I'll have the collywobbles later."

"There are beignets for dessert, so leave room," Nelli said, carefully keeping lemonade and iced tea flowing.

I noticed Faye picked at her food. She moved it around her plate with feigned enthusiasm. She barely ate three bites. According to Rumi, she usually ate the entire menu from Mudbugs in one sitting. *Not a good sign.* Delia noticed my study and nodded at me. *We see the same thing.*

Over fresh black coffee, Faye motioned to Delia, who stood and asked us to listen. I knew there was an announcement coming, but that didn't take special superpowers, simply logical deduction.

"We decided against this, Faye." Gus shook his head. Today's activities gave his cheeks color that this conversation quickly leached back out.

"Today was tops, but merely a reprieve from the inevitable." Faye touched his hand.

I glanced around. *This couldn't be about the wedding, could it?*

While Gus muttered, Faye took a handful of pills and Delia gave her a shot. "My friends, it's time," Faye said.

Gus blanched. "You'll die in your home, Faye."

"No, I won't. You're burdened by me."

"I'm devoted to you. There is no burden," he fought.

"I disagree. This is killing you as much as it is me."

"May I?" Delia gently inserted between the two.

Faye and Gus both nodded acceptance.

"It's not about love or devotion. Faye's body is deteriorating rapidly, and I'd like to ask her a question. I'd like you all to listen to her answer. Faye, are we able to fully control your pain and discomfort?"

"No. As much as Gus keeps track of the pills and shots, it's no longer enough. And when I can't sleep, he doesn't either."

"And the tightness in your chest. Is that bothering you?" Delia took notes, but I saw she already knew the answers.

"Yes, it's getting harder and harder to breathe. The cough is adding to my pain."

"The cancer is in your bones, your ribs, so when you cough, those bones react. You might cough and break your ribs."

"But you said she could stay in her home with hospice help." Gus stood and marched around the room, picking up music-related knickknacks and putting them down without seeing them.

"Help, yes, for you, but we've reached the place where we need to have her on an IV, soon a catheter. We need to monitor her constantly to keep her comfortable. The best way to do that is to admit her to the inpatient facility."

"There's a bed available, Gus," Faye said quietly.

He bowed in front of her and clasped her hands. "I'll try harder. You just have to tell me what to do."

"I am." Faye smoothed his hair. "You need to be with me, spend time with me, talk to me. Let them worry about my body while you worry about my heart and take care of it. Okay?" Her eyes sparkled with unshed tears.

Gus's grief overflowed and he hung his head.

"I've already talked to Dolores and she doesn't understand," Faye said. "I need you to understand. I was going to tell you yesterday, but I didn't want to ruin the track today. The freedom . . . That's what I realized in that car. This body of mine has gotten creaky and stiff—it doesn't react the way it used to—but inside I'm still the same girl I was when I chased after boys and swam in the lake for hours." To us, she said, "You forget, because it's so slow and gradual, how much these bodies can fail. Until a moment like today, when the wind was in my face and stealing my laughter from my belly. I will be glad to leave this body behind. Death will be freedom."

Gus cried silently, wiping tears from his cheeks in angry swipes of tissue.

"Would you like help packing?" I asked, bending low to her.

She shook her head. "Delia took care of that already. I don't need much."

I glanced around Faye's house. She'd been parceling out her belongings since the diagnosis. But there was still an awful lot of stuff here. She needed none of it now. Sheet music and porcelain figurines, mingled with cases of instruments and old vinyl records, competed with stacks of books.

Faye held out her hands to Juliet and me. "But you can do something, Meridian, Juliet. Can you promise me you'll be with me? You'll carry me across?"

"Of course. We will. At least one of us will be with you," I said.

Juliet nodded her head as well.

Faye's eyes shadowed as she gazed at Gus, at the walls around her, as if seeing them for the last time. *Or the first time.*

"Why don't we call it a night and let you and Gus have time?" Tony rose. "You'll call when you're settled and we'll come."

As we walked out, I tugged Juliet aside in the gardens,

mostly overgrown with weeds. "Are you okay?" She'd grown paler and stopped sneaking beignets.

She struggled for words. "It's just so familiar. Sitting and waiting for someone to die." Juliet's voice broke and she flinched on each syllable.

I'm a bitch.

"I didn't think about that. I'm sorry." Of course this was so much more her norm than mine. *How do I fix this?* "I can handle it alone. If that would help? You don't have to be there. Everyone will understand."

Juliet shivered and gave nothing away. "It's fine. She's been good to me. Why wouldn't I be there? But it makes me think of"—she paused and swallowed—"all the people I've loved and said goodbye to."

"Did you grow close to the dying at DG?" I asked carefully, hoping she'd share. Only Mini's intervention near Juliet's sixteenth birthday kept her from getting tangled in the dying's energy. It was no wonder Juliet shielded herself from us. *Caring equals hurting in her world.*

"After a while, I tried not to. I tried not to care. To focus on the kids more than the elderly. But I had favorites. They taught me things." She twisted her cuticles and snagged hangnails as she talked.

"Like what?" I liked this side of Juliet. Having a conversation with her. Talking about DG was something she rarely allowed. *Please keep talking. Please let me in!*

"Well . . ." She paused and shook off the moment. My chance gone, she merely shrugged and said, "Silly things."

"Oh, but—" I saw Tony walking toward us. *So close!*

"Juliet, we need to go!" Tony called, oblivious that he'd offered her escape yet again. I wondered what would happen when Juliet could no longer run. *Will she crack? Will she become a force for herself? Will I be here to see that day?*

I watched her rush away and leaned against the shed behind Faye's gardens. At once, I was at the window beside a tall man with scars crisscrossing his arms and chest like railroad tracks.

Rags hung from his body, and the whites of his eyes were big in a face full of angles and bones. He gazed beyond. I saw a giraffe wander by, and the savannah flowed endlessly beyond the horizon. Somewhere a lion roared welcome.

He said something I didn't understand; I pointed through the window. "Home—go on."

I wondered if he was one of the escaped slaves who had gone through here on the Underground Railroad. *He's been waiting for home, here in this garden, for a century and a half.*

I began to turn away when a voice called, "Meridian!"

"Howie?" Dressed in clean clothes that were the vibrant twins of his earlier outfit, he looked at me with eyes that were clear hazel and a face that was whole. I hadn't seen him at the window since we'd buried him and prayed over him.

"You can see!" I yelled.

His handsome face was unblemished and younger.

"I'm free! Thank you. I'm heading home now. For real."
He leapt upon the back of an elephant and waved as they
walked out of my sight.

"Meridian? Merry? Supergirl?" Tens bracketed my
face and peered into my eyes. "Where'd you go?"

"Africa?" I smiled.

CHAPTER 18

Juliet

fara paced the outlines of the room. "You have to give it back to Rumi."

"I know. How?" I shook my head. "And tell Ms. Asura what? She'll come after all of them." *And never tell me about my parents.*

"You cannot protect us all. You have to stop trying. You are not alone in this world."

I knew Fara had more to say. I braced for it when a car honked below. "That's Nelli," I said.

Fara closed her mouth, then simply picked up her

hobo bag, slung it over her shoulder, and waited at the door for me. As I brushed past her, I smelled cumin, oregano, and candied lemon peels.

The statues all over Carmel's Art and Design District were creepy on the best day. A policeman directed imaginary traffic. A dad helped a kid ride a bike. A street musician played silent sonatas with a very open, very fake violin case at his feet. *They watch me. Judging.* The same way Mistress could see and hear everything at DG. I was afraid to look at the statues directly in case they, too, could read my thoughts and report back.

It was silly. *Childish. Irrational.* As many times as I told myself they were fake, I couldn't shake the feeling. *They are art. Doesn't matter.*

"Change of plans," Nelli greeted us. "Bales found another set of remains in a completely different area of town. Do you want to go with me, stay here, or sort papers without me? Meridian and Tens are meeting me there."

Stay here. I glanced at Fara, who gave me no clues as to what she wanted. "Your choice." She shrugged.

"We'll go with you," I said.

Nelli nodded. "Do you feel okay? You look a little pale."

"I'm fine." *No, I can't sleep and food appeals only intermittently. Someone is watching me all the time. I keep dreaming of Kirian calling for me. I don't know if I'm going crazy or if he's really trying to reach out.* "Fine," I repeated, trying to force strength into my voice.

Nelli stayed silent as if she didn't believe me and judged my lies.

"These bones belong to one of your missing?" Fara asked, touching my arm daintily as if to reassure me.

I inhaled.

"We don't know. I think so. The file's description matches a name Howie mentioned to Meridian. Hopefully one of you can pick up on something if the little girl's soul is still around," Nelli said.

"It's a girl?" I asked.

"We don't know yet. I just hate using impersonal pronouns to describe the unknown dead. Feels icky to me." Nelli shuddered.

She's too sensitive for this. She's going to get hurt.

"Where did Bales find her, then?" Fara asked.

"They were cleaning up a demolished building downtown and digging a foundation for a new one. Found the remains, but I didn't get information about it before she was moved to the labs. The coroner called me because the clothing scraps match a description of a missing child. She was taken from a foster family and disappeared. Her name was Aileen."

"So where are we going?" I tried to focus on the information and not the memories that bombarded me.

"To the Indiana University Pathology Laboratory."

"Will they let us in?" Fara asked.

"Probably not, so we'll have to play it by ear. The medical examiner is a friend, though, and knows how important this case is to me. I'm more worried about residents and fellows hanging around, asking questions. I sent Sergio ahead to check it out and come up with a cover story."

Tens, Meridian, and Sergio met us in the parking lot wearing scrubs the color of blue raspberry candy and lab coats smelling of sauerkraut. They had matching sets for Fara and me. *Goody.*

Meridian snapped gum and wore crazy neon sneakers. With her hair in pigtails and glitter on her eyelids, she was perfectly cast for the part of high school student. They even had spiral notebooks and pens to take notes. "Thanks so much for arranging a tour for us today. We're Carmel High School Greyhounds, eager to learn all about pathology."

"Have I mentioned lately how brilliant you are?" Nelli asked, laughing, as Fara and I ducked into Meridian's van and slipped on the clothing. The van smelled of old coffee and cheap hot dogs.

I watched Fara finger her knives, one clasped along the outside of each thigh. "You can't take weapons in," I whispered. "We'll get in trouble." *I hope. What do I know?*

She nodded and tucked them under the carpet.

"If you can't handle this, you don't have to go in," Meridian said to me as we rejoined them.

Stop coddling me. "No, I want to go."

"Okay, sit down if you feel ill. I'll try to handle as many dead as I can."

Sometimes her superiority is too much. We were surrounded by medical facilities and hospitals. *Plenty of dying going on.*

Her mouth snapped shut as Sergio brushed against me. "I'll be right here if I can do anything, okay?" Sergio patted my arm awkwardly like he wanted to hug me or hold my hand but didn't know how to start. "I know stuff like this can be scary."

I stepped away from him, nodding. "Thanks."

I tried to appear confident and excited, like a high school student should be on this kind of tour. I followed Meridian and Fara's lead, chatting loudly about the latest hot guy on the silver screen. *I have no idea who they're talking about. But I know how to lie convincingly.*

Sergio never left my side, ready to steady me when we bumped into each other. His touch felt too familiar, too easy on my skin. Like leftover cold and crusty spaghetti sauce from a jar. *But he knows what it's like to not have a family. Talk to him.*

"No, I have to take it with me," Sergio explained to the guard, insisting he needed his computer.

"You have to," the guard persisted.

He's very attached to technology.

"But it's too valuable. I can't—"

"Sergio, leave it. It'll be fine," Nelli assured him. She got us through security and signed us in. No one questioned us after she waved her hand and declared us the Future Doctors of America Club.

There can't possibly be such a club, can there? I know so little about real life. The thought broke waves of sadness over me.

"Here we are." Nelli knocked and opened a door to the pathology department. "Frank, so nice to see you!"

Smelling like peppermint and rotting meat, Dr. Frank

introduced himself easily as if kids toured his office all the time.

"These are my friends. They're doing an internship with me, investigating those cold cases." Nelli named us all.

"You have strong stomachs? Any fainters among you?" he asked with a strange twinkle in his eye, as if he knew better than to take our word for anything.

We smiled and shrugged.

"Let's go through here and I'll fill you in on what we know so far."

I followed with Nelli beside me, as we were closest. It didn't occur to me that I might regret going first.

As he pulled open a drawer, light poured forth. *Uh-oh.* Immediately, I sat at the kitchen table. My window belonged to the photograph of a pricelessly appointed kitchen and dining area. In March, Meridian asked me to pick a location with a window to visualize. I'd seen this once in a magazine Kirian stole for me. *For me, the closest a soul can get to heaven is through the kitchen.*

A tiny girl, very young, was balanced at the counter, watching out the window. Her hair was the color of brown sugar. Her dress, once yellow but now threadbare, seemed more mashed potato than banana. She pressed her hands against her head as if trying to block out horrible sounds. I followed her gaze toward the window and wondered what I was doing wrong. *There is nothing beyond. A void. Empty. What's going on?* Panic flared my pulse.

"Hello?" I said, but she didn't turn toward me. I stepped closer, into her line of sight.

Her ears were melted with her hands covering them, stuck and joined like pieces in a macabre creation. Her eyes widened farther when she saw me. She began to shout, sounding as if she were underwater, but as hard as I tried, the sounds she made didn't correspond to words or phrases.

She couldn't pull her hands from her ears. *She can't hear.*

"My name is Juliet. What happened?" When I spoke, she didn't seem to hear me and became all the more frantic. Hopelessness engulfed me. *How do I help you? I can't even do this right.*

Tears rolled out of the girl's eyes and her expression radiated deep pain. *Is this how my mother feels? Does she scream silently too?*

"Juliet, go back." Meridian startled me. "I'll get her through the window."

Meridian had appeared at the window with me only once, the night of my birthday.

The scene changed from my kitchen to a white room with billowing curtains. But the window still didn't reveal a scene beyond. "Why is that—"

"Go back. We'll talk later," she demanded.

I looked up, blinking, lying on my back, with a bright white light peering into my face.

"You said you weren't a fainter." Dr. Frank bathed my forehead in rubbing alcohol, which made my eyes water.

Sergio held my hand and made funny little circles with his thumb like he was tapping out Morse code.

"I'm sorry," I apologized. *I've made a scene.*

Sergio and Fara assisted me to my feet. I leaned heavily on Fara.

"No problem. If it happens again, you may want to explore other careers." Dr. Frank tried to make a joke that fell flat.

He has no idea.

I glanced at Meridian, who looked as though she'd never left her body. Cuddled against Tens like a couple who couldn't keep their hands off each other.

Nelli bustled back in. "I'm sorry. That was my boss. He wanted to be told immediately if these remains belonged to Aileen. Are you okay, Juliet? You worried us."

"How long was I out?"

"Missed the whole thing." Dr. Frank seemed to find me humorous. To Nelli he said, "Looks that way. We'll know more when the tests come back," he added with a nod.

"When you're finished, I'll take possession of her remains," said Nelli.

"Can't she be buried with this semester's cadavers at the med school?" Sergio asked. "Isn't that policy?" The interest in his question seemed overdone.

"No, a proper burial is the least I can do." Nelli shot him down and shook Dr. Frank's hand. "Thank you for calling me."

Meridian moved like corn syrup in March. I felt like I

had lost a battle with a bulldozer. *Someday this gets easier. Yeah, right.*

Tens guarded the ladies' locker room while Meridian, Fara, and Nelli pushed me down onto a bench until they declared me the right shade of living.

"Are you okay?" Nelli asked. "If I'd known you would have such a hard time, I never would have let you come with us." Agitated, she blew her nose.

"It was weird, Nelli. She's possibly Fenestra too. She has similar wounds to Howie's and Roshana's. Juliet wouldn't know." Meridian turned to me. "Did the bones glow for you? Did you see that?"

I nodded. "Was there really nothing at her window?" *Is that how my mother's is? Can she only see the cornucopia of living colors when she appears at others' windows?*

"Yes, but I was able to get her across. I think that once her bones are laid to rest, it'll fill in. That's what ultimately made the difference for Howie. I think." She frowned. "I'm not sure yet. I need to talk to Rumi about his prayer. He's always saying words have power. Maybe he's right."

Whispering, I asked, "What about my mother? Will she never be able to go beyond without her—" I couldn't make the word *bones* come out of my throat.

Meridian shook her head and said softly, "I don't know. I think maybe that's why Auntie can still find me at the window. She's not been given a specific grave yet either."

Oh, Mommy, I'm so sorry. I promise I'll do whatever it takes to find you. Anything.

* * *

After an hour of sorting papers in Nelli's apartment, the names blurred. Fara watched me, her eyes jabbing into me like a meat thermometer. She opened her mouth, but each time I moved away before she spoke. *I know what you're going to say.*

"Why don't we give her a fake?"

"Who? What?" I shook my head. *Not what I thought you were going to say.*

"This book you have to give to the Nocti—we draw our own. Give Rumi his back," Fara said.

"I don't know what they're looking for." *I can't trick Ms. Asura. I'm not smart enough for that.* "Rumi can't know I took it. They'll never forgive me."

"Meridian talks to you, yes? And you stole her scarf."

Shame washed over me in waves of nauseating heat. *I don't know why I take things. Why I hide them. I can't stop.*

I focused on the papers. Anything that might shed light on the truth, anything that might give me control. Miss Claudia and Paddy's files were there. My first almost-grandparents who I loved and who died so quickly. Dozens of patients. *The closest people to grandparents I ever knew.*

And dozens of kid files too. Ones I'd seen come and go. Faces I remembered but whose names faded with time.

Kids I thought turned sixteen and went off to boarding schools, jobs. Like we were told. *Not death. Not service to the Nocti like Kirian. Not this hellish wounded in-between!* Frustration boiled up and spilled over.

Each piece of paper crumpling, rustling, was a thwack, a jibe. *Outsmart the Nocti? Fake a book? What are the potential ramifications? Who will Ms. Asura hurt instead of me?*

My head ached.

Kirian's file was there. He'd never gone anywhere. *Nowhere.* Those postcards were lies. The Eiffel Tower never soared over him. Venice never lapped itself into his heart. All lies. *Did he love me? Really?*

I shut the bathroom door behind me and turned the faucet on full. I splashed water on my face but tasted the familiar metallic edge of blood. I'd bit my tongue again to keep from screaming. *To feel something other than anger. Fear. Frustration.*

Memories of Mistress beating me came rushing back. *Useless.*

Stupid.

I let the towel fall to the floor, pressing my hands against my eyes. *Run! Run! Run!*

"I can't stay." I fled past Fara and out Nelli's door, deep into the woods along the estate. I imagined the sound of the creek gurgling in the distance, calling me. The trail merged ahead and I let my legs go.

Fara called, "Juliet! Juliet!"

Run. Run. Don't stop.

I left her there, running behind me, ducking between cars and through brush. Step after step. Mile after mile.

Push. Harder.

I needed my creek. I needed the Wildcat. *I need water.* I ran until my foot's ache became a full-fledged throb and the bandage rubbed against the wound. My tongue stuck to the roof of my mouth, sticky like spun sugar. Sweat poured off of my face, between my shoulder blades, down my legs.

There it is.

Not slowing, I waded into the cool creek water until I sat down against a log, only my shoulders and head visible above the rushing stream.

Little minnows darted and picked at my feet. A turtle raised its head out of the water like a periscope and dove back under. A catfish, with the mouth of a grand canyon, swallowed a tub full of water, then thrashed its tail at me. Above me the birds gathered. *Their lives go on, day after day, until they stop. None of these animals has the fear and self-loathing and rage eating them from the inside out.*

Rustling and footsteps should have put me on the defensive, but I didn't care. I didn't move.

"I brought you bread." Fara held out a loaf of Wonder Bread by the top of the plastic sleeve.

When I didn't move to take it, she swung it closer, letting it splash into the water near me. "For the animals. Yes? Ducks eat it?"

"You followed me all the way here?" *Am I that predictable? She must have driven because she's not even sweating.*

"Of course. Didn't you want me to?" Without removing her boots or leather jacket, Fara waded out and sat down as if the middle of a rushing creek was a normal place to have a conversation. *She's crazy.* "Don't you Americans feed everything? Make everything into a pet?"

I laughed. "Maybe. Some." I thought of the bedtime stories I'd told to the younger kids at DG. Two parents. A goldfish and a dog. Hugs and kisses galore.

"You have the kitty cat." Fara's hands drifted with the currents.

"Minerva? I don't think I'd let her hear you call her a cat. She's a goddess in a cat's body."

"I know. I know. She's of the Creators, but still. A cat. We call that lunch." Fara winked.

I thought she was teasing but my face must have betrayed horror because she smiled at me. "Kidding you."

I tasted tomato soup and grilled cheese, cold cereal crushed into ice cream. *I need to cook off those last souls.* The little girl, Aileen. Simmering anger flared hot again. *Ms. Asura did this. Who will make her pay? For all the children? My mother? All the elderly? The pain? The lies?*

Fara reached out. "You are upset?"

I didn't answer. *Why isn't everyone screaming with me?*

"Ah, dumb question?" Fara tried again.

"No, not dumb. Yes, I am upset."

"Tell me why? Please?" She waited.

"Because I can't *do* anything to stop her. To keep from hurting everybody, I need to find this mysterious document Ms. Asura demands, and I need to do something

more than look at notes and papers collected over decades. I suck at reading. I HATE IT!" I shouted, startling
ducks, which flew up and away.

Fara didn't react. "What would you do?"

"About?" I splashed the water.

"Instead of this reading, what is this something you
would do?"

"Find the Nocti and make them tell us what is going
on." I let passion flavor my voice jalapeño hot.

"And then what?"

"Then kill them. Dead." I pointed an invisible gun
and pretended to pull the trigger.

She shrugged. "And that makes you like them. Living
in a haze of hate and retribution."

"They deserve it!" I couldn't believe she was defend-
ing them. *How can anyone forgive them?* "Just go away," I
pleaded. If she wasn't on my side, she could leave.

"You want me to go, leave you here?" she asked.

I glanced up. I could tell her the truth, or lie to her.
"Yes."

"Okay. I leave if you promise to come back home soon?"
She started to rise out of the water. Her heavy layers of
fabric soaked up creek water and released it in a *whoosh*.

Thank you. Go. "I promise." I nodded.

"No." She sat back down, sending water splashing into
my eyes.

"What?" Shocked, I coughed up water I inhaled.

"I do not leave you. We will be friends." She crossed
her arms.

"If you want to be my friend, you'll leave me alone."

"No."

"Then I'll leave." I rose.

"I'll go too."

I sat back down. *Are we three years old?* "Why?"

"Because you are not alone," she declared.

"I'm not?" *Really?*

"You never have been."

"That's bullshit." I slapped the words.

"Maybe. Maybe you cannot see it now. Your eyes might not always see, but you have never been completely by yourself. And now your eyes can see me, see Meridian, see Tens, see Tony, see the world of your window that is bigger than this one can ever be. Until you feel this, I will follow you. Into your anger, your hate. Into your light. Wherever you go, I will go, and I will not leave you alone."

The fight gone. I laid my head on my knees. "You sound like Nicole."

"Tell me of her?" Fara asked.

"She was an angel. I didn't know that; I hurt her feelings when I insisted angels don't roam Earth."

"She told you to believe? To have faith?"

I nodded, lifting my head.

"My baba, he used to say that all the good in the world is nothing when faced with self-doubt." She smiled at me, flashing a dimple.

My teeth began to chatter, which made us laugh.

From the woods across the bank, a voice called out,

one I instantly recognized. "Can't stay away, can you, Juliet? We're in your blood." Ms. Asura's voice carried over the lazy water and kicked at my already frazzled reserves.

I didn't answer but grabbed Fara's hand underwater to keep her from standing and heading toward Ms. Asura.

"Introduce us." The Nocti clicked closer, her heels hitting rocks, but her face remained hidden. "You will answer me, Juliet."

"Or?" I dared, unable to figure out what tree she hid behind.

"Or I'll decide not to tell you where your mother is?"

I growled almost as if I had no control over it. Fara squeezed my fingers hard as her head swiveled around us, silently surveying the underbrush.

"Ah, that got your attention, did it?" Ms. Asura's perfume chased away the scents of spring.

"This is Sally," I lied, hoping to shield Fara. "What do you want?"

"You need to be polite. Say please, and tell me, do you really believe that I'm senseless enough to buy that Sally isn't Fara, your Protector?" She tsked.

I stayed silent. *Who told her?*

"You won't live long, Fara, if you hang around here." Ms. Asura actually sounded like she cared.

"You do not scare me." Fara's tone gave away nothing.

"Pity you're as stupid as your friends."

"She's not stupid!" I shouted, standing.

"Sheath your claws, Juliet." Ms. Asura laughed, bitter, fragile chuckles. "Do you love your idiotic little people, Juliet? Like you loved Kirian? Will it hurt you when they scream?"

"What do you want?" *Be nice to her.* As an afterthought, I added, "Please."

"Good girl. I wish I had a cookie to give you." The slap of running feet against pavement drew her attention. "Your father begged me to kill him. He couldn't stand the idea of having a daughter such as you."

Runners in matching blue and yellow tracksuits paraded by. A few gave us odd glances but kept going. "Ah, the little Greyhounds' track practice. How cute. I wonder if they can outrun the Dark?"

"Of course they can. The Light always wins," Fara said.

A hearty laugh carried far over the water. "That's priceless. If I thought you actually believed that, well . . . Thank you, I haven't laughed that hard in ages. Fara, your knives can't hurt me."

"The Light can." Fara pulled me to my feet and shoved me toward the opposite bank. "You will not hurt Juliet again."

Ms. Asura's voice carried over the water. "We will meet again, Juliet, and you'd do well to have an attitude adjustment. Or your new daddy Tony will burn too."

Fara helped me stay upright, dripping, my fingers and toes numb from the cold. She whispered, "I need to follow her trail, see where she goes."

"Don't leave me, please don't," I answered.

Tony's voice rang solid and warm across the field. "Juliet? Juliet! Fara!"

I stood on shaky knees, hoping he wouldn't notice the fear that made my tongue rough. "I'm right here." I stepped toward him. *Thank you.*

He hugged me, crushing me against him, ignoring my sopping wet clothes. "Nelli called. I couldn't find you at home. Couldn't find Fara." He babbled and I let him. *He doesn't deserve the worry I bring him.*

Fara disappeared into the trees. I closed my eyes and hoped Ms. Asura wasn't watching. *She is. And always will be.*

CHAPTER 19

After finding the college kid photographer a dead end on campus, we spent the rest of the day trying to track down a rare book about Renaissance art and symbolism at the university's library. Turned out artists in the sixteenth century believed the adage "the eyes are the window to the soul" to be fact and painted windowpanes into the pupils of their subjects. They also painted clues to the history of Fenestras. Not easy slogging through that. My eyes crossed and my brain overflowed. The cottage lights were bright and shining when we arrived home. *I want a bubble bath and kisses.*

Tucked in the front door was a piece of creamy stationery. Tens glanced around. Nothing seemed out of place or odd.

"Rumi probably stopped by to see if we found the book and any clues," I said, reaching for the paper.

"Careful," Tens cautioned.

I opened it to see the tree, exactly like the photographer's hat, and the initials WoW. In beautiful calligraphy script, it read,

Gates open at seven.

Meet at Meridian Laine Fulbright's stone.

—Woodsmen of the World

Huh? Clandestine meetings at the cemetery? The man who took pictures of the gravestones wants to meet? And calls himself a Woodsman of the World? Is this an ambush?

"What do you think?" I asked.

Custos barked off to our right. Startled, I dropped the paper. I felt goofy to be so jumpy until I heard her growl and the hair on the back of my neck prickled. Tens swore, pressing me back against the door.

Yelp!

Pow!

Snap!

A fight? Custos? I'd never heard these sounds before. Bushes along the trail creaked and cracked. Tens grabbed my hand and took off toward the sounds. I ran behind him, two strides to his one.

"Custos! Custos!" he called.

As we drew closer, the gut-wrenching sounds of snapping teeth against bone devastated the night around us. Nails scrabbled on the sidewalks. The fearful yelp of pain. Custos?

I wanted to scream. *Stop! Stop!*

"Stay behind me, Merry. Stay back!" Dropping my hand, Tens put on another burst of speed and drew farther into the darkness.

As we rounded a corner, we saw Custos with her back to us. Mini lay inert on the ground. They were surrounded by three mangy, starved coyotes growling low and holding their ground.

I stepped on a stick, cracking it. Their heads turned toward us, but one advanced on Custos while the others seemed to call dibs on Tens and me.

"Merry, climb the tree," Tens commanded.

"But I can help." *A large stick, a rock, anything? I can help.*

He didn't raise his voice, but said, "Get out of the way. She's protecting you."

"You too." I wanted to stomp my feet. *She loves you more.*

"Up the tree." He kicked out as a coyote roared toward Custos's undefended back. The coyote ricocheted against a bench and shook its head.

Tens leveled his gun, ready to shoot, but they lunged so fast that one minute they were by Custos and the next they were near me. *Oh hell. This is what you get for arguing.*

I backed up. Swearing, Tens tried to get a shot, but there was little ambient light. I knew why he hesitated—he was as likely to hit Custos or Mini.

I grabbed the lowest branch of the tulip tree and half walked up the trunk, clawing my way onto the top of the branch to climb higher still. The leaves obscured my vision of the ground. But Minerva had disappeared from the sidewalk. I wondered if she'd crawled off to the safety of the bushes or used her ability to materialize and dematerialize. *Why did she and Custos stay to fight? Why didn't they disappear to safety?*

The coyotes lunged, trying to take Custos down as a team. I smelled the metallic stink of blood. I broke off dead branches and hurled them down with all my strength. Tens winged one with a shot.

The suppressed blast allowed Custos to pin another with its belly up. She ripped at its guts, disemboweling it with a quick slice of her powerful teeth. The survivors raced off into obscurity.

Tens placed the muzzle of the gun at the dead coyote's head and pulled the trigger. The suppressor kept the sound muffled, but I saw the force of the blow against the coyote. *Better safe than sorry. I should be sad at the loss of life, but I can't be. Custos and Mini are hurt.*

Custos collapsed, blood and saliva dripping from her jowls. Tens knelt beside her, trying to check for injuries.

"Is she hurt bad?" I called down.

"A few bites. Nothing critical. Where's Mini?" Tens answered.

"I don't know. I didn't see her go." I scooted along the tree. "I'm coming down."

A plaintive meow grabbed my attention. I froze. Who was that?

Tens tilted his head, trying to place the sound.

I glanced toward the meow. Mini had made it onto a branch near me.

"She's up here," I said quietly.

"Can you reach her?"

Carefully I reached out, unsure of how to touch her. It was as if Mini's claws had been ripped from her bloody front paws. One eye swelled shut, and the side of her face was mangled as if she'd had her head in the mouth of a monster and barely escaped with her life.

"Minerva?" I wrapped my legs tighter around the tree branch and reached for her. I had to get her before she fell to the ground below us. *Please don't let me hurt her more than necessary.* As soon as she was in my arms, I felt her body relax and go limp. "Mini?" I felt her chest move shallowly; she was alive. Barely. The sticky warmth of blood dripped along the crease of my elbow.

"Tens?" I said.

He turned on a penlight and shone it up at me. Blood dripped off Mini's tail. "How bad?" he asked, his arms extending up.

"Bad." I let him take her from me, then swung down to the ground.

His expression full of worry and concern, he said,

"Coyotes are timid animals. They don't do this kind of thing."

"I know, I know." If I hadn't seen it with my own eyes, I never would have believed it.

Custos pushed herself to her feet and whined in the direction of our cottage.

"Okay, girl, we're going," Tens answered her.

"I don't understand it." We walked as quickly as we dared.

"Me neither. Things with the Nocti are definitely escalating. This has their stink all over it."

"We need a vet first." We laid Mini on towels and tried to get the bleeding to stop by applying pressure.

Custos limped over to us and cried, pressing her nose against Mini's side.

"I'll call Rumi." Tens grabbed the phone.

CHAPTER 20
Juliet

If I can find my mother first, I can kill Ms. Asura. We can be free. Determined, I loaded the shovel and gloves into the back of Tony's car. *I'll figure out how to kill her later.*

"You can drive?" Fara asked. It was as if she appeared from nowhere, leaning against the lamppost in the parking lot.

Shocked, I dropped a spade, which clanked down on the sidewalk with a cake-falling clatter. "I'll figure it out." *I have to. Lives depend on it.*

Fara held out her hand. "Keys."

When I hesitated, she said, "I know how. Safer."

We got in, and she waited until I'd buckled my seat belt. "Where are we going?"

I hesitated. *She'll just badger me until I tell her.* "Go straight, then left at the roundabout."

Fara merely accepted my directions as they came, and soon we were at the gates of DG. I saw ghosts of the fencing and the echoes of the house outlined as if it still stood. Even the trees in my mind were their pretornado selves. *It's all still here. As if I never left.* I blinked and it was dark, all gone.

Shadows grew limbs and crooked their fingers in welcoming seduction. Above our heads, bats flew low to and from the creek. In the distance, I heard the Wildcat calling me to sail away.

"We are back here again? This is your home, then," Fara declared with a troubled frown.

No! "Not my home. Never a home." *Homes are full of light and warmth and love. Not fear and pain and cold.*

Fara turned off the ignition. The headlights cut through the darkness, illuminating a crumbling foundation and the deep pit of the storm cellar beyond. She stared into me, her eyes eerie in their intensity. "Why do you keep coming back here? Home doesn't always mean sweet and warm. It means where we are from, where we rise from."

"More wisdom from your father?" My tone was snotty.

She shrugged, a very Meridian gesture that I hated. *What does that mean? Shrugs say nothing.*

I climbed out of the car and let her help me haul the tools to the old cellar. There was police tape on the ground, ripped and trampled. I wondered if local kids dared each other to come out here, go into the cellar, and come back out alive. *Unlike my friends? Are they buried here somewhere?*

"What are we doing here?" Fara asked again.

Making sure no one is waiting. I handed her a flashlight, picked up a shovel, and tripped my way down into the damp, dim cellar. "Howie and Aileen were dumped in old buildings."

"Right." Fara's distaste for the place was evident.

"What if they had to take them somewhere else because there wasn't enough room here anymore?" *Makes sense to me—wouldn't they start here?*

Fara shook her head. "But you've been down here— the whole group hauled boxes out to Nelli's. Yes?"

A few inches of water puddled near the door; mosquitoes attacked my face and arms. I nodded, my eyes on the muddy floor. I was looking for a glow, a white sign of bone. *My mother?*

I shone the flashlight at every wall, every corner. At the floor, the empty spaces. *Where are you?*

"No one saw anything before. Right?" Fara simply waited until I paused. "Juliet, no one's down here."

I broke. "You don't know that!" I shouted. "What if they are? What if they've been here the whole time and we left them?" I pointed randomly. "There. Start digging." I sliced my shovel into the dirt, hard-packed like cement; it sang up my arms. *Damn!*

After a few moments of watching me maniacally bang and hiss and spit, Fara pulled out a pair of leather gloves. They were her usual fingerless gloves, studded and padded. She wore them to protect her hands from the chains.

The sounds of carving earth—cutting through, lifting, and throwing—were punctuated by the drip of water. Our breaths mingled and competed with those of mice and spiders. After digging several feet down, I'd found only a few rocks the size of my palm.

I turned around and picked another spot. Hit the dirt with all my might.

"Want me to move too?" Fara asked. "There's nothing here. Rocks. No people."

"Yes, anywhere." I bit the words out as sweat dripped into my eyes and down my sides.

I heard the frisk and squeak of rat conversations. I'm sure they were all around us. They probably came to watch the show. *Who is the crazy girl digging?*

"There's nothing here, Juliet." Fara's voice blew across my spine and I shivered.

"Keep digging." *I won't give up.*

"Are we digging up the entire floor?"

"If that's what it takes." *My mother? My father? Where are they?* "I'll know."

Fara snorted. "You don't know too much right now, cookie."

"What's that supposed to mean?" I threw down my shovel and straightened, my hands fisting.

"You're believing a Hashshashin over our kind. She's playing you."

"With me? She's playing with me?"

"No, like a settar, a guitar. She say do and you do." Fara's fingers steepled, her palms pressed together in an entreaty I couldn't allow.

"My mother is caught in the window because her bones are lost."

"And you think she is here? That she would want you to give up your friends' lives and safety for this? For her?"

I shook my head. "She's in pain, not at rest. And they don't care. They want to stop the Nocti more than they want to help my mother." If I heard another homework assignment or lesson about fighting this grand battle of good and evil, I was going to hurl. *I'm all I can count on.*

"They've risked nothing for you?"

"Of course they did." *At the beginning.*

"Ignored your questions for help?"

"Yes!" I shouted. *They should know how important this is.*

"Really? You have asked them? Told them of this great Asura and the threats she makes of you?"

"No." *Never. They'd never understand.*

"Meridian, she uses you? Asura wants only what is best for you?" Fara's voice stayed level and calm, sending my pulse racing.

"No!" *You don't understand.*

"She is honest? You do her wishes and she will give you truth?"

"No!" *Dammit, just leave me alone. Help me or get out of my way.*

"Why are you so angry at these people who love you?"

My heart stuttered and I felt the hair on my arms rise. A soul found me. I tried to sit down quickly but said instead, "Fara—" My knees gave out, but I stood at the kitchen window, holding the hand of a young girl.

"Where am I?" she asked me.

I thought quickly. "You are going on an adventure." Explanations like these were new to me.

"Where?" she asked.

I pointed. "Through that window." I watched kids and maybe her family members gathering. Outside my kitchen, we were at a park, in the summer, with a jungle gym and puppies running everywhere.

"Can I have ice cream?" she asked.

"Go find out." I lifted her up and over the sill. I tasted chicken nuggets and tater tots.

She raced toward a couple. "Mommy! Daddy!"

"Juliet! Juliet!"

I turned and saw Auntie holding my mother's hand. My mother seemed to speak out of the side of her mouth not crisscrossed by scar tissue. Quietly, so low I couldn't hear her. I wanted to climb across the window and join her. Wrap her arms around me and have her sing me to sleep.

"She says she's okay, to stop. She's"—Auntie frowned—"in the shade."

Mom shook her head. I heard yelling; a commotion brewed in the world behind me.

"Trust them. Meridian's heart is your heart." Auntie raised her hand, and in a moment I was back in the cellar, in my collapsed body.

Cold water soaked along my back, chilling my flesh. I blinked, trying to shake off the confusion that rattled me every time I moved back and forth to the window. Meridian said it got better with time and use, but I wondered. She'd only just begun staying on her feet a few weeks ago.

Fara's voice was full of heat and spice. I blinked up at her.

"You can't kill me with a shovel," Ms. Asura offered.

"How about a knife?" Fara asked.

I realized I lay in Fara's lap.

"Ah, Sleeping Beauty is awake." Ms. Asura stood above us. The side of her face was puckered and webbed, but her mouth was untouched. Her black hair was loose and fell over her shoulders, seeming to ripple without wind. "Tsk, tsk, tsk." She clicked her tongue. "It looks like you don't trust me, Juliet." She glanced at the holes we'd dug.

I swallowed past the bread crumbs in my throat. "Why do you think that?"

"Ah, you're almost adorable when you're imprudent." She toed a shovel handle. "Digging around for the past, are you? Don't think I'll tell you where to find your mommy and daddy? Or are you trying to find Kirian here? Pity how they can't move on."

I sat up, freeing Fara. I reached into the mud for a rock, anything. *Nothing.*

"Leave her alone." Fara stood, holding a knife in front of her, planting her feet.

"Or what? You'll cut my steak into small bites for me? You two are suited for each other. Congrats."

I opened my mouth to speak but she cut me off.

"Stupid—"

"Hello? Is someone down there?" From the shadows above us, a flashlight sliced across my vision.

I knew that voice. *Who is it?*

"Juliet? Fara? Are you okay? Who are you?" His voice dipped deep into his chest.

"Sergio!" Fara called out. "Go back out, call the police."

He clamored down the stairs. "You need to leave," he said to Ms. Asura, and picked up a shovel. As he moved toward us, we became a threesome. *But the odds aren't in our favor. The odds are never in my favor.*

"Who are you, little hero?" Ms. Asura licked her lips and clacked her teeth.

"You're trespassing," he said to Ms. Asura, tossing his cell phone in my direction. "You can leave or you can explain to the police why you're bullying these girls." Sergio protectively stood between us and Ms. Asura.

"Ooh, I know when I'm outwitted," Ms. Asura cackled. "I'll leave." She held her hands open in front of her. "Please don't call the police. Please, please." She moved back toward the stairs but paused near the top step. "I left your cat with a present. Thank yourself I didn't kill her. Yet. Just a warning, Juliet, dear. Don't fail me. You have four days left, or your friend here and an army won't be able to protect that ragtag band of annoyances."

"What did you do to Mini?" I shouted. Fear wicked up my spine and brought bile to my throat.

"What I did to your mother so she'd tell me where you were hiding with your daddy."

"You bitch," Fara spit the words.

"Get out of here!" Sergio yelled, shifting his weight.

"Thank you. Now, if you'll excuse me, I have dinner reservations with my beau. Find it, Juliet, or . . . Well, you're not too smart, but I do think you have quite the imagination, don't you?" She picked her way outside.

I threw up and tried to catch my breath. Adrenaline tasted metallic and bitter like old onion salts. I asked myself for the millionth time, *What do I do?*

CHAPTER 21

I sat on the floor with Custos half leaning against me, half draped across my lap. She let me tend her while Tens and the veterinarian worked on Mini. I barely registered that Custos was trusting me at her most vulnerable. Rumi blubbered, unable to do more than cry.

Dr. Jones shaved most of Mini except for the tip of her tail and her ears. After injecting her with general sedation, the doc cleaned and stitched all of the cat's numerous puncture wounds. Shaking her head, Doc said, "I don't know how she survived this. The blood loss alone should have killed her."

Please be okay. Please be okay. I kept my hand on Custos, trying to reassure her.

Custos whined and nudged my hand with her head. I focused on petting her, giving what little comfort she asked for.

Minerva looked like a mummy all wrapped in tight white dressings. We were instructed on how to give her oral pain medication from a needleless syringe.

Dr. Jones continued. "Let's keep her as medicated as she needs to be for the next few days. We don't want her moving around and tearing her stitches."

We'd laid Mini on a makeshift bed on the floor so she wouldn't accidentally fall off the furniture. With the wraps and the meds, her reflexes were impaired at best. Why didn't she disappear and heal herself? Were the coyotes the Nocti equivalent of our creatures? *Why didn't Custos and Mini simply vanish to a safe place? Why stay and fight?*

"I don't think she'll ever have claws again. It looks like she lost parts of each digit. And you say this happened how?" the vet asked.

"Poor cat, what ailurophobe cat hater would do this?" Rumi wiped his eyes on a handkerchief.

Tens answered Dr. Jones, "We don't know. But coyotes were attacking her and then us. She was up in a tree."

"Maybe they yanked her off the tree?" Dr. Jones shook her head. "I wish animals could talk, tell us the whole story of what happens to them."

"Me too." I smiled. Sadly, I really wish that. Tens hadn't received more information from Mini since February; I rarely got Custos to stay in the same physical space as me, let alone give me any gifts of knowledge.

Dr. Jones finished tending Custos, who needed a few stitches and antibiotics. "Call me if you need anything else. If Mini's condition changes at all."

Rumi walked her out to her car, helping carry her toolbox and bags of accoutrements. I shut the door to the cottage. *Leave it to Rumi to know a house-call veterinarian.*

"What time is it?" Tens stretched his legs straight and leaned back against the couch.

"It's after three." I checked the rooster clock hanging in the kitchen.

The birds would soon be coaxing the sun from its hiding place.

"That's why I'm so tired." He rolled his head on his neck; the popping sounds made my toes curl.

"Where is Juliet?" Rumi reentered, asking. "Wouldn't she want to be here?"

"We called Tony, but Juliet and Fara are missing. As is his car," I said.

"He must be worried sick, going fantod." Rumi trembled.

"There's something going on. I'm afraid for her," I said.

"She battles the energumenical demons of her experiences, doesn't she?" he asked thoughtfully.

"I think not knowing her parents is harder on her than she lets on. And now thinking that her mother isn't at peace? I think that's tearing her up." But maybe there was more to it? *What am I missing?*

Running footsteps had Tens bouncing up and reaching for his gun. Juliet knocked at the door as she flung it open.

"Where is she?" Juliet was covered in dirt. Her braid hung limp and wet down her back. Mud crusted and flaked off her with every movement. She smelled like sewage and ammonia.

"What happened to you?" I asked. *You look horrible.*

She shook her head and collapsed near Mini. She cried quietly, plaintively.

Fara was right behind her, looking as bedraggled and smelling worse. "Asura."

Ms. Asura? Tens and I exchanged a glance. As I opened my mouth to question them, Sergio barged in, talking on his cell phone. "Right, yes, I agree. I'm sorry. I thought I was helping. No, I don't know who she was."

For our benefit, Fara explained, "He's talking to Nelli on the phone. Rumi, can you call Tony, please?"

"Sure, lass." Rumi leapt into action.

Juliet kept whimpering, tears and snot flooding her face.

"Tens?" Fara jerked her head at Tens, who then disappeared with her out the front door.

Rumi and I tried to soothe Juliet, but she wouldn't relax into any of our touches. She was drawing away. *I can feel it, but I have no idea how to stop it.* It was as if she had to decide of her own free will to be one of us.

"What happened?" I asked Sergio, unsure if he knew anything or even if he could be trusted.

"I, uh, well, I wanted to see the old foster home, Dunklebarger?" Sergio blushed. "I know I shouldn't have been trespassing and everything, but working with Nelli made me curious and I thought, you know, I could maybe find something useful." He paused.

"So?" I pressed.

"Um, I, uh, heard voices and shouting and saw flashlights in the cellar, and I thought maybe I should call the police, but then I heard Fara's voice and Juliet and I kinda stormed in." His cheeks pinked.

"Who was in there with them?" I kept my voice even, trying to make sure there was not a hint of my adrenaline evident in my tone.

"A freaky-looking scarred homeless lady. Right?" He turned to Fara as she and Tens walked back in.

"Yes, I think she was living there." Fara moved toward Juliet. "Thank you for your help," she said to Sergio.

"Can I give you a lift home, my boy?" Rumi asked, understanding my silent plea to get Sergio out of here so we could speak freely.

"That would be great, thanks. I left my bike out at Dunklebarger. Um, I hope you feel better." Sergio stumbled over his feet and seemed to think better of approaching Juliet.

"DG," Juliet muttered.

"What were you doing there?" I asked Fara.

"We went to look for—"

Juliet interrupted Fara, asking, "What happened to Mini? Who did this?"

"Merry, we're going to be late." Tens's expression was drawn and troubled.

I glanced at the clock. Six-thirty. We had been summoned to the cemetery by the Woodsmen of the World. "You still want to go?" I asked.

"I think we have to."

I glanced at Juliet who was watching Mini sleep as if she couldn't hear us.

Fara saw the direction of my gaze and said, "We'll stay and watch Mini. Try not to worry."

* * *

We drove through Riverside's gates without trying to hide the van. We needed it for protection and for escape if this went very wrong.

"What's your plan?" I asked Tens.

He shrugged. "I was hoping you'd have one." Then he smiled. *Teasing me on no sleep? That's living dangerously.*

"Good, glad we've got that covered." My stomach pitched against my ribs. "Tens, check out the headstones." Roshana's was the same, but Auntie's marker was replaced with an elaborate window, much like those we saw in other parts of the cemetery, like Rumi's Fenestra ancestors.

"They've changed one but not the other?" Tens asked, studying them.

It wasn't long before the sedan we'd seen the photographer driving came around the corner, followed by an SUV and another truck. A convoy?

"We've got company." Tens slid a gun into my hand. "Please."

I gripped the gun. *Please don't make me use this. Not again.* "They could have killed us at the cottage, right?"

"This has more ambience?" Tens tried to joke.

The kid we recognized assisted an elderly man out of the SUV and into a wheelchair. Balding and fragile, with pale skin that hung in deep wrinkles covered in liver spots. None of the rest of the group gathering wore sunglasses and all of their eyes were very human. *Not a blank void of dark in sight.* I relaxed a fraction. *Not Nocti doesn't mean friendly.*

The man situated himself before addressing us. "Good morning. I see you got our note. I am Timothy. We are all Timothy, or Tim, or Timmy. Your choice."

Uh-huh. Odd. Very, very odd.

Tens nodded, as if such declarations were common. "We didn't get much sleep last night. Can you tell us why we're here?"

He ignored the question. "Don't the new stones look nice?" He wheeled up the path toward us and pointed.

"Yeah, why'd that one get changed?" Tens asked, rolling up on the balls of his feet.

The man stared at me as if he could see secrets I didn't know I had. "I suspect you know the answer to that."

"Humor me," Tens said, directing the man back to him.

"Breakfast?" Another young man accompanying Timothy unfolded a picnic blanket and poured mugs of coffee from thermoses. Another gave him a picnic basket that he peeked inside of with a satisfied expression. *Breakfast at the cemetery? A contingent of frat boys as servants? Everyone named Timothy?*

"No thanks, we already ate," Tens spoke.

"Pity." He handed the basket to a kid, who carried it back to the car.

I watched the display with curiosity. *What is going on?*

The old man said, "There are no bones here. Not of these two ladies. Where are they?"

"How do you know?" Tens shrugged. "Does that matter?"

Timothy dismissed Tens's questions. "They need to be at rest. We must say the words. It's not natural to leave them in the void."

It was like a perverse chess game of male egos. "Ah, of course." *Not natural?* I rolled my eyes. "Are you Nocti? Some sick sympathizer? Do you work for Ms. Asura?" I was tired of beating around the bush. *Attack us or let us get some sleep.*

"Are you? Do you?" He swiveled his piercing gaze to me.

"What?" Tens roared. "Are you kidding me?" He freed his gun and held it at his side.

The men dropped their coffees to the ground and reached for weapons.

"Hold on." The old man held up a hand to stop them.

Interesting. He absolutely controls them.

We stood, holding our breaths for what felt like forever.

"We seem to be at an impasse." He nudged his chair toward his guys. "Take a walk."

"But—" they argued.

"One of you stays; the rest go."

As they ambled off, muttering, Tens relaxed his gun arm, but only a fraction. Never underestimate a potential enemy. *Just because he hasn't killed us yet doesn't mean he won't.*

The old man said, "There's a very active Novelty in the area. They've been trying to flush us out for years. Your arrival in town stirred up the evil. I needed to see if you're on our side or theirs."

A Novelty? A huh-what?

We kept silent.

"My name is Timothy Baumhauer. We are Woodsmen." He waited for us to recognize his name or affiliation. His face fell in disappointment. "Did no one tell you of us?" He looked at me. "We were asked to watch Juliet this spring. You know nothing of us?"

I shook my head. Tens stayed still.

"Get me the basket," the older man yelled over his shoulder to his lone sentry. "Careful with it," he barked.

What is going on? How do they know about Juliet? Who asked them to watch her?

A boy about our age set it on the ground between us and opened both lids for a second time.

"You know yourself to be a Fenestra, yes? And I assume you're more than eye candy?" he poked verbally at Tens. "You've heard of the Templars? Knights of the

Round Table? White Lions? Emerald Society? Druids?" When we didn't respond, he grew frustrated. "Where is your education? Your knowledge? Have you not studied your history? Our history?"

"We're new," Tens answered him without apology.

Timothy considered this, then said, "In the basket is what we call a Celestial. It belonged to my great-great-great-great-grandfather. When it lights from within, we know we are among friends. When it blackens, we know we are not. Take a look."

Tens motioned me behind him, but I marched next to him and peeked into the basket. *Oh, pretty. What is it?*

I'd thought perhaps a lantern or flashlight was on inside, until I peered into a Spirit Stone like Rumi's, but oh so different. "Wow." I swallowed back my surprise. *Could we truly have an alliance with these Woodsmen? Do we have friends? Generations of history working together?*

The old man smiled. "Yes, wow."

I squatted closer. The ball wasn't perfectly round. It was filled with bubbles, opaque off-white glass that looked more like granulated sugar or a stream full of sediment. *It's very, very old.* To my untrained eye, this appeared ancient. It even had a crack or two that seemed to cleave it almost in half, as if it held together by sheer will.

"We know these as Spirit Stones. We have a friend who makes them," I offered before I could second-guess myself.

Timothy shook his head in disbelief. "You can't. The

magic was lost long ago. This is the last of them." The men along the perimeter glanced at each other in question.

I shrugged. "His work too." *Okay, don't believe me.* "Why would I lie?"

Excitement lit his features and rushed his words together. "You must introduce us. We are in great need. We are very vulnerable without them."

"Maybe," Tens said, unconvinced.

To the world, he seemed cold and distant, but I saw him thinking, his mind churning. *Always thinking.*

"What proof do you need?" Timothy asked.

"I don't know yet. Keep talking." Tens shrugged again.

"Will you sit, please? My neck is not what it used to be."

I settled onto the grass. Curiosity overshadowed fear. If this, too, was a Spirit Stone, then it would darken if Nocti were in the area. *So far, it blazes.*

The man's face took on a faraway expression, as if he saw into the distant past. "We came on the first waves of immigrants, way before this land was a country. We came with Fenestra who'd survived the Spanish Inquisition, the pogroms in Eastern Europe, the religious cleansing in the British Isles. We settled many places. Made alliances with others like us whose way of life dictated everything about their existence."

Interesting. Reasonable.

"Such as?" Tens asked.

"Quakers. To this day, Quakers are our friends, which is how we came to be in central Indiana in the 1800s."

"Why?" Tens asked.

"Quakers moved here from Ohio and Kentucky to open a railroad depot to the north."

"What?" I couldn't help my disbelief. *A train? Seriously?*

"Not a locomotive, child—it was for the slaves. The Underground Railroad? Took many hands to make those moves. We settled in Westfield, north of here, to battle for Light. Woodsmen have many religions, Gnosticism and Christianity, Islam and Judaism, Buddhism and Hinduism."

"How is that possible?" I asked.

"The heart of all faith has nothing to do with walls or rules. It is believing that love and light are worth dedicating every breath to. You've never heard that faith is a noun and to believe a verb? Faith you hold in your heart. It's a tangible gift you give yourself. But believing requires action, doing. A manifestation of love."

Auntie's long-ago declarations of a similar nature echoed in a sudden flush of tears. *She would like this man and his cadre of Woodsmen.*

Tens licked his lips. "So, you do what?"

Timothy looked at me. "Your job is to help the soul?" To Tens he said, "And yours is to protect her form so her spirit may walk in both worlds? Ours is to guard your families, your history, your stories. We are your friends." He rolled closer to the headstones. "As part of that, we mark the earth in special ways to denote a Fenestra, a Protector, a Woodsman. We say the sacred words to aid the souls and ward the dust our bodies return to."

"Do your gravestones look like this?" I pointed at the windows now adorning Auntie's and Roshana's plots.

Timothy shook his head. "No, we are trees. Many cemeteries have them; you'd be surprised. The height, what is on the stone, the carvings—all of those mean something to us. Like signs, we can read them at a glance. Masters, those like me who've seen the great darkness and lived to tell about it, have their stones marked with 'WoW' mixed in among the symbols."

I glanced around the hills of Riverside as the sun drew higher in the sky. Stone tree stumps of varying sizes were all around us.

"How did you hear about these graves? How did you know?" I pressed.

"Ah, we have a network. It's shrinking, but it's there. We get word to each other. A special friend contacted me months ago and asked us to watch your Juliet. We saw you were like her. And so on. There are more humans with gifts similar to yours"—he pointed at me—"who feel when another has died. Some who can talk to the dead also get word to us. I do not know how they know. Secrecy is part of how we've lived this long. Kept ourselves safe from the Dark Ones. We know each other close in the circles, but as we go farther out, we don't even know names. We are all Timothy when we interact with outsiders."

"So he's not really Timothy? And you're not really Timothy?" Tens blinked, pointing at them.

"No, coming of age for us is at twenty-one years. They have much to learn before then." His face clouded. "But we are living under a yellow flag of caution; the Novelty is growing stronger and more desperate. Our numbers shrink. Your numbers are less than zero."

A chill zinged down my back. *Zero? I don't count?*

"Novelty?" Tens asked.

"A group of Nocti is called a Novelty."

"Why are you coming to us now? What's changed if you've been watching us since when?" I asked.

"Since February and the exposure of the Dunklebarger scandal, we have been checking on the progress of Miss Ambrose. The Novelty is active. We are afraid they are planning on a significant event. We don't have details yet, but without help, we fear you might all be killed and many more innocents will die."

"Who's your friend?" Tens asked.

At the same time, I queried, "How did you lose the use of your legs? Was it Nocti?"

"I helped a young man and his girlfriend escape capture. I was injured in a car accident with the young man. This is the friend I'm talking about."

Someone who knew Juliet at DG? "What happened to his girlfriend?"

"I was told she was killed as well, but we were near the rendezvous. I don't know. I do not remember the accident. And I was the only survivor of my kind. The young man moved on. I hadn't heard from him until he contacted us."

"What is his interest in Juliet?"

"I do not know his relationship to her, but I would

bet my life that it is only good. I lost family in that accident and he lost his. We are bonded by battle."

My heart broke a little for Timothy's obvious pain. "I'm sorry for your loss."

He brightened slightly. "Ah, the point is to have love to lose, isn't it? What a horrid place this would be without love."

"What do you mean about a rendezvous?" Tens ground his teeth.

Still thinking.

"Ah, we operate a bit like the Underground Railroad, with relaying messages and transporting your kind. We break up the parts to keep each other safe."

Tens nodded.

"Good, I am afraid the Novelty is preparing to strike. We have uncovered some of the plans and I've put out the call, but I do not know how many of us will come. Things are not as they used to be. I know of none other like Meridian and Juliet."

"What do you know about the Nocti's plans?"

"You will know all we know. Perhaps we could meet with your glassblower as well? And Juliet? We must collaborate in order to stand a chance."

Tens glanced at me. I nodded. *We need all the friends we can get.*

CHAPTER 22
Juliet

Be okay, Mini. Please be okay. How will I live without you?

Mini was stable, though I didn't stop my fervent hopes. Fara woke after a short nap and after staring at me intensely, she broke into a flurry of activity like a whisk at high speed. She'd yet to explain to me the necessity of all this commotion.

I held my mother's words in my hands. She'd written notes in the pages of a book of sonnets. In tiny, short sentences, in cryptic code that left most information out.

She probably thought no one would read a book of expired poetry. She'd left me all of my tangible history. The CD she'd tucked into it was the soundtrack to a movie called *Ghost* I'd never heard of. *Why is this CD more important than my father's name? His address? My grandparents?*

A knock at the door of the apartment forced me to move from the couch watching Hurricane Fara make calls and lists and pull ingredients from grocery bags to lay upon the counter like row upon row of little soldiers. Fara tried to make it to the door first, but I beat her because she had chicken juice on her hands.

I glanced through the peephole and waved Fara off. Sergio stood outside clutching a bouquet of wilting daisies.

Why? For whom? I swung open the door. "Hello." *Go away.*

He smiled as if I was exactly the person he most wanted to see. "Juliet." He shifted from foot to foot as we considered each other. "Oh, these are for you." He held out the flowers.

I don't want them. "Thank you." I couldn't make my hand move to take them. He smelled of stale potato chips and old tuna salad.

"Here." He shoved the flowers at me.

Reluctantly, I grabbed them, my fingers brushing his. The stems were sweaty and warm. I stepped back. *He looks too much like Kirian.*

"Hello, Sergio," Fara said from behind me.

"Fara." He dipped his head respectfully as if she were my mother.

"Would you like to come to dinner? We are having a party tonight," she asked in a tone that made me whip around and stare at her.

What are you doing? What party?

Sergio leapt at the invitation. "Oh, yeah, that would be great." His smile filled his face like a cartoon character.

"Don't tell Juliet; it's a surprise." She scribbled on a piece of paper and handed it to him. I tried to grab at the paper, but she was too fast for me. "Can you bring this?"

He read the note, nodding.

What does it say? Upside down and at an odd angle, it could have been written in Chinese. I peered at it, trying to read the crazy squiggles and lines Fara called handwriting. *I don't think it has anything to do with my reading problems; she simply writes horribly.*

"Sure," Sergio said.

"Okay, we will catch you later." Fara pushed me out of the way and started to close the door.

"Oh, yeah, okay later." He seemed shocked as the door swung shut in his face.

"That was rude," I said, dropping the daisies onto the floor.

"We have important duties today. He'll come to dinner. Do you like him?" She tilted her head and narrowed her eyes until the black liner around them seemed to blend into a black mask.

"He's okay." *No! But I don't want to talk about why. You'll ask me about Kirian.*

She didn't let up. "He has much desire in his eyes for you."

"He doesn't desire me." I shuddered. I'd been there once. Kirian loved me. Wanted me. Left me. Betrayed me. *No, thank you.*

Fara shrugged. "Whatev."

I laughed at her atrocious accent and parody of an American moron. "Are you going to tell me what you're doing?" The kitchen was my domain. I wasn't sure how I felt about sharing it.

"You are always saying you don't know enough about me. I'm sharing."

"Now?" I asked. Everything, all at once?

"Do you have to be so annoyance-ing?"

"Yes." I smiled, laughing.

Earlier, Tony mysteriously disappeared but left Fara with the car keys. And without a lecture about scaring him. *He must know what's going on.*

She shrugged her shoulders and tossed her hair— or tried to. There was so much goop in it that it didn't move at all. Her expression grew serious. "I miss the tastes of my father's people. You understand this? You will help now?"

What of my father's people? What do they eat? I was too tired to argue. "All right, what are we making?"

We settled into a rhythm of Fara directing me to chop green leafy herbs: parsley, cilantro, dill, mint, and tarragon. Soon the scents of garlic cloves and cardamom pods layered themselves in. The kitchen became exotic and fresh. I was transported, unclenching the tight grip of my control. I usually knew exactly what flavors went where, but I had no idea what our end menu included. *I should feel awkward with Fara bossing me around in the kitchen, but I don't. Why not?*

Next, I chopped tomatoes while she prepared to cook the rice and chickpeas. Silently, I did as she bid. She'd turned into an expert, confident and demanding. Soon, she began to talk.

"I first made Kuku-ye Zabzi Zereshk—you can call it Kuku—with my father when I was three years old. He had me crack the eggs carefully in the bowl after he'd chopped like a superhero with big knives, and fast hands, all the herbs."

I listened, watching her expressions animate with these wonderful memories.

She continued. "We made this over and over again until I'm sure I murmured the ways in my sleep. Then he added Ash-e Reshteh, noodle soup, when I was five. I picked the bad chickpeas and beans out of the dried mix. Very important job. But if you wish while you make it, the wish comes true." She laughed.

She motioned for me to chop scallions and more garlic. She burst with fussy.

"Then came Mast-o Khiar. A yogurt sauce." She squeezed limes over a pot of rice, onions, chicken thighs, and tomatoes. She dotted the top with tiny saffron threads. "Rice and green beans is called Lubia Polow."

I practiced pronouncing her words until my tongue tied. *I don't know the names but I know these flavors.*

"This smells of my father." She held a small cardamom pod, dried and green, under my nose as she broke it.

I nodded. Food piled higher around us on every surface. All of the hungry in our city might be satiated by the volume of this meal. *Why a party now? What is there to celebrate?*

"Sabzi Polow is a spring rice, green like your grass." She heated a large pot of oil and pulled catfish out of the refrigerator. "Mahi-e Tanuri, like Rumi's catfish fry?" She giggled and I laughed. He never missed an opportunity to eat fried fish.

Fara kept up a steady stream. "When I knew each of these dishes and how to pick the best, the freshest parts, my father added in sweets, cookies, and frozen creams to our practice. But these foods, they were the most important. Each family has their own recipes, their own way, yes? This is our way."

I inhaled, relaxing with each breath as the scents of cooking food, spiced with life, filled the condo.

"This is a lot of food." I glanced around. "Is everyone coming to dinner?"

"Ah, we go to them. Sit." She pointed at a chair.

I sat as she handed me a cherry fizz drink that made my mouth pucker and my heart sing.

"Your day to begin is Nowruz. The day of the New Year, a day of new beginnings and fresh spring. I was to be here. I was supposed to cook with you this meal. We were to make you fresh, clean, welcome to the new you." She spit out a string of words I didn't understand. "Translate is hard." She paused in frustration.

"We write down all the wrongs of the year before, all the mistakes." She pushed a pen and paper toward me.

All of them? Where do I start? "Do you have more paper? I'm not sure this will be enough," I tried to joke.

"No joking. Write. What makes your heart hurt? Your soul cry? Put on paper. Takes much time." Fara went and checked the food and left me to stare at a blank page. As she clanked around the kitchen, I began with a single word. *Kirian.* Then *Mother.* Added *Meridian.* And soon the words began to pour forth as if my pen were a mere extension of myself. I didn't believe Nicole. I didn't save more kids or elderly. I let Ms. Asura make me doubt and hate. *How did I give her permission to make me feel these ugly, horrid things?* I paid no attention to the possibility anyone might read what I wrote. I knew what it said. Every word.

I glanced up and saw Fara studying me. "My baba told me love has only one enemy. Not hate. Unknowing." She searched for a word. "Ignorance."

I nodded.

"Nowruz is about knowing our soul clean again. Loving each other. Chasing the dark away and welcoming the light back. It is a clean start. You see? Write more. Write it all." She waved toward the paper and turned away.

I nodded, though I felt like I was in the middle of a crazy crash course. I kept writing until my hand cramped and kept going even when my fingers hurt so much the words were no longer recognizable. Not only a year of wrongs, I wrote my lifetime.

Fara quietly tasted food in pots and wrapped the fried fish to keep it warm.

I laid the pen down and stretched.

Fara nodded. "We are ready. Let us load the car."

Night fell like velvety ganache down the sides of a chocolate cake, which meant hours had passed as we'd cooked. As she'd told me stories of Nowruz, Baba, and traditions.

After making several trips to load the food into the car, Fara declared, "We are going now."

"Where?" I asked, buckling into the passenger's side.

I wasn't sure she was going to answer, but after a few moments, she said, "Home."

I frowned, wondering where she meant until I saw the turn toward DG. "Why? No, turn around." *This is no home.*

Panic rose in me like dough in a warm oven until I couldn't swallow past it. *What are we doing here? A party? No parties ever happened here. The opposite of parties is DG.*

"No. We go." Fara's resolve shut down my words, but my fingers cramped along my thighs as I tried to hold on to the calm and confidence I'd found such a short time ago.

We pulled up among many cars, and I recognized all

of them belonged to people in our coalition. Including Joi and her husband. Bodie and Sema shrieked joyfully as I got out of the car. My heart lifted seeing the littlies. They seemed so relaxed, happy, and cared for. *They look like children who are safe and cherished with no worries except what flavor of frozen custard to choose.*

"They're back?" I asked Fara as the kids ran toward us.

"Just for tonight. They needed to be here too." She smiled as they approached.

Bodie and Sema raced toward us wearing crimson hats and red satin capes. They banged pots and spoons in a cacophonous racket all around us.

Bodie sang out, "Like this, Fara? Are we doing it right?"

I swept them into my arms for a brief hug before they danced away, intent on performing their task.

"Yes, little one, all around us. Chase away the bad! Dance in the Light!" She danced with them and sent them off banging around the edges of the property. At my questioning glance, she explained, "They are the Haji Firuz. They scare away evil and help us celebrate Light's victory over Dark."

Sergio and Tony came toward us to help carry all the food from the car. Tony stopped by me, hesitated, then kissed the top of my head, as if saying hello. *Or goodbye.*

"You all know what this is?" I asked him as he loaded up his arms.

"Fara's a good general; she delegates well." He shrugged. "We're only following orders."

"Uh, yeah, she gave me that note and it took three

hours." Sergio grinned ruefully. "Next time I'll remember not to agree so easily."

Fara laughed and waved them off.

A huge bonfire blazed on what used to be the back lawn of DG, nearer to the creek than the road. Gus and Joi set up tables and chairs. Tony helped Rumi light candles under colorful glass bulbs.

Beautiful. Magical. I almost forgot where we were.

Nelli and Bales draped garlands between the trunks of two skeleton trees. Fara pointed out the objects strung together. Apples and oranges, bunches of grapes, tiny mirrors dangled and reflected the bonfire. I saw faces I recognized in the photographs hanging down too. Everyone was there in candids and poses. Meridian's silhouettes were light but blurry; mine were balls of light with no human form.

Fairy lights twinkled amid the candles. Fara pointed up. "Light is the symbol of Nowruz."

Rumi even strung a few new Spirit Stones from the branches of the trees. Mini lay beneath one, still bandaged but alert, with Custos as her side.

As we unloaded the food onto the tables, Fara taught everyone the names and which ingredients were in each. The aromas blended with the warm air and earth around us like a delicious promise. My heart beat easier. My lungs allowed in more oxygen-rich air.

I listened to the creek giggle and laugh behind us in approval. I wondered if my mother was watching with Fara's baba. If Kirian knew where I was.

We ate, laughing, Fara orchestrating the conversations to stay airy and silly. Bales seemed to blend into the shadows of the perimeter as if he was guarding the event. When had Tens, Fara, and he discussed it? As we finished eating, Fara opened up about her father and their Nowruz traditions.

"There are seven kinds of immortals, seven of our kind who guard all of the Creator's domain. With the light, we guide our ancestors' spirits home and chase away the evil." She moved to the table lit by green pillars. "Sofreh-ye Haft-Sinn, the holiday table." She frowned.

We gathered around in a circle. Sergio moved close to me but paid me no attention. His focus was completely on Fara's words and actions.

"We're sorry. We did the best we could on your list," Tony apologized.

Fara composed herself. "My baba taught me to adapt. This is fine." She smiled and held up the apple. "For life in all its kinds." She placed it down and picked up the bunch of peonies. "For our noses, fragrance." The bottle of vinegar was next. "Pickles? Yes? Last a long time? Eternity." She glanced at me. "You love this one—garlic represents health."

I laughed and shrugged. I do love garlic.

She held up a bowl and glanced at Nelli, who said, "Olives."

Fara nodded. "Ah, olives are for love, two parts in one. And the lemons must be for fertility?"

"We couldn't find sumac, and the Internet suggested this as a substitution for recipes," Tony added.

Fara flashed a dimple. The glow from the bonfire and colored glass shades filled the yard with warm rainbows. "Lemons. So the earth and our families continue growing for generations." She pointed out other elements, including the mirrors. "Reflecting the light of the Creators and reminding us of the beautiful world around us."

Sergio began writing on the back of his hand with a pen. *Odd.* It seemed as though he jotted down notes each time Fara spoke. *As if there is a quiz later.*

My pages of mistakes dragged down my pocket. A tension built in my gut as Fara became very serious. With each new word, I knew she was going to make me read my list. *When will she make me share my letter of mistakes?*

But instead she asked Meridian, "Did you bring Auntie's diary?"

"Yes." Meridian grabbed her bag. The thick book of leather and parchment seemed to radiate the power of many lives, many words of wisdom and past mistakes. I wish I had that much to my past, my history. *Is that the book Ms. Asura wants? Can it possibly be? How will I ever get that away from Meridian and Tens? I can't steal it, betray my friends and live with myself. I'll have to leave. If I do this, it means exile.*

My lungs felt like overcooked noodles. Saturated and falling apart, they were unable to take in air.

Sergio reached to take the journal from Meridian and bumped her arm accidentally. The journal thunked against the ground. "I'm sorry. So sorry." He clumsily picked it up and dropped it again until Tens stepped between them.

Sergio moved closer to me instead, his face doused with embarrassment and his hands shoved deep into his pockets. *I feel sorry for him.*

Fara reached into her jacket and pulled out my mother's book. "I have the sonnet book."

"When did you grab that?" I asked. *Is this the book? Do I have to give Ms. Asura the only thing my mother left me?* But I'd never seen that symbol on its pages. *It can't be the one.*

My voice must have carried more upset than I knew, because Sergio jumped in. "Do you want it back?" he asked while advancing toward Fara.

"It's fine," I said quickly. I stepped back and around him, careful not to touch him until I was next to Fara again. He stood too close, wanting something I couldn't give him.

Fara simply ignored him and asked that we all sit by the bonfire. "The tenets or pillars of my people, of our people"—she waved her hands to include all of us—"are knowledge and love. When taking on enemies, these are powerful weapons. Love is Light. Knowledge is Light. Light is our most pure form."

Bodie and Sema both crawled into my lap. It was almost like old times with a story for bedtime. *Once upon a time, there was a girl trapped in a castle with no one coming to rescue her.*

"Think of a question in your minds. Something you very much want guidance with in this coming year. We use our holy texts, our ancestors' writings. Baba tell me to use those most special to you. Now everyone wish for an answer." She waited a heartbeat or two, then asked, "Ready?"

Fara looked at Meridian, tapping her temple. "You think yes?"

Meridian nodded. Fara randomly opened Auntie's journal and pointed.

> **You will know when the time is right. Know not just in your head, but your bowels & your heart.**
> **—Cassie Ailey, March 1871**

She turned to Tens, who nodded that he, too, had a question in mind. After closing the book, she repeated her flip and point.

What questions are they all thinking? Can these point-and-speak answers possibly impart any wisdom?

> **Patience, the knowing will come when you need it most.**
> **—Melynda Laine, November 1939**

To Nelli and Gus, she also asked them to think of a question. Their answers were both from the same writer, Jocelyn Wynn:

> **To love a lifetime or a breath is all the victory we need.**
>
> —1822

> **See the past in the future and the future in the past as we live again and again and learn nothing.**
>
> —1804

All their faces registered surprise and understanding. Then she gave the book back to Meridian and held my mother's. "Tony?"

She swiveled to read the margin notes. To Tony she read, " 'The sun is relentless this week. For all I'd like is a tall glass of punch and a nap in the cool shade for all time.' "

He nodded, thoughtful, though I was unable to decipher what he was thinking

Finally, Sergio's turn arrived. "Which book is your most sacred?" Fara asked.

"Uh, yeah, I don't know—why don't you just skip me tonight? I didn't bring it with me."

"But—"

An electronic beeping interrupted. "Sorry, sorry. That's my cell." He dug into his back pocket and read the screen before tucking it back. "I have to leave in a minute. Why don't you go on to Juliet now?" he insisted.

I squirmed, feeling all their eyes on me. Not even the sleepy heartbeats of my littlies in my arms calmed me.

Fara turned to me. "Think of your question."

Mommy, what should I do? I can't go on this way. I don't know which way to go.

She again randomly opened the book, pointed to a section, and read, " 'If my daughter learns nothing from me but trusting in good, I will consider myself a worthy mother.' "

I felt as though I'd been punched in the gut. *Is it rigged? It can't be.* I grabbed the book and read her words slowly, focusing completely. My heart tore. I had done nothing but distrust and second-guess, undermining myself and my friends. *No, my family. These people are my family. The good.*

Fara held the book back out to Tony with a smile on her face.

"Wait, what about you?" Meridian asked.

Fara paused and gestured all around us. "This is my answer." When she looked at me, it was as if generations I'd never met held their breath. "For Nowruz to complete, we must all clean our hearts, give up the wrongdoings, drop the burdens. You brought your lists?"

Everyone dug theirs out of their pockets or purses. I was surprised to see mine wasn't the only one of several pages.

"I'm sorry, I can't stay." Sergio abruptly stood up,

tossing blank pages on the ground behind him. Sweat beaded along his hairline and his face flushed as if he'd sat too long by the bonfire.

"You must stay." Fara picked up his paper and tried to hand it back to him. "This is important."

He shook his head, looking like he felt trapped and scrambling for a way out. "I'm late for a school thing. I can't miss it. I'll see you at work tomorrow?" He nodded to Nelli.

"Sergio, wait!" Nelli called, but Bales stepped out and shook his head at her.

Nelli fell silent as Sergio wheeled his bicycle away from a tree stump and down the driveway. Bales melted back into the trees and Nelli frowned.

None of us knew how to respond. No one said anything for a few moments as the flames cracked and hissed and the night settled back around us, but then with a shrug, Fara continued. "It takes strong hearts to see our mistakes. Faith that we can change the path before us is maybe scariest thing. Some people cannot see, cannot change."

I swallowed. *She's talking to me.* My throat closed and I hugged Bodie and Sema so tightly they woke fully with giggling complaints.

Fara said, "Normally, we would all share these, to make amends, but that would take us years." A half smile on her lips, she studied us all in turn. "Instead, we will burn them. But if they belong in this circle, with us, to shed light into our souls, then please tell us all."

She's talking to me. She wants the impossible. I'm not brave. I can't do this.

She led the way to toss hers on the fire. No one seemed to hesitate, but I kept hearing Fara demanding that secrets come to light. The elders followed quietly, discussing how truthful and honest their textual answers felt, but all I heard was my heart beat in my head. Pounding. Beating. *Be brave. Speak up! Give them a chance to help!*

With each step toward the fire, I felt heavier and heavier. I crumpled the papers in my fist. Sweat dripped down my spine.

Tell them. Tell them. Ms. Asura wants you to keep silent. Find your voice. Take back your power. Like with reading, like with cooking, be you.

Tony tossed in Bodie's and Sema's crayon creations. They'd drawn pictures of DG and a blackened blob of harshness that could only be the headmistress.

Meridian waited next to me. I felt her glance. *She knows I'm hiding. She knows my lies.*

I cleared my throat. I started in a whisper but each sound gained potency and depth until I lifted my head, pouring my guts out. "I have something to say. I can only hope you'll forgive me."

CHAPTER 23

"They shouldn't be here." Tony pointed at the kids, who listened with wild eyes.

"You're right." Juliet hugged Bodie and Sema.

"Are you all right?" Bodie whispered in a stage voice. "You're scaring me. Is she back?"

"You don't need to be afraid." Juliet's voice was strong and forceful. "Joi and Robert will chase away the monsters."

Bodie nodded but dragged his feet as Joi loaded them up to take them back to the lake. The bleak defeat in Juliet's eyes broke another piece of my heart. *She thinks she's lost all of us already. Oh, Juliet. How can you bend and not break under this pain?*

Listening to Juliet spew her truth, her words, pained me. Grief's drab and hostile colors radiated around us. Sadness enveloped me, wrapped around my heart with icy fingers. I shrank under the obvious wounds Juliet flayed for us. Like cleaning out a gangrenous, putrid limb, Juliet bore down with everything she had and opened herself up. Anger would have been an easy response, but not honest.

How had I failed her so badly that Ms. Asura had any power over her? *What should I do differently?*

I had tried to give her what I'd lacked from my mother and during my transition. We'd had time to prepare for hers, so I'd done everything I'd wished for last December. *Maybe what she needs isn't the same thing I do.* How had I been so oblivious to her need to protect her mother and find her father? *Maybe because mine betrayed me so badly.*

"Is that everything?" Tens asked quietly.

Juliet nodded and Fara confirmed as well with a gesture. "She offered me a trade"—Juliet swallowed—"and I didn't say no."

Ms. Asura promised to give Juliet the location of her parents' remains in exchange for finding information. *Wild-goose chase? Something bigger? Can it really be considered a trade when not cooperating meant threats against the rest of us?*

"What does she want you to do exactly?" Gus

questioned, his arm wrapped around Nelli's quaking shoulders.

She's taking this personally.

"Find a book with this symbol on it." Juliet picked up a stick and drew in the dirt.

We crowded around trying to make sense of it. She's either not that good an artist or Ms. Asura wasn't terribly helpful. Based on how Ms. Asura and her cronies toyed with the kids at DG, it wouldn't surprise me if Juliet was given an impossible task that would leave her feeling guilty when the Nocti attacked us.

"That's it? Wings and a stick? Is that a snake?"

"A candle?" Rumi asked.

"What's that circle in the middle?" Nelli questioned.

Juliet seemed near tears as she muddled the picture, trying to make sense of it. "The ink ran all over the page. I don't know." There was no hope in her voice. As if she'd already given up.

"Then we have to find out exactly what this symbol is," Tens said.

"Why ask for a book, though? Is it one of the ones we've started studying?" Tony asked.

"I think it goes back to the knowledge thing," I added.

"We know something they don't?"

I nodded. "Maybe we don't even know what we have."

Tens glanced at Juliet. "Okay, you find and hand over this book or information and then what happens?"

"If I did that, she would tell me where to find"—Juliet's

voice cracked—"where to find my parents. And leave you all alone."

"That easy?" Tens questioned. "That's too easy, Juliet."

Juliet's tears fell down her face and Fara held out a tissue. "I know, but I didn't know what else to do. She's always around." Juliet scanned the area as if she expected Ms. Asura to jump out and scream, "Boo!"

"I should have realized she was threatening you." Tony dipped his head low, his rosary clutched in his fingers.

"What do you mean she's always there?" I asked.

"At the condo. At the creek. On the path near your house. It's like she knows where I am before I do."

What if they're watching us? How? Is there a traitor in our group?

"She's been inside our house?" Tony leapt to his feet.

"I don't know. I smell her after. She chases away food." Juliet began babbling as if once she let go on the firm hold over her tongue, she couldn't catch up.

"Did you break the Spirit Stones? Vandalize my shop?" Rumi asked.

Juliet paled and gasped. "No, I promise you. I wouldn't let you, any of you get hurt, I swear. I thought it wouldn't matter. That—" She stopped and inhaled. "I took your leather folio, but I didn't give it to her. It's in the closet."

"I never thought I'd be pleased to know a thief," Rumi muttered.

"It was before that. I tried to put it back, but they'd already been there."

"That's what you were doing going to Rumi's?" Tony asked.

She nodded. "I thought no one would be hurt if I did what she asked."

"Did she threaten to harm you if you said no?" Nelli wiped away tears.

Juliet shook her head. "No, not me." Her words hung in the air.

"Who?" My question was quiet but important. If she wasn't worried for herself, then who?

"All of you." Her words were low and almost silent.

"Everyone we've asked you to depend on?" Tony asked, reaching a hand out to grasp her shoulder. "I wish you'd told me. We could have figured this out together."

"She tried to say no. Several times. We were trying to make a fake book," Fara inserted, as if this clarification was monumental.

All I saw was a girl tossed into a world she didn't know, being asked to choose between what she most wants in this world and inflicting pain on others. *Avoid pain and get what you want—that's basic survival instinct.*

Rumi broke his unusual quiet. "No one knows the truculent hell you've been through, lass, but this is a minatory, threatening revelation. I fear for all of us. That is difficult to let go." Rumi crossed his fingers and frowned. "Not impossible, but now I feel as though you must live up to your photic soul instead of down to your weaknesses."

Juliet nodded, her gaze set on the fire's blaze.

She didn't need us to make her feel worse or she'd curl into a ball and be useless in the coming fight. "Rumi, Ms. Asura and her group know us. If they want to come after any of us, at any time, they will. They don't need Juliet to do it. Right?" I asked him.

He nodded in agreement.

How do we salvage this? Repair the damage? Rebuild on truth? I glanced at Tens, wishing he could read my mind.

Of Juliet I asked, "Does Ms. Asura think you're co-operating? Right now, does she believe she's scared you enough and motivated you enough to follow through?"

"I don't know. She's been showing up more, like she's watching me all the time. And when I tried to buy time, that's when Mini was . . ."

"Attacked?" I filled in.

"It was a warning, then. If she can get to creatures of the Creators, she can get to any of us." Tens began carving a tree branch. I knew he did his best thinking when his hands were busy.

Movement at the edge of the woods caught my attention, but Tens's voice brought me back.

"She attacked Mini to prove you're more vulnerable and will believe her threats. You won't disobey again," he said.

"She thinks you're going to go along with it, right?" Tony asked.

"It appeared that way to me," Fara said.

"And she's not threatened by your presence?" I asked Fara.

"No, she does not see me as powerful." Fara grinned. "She is the stupid one."

I nodded. "Good. We let her think that. You'll have to talk to her again. Convince her you can find the book with more details from her." Not only would this give us more information, but also Juliet needed to make restitution for her own well-being. We could tell her we understood or that she was forgiven, but until we proved that and she demonstrated she was worthy of our trust, nothing else was going to matter. *Not really.*

"Okay," Juliet said tentatively.

What is she thinking? "What is it that you want? Honestly?" I asked her, forcing myself to slow down and really listen.

Her brows furrowed and tears chapped her cheeks. "My parents. I can't stand the idea they are hurting and trapped between the worlds. I want my mother transitioned beyond the window and healed. And I want to know who my father was, if he's dead too."

Oh, Juliet, how can one person be so lonely? Especially when you don't have to be.

Tens's voice carried over the crackle of the wood fire. "Juliet, think about it. If your father was dead, he'd be at the window too. He'd be there waiting for you. If they'd desecrated his remains, he'd be there, too, caught as you say."

Brilliant! Why hadn't that occurred to me? *Of course he's still alive.* Her head snapped up and she focused on Tens. "What do you mean?"

"I don't think he's dead. I don't think Ms. Asura knows where he is."

Tony thoughtfully circled. "That makes sense. Maybe Roshana didn't know either."

"It's the number-one rule in interrogation—leave lots of blanks and let the suspect fill them in. You learn the best information when they assume you know more than you do," Nelli pondered out loud. "What else do we know about your father?"

"He's out there? Really? You think it's possible?" Juliet's voice blossomed with excitement.

"Hiding," Rumi added. "Or when the news broke about DG, he'd have seen you. By all accounts you look like your mother, yes?"

Tony answered all of them, "We think he was with Roshana at DG, but how they got north to me I don't know. She wouldn't talk about him at all. And, yes, Juliet looks almost exactly like her."

I wondered if Roshana's eyes held the same tortured sadness as her daughter's. *How do we break this cycle?*

"Maybe he thought he'd put her in more danger if he came forward. There would be questions he couldn't answer," Nelli pondered. "Bales started looking for a man with the last name of Ambrose about the age of Roshana. That'll only work if she took his last name. He doesn't have anything solid yet. But he's the best; he'll find your dad."

"Where did Bales go?" I asked, noticing that Bales was missing out of this discussion.

"He had a lead," Nelli said, breezing over my question.

"Juliet, you still have to be accessible to Ms. Asura. We have to let them think we aren't working together against them. Can you do that?"

"How do I behave as if you don't know what's going on?" Juliet didn't sound as if she believed her. "How can I pretend nothing has changed tonight?"

"We must all be Tartuffes and operate under pretense," Rumi said.

Nelli nudged Gus. "Uncle Gussy, tell them what you told me."

"No, Nelli, it's not the time. Forget I mentioned it," Gus declined.

"It's exactly the time. If we're busy throwing a wedding, the Nocti will think we have no idea what they're up to. It's perfect." Nelli nodded.

"Wedding?" I asked.

"Faye changed her mind. She said yes." Gus sighed. "But it's not as important—"

I could hear Auntie's voice in my head as crystal clear as if she stood next to us. So I said, "Gus, loving is the reason for living. It's the only way to fan Light brighter."

Juliet smiled through her tears. "If you'll let me, I'll make the cake."

CHAPTER 24

Throwing an impromptu wedding required all of us and then some. The hospice staff fully supported our plan to surprise Faye. I walked down East State Street to Rubia, an old gas station converted into a European-style flower market. Rumi told me their buckets and tubs, overflowing with every possible color and fragrance, would meet our needs. It was like walking into a van Gogh or Monet garden come to life. *Perfect*.

"I'm Sarah. How can I help you?" With bright blue eyes and deep dimples, she welcomed me into the shop and instantly felt like a friend.

I glanced at the clock. "I need to put together a bridal bouquet and a groom's boutonniere."

"Okay, let me get an order form. What date are you looking at getting married?" She bustled to take my order.

I cringed. "I'm sorry. I mean now, um, for today. We don't have much time."

To her credit, she merely steered me toward the abundant peonies, roses, and daisies in stock. "I can have it ready in thirty minutes. Does that work?"

"Thank you." I grinned.

While she worked on that, I headed down the street to Pillowtalk and picked out a beautiful white linen and lace nightgown.

Rumi assured me he had Gus's attire under control as well as the jewelry. Tens was picking out and delivering decorations for the tiny terrace patio. Nelli and Bales kept Faye occupied watching television and writing goodbye notes to out-of-town friends.

Tony covered the ceremony vows that Faye mentioned as being so important to her. Juliet and Fara composed the celebration's food; Juliet seemed lighter and more hopeful than I'd ever seen her. *I hope it lasts.*

So maybe it wasn't traditional to get married in a hospice, while waiting for death to creep closer, but it was living until the very end, and that was Faye's number-one goal.

To fully live up, until life continued beyond this world. It's a good goal.

After picking up the flowers and meeting Tens, we headed to the center. He left me at the front doors while he snuck his assembled Eden around to the back. Faye's hospice team knew all about the plan. Faye, and even Gus, not so much. I liked surprises when they happened to other people.

Before the ceremony, though, I needed to prep the facility for Juliet to enter. Her time at the window still drained her. *I'm lucky it's getting easier for me.* I headed inside to clear the space for Juliet. If there were willing souls, they needed to use me today. I was almost to the point I could control my physical self while operating the window. *Closer, anyway.*

There was a comfortable living room space near the front doors, so I planted myself in the corner of an alcove. I hoped I appeared to any onlookers like I was meditating. I didn't have long to wait for the first soul to find me. Delia knew they might have more empty beds today than expected.

The window scene opened before my eyes like the curtain of a dressing room.

"I haven't been here in years." A well-dressed coiffed and set lady wearing a mint-green skirt suit, white gloves, and a pillbox hat stood next to me at the window.

"Where are we?" I asked. It was a restaurant with floor-to-ceiling Greek-inspired white pillars and shining crystal chandeliers.

"The LS Ayres Tea Room, dear. I modeled here when I was young."

"Really?"

She nodded. "We'd wander the tables while ladies

lunched. Before those reality shows, you know, there was actual reality," she said with a sparkling smile. She waved to a group of similarly done-up ladies. "There are my girls. Five daughters, three grand, are at that table right there." She pointed, then frowned. "I have to wait for the rest to come over, don't I?" She turned back behind us.

I tried to find words to reassure her. "I don't think it feels like very long."

"Thank you, dear." She patted my arm and gracefully walked through the window.

I blinked, hearing a rhythmic thump and squeak. Hardwood polished to a high sheen, a whistle blew and a basketball court filled with boys running drills. Their shorts were tiny, their socks pulled up over shins high above canvas sneakers. The seats of the pavilion were full of cheering spectators. Chanting and excitement echoed off the rafters high above.

"Wow." The scoreboard seemed captured at halftime of a game. *What decade is this?*

An old man shuffled next to me. "1954. Hinkle Field-house. We beat Muncie for the state championship." He hesitated. The crowd started to chant a name and he stood a little taller. "That's me."

"What are you waiting for?" I asked.

"What if I've lost my shot? After all these years."

"I think it'll come back to you as soon as you hit the court." I took his arm to aid him.

As he crossed over, his slacks and flannel shirt changed into a matching basketball uniform, and he rewound into the height of his youth. He turned, saluting me with a big smile as the announcer called his name.

I opened my eyes back in the hospice. The room was empty, and no one, dead or living, came near me. I waited a few more minutes, then called Juliet's cell phone. "We're good to go here."

"We're just pulling in. Thanks for, you . . . you . . . know," Juliet stuttered.

Why are you thanking me for caring about you? "Of course." I hung up, walking down the carpeted hallway. *What is different about this place?* I can't describe the feeling, but there wasn't the rush I experienced at hospitals. These were souls not-quite-ready, or ready but not in such distress they needed to leave their bodies at the first opportunity. *There's a calm expectancy, but no hurry.*

Extra-wide doors opened off the hallway much like an apartment building. The halls all radiated out like spokes on a bike wheel. It was softly lit and quiet, a feeling of hush-a-bye pervaded the air. Like a library. As if no one wanted to interrupt very important work.

To my left, rainbows spilled into the hallway, bright and iridescent, shimmering with all the colors of existence. Curious, I moved forward. I squinted at the rays, as if I couldn't quite make out or focus on all the shapes and layers within it.

A man's voice called out an invitation. "Come in, please?"

"I'm sorry. I saw——" I waved my hand at the light that seemed to be everywhere and come from nowhere.

"You're right on time." A tiny man who barely made a shape under the sheet nodded.

"Do you need a nurse? Is there someone to call?" I asked.

"You're here. I am ready."

I felt like I missed pieces of this conversation. "To die?"

"To be released, to be freed from this body."

Why aren't we at the window? I felt the same woogy, shaky feeling I got in my knees when someone crossed over. However, I was firmly planted in this room. *No fainting, no light-headedness, no needing to sit down just in case.*

"Come closer," he instructed.

"I'm sorry. I don't know why it's not working," I said, struggling to will us to the window.

"It's working perfectly." His voice was serene and warm.

The colors seemed to shrink, coalescing, to move across to the head of the bed. The room shifted so its corners rounded in. It was as if the geometry of the world was swooshed into a new shape.

"Can you see me?" I asked. *Is he dying? Does he see light in me, or have we reversed our roles?*

"Yes." The light moved across the bedding and combined above his head like a mist.

He sat up and arranged his body in what I can only guess was a meditation pose, with his legs crossed and hands on his knees. He smiled at me beatifically. "Tell them to rejoice as I go on now. To the place beyond the windows, to the light itself."

His eyes closed and the iridescence shimmered, bursting like a firework from the top of his head. His body stayed upright in the seated position even as a drop of blood trickled from his nose.

He's dead. I went to get a nurse.

She seemed visibly shaken when she entered the room and saw him sitting upright. He seemed frozen in what she called the lotus position. "Did you help him? Lift him? He hasn't moved on his own in two months."

"He said he was—"

She gasped. "He spoke?"

I nodded. He'd sounded fine.

"He had ALS. He hasn't said anything to anyone for six months, long before he got here. His nephew brought him."

The door was pushed open and a young man in his thirties stood there. "He's gone?"

"I'm so sorry. Your uncle passed moments ago," she said.

The man nodded, resolved in his grief but as if relief lived in him too. "You were here?" he asked me.

I nodded, not sure what to say. "He was at peace. He smiled at me."

"He came to me. I know that sounds crazy, but I woke up because it was like someone turned on all the fixtures in my apartment, but no lights were on. He was standing there. And he said it was time to go but not to worry, that he had company. A girl of the window."

"He said he went to the light beyond," I said, because he seemed receptive to the information.

The man shook his head. "I'm sorry. You must be mistaken, because he doesn't know English. He's never spoken a word of English even when he could talk."

"Maybe he's been listening to us all," the nurse offered, trying to explain away the mystery.

"I must call the temple, maybe the elders or the abbot will have an explanation. This doesn't make sense."

Or maybe it didn't need to make sense. I tried again. "He was happy."

"Thank you." The man walked down the hallway shaking his head, pulling out his cell phone.

The nurse said to me, "Maybe he was a hidden yogi. In my homeland, this is what we say."

When I reached Faye's room, Rumi glanced at the clock. "Are you okay? You look shaky."

No kidding. I felt off kilter. "We need to add hidden yogi and Buddhist death practices to our research."

"What happened?"

"I was just informed there's a way to go beyond the windows, to the Light itself. Are they keeping you comfortable?"

Faye smiled. "That sounds intriguing. Rumi's awfully dressed up today. What are you wearing, Meridian?"

"A dress." It didn't seem right to be casual simply because the bride couldn't see my clothes.

"You and Rumi have a date later?" She laughed into a cough.

"Maybe. Sure." Rumi did look quite smashing in a white lace-up shirt and kilt. I noticed he had pulled the curtains so the view to all the preparations outside was blocked.

"I'd like to open the French doors for a little air," Faye grouched.

Rumi shrugged his shoulders. "They're not quite done with the landscaping, and you know how loud and obnoxious those leaf blowers are. We'll open them as soon as we can, I promise."

"This is nice," I said, making small talk, too nervous about this surprise to say anything remotely intelligent.

Faye's room had very little of a hospital feel to it and seemed more like a guest room in a not-so-fancy home. "Yes, this is as good a place to die as any."

"You feel like doing a little more living before then?" I asked.

"What do you have in mind?" Her eyes brightened with a spark of curiosity.

I held up my shopping bag and shooed Rumi from the room.

Delia came in behind me with another nurse. "What's going on?"

"Trust us?" I asked her.

"I do, child."

We gently changed Faye into the fancy lace nightgown and robe. One nurse brushed her hair and styled it while

Delia and I covered her bed with a white tatted coverlet.

"I almost feel pretty." Faye sighed as Delia dotted blush and coral lipstick on Faye's astonished face.

"Are you warm enough?" I asked when I saw Tens crack the door. Our signal.

"Yes."

The terrace's transformation was as much of a surprise to me as it was to Faye as Tens swept open the doors.

Nurses crowded around behind us, wanting to glimpse this occasion.

Tens had packed the van at a local nursery with blooming rosebushes, dwarf lilacs, and hibiscus trees. Petunias draped from baskets and sparkling hummingbird feeders were tied from the rafters all along the lattice overhang. Honeysuckle and clematis twined along the privacy lattices on the sides.

"Oh my," Faye sighed.

Dressed in a dapper three-piece suit with a deep maroon peony pinned to his lapel, Gus waited outside. His chin quavered, but he didn't drop a single tear.

Custos wore a blinged-out top hat and Mini wore a matching bow tie over what was left of her bandages. Nelli placed the peony and lily bride's bouquet next to Faye's hand on the bed. Then she sprinkled rose petals and confetti across the coverlet.

Delia and I pushed the bed closer to the patio. Faye grabbed my hand, clinging with a grip of someone who spent a lifetime of promising tomorrows and missing todays.

I leaned down and whispered, "Live a little more. It's okay."

She kissed my cheek and reached toward Gus.

Flocks of goldfinches and cardinals gathered to witness and chatter.

The sky was a brilliant blue and white as if the heavens rolled out its best-dressed ensemble for the occasion. A warm breeze dispersed the marvelous scents of flowers and fluttered the petals.

I moved over by Tens and twined my fingers through his. "This is gorgeous."

A delicate table held a beautiful and simple white frosted cake that I knew was deep velvety red on the inside. A pitcher of iced sweet tea sweated next to a pair of crystal champagne flutes.

Nelli snapped photographs as Tony cleared his throat. We knew Faye had little energy, so efficiency and timing were everything.

"The love of a husband and wife is transcendent. Gus and Faye, you built your love on a foundation of friendship and spent many years climbing the mountains of time, travails, and joys together. With Sunday brunches and midnight phone conversations, you wove your lives together into a rope. A rope to catch you when you slipped on the unexpected, to anchor you in safety and shelter. You held each other in those moments when alone you were too tired and empty to hold yourself. Your love as a couple spanned the canyons and crevasses of human failings. Today before God, before your family of friends, we celebrate this bond and the promise you've made to each other."

Beautiful. Honest and true.

At Tony's signal, Tens stepped forward bearing a pillow that held both a silver ring and a silver bracelet. Faye's fingers were too swollen and painful for a ring, but the bracelet could be adjusted and easily removed. The circle symbolism was the same.

Tens held the bracelet out to Gus, who took it gently.

Tony asked, "Gus, do you promise to love, to care for, comfort, and aid this woman, in this life and the next, until you meet again?"

Gus gazed into Faye's eyes and said, "I do." Then he slipped the bracelet around her wrist.

Tens stepped forward and gave Faye the ring. She held it in her fist.

"Faye, do you promise to love and hold precious this man, allowing him to comfort and aid you, in this life and the next, until you meet again?"

Her voice, stronger than it had been in several days, shouted, "I do!" She was able to place the ring on Gus's finger without assistance. Happy tears tickled my lashes.

"By all that is good and light, and all that is love, I pronounce you husband and wife! You may kiss your bride." Tony smiled.

Gus bent down and placed the most tender kiss I'd ever witnessed on Faye's lips.

I turned my head and surreptitiously wiped tears away

as the nurses and other families from the rooms around us clapped and congratulated the newlyweds.

Faye had a single bite of red velvet cake and declared it perfect before dozing off with a smile on her face.

Gus hugged me tightly and for far longer than I was used to. As quickly as we'd descended, we left. The flowers and plants would stay on Faye's terrace for the duration.

* * *

That night, back in the cottage, Tens and I lay on our sides facing each other. The light from the streetlights outside breathed shadows and strange angles across Tens's face.

We so rarely had time these days to just be together and enjoy each other. I grinned, going over the wedding in my mind. Perfect.

"We pulled it off," I said.

"Yes, you did. I only did what you told me to." He evaded credit as expected.

"You'll have to plant all the stuff now." We'd offered to plant all the flowering plants among the gardens and terraces at the hospice. It seemed only fair. As we left, I realized Juliet had made several larger versions of the cake for the nurses and the family goody room. *I don't know why I'm surprised by the way she whips out complete confections in the amount of time most people read a recipe.*

He shrugged. "Did it make you . . ." He trailed off,

breaking eye contact. His fingers slid down my arm, from shoulder to fingers, making the little hairs zing and sending a delicious quake along my spine.

"What? Want a wedding?" I asked, thinking perhaps that's where he was going.

He nodded.

"Someday." I wondered how to articulate my feelings. *A future?* I never thought I'd have a future. "I've never been able to picture myself in a white dress, my father walking me down the aisle. Who would be my bridesmaids? Who would I invite?" *I've never had that kind of family, or friends, for that matter.* Never been the little girl who played pretend wedding. There hadn't seemed any point to dreaming.

"Me." He kissed my hand.

"Oh, well, I thought you'd be the groom, but if you really want to wear a puke-green satin ball gown covered in ruffles as my maid of honor, we can talk about that."

We both laughed. What a picture.

I frowned. "It never seemed like my life. Like it was possible. Until you, I didn't know anyone could love me." *Maybe if my mother had allowed Auntie to raise me as requested, I wouldn't be so surprised all the time.*

"But now that you have me?" There was a hitch in his voice that I wasn't certain about.

I shrugged. "I don't need the dress, or the cake, or the bouquet toss to make that real. You don't want one, do you?"

Does he? His expression grew thoughtful. "I think I

do. We're special and I think I'd like to celebrate that with our friends watching. Not soon. Someday."

Oh. "I'm not against it. I never dreamed about it. You'll tell me? When you're ready?"

"Tell you what?"

"When you feel like it's time for you? For us?"

"Probably before our seventh kid is born."

"Seven? Kids? Now you're freaking me out!" I yanked the pillow out from behind his head.

"Hey, I was using that!" He grabbed me as I reached for his ribs. "No fair. I'm tired!"

He pinned my hips with his and slid down me. I wondered if I'd ever grow tired of feeling his weight pressed against me. Of looking up into his eyes and seeing the best parts of myself reflected down at me.

He dipped his head and nibbled the edge of my mouth. "Hmm, frosting."

"No! I . . . I washed my face," I sputtered, until I realized he was laughing at me. "I guess you don't want the extra piece I grabbed for you, then, huh?"

"Cake?" Tens perked up.

Always hungry. "I'm not telling."

"Here?" He licked and kissed behind my ear until I shivered. "How about here?" His lips drew down along my throat and found the rapid pulse.

I shifted my hips and felt him slip snugly against me.

His hands spread under my shirt and cupped my breasts, the calluses on his palms creating a pleasant friction.

I tugged my T-shirt over my head. His shorts rode low on his hips and his stomach rippled under my fingers.

"Here?" Tens dipped his head deeper, touching his mouth to my nipple. I arched against him as all thoughts fled my brain.

At my most vulnerable with him, I was home.

CHAPTER 25

Juliet

I pleaded a headache and disappeared into my bedroom as quickly as I could after the wedding. Faye and Gus might be married for a week at best. *Until death do them part.* So little time. I shuddered. Did my parents have any time together? *Any? Would they have gotten married? Made us a family?*

I heard Tony and Fara whispering in the living room, probably about me. I held the book of sonnets, practicing my reading. My mother's scribbled notes in the margins were cryptic at best as I looked for anything that might be what Ms. Asura wanted. As if she'd been afraid some- one else might read them, as if she were protecting more than me. *My father? Her parents?*

Back and forth, back and forth, I slid the medallion Nicole gave me across the chain on my neck. *Nicole is gone. And I need to let her go.*

My head hurt.

I waited. Even now, I waited for the feelings of uncer- tainty and fear to dissipate.

"Can I come in?" Fara knocked. "Please?"

"Sure." I sat up and wiped at my face.

"Tony went out to get you frozen custard. He heard today's flavor was grape."

I tried to smile. He tried so hard and I didn't know why he continued to bother. *All I do is make messes and problems for him.*

Fara stared at me without breaking eye contact. "Want some air? It's awfully stuffy in here." She abruptly turned to the window, and before I could ask her not to, she opened the curtains and threw the window open wide.

I gasped, terrified my room would smell like Ms. Asura again. *No, just food.* Cooking rice, garlic, and fried chicken were the only recognizable scents on the breeze. I sighed.

Fara sat at the edge of my bed. "My baba called them Hashshashin, these Nocti of yours. For thousands of years they are the dark Hashshashin. I find out from Tony that the word for this in English is *assassin*."

I picked at my fingers. Watched blood ooze between my nail and skin.

"They do not just kill bodies; they kill love, dreams too. Do you know what my baba said to me about them?"

"What?" My mind turned over and over again the conversation about Ms. Asura at DG.

"He said it is easy to give up the body, for it is fragile and from the earth. But that I must never let the Hashshashin speak to my heart. I must give my blood to save my light. They promise miracles and prey on ignorance. I have seen much ignorance in this country of yours. Much fear of difference, no tolerance."

"Turn on the television and it's the same everywhere." I brushed off her stinging criticism. *We aren't different from anyone else.*

"Maybe, but it doesn't have to be. What do you say, sink or fly?" She reached out and touched my cheek until I raised my eyes.

"Sink or swim?" I asked.

She shrugged. "You can fly, be above, not sink below."

I blinked at her, waiting for the next fault she might find. *What else am I doing wrong?*

With narrowed flashing eyes, she asked, "What do you think of this wedding? Was it the perfect American wedding?"

I couldn't help snorting back laughter, which made her smile.

"I guess the dying is not so perfect?" she asked.

I shrugged. "I don't know. I've never seen one." *Will*

I wear white? Find a man to cherish me and treat me as the precious person brides always embody? If I can't love myself, how can someone else love me?

"A wedding?"

"No. Never been to a wedding." People died, left, and disappeared in my world; they didn't commit to love, honor, and cherish.

"Oh." She nodded. "Tens and Meridian seemed to think it was good."

I shook my head. "They are in love. Even crap smells sweet to them." I blanched, not sure where the venom came from.

"Ah, you're jealous of them?"

I stayed silent.

"Me too." She poked at my leg.

I wondered aloud, "Tens is Meridian's Protector and her soul mate."

"Uh-huh."

"Are you my soul mate too?"

"Maybe. I don't know." Her expression closed.

"How do we know?" I pressed, pushing at her buttons, hoping for a reaction.

"What are you asking me?" Her brow furrowed.

"Are we going to fall in love like them?" *Am I destined to fall in love with a woman?*

"Ah, you Americans always focus on the sex, don't you?"

A scalding blush flowed over my cheeks but I held my ground. "Oh, please. You only bring up the American thing when you need to buy time to formulate an answer."

"Noticed that, did you?" She smiled. "There is more than one kind of soul mate, Juliet." We heard the front door. "Tony is back. Do you want to eat anything?"

I shook my head. "I think I'll practice my reading." *Formulate a plan to confront Ms. Asura and find my mother.*

"Do you want help from Tony?"

I frowned. "Not tonight."

"What are you thinking about so frowny?" She paused. "The book?"

"Nothing." I didn't want to share yet.

"You will tell me before you run away toward what it is in your heart? You will let me run beside you."

"Are you asking or telling?" I bit out the words. I didn't need a babysitter.

"Yes." She stepped away. "You are not alone."

"Sure." I already regretted putting everyone in more danger by being honest.

"Do you want me to stay?"

"Not right now." I couldn't tell if I hurt her feelings or not.

She nodded and stopped at the door. "We are on your side. Give what little trust you can, please? It becomes easier with practice."

I lay flipping through pages, trying to read between the lines of my mother's lines and squiggles. The only words I had to tell me what I longed to know. *What is my story?* I whispered her words out loud:

" 'Did he make it out? Did they help him go on as we'd planned? Does he see this moon tonight?'

" 'My daughter will be strong and grow up laughing. She will eat ice cream for dinner and take naps for no reason. She will not work until her fingers bleed. She will know her worth.' "

I shivered and rose to close the window. A new statue installed in front of the new construction site across the street sat across from my window, gazing up at a yellow balloon trying to float into the sky. The fake man stared vacantly, directly at my room, at me. *He's only a statue.*

I quickly pulled the window handles, trying to shield myself. They stuck. The window wouldn't shut. I opened it again and leaned down to see a piece of paper, of cardboard, wedged into the frame. *What is this?*

I lifted it out and realized it was a postcard. A sunset at a beach. Just like Kirian and I talked about so many years ago. We'd live on the beach and eat coconuts and crabs. *Oh, Kirian! Why did you betray me? How did this get here?*

Written in red ink like blood were the words:

You're losing lives like your cat. You will suffer foolishly.

I dropped the postcard, my heart skipping and stuttering, the air impossible to inhale. I watched it blow in the breeze toward the ground. I slammed the window shut, sliding to the floor. *Is she out there? Is she watching?*

I gagged back bile. *Ms. Asura has been here.* While I'd been making cakes and serving them. While I'd wondered if my life might ever contain the love that I saw reflecting in the eyes of Meridian and Tens, Gus and Faye, Nelli and Bales. *She was here.* Spreading poison and reminding me there was no escape.

I crawled along the floor until I could nudge open my closet door. I felt for the telltale bulge of Rumi's folio. My fingers ran along the back seam of the carpet until I could lift it. I tugged.

"No, no, no, no." I lifted more of the rug. Maybe it shifted. Maybe it moved over.

I flicked on the light switch. Nothing. Bare plywood. No leather. No folio. Nothing. *Rumi's book is gone.*

This is all my fault. I did this. I should have given it back yesterday instead of making the cakes. *I should have, I should have, I should have—* I opened my mouth to call for Fara, but nothing came out. *What can she do? We're doomed. We're going to die and it's my fault.*

Shutting the door behind me, I curled into a ball on the floor of my closet, wishing for Mini, who'd planted herself at Faye's side after the wedding. I tucked my head deeply against my knees. *Why now? This is too much. They won't forgive this.*

I felt snot ooze down my cheek, my eyes scratchy from so many tears. At some point, I dozed off and dreamed of freight-train tornadoes ripping my family away. Of DG. Of children crying. Of Kirian reaching for me. Of my future spreading out in front of me as nothing but a void.

CHAPTER 26

"Supergirl?" Tens turned around, hopping backward, making it clear he was waiting for my slow ass.

Tens decided we needed to run a few miles to expend all the adrenaline of the last week and clear our minds. I was pretty sure I could clear my mind during a massage and manicure, but he thought this was good for me.

I grunted. I saw the cottage and sped up. *Grape soda and a flat surface. Hallelujah.*

A Timothy had left the day's newspaper on our door with a note on their signature stationery.

Related?

The headline read LAST YEAR'S WINNER AND

CURRENT FAVORITE COLLAPSES WITH MYSTERIOUS ILLNESS. The accompanying note said, *"The article was vague. Nocti?"*

Tens booted up the laptop and I turned on the television. Tens's fingers flew over the keys. "Merry, listen. 'The team's owner reported that Roberto Tonsa started experiencing severe symptoms earlier in the day yesterday. He remains hospitalized under round-the-clock care. The backup driver was flown in from Charlotte last night as a precaution, but they were hoping Tonsa would be better today with the IV medications. They are unable to identify the toxin in his system. The backup driver, Eddie Smith, will try to qualify the car.'"

Could the Nocti poison someone? Sure. What did they have to gain by poisoning one driver, though? That didn't make sense.

Tens continued. "'If Tonsa is not cleared to race Sunday, Eddie Smith, who did practice here earlier in the month, will take over the car.'" He frowned. "They say it's a risky choice since he hasn't been up to speeds or practiced in current race conditions. But they have every confidence the veteran driver, but Indy 500 rookie, will race well. Smith has been off the circuit for several years amid rumors of addiction and gambling debts. When asked about this opportunity, Smith said he owed his family everything for sticking by him. Racing Sunday would pay them back for all the pain he'd caused."

I battled to see into the future. *Just a glimpse. Anything.*

"You're making me dizzy," Tens grouched.

"Are you picking up on it?" I asked, excited. Maybe we'd broken through the silence and could communicate telepathically. *Finally*.

"You're mumbling and pacing," he said without looking up.

"Oh." *That's disappointing*.

"You think this is Nocti?"

"I don't know. I don't get what they'd gain."

"Giving one driver a chance at redemption? That's not like them."

"Eyes open, right?"

Tens's phone rang and I picked it up.

"Can you come by the shop, please?" Rumi's agitated voice galloped over the phone line.

"Now?" I asked, watching Tens leap into action at the tone in my voice. "Rumi," I mouthed at Tens's silent question.

"Yes, Timothy is here with news."

What are the Woodsmen doing there? "We're on our way," I said, hanging up. "Is it a trap to meet W.O.W. at Rumi's?"

"I hope to hell not." The quickest way over was by car, but the care Tens took loading up weaponry slowed us way down.

The few Spirit Stones Rumi had rehung went from normal to bright as we approached. *No Nocti*.

Rumi's store was full of shoppers. All male. All trying to look inconspicuous. Because I was pretty sure they were all Woodsmen, I bet they'd all turn if I yelled, "Timothy!" I was half tempted to try it just to see how they'd respond.

"Thank you for coming." The elder had pulled his wheelchair next to Rumi's seating area.

"What's going on?" Tens asked, standing at attention.

"We need your help," Timothy replied.

Rumi returned with grape soda and Coke for us. "I think you'll need this," he said, his expression grim.

I fingered the notebook in my pocket and dragged it out to take notes.

"One of our brothers was found dead this morning."

"I'm sorry." I blanched.

He nodded. "We know the risks."

"You think he was killed?" Tens asked, already skipping forward.

"Yes, deliberately. We think he saw something."

"Something?" I let the word hang there. I wondered why Timothy seemed to think Fenestras were also mind readers. With no idea where he was taking the conversation or what he expected from me, I waited.

"Part of our vow is to stay in this world, fight the pull of the Dark, until we can help our brothers. We need you to find him and see if he knows who killed him or why."

"Wait, I'm not a physic. Not a medium like on TV." I shook my head.

"I know that. Hear me out. He was found dead at the track; he was in charge of making sure the grounds are safe."

"The Indianapolis Motor Speedway? That track?" Tens shook his head. "What does that have to do with us?"

Timothy wiped his brow with a handkerchief. "I'm sorry, I forget you're unschooled. There are places in the world where the veil of time and energy is thin. Where it's transparent. Sacred places like Easter Island, the pyramids, the palace of Machu Picchu. Places human beings congregate over time—these absorb energy and feed the universe. It's similar to the belief that saying the name of a god makes them more powerful. Prayer and thought convey strength to those they are directed at."

"Mythology?" Tens asked Rumi.

"You have been paying attention, haven't you?" Rumi looked pleased.

"So these sacred places get more or less powerful with human interaction?" I tried to follow.

"Yes, close enough." Timothy nodded.

"And you're comparing the race track to Giza?" Tens queried.

"Not the track itself but the land it's on. Yes. For centuries it was of the First People, but with settling of these lands, the ancestors of Polly Barnett took ownership. She then inherited it from her family; her husband was a WoW member. They settled there to protect the land, the veil."

Where had I heard that name? "Wait, Polly Barnett, the one who wandered around with a black cat looking for her daughter? That one?"

Rumi nodded.

"The same. We do not know much of the details, but in a battle with the Nocti, her daughter and husband were killed. Polly never recovered her mind, but her death allowed the land to be sold outside of the family. In 1909, it was sold again to developers who needed a racetrack for the burgeoning automobile industry."

Trying to keep up, I asked, "The Indianapolis Motor Speedway is built on the sacred land?"

"Yes, and at every event, Woodsmen from this region converge to protect the people and the veil. We volunteer and man every position possible. What we cannot manage, our families do."

"Do they know? The racetrack owners?" Tens asked.

"How could they not? They turn a blind eye to us because we all want the same thing. A safe and harmonious place. But every century, the Nocti converge somewhere in the world to elect a new Commandant. The elder is killed, his essence absorbed by his successor in a secretive ceremony."

My stomach dropped. "Let me guess, this year Indy is the selectee?"

"Based on the chatter and rise in incidents there, that's our guess exactly. We've sent spies in among them, but they're always killed. We're afraid that this year they are coming to the Barnett farm, the racetrack. Every place they converge, a terrible catastrophe ensues, usually with a huge loss of human life."

"Why here and now?" Tens pressed.

"It is the Centennial Race—generations of race goers

will show up. What better timing than to congregate at the race with hundreds of thousands of people? The more innocents the better. But we also think they are scared of this new Fenestra generation. You are stronger than you've found or accepted."

Oh, really?

Tens turned the discussion back. "And the man killed?"

"He was a good man. He wouldn't turn on us, and if it was possible, he'd stay and try to tell us what he knows." Timothy's confidence sounded sincere.

If a Nocti killed him, he wouldn't stand a chance. A human sympathizer pulling a trigger, *maybe*. Tens and I shared a look that spoke without telepathy.

"Will you try, please?"

The pleading in the old man's voice undid my reticence. "Sure." What else could I say?

"Sir, we should turn on the television," one of the young men interrupted us as he talked into a cell phone. "It's the track."

Rumi flipped on his new flat-screen television; every station he clicked through showed a local news crew. We sat silently stunned as images were replayed.

An Indy car smashing into a wall was obliterated in slow motion, while a newsman voiced over, "One of the worst crashes in racetrack history happened early in race practice for qualifying today."

Fire spewed along the asphalt, up into the bleachers. Pieces of the car shattered and flew like shrapnel.

"The driver was pinned under the chassis of the car, lodged against the safer barrier for several long minutes while safety teams worked to put the fire out and rescue him."

The camera cut to a person lying inert on a gurney. Thankfully there were no close-ups. "And what's the latest on his condition? Have you gotten any medical updates from Methodist?" asked the studio announcer.

"Yes, here's what we were told moments ago. His eyes are bandaged and it'll be several days before we'll know whether he lost his sight. Both legs are broken and he suffered a collapsed lung. Most concern is focused on his head trauma and the brain swelling over the next twenty-four to forty-eight hours. It'll be touch and go."

The pertly made up newscaster said into the camera, "We do know this driver's dreams of racing in the 500 this year are over. We're praying for him. The whole team must be shaken. Do they know what happened?"

"They're speculating that there was a radio miscommunication."

"This is the third mishap or accident at the track this month. It's shaping up to be a very dangerous time at Indy. What do you think is causing all the trouble? Is anyone saying?"

"I've heard everything from tires to weather. Seems like no one, not even the veteran owners like

Foyt and Penske, can pinpoint why the track is so edgy this year. Hopefully the weather will cooperate for the rest of the month."

By the second replay, I was sick to my stomach.

"It's beginning already." Timothy lowered his head to his hands. "Will you go?"

"Yes." My stomach pitched to the floor.

As we headed back to the van, Tens's cell phone rang. After his conversation, he reported to me, "Nelli has news. The second set of child's remains have disappeared and Bales uncovered the rat among us."

A rodent or a human?

CHAPTER 27

Tens and I drove down Nelli's driveway and parked behind her car. Bales and Nelli waited for us with grim expressions.

"I'm so sorry." Nelli hugged me as soon as I stepped out of the passenger side.

"What's going on?" I asked, unsure.

Bales stepped forward and ushered us inside, closing the door. "I've been working on who in Nelli's office is corrupt."

"It's my boss." Nelli's lips quivered. "And Sergio."

"I followed Sergio the night of Nowruz," Bales said. "The kid just didn't add up to me. So I've been dogging him. He's got some interesting older friends, including Nelli's boss."

"That's not surprising, though, is it? For Sergio and his boss to meet?" I asked. My stomach clenched. *Sergio? The boy who empathizes with Juliet and is so helpful?*

"Not on the surface. But at night and in the dark along the river canals? They were sneaking around, pretty classic body language. But it wasn't until a woman showed up that I was able to link them to the Nocti. I think Ms. Asura was there."

Tens perked up. "Can you describe her?" he asked Bales.

"Sure. Tallish for a woman, though she wore stilettos of five-plus inches. Black hair, worn straight and long. Nutmeg complexion, naturally smooth, no moles or spots, but her face was webbed as if she suffered in a terrible fire. She dressed in a silk skirt suit with a matching scarf and hat, though when she spoke to them, she removed both."

"You think she wanted them to see the scars?"

"I do."

This sounds exactly like Ms. Asura.

Bales continued. "She wore lots of silver jewelry, rings of colored stones and long earrings. I didn't know immediately it was the same woman Nelli described to me, so I got as close as I could without them seeing me. I listened to their conversation." He paused. "Took photographs."

"What did they talk about?" I asked, butterflies flying in my stomach.

"It could be out of context; I didn't hear the whole thing," Bales warned.

"Just tell us," Tens demanded.

"They were discussing needing the book and using Juliet to retrieve it. Almost exactly what she said at Nowruz."

"Did you hear other threats? Anything else?" Tens asked.

"They spoke in a shorthand code, not a language I recognized. It seemed like Sergio was newer to the plans than the others, though. Sergio stared at his feet a lot, kicked the ground, and stooped in on himself."

"What does that tell you?" I asked, intrigued.

Demonstrating, Bales went from standing straight and upright to curling his shoulders and folding down. It was an instant transformation and I saw immediately why he'd mentioned it.

"He was uncomfortable?"

Bales nodded. "And afraid I'd say. Coerced most definitely."

"So maybe he's not working for them; maybe your boss is trying to get him to, but—"

Bales and Nelli both shook their heads.

"What are we missing?"

Bales pulled out photographs of extreme close-ups, enlarged to the point where the pixels were grainy. "He handed her papers. Now, I couldn't get great photographs, but you can read some of it."

I saw a list. Instantly recognizing what it was. "Details about the Nowruz at DG?" I asked, noticing our names and things like the bonfire and ritual prayers in larger shaded lettering.

"Uh-huh. Keep looking." Nelli's tears escaped down her cheeks.

"That looks like a page from Auntie's journ—" I broke off, gasping.

"He ripped a page out?" Tens scrutinized the photograph.

I sat down hard. *Which page? Anything important? What's not important in there? Why?*

"I think he only got one. He wasn't ever alone with the journal during the ceremony."

"We don't have it with us." *Oh, Auntie, I'm sorry.*

Tens frowned. "We'll look when we get home. He couldn't have had time to be picky, could he? A rip and stash?"

"They probably just want to get a sense of what we know and don't know. If these were humans, I'd have a better profile, but my guess is Asura has something Sergio needs or wants desperately or she's threatening someone he's trying to protect."

Like she's doing with Juliet.

"The Nocti know who we are. Why aren't they simply coming after us?"

"We have something they need? Does Auntie's journal say more than we think it does?"

"There's more. I know where they're camped out." Bales showed us a map of downtown.

"How do we tell Juliet?" My heart broke.

"Do we have to?" Tens asked.

I nodded. "Of course. Not tell her? We can't keep her in the dark."

"Will she be able to pretend she doesn't know?"

"We can't let him continue to be around us. Or her."

"We have to, Meridian," Nelli disagreed.

Tens agreed. "She's right, Supergirl. It's the only way to find out what they know or think they know."

Bales said, "I think Asura's living in the bottom of the Indiana Medical History Museum. It has signs all over it that it's closed for renovation and remodeling, but she went in the basement door. Didn't come out before I left. I saw a few more men and women come and go from the backyard. If I was still on the force, I'd say it was a drug house, but maybe it's just your Nocti. Do we need to go take it out?"

"It's not that easy," Tens said. Then he and Bales broke off into a conversation about the pros and cons of trying to confront Ms. Asura on our own.

I was still stuck back at Sergio playing both sides. *How could we miss that?*

I tuned back in in time to hear Bales say, "I'll keep an eye on them. I think there might be a connection between Juliet's father and the Woodsmen."

"Anything specific?" I asked. *That's a huge leap.*

"I don't know. A hunch. When I know something, I'll tell you. I'd rather have concrete proof." Bales wrapped

Nelli against his chest. "Don't be crying, Nell-Bell. We'll make this right."

I turned away to give them a moment of privacy and laid my hot face against the cooler windowpane.

Tens slid his arms around me from behind. "Fara will help us convince Juliet to keep going."

"Are you sure?" *Won't she protect Juliet at all costs?*

"I'm sure. We've talked about the Protector code. There is one thing ancient cultures understand, and that's biding time to strike back."

"The what code?" I asked, peeking over my shoulder at his face.

"Her father instructed her that her allegiance is first to her Fenestra, then to other Protectors and Fenestras. But not at the expense of the other. She has to tell us if there is danger. Our safety cannot be sacrificed even for herself. It is how her bloodline stayed strong for so many generations."

"Then won't she sacrifice us for Juliet's needs? Even if that means Juliet never knows what happened to her mother and father?"

"It doesn't work that way."

"I hope you're right. We should go talk to them now." I sighed.

"We promised Timothy we'd check out qualifying. See if we can't get more information about what the Nocti have planned."

"Are you sure we shouldn't go right to Juliet?"

"I don't think a few hours will matter, will they? Pole Day is today only."

"Okay, we'll wait." I had a bad feeling. Very bad.

* * *

Tens flipped on the news radio and listened for any tips on navigating the traffic as we headed toward the Indianapolis Motor Speedway. I listened with half an ear until I heard a controlled radio voice say:

"*Now an update from the Speedway. Jessica Martin, what can you tell us?*"

"*This race month gets more bizarre with each passing day, Jonathan. Earlier today, a team of wildlife experts was dispatched because a coyote was seen roaming the infield.*"

"*You're kidding!*"

"*No, it was chasing geese in the lake. There are reports it was seen in a concession stand and also near the garage area. No one is sure how it got onto the property or where it's hiding. Officials are asking that no one approach the animal. It is wild and will probably be on the defensive.*"

"*We don't want folks getting hurt.*"

"*Be on the lookout, folks—it's a jungle out there.*"

We drove toward the main gate of the Speedway track entrance. A mobile home park across the street turned their neighborhood into a paid parking zone. *Entrepreneurial and convenient.*

"Coyotes don't live in the jungle," Tens said to me as

we joined the throngs heading toward the ticket shacks.

Our recent bout with coyotes put us both on edge. "I think she was trying to be funny," I said.

"She wasn't." Tens's usual stark demeanor was shadowed by Bales's explanations and worry. I knew him well enough to know that he would stew, brood, and contemplate until he was ready to speak. I'd relaxed into understanding his processing took time that mine didn't. *Isn't that what love is? The real kind of lasting love, like Auntie and Charles shared? Understanding the other person as he is and not changing him to suit me?*

Yet again, I wished Auntie were able to give relationship advice to me. Even if my mother were around, I'd die before sharing with her or taking her advice on anything.

"I know." Over the brick Speedway gates hung a huge golden wheel with wings that seemed to be the emblem for the Speedway. "Tens—look up. Is that the symbol?"

"Could be, but where's the stick thing Juliet drew?"

"I don't know."

Tens handed over a couple of twenties for our tickets. "No assigned seats?" Tens asked.

"Open seating, folks. Go anywhere you like. Don't sit on anyone's lap unless you ask nicely first." The ticket taker cracked himself up.

Everywhere I turned, people wheeled coolers, held the hands of children, generations massed together all heading inside. They wore tank tops or T-shirts and shorts of every color of the rainbow. Most of the guys wore ball caps. I couldn't peg the demographic of the crowd.

It seemed like everyone was represented, from glammed-out designer labels to guys who looked like they hadn't heard of bathing or doing laundry. There were even soldiers in uniforms wandering in the crowds.

The ticket guy saw our expressions. "This your first Pole Day? Like it better than the race myself. You can go anywhere you want to—infield, up in the expensive seats, any turn, any place. If you aren't allowed, someone will tell you. Just look for the guys in yellow and black if you have a problem or a question. Enjoy yourselves. They're just about ready to reopen the track to qualifying."

"Are there accidents often?" I asked.

He nodded. "Every year—rookies who don't know what they're doing, changes in the tires or the cars. Remember, the cars are supposed to break apart to protect the drivers—so often crashes look much worse than they are." He lost his smile.

"Is this year different?"

"We've had more serious injuries. More fender benders than usual. But the weather is fluctuating wildly from cold to hot. Hot weather makes the track slicker than a Slip 'n Slide."

"If it's so unpredictable and dangerous, why don't they cancel it?"

"Haven't canceled a race since the second World War. Drivers and owners know this is a dangerous sport; that's what makes it exciting. Defying gravity and death at two hundred twenty-five miles per hour." He whistled. "You don't stop a horse race just because one horse breaks a

leg. We don't stop a 500 because a rookie hits the wall."
He turned to the people waiting behind us. "Enjoy your
day, folks."

"That's kinda fatalistic," I said to Tens.

"He's right, though. Death is everywhere. We know it."

The scents of roasting turkey meat and fried potatoes
wafted on the breeze.

"You hungry?" Tens pulled out cash and headed for
the shish kebab stand. With meat on sticks and lemonade
cups, we looked more like we belonged.

"You have any idea how this Pole Day works?" I asked.
None of the Woodsmen schooled us on what to expect.
*Will I see their dead brother, or anyone else hanging out at
the racetrack waiting for my window?*

"Nope."

I knew that behind his sunglasses, Tens was ultimately alert for threats of all kinds. I wished it were night
and Nocti would have to show me their eyes. As it stood,
in today's sunshine, not wearing opaque shades became
the oddity under the bright sun and its broiling rays.

We'd have to eavesdrop to get our information. *That's
nothing new.* I was getting really accomplished at looking
one direction and listening fully to someone behind me.
Somewhere around us, maybe in yellow and black, too,
were Woodsmen scouting and seeking information.

Stairs of scaffolding-like metal crisscrossed behind
bleachers three stories tall. Underneath them were storage areas covered and fenced but still visible and accessible to the highly motivated. The caverns contained

empty blue trash bins, while others were filled with white rocks the size of my fist and fenced off. Only chain link seemed to separate us from the actual structure of the bleachers.

The bleachers were stories tall, leaving storage areas below. When we'd come with Faye, I hadn't been thinking of weaknesses in the structures that could be exploited to kill or maim. Now I saw them everywhere I turned. Today there were thousands of people here, but next week, there would be an estimated quarter to a half-million souls present. *How many Nocti? How many Woodsmen on our side? No clue.*

Tossing his licked-clean skewer into a trash bin, Tens asked, "Let's walk around the outside perimeter for a while? The wind's picking up."

Rock music blared from amplifiers, so loud it shook my body. I didn't recognize the song but what the band lacked in melody, they made up for in enthusiasm. Screens showed the track being cleaned. All of the earlier debris was gone and the only things visible were scorch marks and tire tracks. *Very efficient.*

Wind socks and flags in white, green, red, yellow, and checkered rattled on poles blowing above the stands. "Is that Pole Day?" I pointed at them.

Tens ignored me, keeping his head swiveling and his pace at a forced march.

"Uh, Tens, isn't this like two miles around?"

"Two and a half according to Gus."

Way to pick up on my subtlety. "So we're going to walk

the whole perimeter?" I didn't know if it was even possible to walk the entire outside, but everyone was heading up into the stands or toward the tunnel underneath to the inside.

He paused and quirked an eyebrow at me. "Want to head into the bleachers?" *Which translates to, "If only you'd run five miles with me every morning instead of a couple of miles every other day, you'd enjoy jogging the perimeter of the track."*

"Yeah. Maybe we can see more if we go on the other side of the bleachers?" I answered him.

"Any souls?" Tens asked.

"Nah, not yet."

We climbed flights of stairs and stepped out above the track, across from the glass Pagoda. True enough, we could go almost anywhere we wanted to. I forgot how expansive the infield was; there was an entire park inside the track with large trees and rows of buildings.

People far down in the stands, in either direction, looked like dots of color in a sea of gray. *What horror is planned for these people?*

"There are so many people here," I said to no one in particular. The masses in the bleachers only emphasized the antlike frenzy on the track. Cars were lined up, loudly painted with sponsor logos and website URLs. Each team seemed like they were trying to be recognizable at a glance and different from the rest of their competition. Neon green, bright blue, blood-red, tangerine, and camouflage competed with fonts screaming for attention.

Similarly uniformed groups of men scurried around the cars, talking into headsets.

A fleet of trolleys with little tractors carried huge black tires stacked four and five tall. They drove purposefully between teams and a gasoline alley that led back toward the buildings behind them.

Television crews and photographers seemed planted with cameras raised, waiting for a sweet shot, like paparazzi with celebrities. *Some of these drivers are celebrities.*

"That's gotta be the Pole." Tens nudged me, pointing at what looked like a giant Tootsie Roll, only all four sides had numbers. White paint on black listed 1–33; beside them were corresponding lighted numbers, changing positions as I watched.

"The track is open, race fans!" the announcer called, and all the spectators surrounding us cheered. A car revved and tore out onto the oval. The announcer said what sounded like a name, not that I knew any of them. People chanted and clapped as the vehicle went by again. And again. I kept my ears plugged with my fingers. If we came back, I'd want the serious-looking headphones a lot of the old-timers wore.

"Anything?"

I shook my head.

Tens took my hand and we finagled our way into the flow of human traffic under the track.

"And he's done it, ladies and gentleman. Danny Jones has the fastest speed and currently holds the pole."

So it's the order they start.

Tens glanced back at me with a smile. *Gus told him more than he'd let on.* "Only thirty-three cars get to race next Sunday. Today they're trying to get places at the front of the pack and qualify to race next week."

I playfully swatted his butt. "Have no idea what Pole Day is, huh?"

"Thought about telling you all the girls had to dance on a pole, but I figured you wouldn't buy that." He tried to say it with a serious expression.

"Oh, I'll dance on a pole for you, baby cakes." I gave him my most lascivious stripper strut.

He grinned bigger, even showing me sparkling teeth in an attempt to call my bluff.

"Unfortunately, you missed your chance." I laughed. *As if.*

As we explored the grounds, we walked down into a tunnel. Above us, on the ceiling and on the walls, pipes and cables were easily accessible. Peeling paint and crusty floors made me think these weren't the most inspected areas. *Quick to slip something in or drag a cooler filled with nasties to accidentally leave behind.* I shivered. I wanted to hurry out of there.

Tens frowned. "You okay?"

Nope, catastrophic extremist threats make me ill. I shook my head. As we exited the tunnel into the infield, I was overwhelmed by the sheer volume of people. Coupled with the amorphous threat, I didn't even know where to begin.

Tens spun me around and I saw an alcove with a couple

of the yellow-shirted officials having lunch. What interested me, and I'm assuming Tens, was the fact that official yellow gear was hanging on pegs and hooks. *Cause a commotion and it wouldn't be too hard to snag those.*

Behind us, another car roared to life and sped around the track.

Inside the asphalt oval, we were in the depths of food booths, a music stage, huge screens, and souvenir shops. *Like an outdoor food court.*

Around us there were alleys behind bleachers, scrolling doors to storage spaces or garages, people everywhere, lots with drink cans in their hands, lost in having a good time.

Superfans wandered among us, wearing outfits made of car parts and ponchos.

One guy wore a miniature speedway on his head, complete with the flags, pole, and Pagoda. What was odd, though, were the number of people taking their picture with him as if he were part of the spectacle itself.

The crowd stopped while one of the red and white cars was wheeled past us, back behind a section that seemed to require credentials. Girls in bikini tops tried to flash their own credentials to get past security. The number of golf carts made me wonder if in the off-hours there weren't drag races around the oval.

In the distance, several military helicopters were parked for people to tour. And semi trucks unloaded pallets of soft drinks and beer. Motorcycles and sports cars were parked around the semi-trucks and trailers as if this were a giant parking lot. If seeing the activity from the bleachers around the outside was overwhelming, this small city inside was even more so.

Holy hell, where do we start?

Below us, by the rows upon rows of garage doors, a motorized wheelchair was surrounded by guys in jeans and green hats. "Sergio's talking to Timothy." I grabbed Tens's arm to snag his attention. "Over there." I stepped up on an air conditioner to try to get a better look. "He's surrounded by Woodsmen."

It looked like the intern was wearing a volunteer's green ecological vest, but he was writing notes and joking with the men.

"Come on!" Tens grabbed my hand and we shoved our way between people, down flights of stairs and against the flow of traffic. Because of his height, Tens had a good bead on the group.

"Crap!" I saw a group of fans chatting together, waving excitedly in my direction. A Woodsman walked with them, his WoW insignia seemingly bleeding through his T-shirt from his wounded chest. *Do you see this?* "Tens?"

"Supergirl?" Tens responded distractedly.

"You don't see him, do you?" I stopped and leaned back against the wall of a building. "Go on, make sure Sergio isn't up to something. They don't know to distrust him."

"I can't leave you—" Tens stopped too.

I shoved him away. "I'll be fine. Go."

He nodded, hesitated, and left just as the souls arrived. If anything, I hoped my sunglasses and stoned expression might make people think I was drunk rather than splitting my time between two worlds.

"Hello," I said as we appeared at the window as a group. Thick Indiana accents peppered me with questions and commentary as if they'd waited decades to talk to someone new.

The view out their window was an almost exact replica of the track. *Talk about déjà vu.* Only there were more people present and their clothing ranged from early twentieth century to present day. More than a few superfans wandered in elaborate hats of their own.

"We won't miss anything, will we?" one man asked his friend.

"I'm telling you we should stay. There's something wrong with those tire guys. Have you ever seen that happen?"

The Woodsman stayed in the background, not interacting with the other souls or me. His lips were moving, but I heard no sound.

I inserted myself into the group. "What are you talking about?"

"Something's going on. We should stay."

"Can you tell me what's happening?" I asked.

"I don't know. Do you know? How do we know?" They seemed confused and anxious.

"I want to go now." His companion leapt through the window without a backward glance.

"What do I do?"

"There's nothing you can tell me?" I asked.

He shook his head, not taking his eyes off the scene beyond the window.

I sighed. "I think you'll be able to see everything there." In my peripheral vision, Auntie and Roshana stood together. It wasn't the first time I'd seen them, but oddly both had changed their outfits to black and white dresses. Checkered accents sashed their waists and matching sun hats. I frowned. *What are they trying to tell me?*

"That's my wife. What's she doing here? She never comes out to the race with me—"

That seemed to be all the encouragement he needed. As he crossed over the threshold, the scene at the window changed. Everyone was gone, including Auntie and Roshana. Where the Pagoda and garages sat currently, a huge old growth forest sprang to life, almost like the world was on high-speed rewind.

The Woodsman moved closer to me until we stood shoulder to shoulder. A log cabin sprang into being, wood smoke drifting out of the chimney. I watched a young girl, my age maybe, come running across the yard with a basket in her arms.

"Mama! Mama!" she called.

"This was the farm before it was the track," the Woodsman said. "Know they will make snake pit real. Find the old artesian before the last yellow. They've got a driv—"

"Art what? Who? What snakes?"

He watched the farm, ignoring my question, as a terrible clatter and smash erupted from inside the cabin. I felt the pounding of hooves shake the earth.

"Tell me more!" I pleaded.

His lips moved, but his words faded, as did his form. *As if all the strength he has in his soul is depleted.*

A scream rocketed around me. I didn't know if it was at the window or in the real world. I flinched, losing my focus, and he was gone across the window, moving toward the cabin, picking up a branch as a weapon.

Back in reality, I blinked as my body was jostled and pushed. Another terrible gasp rocked through the crowd. People ran for the jumbo screens or toward the track to see. I tried not to get trampled and stared at the screen nearest me.

Sirens sprang to life and a legion of emergency vehicles sped out onto the track.

I couldn't make sense of what I was seeing. Several cars were tangled and engulfed in flames. Explosions rocked the cameras and shook the infrastructure around me. The sounds of tires thumping and bouncing, metal fencing tearing and ripping, and the ping of debris as it ricocheted off—all these echoed around me like sounds of combat. People thrust past me to get a better look; I wasn't tall enough to see anything over most of them. Those listening to the radio in their headsets shouted updates, trying to tell us who was in the cars, who was walking away, who hadn't moved yet.

Another crash? This can't be a coincidence. The Woodsmen

must be right. The Nocti are going to strike here. But when? Today? How?

As if to punctuate the carnage, the wind picked up, unexpectedly blowing black clouds over us. They churned and sputtered. Lightning strobed the sky in the west. Thunder boomed. Without warning, sheets of rain began blanketing the track and all her spectators. Now people ran, not to see better but to get under cover. *It's as if they think they'll melt.*

Large drops, snuggled against each other, drenched everything in a matter of breaths.

I merely tried to keep from being trampled and stayed as close to where Tens left me as possible. *Where is he?*

The bleachers emptied, overhangs filled. The announcer boomed, *"The National Weather Service has advised us that storm cells are popping up on the radar from the southwest. The severe weather makes it unsafe to continue this afternoon. Please evacuate the stands and head toward storm shelters. Volunteers will direct you toward safe structures around the Speedway."*

People hustled for parking lots. Smoke choked from the crash across the infield in acrid black swaths.

"Supergirl!" Tens stood on a trash bin trying to spot me in the commotion.

I waved and waited for him to fight through to me.

"What happened with Sergio?" I asked him.

"They disappeared into a garage. I couldn't get past the state patrol guys who showed up when the crash happened in turn three." Tens's hair hung lank, dripping into his face.

"Did you see it happen?" I reached out, needing skin-to-skin contact as reassurance.

"No. Did you speak with souls?" He leaned down briefly and kissed the top of my head.

"The Woodsman was with them. I didn't understand what he tried to tell me. Auntie and Roshana were there too."

"We have a lot to talk over, but we have to go to the hospice. Tony texted me—Faye's slipping quickly."

I blinked at my sudden tears. "It's time?"

"Sounds like."

As a crowd of yellow shirts bustled by us, a bandage hung off of one man's forearm. But there was no wound, just a tattoo that looked eerily familiar. Like the one on the hot-air balloon. Like the mashed-up symbol Juliet drew for us. *That's it.* I grabbed Tens's hand, but by the time we turned toward the group, they were gone into the melee.

CHAPTER 28

Juliet

"No, we have to go get it back." I stamped my foot in emphasis. I refused to think through how much like Bodie throwing a temper tantrum I might seem.

"We don't know where she is." Fara shook her head again.

"She'll show up. She always does." I paced the living room. I'd tried to think of everything. There weren't other options.

"And what are you going to give her instead?" Fara cocked her head as if she knew the answer.

I held my mother's book in my hands. "This." My heart lurched at the idea of parting with it. But I stole Rumi's history; it seemed fair to lose mine in return. He always spoke of karma. Maybe this was mine.

"Does it have the symbol in it?" Fara asked.

"No."

She shrugged her shoulders. "She's not going to want it. She's not going to give you back Rumi's things either."

A knock at the door stopped us. Fara checked the Spirit Stone and then opened it. "Sergio?"

"Hi, is Juliet home?" He sounded hesitant and awkward.

She stepped back and motioned him toward me.

No! I tried to smile, but I think it was more like a grimace. *Don't take this out on him. He's been nothing but kind.*

He shuffled inside. "How is the cat doing? I brought you tickets for the race. I don't know. I thought maybe you might want to go with me?" He held out shiny, colorful tickets.

"Oh. Uh. She's better, thanks." I hated small talk.

"Juliet's not sure she can go," Fara answered for me. "Want a pop?"

"Sure." Sergio sat down on the couch. He had to feel the tension. "Why not go to the race? It's pretty cool. You should see it once before you decide." He swiveled his head between me and the kitchen. "What's going on?"

"I'm . . . I'm . . . ," I stammered, unsure and uncertain.

"Is it that lady again?" He couldn't seem to let things

hang, as if he were forever impatient. "Is she bothering you still?"

I nodded, latching on to any feasible explanation.

"Want me to teach you some self-defense moves? I took a class." Sergio did a few staggering, comical chops and kicks that had Fara laughing so hard she couldn't speak as she came back in.

"Um, no thanks?" I said as he sat back down. "I'm sure you're really good, but that's not my, um, style." *Complete sentences, Juliet. Try them.*

He nodded. "No, really, what's going on? Nelli come up with something more about your family? I've been inputting data as fast as I can." He wiggled his fingers as if to demonstrate.

"I'm looking for my dad," I said, because he seemed to already know that. *Nelli must have told him.*

"Is he alive? My mom died in a car crash. Do you know what happened to yours?" Sergio's expression was sober and caring.

"She died too. I don't know about my dad."

"Wow, I'm sorry. I hope he's okay."

Fara asked, "Do you have any brothers? Sisters?"

He shook his head. "A brother. I'm trying to find him. We were sent to different foster families when we were little. I don't even know if he's still in Indiana. He'd be fifteen now."

My heart bled a little seeing the pain in his eyes. "Now I'm sorry. That must be really hard," I said. I knew what siblings who were split apart went through—so many came through DG not knowing where the rest of their family was.

"Yeah, it is. I'd do almost anything to find him. Be a family again." Sergio drank a huge gulp of his Coke. He pointed to our shoes. "Did I interrupt something? You look like you're getting ready to go out."

"Uh, well . . ." I wasn't sure how to answer.

"Juliet thinks she dropped a book at the cellar the other night. We were so scared we didn't have a chance to go back."

"Let's go." Sergio leapt to his feet. "I'll go with you."

"Oh, you don't need to do that." I felt panic well.

Fara didn't try to rescue me. I knew she wanted to sabotage my plan. "I'll drive."

"Cool." Sergio left the soda can and tickets on the coffee table but picked up his backpack.

I squirreled my mother's book into my bag and followed them. *Ms. Asura won't talk to us in front of Sergio, will she?*

* * *

"I don't see anything." Sergio swept the cellar with his flashlight again. "Are you sure you left it here?"

"I don't know." *Think faster, Juliet.*

"Back so soon?" Ms. Asura's voice preceded her descent down the stairs. "And you, how interesting." She spotted Sergio but didn't hesitate to continue. She stayed on the steps blocking our only exit.

"Did you pick up a book around here?" he asked, setting his jaw and stepping forward as if he could protect us.

"A book? Here?" She laughed. "I like to read dirty stories, but not this kind of dirty."

I cleared my throat and said, "If you did find something, I would trade you for this." I held out my mother's book.

She nodded to Sergio. "Hand me that, young man."

He frowned and I had to shove it into his hands. He leaned forward rather than walking too close. *Even he knows she's not a good person.*

She flipped through it. "This? This doesn't interest me." She threw it into the mud at our feet.

"Hey, that was uncalled for." Sergio knelt and tried to wipe the dirt off the cover with his sleeve. He reached into his backpack for a napkin.

"You're becoming tedious." Ms. Asura sighed. "The key. We want the key."

"The key to what?" Sergio stood up, shaking his head. "This place isn't locked."

She rolled her eyes. "I don't have time to play games with children. Find it. You're running out of time." She turned to leave.

"Wait!" I yelled. "I need to know more. I don't know what to trade you to get back what I left here." I glanced at Sergio, hoping he wasn't smarter than Kirian and that speaking in vague terms might go over his head.

"Not pretty pictures. You might want to go take a

gander along the banks of the creek. I think you dropped yours out there."

By the time we'd clamored up the steps, she'd disappeared down the drive in her sports car.

We ran along the property to the edge of the creek. There, hanging from the branch of my tree, was Rumi's open portfolio. Below it, swirling in the water's currents or heading downstream, were bits of dissolving papers. Rumi's ink drawings of windows, notes, collections of letters.

I threw myself into the water, Fara and Sergio beside me, collecting the pages as quickly as we could.

"What is all this?" Sergio called, heading into the worst of the eddies to get to the ones stuck near the other side.

We didn't answer him as we relayed pages and ripped pieces to the shore. *Ruined. It's all ruined.*

Huffing and puffing, we fell against the grass when we'd collected everything we could. The old leather swung from the tree above like a macabre reminder I'd never have the upper hand on the Nocti. Never escape from the pain that I brought to those around me.

"What was all this?" Sergio pressed, trying to spread the crumpled mush flat.

"It was all I had to find my parents," I whispered.

He nodded. "Maybe when they dry out? Maybe you can read it then?"

"We need to take them to our friend. Maybe he can fix them." Fara clasped my hand and pulled me to my feet. "We need to go now."

Sergio carefully helped load the sticky, disintegrating pages into the trunk of Tony's car. "Do you want me to go with you? I have a class, but I'll skip it if you need me—"

"No, thank you," Fara answered him. "You are very helpful, but there's nothing else you can do today."

We drove in silence, Sergio sneaking glances at me. I didn't have the ability to reassure him at all.

"You can just drop me off up there at the bus stop. I'll, um, call you tomorrow? Okay?" he asked me. He reached into his backpack. "I almost forgot—here's your book. I don't think the dirt hurt it too much."

I think I nodded. I had almost let him walk off with my mother's sonnets. I clutched it to my chest.

When Fara parked outside of Rumi's shop, she paused. "This is part of your path."

"He's never going to forgive me."

"He will when he knows you tried to give up yours for his. That's something."

"It's not enough." I swallowed. "It's never enough."

CHAPTER 29

Faye was sunk in on herself. Barely a shell of who she'd been at the wedding even three days ago.

"She's been nonresponsive since late last night." Gus hugged us. He, too, seemed to have aged and worn thin at the edges.

Rumi arrived bearing bags of takeout—burgers and waffle fries from Bub's, pizza from Uno's, doughnuts and sandwiches from Auntie Em's, lasagna and meatballs from Donatello's. As if he'd picked up food from each restaurant on his way down Main. "Comfort food." He shrugged. He'd already strung newly blown Spirit Stones, glass birds and fireflies, along the terrace doors and windows. *To make all these new pieces, he must not be sleeping.*

A vase of wedding flowers with butterflies and birds on sticks tucked between the stems was another gentle reminder that life was lived in breaths and moments. Nelli fussed with them, changing the water, rearranging the blossoms.

It was as if we were all trying to do our best to do something, anything. And yet, all we could do was let Faye's body let go one cell at a time.

A big-screen television played in the corner of the room, the only reminder that life in the world around us continued to spin and turn, even though in this room it felt as if time stood still.

"Were you at the track when the crash happened?" Gus asked Tens.

"Yes, but we didn't see it. I was tailing a group of suspicious guys." We'd decided this was not the time to tell Gus that Sergio was playing us.

"You track them down?" Gus asked.

"Not fast enough."

"Did you see it here?" I asked Gus. "What happened exactly? The radio commentators were all over the place."

His face full of sadness and disbelief, he reported, "One of the drivers is in critical condition. Two others are in serious condition. Brain trauma, broken bones, burns."

"Are they going to be okay?"

"No one's saying. Looked like tires blew out or maybe an engine seized. They're still analyzing the footage."

I grabbed a napkin and quickly sketched the tattoo. "Did you see anyone with this?"

"Is that the symbol Juliet was told to find?" Rumi asked.

"I have to ask her, but it was on the balloon that day and I think I saw a tattoo like it," I answered. I didn't think I'd seen the marking in Auntie's journal or anything that Rumi showed us.

"A couple of the emergency crew wore patches like that maybe? I'm sorry, kid. I wasn't paying that close of attention to know if I saw it or not." Gus sighed.

A deep, resounding exhale from Faye was followed by moments of nothing before her chest gulped air. We all froze and then continued.

I shook my head. "Don't worry about it. I saw a couple of impressive race fans." I changed the subject and regaled him with stories about who and what I saw on the other side of the window. By the time I'd finished, we chortled, because I had to make up words for a lot of what I saw.

"Oh, you mean the crew boss?" Gus chuckled. "It's like listening to Rumi with your made-up talk about the cars and racing."

I'd added layers to my descriptions. Auntie wrote about tears and laughter and being on the same continuum. Seemed to me while we were sitting here talking, eating, and telling stories next to Faye that we were on that continuum ourselves. Waiting for the grief but trying to live a little in the meantime.

Juliet and Fara came in with Tony and helped themselves to food. They sat on the floor. The room wasn't large, but we all wanted to be here. I tried to catch Juliet's eye, but she avoided me, as if she had another secret. I almost sighed. *What now?*

I happened to glance over and saw Mini under Faye's bed, twitching her tail and watching all of us, her stony expression unreadable. The few remaining bandages weren't so white and were picked and clawed at as if she'd felt unbearably confined in them.

Custos nosed opened the terrace door and joined in our vigil. The storm was gone, blown through as quickly as it came up. The sky was a darkening blue, a few stars shone down, but the air was warm. The light breeze blustered with a sweet fruity aroma as if the Creators swigged grape soda before exhaling a sigh across us.

Tony finished opening the doors at Gus's motion. The room felt twice as big and as if we'd invited the world to join us.

Delia came in. "I'm checking in for this shift. I'll be Faye's nurse tonight." She tripped over Custos. "I did not see the dog here"—she winked—"but see if you can't get them to sit across the room, away from the door, just in case someone else has better eyesight?" She smiled as Mini and Custos did exactly as asked. Delia sighed but shook her head. *I'm sure that isn't the weirdest bit about this.* "We have a harpist who will be here in a couple hours. Do you want me to have her play?"

Gus's face crumpled as he said, "I think that would be nice. Music is Faye's life."

"Very good. Call me if you need anything else, okay?" Delia snagged a cookie Rumi held out to her.

Time passed and conversations ebbed and flowed. Tony unwrapped a notebook of more Indiana history and books of history he thought might be relevant to our search. I picked up a book about Buddhism. I was searching for more information on how the yogi had gone to the Light on his own. It might explain how to aid Roshana and Auntie without their remains.

After a time, Bales joined us, beelining for a kiss and a tight hug from Nelli. After hellos, he sat himself near Tens and me. "We need to talk," he whispered low as Gus turned up the volume of the television for the night's newscast.

As they showed the crash and aftermath for the tenth time, we moved to the terrace and Bales leaned close to say, "I got a call from a friend on the force that they're setting up a serial-killer task force. He gave me a list of locations they're waiting to search until next week's news conference."

"Serial killer?" Could humans think Nocti were serial killers? Maybe. Especially if they crossed the line and aided in the bodily death. Fenestras didn't kill people to take their souls to heaven, but DG alone was proof that Nocti operated differently.

Bales nodded. "We're not the only ones turning up

remains. The designation helps the locals put more resources on the case. There's a rumor the FBI is showing up to take over."

We nodded. More resources meant more people poking around, not a development that would make the Nocti comfortable. *And not one important to figuring out where Roshana is buried.*

"I'm going to drive out to an abandoned school and start poking around," Bales said.

"Don't go by yourself." I shook my head in fear.

Bales shrugged me off. "I'll be fine. Criminals don't hang around their dumping grounds."

"Maybe we're not talking regular criminal, though," Tens answered.

"Odds are there's nothing to find. It's a long list of buildings."

"But—" *I don't have a good feeling.*

"Meridian, this is my job. I'll be fine." Bales wouldn't listen.

Tens and Bales continued to talk about what we'd seen at the track while I went back into Faye's room. I watched as Gus tenderly moistened Faye's lips and mouth with a sponge that looked more like a pink lollipop. He brushed her hair off her face and whispered in her ear.

The weather report on the news called for severe thunderstorms moving from the central United States, over central Indiana tomorrow. Even if the track was cleared for more qualifying, which seemed up for speculation, the weather might not cooperate. Besides, after all the accidents and injuries, I didn't understand why the entire event wasn't canceled. But then I knew more people might die. *Maybe I'm biased.*

"How are you?" I asked Nelli, who hadn't taken her eyes off her uncle.

"It's hard to watch him," Nelli answered while Gus massaged lotion on Faye's arms.

Faye's erratic breathing hadn't changed.

Delia came into the room. "Would you like the harpist to play now?"

"Please." Gus nodded.

The harpist set up on the terrace. She closed her eyes as she plucked the strings. The notes were melodic and soothing. I heard the ocean, the rush of waves in the background. I closed my eyes, lost in the cocoon of sound.

She began to play the next song when both Rumi and Juliet startled me by saying in unison, "I know that song."

The harpist paused as if interruptions happened all the time. "Shall I stop?" she asked.

"No, no, what is the name of this threnody, this song?" Rumi begged.

"The hymn 'I'll Fly Away.'"

"Please continue." Rumi hummed along and Juliet merely paled, white and drawn. Rumi began to sing quietly under his breath.

> *"When the sun comes, rising in the sky,*
> *We'll fly away*
> *To the next, dry your eyes and say,*

Let us fly away
Open the window darlings,
Throw it wide
When I die, sing praises by my side,
For I'll fly away
Let me go, for you will follow soon,
I'll so be free
To the Light, unafflicted from all pain,
Let my spirit soar
Broken no more,
Through the windowpane
Without regret I am off into the Light,
For I'm moving on
I'm moving on
Yes, I am
Off into the Light,
When the time's right, see me in its rays,
I'll be the Light."

Juliet lifted her head. "That's my mother's lullaby, but with different words."

"I remember she sang it to you all the time." Tony knelt, wrapping his arm around her shoulders. "I don't remember the words, though."

Maybe I can reach Juliet through this song. "What are your mother's words?" I asked Juliet. "Do you remember?"

Her eyes grew wide and scared. "It was about the creek." Her voice cracked. "She was at DG."

"Sing it for us." Fara gripped Juliet's hand as if imparting badly needed strength. She nodded at the harpist who waited a beat, then started at the beginning of the song again.

Juliet squeezed her eyes tightly shut. Then she sang along, her voice thin and reedy:

> "When you're sad and want to be made glad,
> Follow the Wildcat home
> I will wash those tears off your heart,
> Give your hurts my way
> Send your worries down my stream,
> Let them float away
> I'll hold you close, deep against my heart."

Abruptly, Juliet stopped and leapt to her feet. "I'm sorry. I can't. I need air." She ducked out of the room. Fara scrambled to follow. *Why do Rumi and Roshana both have words to the same song? What is the significance?*

As we composed our faces, Mini bounded up onto Faye's bed, trailing bandage like a second tail.

"Guys?" Tens headed toward Faye.

Her breathing is different. Sometime while we'd been listening and singing, Faye's breathing had changed. Became more intermittent.

We moved as one over to her bed and joined hands. The nurses said it could be any time at all. Tony began reciting the Lord's Prayer at Gus's request. The harpist began playing again, this time a tune that didn't matter; I barely heard it before I was at the window.

I blinked. I felt Tens's hand gripping mine and had the sensation of standing at Faye's side in our circle. Yet I was also outside of my body, my Fenestra spirit hovering at the afterlife's window.

"You told me the truth." Faye sat next to me in a stiff-backed floral upholstered chair. Her voice suddenly as strong as it was when I'd first met her.

I nodded, unsure of what to make of the chair. *No one's ever sat next to the window. What is the reason?*

"It's very beautiful over there, isn't it?" Faye asked.

I considered the view out her window. Huge old trees shaded a light green farmhouse. Fields upon fields of corn swayed in a breeze. "Where are we?" I asked.

"My daddy's farm. I recognize that tire swing tree—I spent hours in the summer up that tree, hunting cicadas. The corn is all tassled up. Ready to pick. I went through pairs of gloves like glasses of water every summer. Corn'll cut up skin like nothing else. There's a pig roasting. Can you smell that?"

Suddenly, the air circulated around us. I caught a whiff of scent on the breeze that ruffled the cornfields and sounded like whispers and rattling. What I didn't see were any people waiting for her arrival. *Her parents should be here at least. Siblings? Her first husband.* Usually there were even souls who simply seemed to welcome newbies.

"Faye?" I asked.

"She's not ready." Faye frowned.

"Who? I think you are."

"Oh dear, I'm very ready, but my daughter, she's not."

"You grew up here?"

"Yes. Now it's a strip mall, but when I was a girl, this was the whole world to me."

"Where is your family? They should be here to meet you," I said, almost to myself.

"Oh, they know I'm not coming today. Ma's probably making her slaw and watermelon Jell-O salad with Cool Whip. Hated that concoction, but she served it every holiday and special occasion. Daddy's got the pig going; he's probably on the porch shucking sweet corn or picking through the ripe tomatoes for the perfect ones to slice and salt."

Does she have a choice? "You're not going?"

"No, I'm sorry, dear, but as much as I'd like to, I must go back, at least for a few more days. Can't you hear her?" Faye's hand trembled as she reached for mine.

In that moment, I tuned back into the conversation in the hospice room. I saw both places, one with my eyes, the other with my soul.

Dolores had blown into the room, moaning and whining and sobbing. She'd draped herself over her mother's lap, carrying on like there was an Academy Award on the line.

I tried to persuade Faye to let go. "She'll grieve you no matter what, you know. If you're ready—"

"Ah, Meridian, a mother doesn't leave her child unless

she absolutely has to. I can tell I have a little more fight in me. We'll be back here again. And now I can tell Gus where to find me."

With a wistful glance and sigh, the window scene slid away and I was firmly back in my body, leaning against Tens's side.

"Mother, don't you dare leave me. Don't you dare," Dolores carried on.

Faye's hand moved and touched her daughter's. "Shush. You'll wake the dead." Her voice was raspy with disuse.

"Mom?" Dolores screeched.

Our chain broken, we moved away to give Faye, and her daughter, some space. Gus didn't go far at all. I didn't blame him.

After explaining, I asked Delia about Faye's rally. "What just happened?" *How did Faye go from not speaking for hours and ready to die to eyes open and talking?*

"It works that way sometimes. The dying aren't necessarily released by the loved and force themselves to stay here. As long as possible. Longer than they should maybe, simply to make other people happy."

"She was ready," I insisted. I saw the longing in Faye's eyes.

Delia nodded. "I'm sure she was. She's held on longer than anyone has a right to expect. You'd think letting go would be easy when you love someone who's hurting that much."

It should be. It really, really should be.

CHAPTER 30
Juliet

Nightmares continued to plague me. Each time I woke, Fara's open and vigilant eyes met mine. "Sleep, no one is here," she repeated as often as I needed, and her eyes glittered in the darkness regardless of when I opened mine. Sometime later, I woke to my bedroom door ajar and the mumbles of conversation. *Meridian? Tens? Nelli? What are they doing here?*

Grabbing a flannel shirt to use as a robe, I padded out as quietly as possible. Fara promised she'd let me tell them about Sergio and the book. I wasn't quite ready to trust her completely to keep her word. But then, she couldn't possibly fully trust me either.

As I entered, Meridian said to Fara, "You look terrible. Are you sleeping at all?"

I cleared my throat, pulling the soft folds tighter around me. "What's going on?"

"It couldn't wait," Nelli said in an apologetic voice, as if she feared I was dreaming of happily-ever-after. *Not likely.*

"Sergio is playing both sides. He's feeding the Nocti information," Tens repeated.

I wasn't even completely awake. *I didn't hear them right. I'm still dreaming.*

My legs collapsed and I slid down the wall, as if my bones melted. "What did you just say? How do you know?"

Fara grabbed my hand.

"But how? He saved us from Ms. Asura. Twice. He helped me!" The shrill in my voice gave me the taste of fizzy vinegar on the back of my tongue.

"You know this for certain?" Fara asked Tens.

"Bales followed Nelli's boss. He's got photographs of Sergio passing Ms. Asura a page out of Auntie's journal and Rumi's folio."

"And Bales is good guy? For sure?" Fara asked.

"Yes," I answered for her. "He'd die to protect Nelli. He knows how important we are to her."

Bales proved himself. Me? I kept proving I'm not worthy.

Meridian and Tens nodded their agreement.

What did I say to Sergio? He asked so many questions.

Did I trust him with too much information? What if he gives them details to use against us? There will be blood on my hands. Again. I frantically tried to remember every word, every gesture, every interaction with him.

"Juliet?" Meridian knelt in front of me. "This is not your fault."

"I told him secrets." My voice was small and undignified.

"About?" Tens's question was backed with steel blades in his tone.

"My father. I told him we were looking for my father. How could he do this to us? He said he was searching for his brother. Was that a lie too?"

"Maybe. Maybe not."

"What if the Nocti promised him his brother in exchange?"

"That might explain how he got involved with them," Tens said.

I sniffed back my tears and forced my spine to straighten. "Does he know we know?"

"We don't think so."

"He talked up the race and the parade. Wanted to get us volunteer tickets in a special area."

"That was probably part of his assignment. To get us all in one place for the Nocti."

"Oh, Nelli?" I turned to her. Puffy eyes and chapped cheeks told me Nelli was taking this betrayal especially hard. *She'll be devastated to be the one to introduce us. She already takes way too much responsibility for DG.*

"I'm sorry. I didn't think. I should have known."

"How?" Fara asked.

Nelli shrugged. "Somehow."

I pushed myself up, making my legs listen. "Someone stole Rumi's portfolio out of my bedroom. Was that Sergio or Ms. Asura?"

"Wouldn't have to be, but probably."

I filled them in on confronting Ms. Asura, Sergio's rescue, and returning what we could to Rumi.

"Are you insane? Why would you go take on Ms. Asura alone?" Meridian gasped.

"It's my mess. I was cleaning it up." My chin notched higher. "Besides, I'm tired of fear. We burned our past, right?" I asked Fara.

"Yes."

"Clean slate. Rumi says the Woodsmen found a book with a similar symbol in it. He's making a fake one like it. I'll deliver it."

"That's too dangerous."

"We've never had the advantage with them. We do now."

"No."

"We do now," I repeated. Between Ms. Asura thinking I'll cooperate and then Sergio. "Yes."

I began pacing. Thoughts whipped through my head too fast to hook on to any of them, but I knew what needed to happen.

"We both will deliver it." Fara stood and wrapped her arm around my waist.

"You don't have to," Meridian said while Tens simply stared at me as if waiting to see if I'd crumble again.

"Yes, I do. We do." *I can do this. I'm sure I can.*

"It's a distraction to keep us from the race events."

"Are you willing to risk the lives of innocents on that assumption? I'm not." Not more innocents.

"We have to try to figure out what they're planning for the race," Meridian pointed out.

"So Fara and I will stall for time."

"Can that work?" Fara asked.

"We will make it work!" I shouted.

"Let's bring the others into the conversation. We'll need their help."

"But how do we ignore Sergio?"

"You can't. You have to keep letting him help," Meridian stressed. "Until we know everything he knows. We have to use him."

Nelli nodded but didn't seem convinced.

As we talked, Fara sharpened one of her knives while Tens whittled a race car with sticks in his bag.

Nelli bit her lip. "I guess we can try."

"I need to." I stomped away and felt everyone pause. "I'm sorry. Sorry," I mumbled. I turned to Tony. "You told me if I learned to read, I'd be taking my power back. This is like that. I can't risk them hurting anyone else."

Tony was the first to speak. "Okay. If you feel that strongly, we'll try, but we can't guarantee anything. And only if Fara can be there with you."

"Then Meridian and I will go back out to the Speedway and see what we can find," Tens said. His phone rang. "It's Rumi." He clicked on the speakerphone and said, "Rumi, what's going on?"

"Are you with everyone?"

"Yeah, you're on speaker."

"Good. Has Juliet explained our late-night rendezvous?"

"Yes, we know."

"Okay, then. I've received a missive from my friend at the university about the writing on the headstones. She initially thought it was Sanskrit and then, unfortunately, discarded that idea. I think we might have a dead end. The Woodsmen only know what to write, not which language it is or even what the words mean."

"Do you have it here?" Fara asked.

"Hang on, Rumi. Fara hasn't seen that yet." Meridian pulled a tiny notebook from her back pocket and flipped through it, then handed it to Fara.

Fara leafed through, squinting at the pages. "It's from Avesta."

"What did the lass say?" Rumi's boom crossed the air as if he were in the room with us.

"My people's words. Ancient words of protection and Light."

"Well, what's it say exactly?" Tens demanded.

She shook her head. "I do not know how to read it. My father had just started to teach me when he—" Tears flooded her eyes and her usual bravado shriveled like an old apple.

I touched her arm. *She knows the pain of a dead parent. We share that.*

"I will try to remember. I am sorry."

"At least it's a place to start." Meridian gave her a small smile.

"Call if you need anything, kiddies. I'll let you know when the dummy book is ready to go." Rumi hung up.

"What do I do about my boss?" Nelli asked.

"Don't let him know you know anything. Act normal," Tens instructed.

Her expression didn't relax, and she didn't seem comforted by that thought.

* * *

"Juliet?" Fara called, after insisting on making sure my bedroom was empty before I entered it.

I turned the corner and she held up a photograph.

"This was tucked into the window."

The photograph showed a girl who could be my twin. And a blob of light next to her. "My mother?"

"She's not a Fenestra."

"My father?"

"Looks like he might be."

She flipped over the photograph and showed me the writing on the back in faded, tiny lettering that matched my mother's notes in the book of sonnets. *Roshana and Argy Ambrose.*

In deep red, like blood, was also scrawled, *"A little incentive."*

"We need to show Meridian and Tens." Fara was already grabbing her bag.

I traced my mother's face with my fingertip and the lighted outline of a boy, featureless and blank. "Who are you, Argy? Where are you?" I whispered before following Fara out the door to the cottage.

CHAPTER 31

Cues were everywhere around us. Hundreds of thousands of people attended the race each year, and maybe even billions around the world watched the Indianapolis 500 on television or live streaming.

Snake pit. Driver. Artesian. Last yellow. What the hell does that mean, Mr. Woodsman?

The Nocti were the worst kind of evil. They had no boundaries. No checks in the universe, but Sangre Angels and Josiah weren't answering my mental pages. I'd been trying.

If you wanted to create chaos, steal souls, and take lives? If you had no soul yourself and no compassion? It made sense. I'd begun to think that part of my destiny was to try to think like my opponents. *Can I think like a Nocti and stay Light?*

We spent hours updating the scrolls tacked to the cottage walls under prints Joi hung there, as overstock for the tearoom. We couldn't risk hanging new ones up at Rumi's after the break-in and their disappearance.

I wondered what Auntie would say about the rings of knowledge and influence spreading farther and farther out. We kept adding to our circle. Each new relationship brought information, but also risk. Consider Sergio— were we taking too many risks?

Tens added maps of the racetrack, blown-up satellite photographs of the area too. The cottage was beginning to look more like a war room at command central rather than a cozy guesthouse.

We were trying to learn as much about the Indianapolis 500, and the land and its history, as possible. "So that's turn one, two, three, and four into the straightaway?" I asked.

Tens studied the list of drivers and team colors. "I wish they wore black and had 'bad guy' written across their chests."

"Why would having a driver matter to the Nocti? What's he going to do, lose the race?"

"Hit someone?" Tens asked.

I shook my head in frustration. "That wouldn't take out a lot of people."

"Not unless he ran into a crowd or had explosives on board."

I glanced down at a book about race history. "This says the cars are sensitive and they're checked very carefully before the race for all kinds of things. No way could there be a bomb in the car."

"Nothing's impossible, Supergirl. Keep looking."

My eyes were dry and prickly as I chugged my fourth soda and the sun slid behind the trees in late afternoon.

Tens's phone rang. "It's Nelli." He hit speaker. " 'Ello?"

For a moment, all we heard was static, then muffled voices. *Rocks falling? Construction? Boxing match?*

"Nelli?" I asked.

Tens frowned, shaking his head and putting his finger to his lips.

Juliet and Fara jogged up onto the porch. I opened the door, inviting them inside but motioned them to be quiet.

Tens hovered over the phone. We all leaned closer.

A voice that sounded like Bales called out, "The police know we're at Jefferson Township School investigating. They'll be coming— *Ooof*." His voice broke off as someone else shrieked.

The response was quiet, almost muffled, and none of us could make out words.

My mouth dried. My palms itched.

I flinched, listening to scuffles and punches hitting a body. *Nothing sounds quite the same as a person being beaten.*

A woman cried out. Nelli? "Don't hurt him!"

Juliet stuck her knuckles in her mouth and bit down. I clenched my jaw trying not to cry out.

"Too late. Why did you have to stick your nose in? This is none of your business."

Fara mouthed, "Ms. Asura?" to us.

We nodded.

The argument grew more heated as it sounded like more bodies were thrown into the fight.

Nelli screamed, "Stop it!"

A large screech of metal or glass drowned out all other sounds as if something collapsed into a pile of rubble. A woman screamed and screamed and screamed. Nelli? Abruptly, the line went dead.

* * *

Tens handed me a holster and a gun. He grabbed his knives and slid them into sheaths along his body.

Fara picked up extras like they loaded up this way every day. Checking rounds and clips. Things that up until months ago I only ever saw in movies.

Juliet packed a backpack of food, water, and clean cloths. "They might be hurt," she said at my questioning look.

If she wanted to think anyone we found alive might be hungry for Lucky Charms, I'd let her continue to nurture that fantasy. "Sure."

In charge of navigation, I typed in keywords and found

us the quickest route to the abandoned school on SR 52.

Once we were completely on our way, Juliet reached into her shirt and pulled out a photograph. "This was in the window of my bedroom. That's what we were coming to tell you."

"I'll give it right back," I promised as I tugged on the photo.

She clung to the photograph as if afraid to lose contact with it.

Her fingers loosened enough for me to take it from her and glance down at it. "Your parents?" I saw her mother clearly, her eyes deep and widely set. Her blond hair was left loose except for a ribbon tied at the top to keep it out of her face. She was smiling at the camera, but her gaze was turned toward her right and an overexposed blob of light that had to be a Fenestra. "You could be twins."

Tens nodded after a quick peek. "Definitely."

"Roshana's not the Fenestra." Shocked, I squinted at the picture.

"Doesn't look like it," Fara answered.

"That means your father is, if this is him with her," I said to Juliet. *Maybe that's why he hasn't looked for Juliet? Maybe he didn't know she'd gotten the genes? Maybe Roshana didn't know what he was either?*

I handed it back to her and chewed my lip.

Tens broke into my reverie. "Guys, we need to focus on Nelli and Bales. We're getting close. You ready, Fara?"

"I never back down."

Tens smiled. "Glad we're on the same side."

"Should be up here on the right," I said, glancing at the laptop screen.

"That's it." Tens slowed as we approached. There was only enough light left to wash the world in grays and mauves and make it hard to see much detail.

Red brick with broken windowpanes, Jefferson Township School wasn't far from the road but was a long way from being a usable, safe building. It was decomposing and decrepit, with the roof appearing to have caved into the top floor. The only vehicle parked near it was Bales's truck.

"Once upon a time, this place was gorgeous," I said as we drove into the old school yard. "So sad."

The front doors were surrounded by limestone carvings, more like a fancy fireplace mantel than doors to a school. Stone-draped urns and cornucopias near stacked stone books made me think they believed in a "bounty of learning." *What are we going to learn inside?*

"There's Bales's truck." Juliet pointed.

"There don't appear to be other cars here," I said.

"That doesn't mean there aren't Nocti. Could be an ambush." Tens shut off the engine; the stillness felt unnatural. "Where is Bales? Nelli?" Tens unfolded from the driver's side and pulled his handgun out. "Bad feeling."

"Me too," I agreed. The world was too silent.

"What's our plan?" Fara asked.

"See if we can get into the basement and work our way up?"

I passed out flashlights. In a few more minutes, we'd be blind in the dark.

"Let's call them?" Fara asked. "Listen for ringing?"

Tens nodded and hit buttons. "Bales first."

A sappy '80s love song started playing outside Bales's truck.

"Ringtone?" I moved toward the grass under the truck bed. "It's his phone." I bent down and picked it up. "Yep, it's his. He wouldn't have left it, not like this."

Tens stopped trying to hide his gun. "Dial Nelli with it."

I listened until I got a weird busy signal, then voice mail. "Nothing on here. Anyone hear ringing around us?" *Inside the school?*

Juliet and Fara shook their heads. *Crap.*

"Stay behind me, okay?" Tens demanded of me as he and Fara took the lead.

We crept around to the back of the property, where the bottom-floor windows gaped without glass. If Tens went first, he'd be vulnerable to attack, but he'd never let me go instead. He handed me the gun. "Don't shoot me." He smiled and I loved him for trying to take the tension down a notch.

"Promise." I knelt near him and gripped the gun. I'd gotten better with my shooting, but not enough to win competitions.

I heard his *humph* as his feet landed on debris and the tinkle of breaking glass.

I leaned in and handed him the gun. "Can you see anything?" I asked as he swept the area with his flashlight.

"No ambush."

Yet.

I slithered into the window hole and he caught me. I took the gun and flashlight, and he helped Juliet unceremoniously join us. Fara was last. Her stony expression gave no hint this type of breaking and entering was unusual for her. Somehow, I felt as if she'd crawled through windows, and worse places, simply trying to survive.

We moved cautiously around the room, dodging rats' nests and pigeon colonies.

A bark startled us. "Custos?" Tens called, lifting his light toward the sound.

She appeared in the doorway, her tail wagging, then turned, heading back into the darkness.

The hair on the back of my neck stood up. "Tens? Soul incoming."

"Do your thing. I'm right here."

"We'll follow Custos," Fara said.

"We're right behind you," Tens said to her.

I panicked, thinking the deceased might be Bales or Nelli, but it wasn't. I leaned against a wall, but my legs felt strong and sure under me as I entered the window space.

A boy dragged his leg behind him, scooting toward me. "Help me, please?"

Trying to manifest my window, I dropped to the floor, hoping to see his face. "What happened?"

"I called nine-one-one. Reported a boy with a broken leg; they decided I shouldn't have lied." He tried to give me a brave smile. "It doesn't hurt too much anymore." His neon-orange nylon jogging pants were torn and bloody at the knee. His T-shirt was hardly legible and all I saw was neon graffiti beneath the grime. "Do you know? Did they make it? Are they safe?"

"Who?"

"Argy and Roshana. Have you heard? Did they make it?"

"I—"

The summer breeze ruffled the curtains at my window, and I glanced up to see Auntie and Kirian just on the other side. Their expressions both grim and determined.

To the boy I said, "We need to get you through the window. You'll feel better over there. I think you might have friends meeting you."

"You come too." He clung to my hand.

"I can't. I need to stay here. But that's my Auntie. She'll help you." Sweat dripped down my face as I staggered under his weight, helping him to his feet.

As his hand touched the window, he seemed to grow stronger and Kirian gently lifted him over and carried him. Kirian's eyes met mine, his full of regret and pain and heartache that I couldn't begin to unravel.

"Meridian, quickly, listen to me," Auntie spoke. "They're moving the children. The bodies are desecrated on both sides of the window. They must know they are loved to heal; they must forgive themselves for not being stronger. Rumi knows the words."

"Meridian?" Tens's voice broke through and pulled me back. "Juliet is calling. Can you walk?"

I nodded, shaking the cobwebs from my head. My body functioned as if waking quickly from a long nap, but I wasn't dizzy or nauseous. Not even a little. Frantic barking urged us faster over rubble and years of trash accumulated by squatters.

Buried under a pile of tiles and fractured wood were Bales's boots and overall-clad legs. The smell of fouled, soupy air overpowered my senses.

"He fell through the floor?" I asked, reminding myself to breathe.

There was a gaping hole above us.

Juliet was clawing at the debris. "Please be alive. Please be alive."

I don't know how he can be.

We got down to him finally and saw the rise and fall of his chest. "He's breathing." Juliet checked for broken bones while Fara held Bales's head still.

It was impossible to tell if his back or neck were broken.

I sidled over to Tens, who was continuing to shift through piles looking for any sign of Nelli. "What do you think?"

"The nasty head wound? I think he fell through the floor from upstairs."

"Hopefully he'll be able to tell us what happened. I got one soul. But I don't see any glow of bones." *And no Nelli.*

"Either they're not Fenestra or they're not here."

"Auntie talked to me—" I broke off as Juliet cried out. "He's waking up."

"Bales, keep still. You were badly hurt."

Custos wagged her tail and licked Bales's face.

"Uh, dog breath," he moaned, and tried to shift.

"Stay still, you're hurt." Tens lifted more rubble around him.

"I'm not hurt bad. They hit me on the head. I'm fine." He tried to shake off Juliet's hands, but Custos put her paw on his chest. "What the hell am I doing down here? Where's Nelli?"

"That's what we're trying to figure out."

"She called you—" He winced. "I can't think. My head hurts."

"We should call an ambulance," Fara said.

"No! Where's Nelli? We were on the main floor. Asura and a bunch of men showed up. Help me up. We need to find her."

Custos barked.

Bales listed to the side like a sinking ship. "My God, they beat me good. We'd just gotten here. Not even long enough to look around. It was like they knew we were coming."

"Did you tell anyone else?" Tens asked.

"No, Nelli dropped a few files off at Juliet's with Tony. She told him. She told Tony."

"Tony wouldn't give you up," Juliet insisted.

"No, no." Bales struggled to breathe.

"Where would they take her?" I asked.

"Back to that museum?" Tens studied our surroundings as if wishing for a clue.

"Yeah, that's our best shot." Bales leaned over to catch his breath.

"I'll call Timothy and see if the Woodsmen can help."

CHAPTER 32

Tens drove Bales's truck while I rode in the backseat making phone calls. Fara and Juliet followed us in the van. Tony and Rumi were on their way to meet us at a Woodsmen safe house along the canal, not far from where we suspected the Novelty held Nelli.

"That's it right there." Bales pointed over Tens's shoulder. "That's the Indiana Medical History Museum."

The redbrick walls and stonework made me think of the school we just left. The museum was in good repair, with the exception of lots of construction signs and a haphazardly set up barricade plastered with NO TRESPASSING signs.

"What's in there?" I asked. Visions of leeches and old instruments, pickled organs, and crazy medical devices that did more damage than healing flit around my brain. *Kinda perfect for nasty Nocti to hole up in.*

"I don't know. I hope Nelli," Bales answered, rubbing his head.

"Are you okay? Are you sure we can't take you to the emergency room?"

"I'm fine. We need to move quickly. That'll take too long."

I wasn't sure I believed him, but when Tens didn't argue, I understood nothing and no one would keep Bales from trying to rescue Nelli.

The Woodsmen hustled us inside their safe house. The rooms buzzed with activity and I heard a range of accented English, from a southern United States drawl to the brogue of Scotland and everywhere in between.

The safe house was central for staging our attack. *Armed with what?*

"We've heard human sympathizers can be controlled with conventional weapons, but defeating the Nocti requires tapping into the Light," a young Woodsman explained to Bales.

"Light?"

"Yes, sir. Love and Light. They are the most powerful energies in the universe."

Armed with love? Hello, Nocti, I love you so much I'd like you dead.

Standing apart from us in the corner, Bales argued with Tens, "Of course I'm going with you."

"It's dangerous."

Bales roared, "I know that. I love her. I'm not staying here waiting."

Tens nodded as Tony and Rumi entered.

"We have eyes," one of the Woodsmen reported from a computer monitor. They'd hacked into the state network and turned on the webcams for reconnaissance. "It's possible we're seeing what they see. We have to assume they have some sort of surveillance on the outside as well."

"That's Nelli." I saw her strapped down to a chair. Duct tape covered her mouth. "What's that behind her?"

"Looks like the refrigerated drawers at the pathology lab," Tens said.

The kind dead bodies are stored in.

"Who is that?" Tens asked, pointing.

"That's Nelli's boss," Bales answered.

"Do you see Sergio? Is he in this too?"

"No, just the boss is guarding Nelli."

"How do we do this?" Juliet asked, yanking at her cuticles. "They'll see us coming."

"Yes, they will," Fara answered. "That's not a bad thing. We do not need to sneak around; they're the ones who hide from Light."

"I could go alone. See if she'll let Nelli go and keep me." Juliet paled. "I deserve that."

"Uh, no," we all said in unison to Juliet.

"Timothy, you survived an attack of Nocti how?" Tens asked.

"I do not know. I wish I did. Our history speaks of working against the Nocti, against their human comrades, but we haven't taken them on in my generation. Not like this. We simply haven't had the numbers or a Fenestra to aid."

"Then, we have an uggred problem. We can't kill her. We've tried. We merely stertiled and wounded her," Rumi said.

Fara gasped. "How do you not know this? You were not instructed on how to shine a Nocti?"

"You know how to kill a Nocti, without a Sangre?" I asked. We'd needed Josiah to kill Perimo and Josiah didn't have a cell phone. *At least I don't have his number.*

"You do too." Fara shook her head. "You all know. We must shine Light on the Darkness. Light is love. You must push everything but love from your heart. Let the light in you chase them away."

"Have you tried this?" Tens demanded.

"No, I have never had the opportunity." Fara shrugged. "My baba did, many times."

"I'd prefer a gun." Tens grunted.

"Guns do not matter for the baddies, only human helpers," Fara said.

"I've noticed."

Fara struggled to translate her thoughts into English. "Baba taught me. You think of the people who you love.

Only that feeling of warmth, of safety, of security. That is a powerful weapon."

"Love?" I asked, astonished. *Love? We think about people we love and then what? Cupid's arrows morph into poisoned darts?*

"It is enough."

"She's right." Rumi nodded thoughtfully. "To focus solely on love without fear is swinking, hard labor."

"Auntie thinks you know the words, Rumi."

"I'll think on it." He frowned.

So all we had to do was get near Ms. Asura and think about rainbows and unicorns. *Easy-peasy. No prob. This is a suicide mission.*

We picked apart every scenario we could think of. None of them gave me a gooshy, Hallmark moment feeling of victory.

"I can go in alone," Juliet repeated.

I shook my head at her. "Even if it was possible for you to convince Ms. Asura to give up Nelli, you know she'd realize we were somewhere waiting to help. We might as well march in together." *If you go alone, it'll be just like February. Asura hasn't lived this long because she's rash.*

"Fara told us to bring reminders of love." Tony pulled out his rosary beads and a Bible. "I have Juliet there next to me, so will these do?"

Rumi held out a photograph of his family for inspection.

"Sure," Timothy said. "Anything that will help you concentrate."

Fara seemed to think she could teach us how to defeat the Nocti. According to Baba, words and intent were our allies or our enemies.

Fara knelt in the corner, praying. She finished and stood. "I must teach you to chant." She rattled off a string of Farsi.

"Uh, sorry, what was the first syllable?" I asked.

"Does it matter what language we speak in?" Tens asked.

She considered thoughtfully. "No, I don't think so. It is the intent in the words. Energy gives words power. Makes them weapons for good or bad."

"Okay, so give us the English translation," Tony requested.

Fara nodded, jotting down scribbles, then squinting at them. "Good words, good thoughts, good deeds."

Rumi gasped. "That's in my nain's papers. But it's Welsh. It's very similar to the Spirit Stone chant."

"Can you say it in Welsh? Maybe that's what Auntie meant?" I asked.

"Of course." He nodded.

If his family knew of this chant, maybe that's why the papers were stolen. To keep us from figuring it out.

"What else?" I asked.

Fara answered, "Good Light, bring us your beautiful colors and take back the Dark."

Rumi translated the Welsh to other Woodsmen while Fara taught a few Farsi. They weren't taking chances that the language didn't matter. I was sticking with English. *Way easier to remember during stress.*

We practiced. "Good words, good thoughts, good deeds. Good Light, bring us your beautiful colors and take back the Dark."

Tony activated his church's prayer line to pray for God's Light to be with us. *I'll take all hands, all prayers, all good thoughts.*

Other than a few, the Woodsmen would stay here. If we failed, they still needed to stop the Nocti's plans for the race.

"You know what to do?" I asked Timothy, who monitored the screens. We dressed quickly in utility jumpsuits and hard hats. We hoped it would allow us to get close enough to get inside without anyone else in the neighborhood thinking much about it. After all, construction workers visited remodeling sites all the time. *Okay, not at night. Hopefully everyone's sleeping.*

Our Woodsmen silently blended into the trees and gardens around the museum. They formed a perimeter we didn't need to see to believe.

"Let's go," Tens ordered.

I watched as Juliet continued to pick at her hands, her anxiety growing exponentially. I dragged her aside. "You have to believe we can do this. No doubts. Stop feeling sorry for yourself. It would be so easy to hate her, but if you do, she wins—again. Focus on Fara; Bodie and Sema; and your father, who is still alive. How much do they love you? Do you love them? You mother gave up everything for you. Let go of your anger, for her."

Juliet nodded and took my hand. "We'll never know what happened to them, will we."

"It's a risk." *Probably not. If we're successful, the knowledge about your parents' whereabouts may be lost forever.*

"We have to defeat her, don't we?" Juliet's expression was torn between fear and resolve.

"I think Roshana will understand. Auntie knows I can't go back to Revelation yet to bury her bones."

"But at least you know where she is." Tears gathered in Juliet's eyes.

My heart breaking, I said, "There's nothing I can say to make this better for you. But Nelli's in there and she might still be alive. Your mom's not." I knew it was harsh to point out, but I needed Juliet focused.

"I know. Let's go." Juliet took my hand. We walked sandwiched between Tens at the front and Fara at the rear. The only light came from a few dim streetlights and a single flashlight.

I had no idea what anyone else was thinking. But the people I loved most in this world flashed through my mind like a slideshow. My little brother was in the forefront of my mind. Sammy. I'd given up hope of seeing him again, of him knowing me at all, to keep him safe. My father who might never understand what my destiny was. Tens with his dry humor and carver's hands, who accepted me at my worst and took my best in stride. Rumi's extreme vocabulary that covered a generosity so big any words became inadequate. Joi who took us in, no questions asked. Bodie and Sema with their innocent smiles and ever-ready ability to think anything was possible. Custos with her drool, antics, and hard-won trust. Mini with her attitude and resilience. Tony's scholarship and faith. Faye's fight to live for her happy ending. Gus's devotion to Faye. I even loved Fara's confidence and sass. Juliet's drive to keep us all from harm no matter what the personal cost.

I saw Auntie's reflection as I walked by a closed, dark window. Auntie, who taught me at my most reluctant, who loved me from the first, even from afar.

My fingers tingled and warmed.

Juliet crossed the grass and headed for the front door. We weren't sneaking in. She tried the handle. The knob turned. "It's open."

We crowded into the foyer. There was a layer of sawdust and cobwebs that made me think the remodeling was on hold indefinitely.

"Tea, anyone?" Ms. Asura said from the right.

"No, thank you," Juliet answered as we turned almost as one.

"Pity to die on an empty stomach, isn't it?" She lit a candelabra; the candle flames danced and licked as she held some papers up to the fire, then tossed them into the old fireplace.

I got my first solid look at her face and wondered how we'd managed to inflict so much damage without killing her. "Nice scars," I said. *What is she burning*? Maps and drawings were hanging off the walls as if someone grabbed them down in a hurry. Rumi's timeline too.

"Not very ladylike to point that out, but then you're not a lady, are you." She smiled at me and winked.

"Tell me where my mother is, please," Juliet demanded.

"Or what? You'll get mad? Oh, please do! That'll make this all the more fun."

I wanted Ms. Asura's attention back on me. "Tell us where to find all the remains and we'll let you live."

"Gee, let me think about that. Not going to happen. I don't need to confess my sins. I've done everything I've been asked, or do you doubt the Creators speak to me as well?"

I tried again. "I've seen the souls you've tortured."

"Are you as dumb as Juliet? I've done nothing. Their souls are wounded in their own right. That's not me. As much as I'd like to take credit for it, the fear, the pain, the loneliness, these all eat at the flesh. All we've done is connect them to this plane so they can't move on."

"No one would do that to themselves," I scoffed.

"People do that and worse every day. Why do you think our job is so much easier than yours?" She lit a map of the city, full of red lines and circles, on fire, making me wonder if she was burning their strategies.

Tens's voice sharpened as he asked, "What are you planning?"

She sighed petulantly. "You can't all have marched in here thinking I'd want to confess. 'Oh, Father, please save my soul. I'll do anything.'" She bit off the sarcasm and pretended to faint on a sheet-covered couch. Dust rose like confetti in the candlelight. "Please. You can't possibly think I was planning an attack by myself? Aren't you adorably dullard. Even if you knew how to kill me, which you don't, I am only one of many. The engines have started. The accelerator is to the floor. With or without me, we've won. We live for this; you live for silly ridiculous relationships and *love*." She sneered the word, then continued. "When you have nothing to lose, there is only everything to gain. The checkered flag is ours."

"Didn't your mother ever teach you arrogance will get you in trouble?" I poked.

"Oh, I'm arrogant?" She whistled.

Footsteps pounded up the stairs to our right.

"Yeah, you are," Fara answered as a group of Nocti and humans strode in to flank Ms. Asura. The other Nocti's eyes were also uncovered and black pits of nothingness. *Doesn't get more creepy than that.*

She chuckled as if genuinely delighted by the banter. "Didn't your mother ever teach you not to underestimate the people in power who want to stay there? Oh, that's right—your mothers didn't want either of you, and yours is dead. Pity." She pointed at me, Tens, and Juliet, then poured herself tea with two cubes of sugar.

"Where is Nelli?" Bales questioned.

"Oh, love, she makes your heart race and your life worth living, doesn't she?"

"Where is she?" The desperation in Bales's voice

weakened as if he were using up what strength he had. *Is he hurt worse than he let us know?*

Fara started to murmur under her breath. It was clear we could trade insults all night, but Ms. Asura would tell us nothing useful. The other Nocti glanced at each other as if they didn't know what to make of us and were waiting for orders.

Please let this work.

Rumi added booming Welsh to the Farsi.

Tens, Auntie, Sammy.

It would take all of us.

Tony began the Lord's Prayer, his faith—his truest love, hallowed be thy name.

Fara's voice gained strength.

The back of my neck felt as if the sun had come out from behind a cloud.

Bales and I began chanting at the same time, and for a moment, I was sure we'd added a choir of angels, an army, to our number, so loud were our words, so convicted were our hearts.

Ms. Asura paused mid-sip and I saw her eyes widen slightly. The candles sputtered and flickered before going out. "Hit the switch! We must see them!" she demanded before one of her men flicked on a single lightbulb hanging from the ceiling.

Tens's gravelly baritone flowed over me as he stood at my back. He twined his free hand in mine. Smoke from the smoldering papers drifted over the floor around our feet.

"What, are you meditating now? Isn't that cute. Juliet, why don't you come with me downstairs? I'll show you where your mother screamed for mercy. Let you say goodbye to Nelli before you all die?"

Juliet stepped forward and my voice faltered for a breath, but she reached behind her, grabbed my hand tight, and began her verses. I recognized lines Roshana wrote in the book of sonnets. *Pieces of Juliet's past made present.*

In the distance, maybe below us, I heard shots fired as several of the Nocti disappeared out a door. We shifted so Rumi leaned against the door and no one could come back through. Ms. Asura seemed nervous but not scared enough.

I kept my eyes on her as she tried to take a sip of tea, the cup rattling against the saucer. We all saw it.

Sweat dribbled down the sides of my face and along my forearms, like we'd walked into a sauna. The bulb brightened; all the candles sprang to life.

"You'll stop acting ridiculous right this minute. If you could see yourselves, so serious." She set her tea cup down with shaking hands and scanned the room. There were no other doorways to this room. And the only window was boarded up.

She began her own speech, but even yelling couldn't outpower our volume. We drowned her out.

The single dangling lightbulb shattered in a hail of glass and sparks, but instead of going dark, the light in the room brightened. *The Light is coming. We've called Light.*

My palms grew so warm they felt like they were burning, but around us I felt the light come. Grow. Creeping like a flooded river outside its banks. Moving at a steady pace, over and under, to encompass the whole room.

Ms. Asura swallowed. "This is your last chance."

She means this is her last chance.

We kept repeating ourselves until the words, our sounds, flowed like breaths, like we were one voice, one symphony of light.

The remaining Nocti tried to charge us, but they couldn't come closer. As if they were trying to swim against an ocean current, a wall of light, a shield and a weapon.

Ms. Asura's face reddened, her scars standing out in shrill white. It was as if the tissue had a will of its own.

The light began to bubble against her skin. Nothing in the room was untouched. Light poured from the lightbulb socket, from the electrical outlets, from behind the boarded window, from our fingers and ears and mouths.

Brighter.

Whiter.

Hotter.

My eyes squinted and teared against the intensity of the sensation. It was like eyeing the sun while standing on it. The light began to coalesce, contract, and wrap around the frozen Nocti bodies. It seeped into Ms. Asura's mouth and down into her ears.

I had to close my eyes, but still we called on Light and Good.

I imagined Auntie and Roshana chanting with us on their side. Smiling and sharing their love.

When hot wind blew over my face and tousled my hair, like riding in a fast car with the windows down, I cracked an eyelid.

"You can stop," Juliet said. "She's dead. They're all gone."

Our voices trickled off.

"You watched?" I asked Juliet.

"I had to. I had to know it was finished."

Just then, a Timothy threw open the door with a strength that pushed Rumi out of the way. "Guys, we've got a problem. A big one."

CHAPTER 33
Juliet

She's gone. Ms. Asura is gone.

Woodsmen swarmed in around us. "We saw the Light. Best firework and lightning show we've ever seen."

I couldn't catch my breath. *She's gone. We did it. Took out Nocti.*

"Nelli's down here." We followed Timothy into the basement, Bales tumbling down the stairs in his haste to get to her.

The basement reminded me of maggoty sausage and stinking cheese.

"You okay?" Fara asked me at the top of the stairs.

Woodsmen hung LED lights and flashlights everywhere. We had to act fast. The police were on their way, probably because of the gunshots.

"I don't know." I could barely feel my toes. I felt like I floated above all of us.

"Bales!" Nelli fell into Bales's arms, sobbing. "I thought you were dead." Duct tape hung from her arms and legs. She'd been strapped to the chair.

"Shhh, honey, it's okay. It's over."

On the floor at her feet was the freshly dead body of a man.

"That's the tattoo." Meridian knelt down beside him, checking out a tattoo on the side of his neck.

"And the symbol she had me searching for."

"That's my boss," Nelli cried between the words. "He shot himself when we heard you upstairs. I thought he was going to shoot me, but he just shot himself."

Bales leaned back from her. He pulled his hand away, covered in dark red. "You're bleeding."

"No, I'm not."

"You are." Bales tried to find the wound on her body.

"Bales?" Nelli's voice caught my attention and I walked closer. "Asa Bales look at me."

He was trembling, falling over, his eyes showing lots of white. "Nelli, I love you."

"Bales!" She squealed as he collapsed onto the floor. "Don't you die on me, you hear me?"

I saw a gaping wound as if a bullet had sliced through Nelli's clothes, leaving a trench in her skin. Meridian saw it at the same time that Tens and Rumi began to check on Bales.

"Nelli, you need to sit down." Meridian tugged her. "You're losing a lot of blood."

"I'm not hurt—it's Bales. He's—"

I grabbed a doorjamb, trying to keep from fainting. The hair on the back of my neck stood up and I tasted a menu on my tongue.

I knew the moment my legs collapsed because I sat at my kitchen table. Spread before me were platters of fried chicken, fluffy biscuits, green bean casserole, ears of steaming corn, and the tallest pile of glazed doughnuts I'd ever seen. I brushed the tears off my cheeks. I didn't want to look up, to see who was in the kitchen, at the window, with me.

"I'm dead, aren't I?" Bales asked me.

I couldn't speak, so I nodded, clearing my throat until I could say, "Yes."

"We didn't win after all, did we?"

"Nelli's alive."

"She's hurt." He frowned.

"It's not bad. A few stitches and she'll be okay." I prayed I was telling the truth. Her wound didn't appear life-threatening, but then neither had Bales's. "We should have made you go to the hospital."

"You know I wouldn't have gone no matter what. You

need to know about your father. He's alive. I think he's the reason the Woodsmen made contact—"

A rock band struck up opening chords on the other side of the window. I saw crowds start dancing toward us.

"That's my favorite band." Bales turned back to me, delight filling his voice. "Wow, look at that—my grand-parents are dancing! I have to go now. Tell Nelli I'm sorry. I love her. But I can't stay."

"I will, but what about my dad?" *Wait!*

"Ask Gus about camping in the shades."

"But—" I tried to get him to stay, to tell me more.

Bales slid across the window frame, the food going with him into the crowds.

Kirian held the hand of my mother and both were smiling. "Kirian?" I called. *Why are you happy?*

* * *

I awoke lying on a couch.

"Welcome back." Fara leaned over me. My eyes didn't want to focus. My head throbbed, pounded, and my mouth was sticky dry like salt rocks.

"What happened? Bales, is he really—" I struggled to sit up as Fara pushed me back down.

"I'm sorry, Juliet, he died."

My breath left in a gust. Tears traced into my hairline. "Nelli?"

"She's in the hospital under observation. She didn't

handle it well." Meridian knelt by my head and offered me a sip of grape soda.

Fara whispered, "We found Kirian's body and Aileen's bones. They were in those drawers, with others Nelli searched for. They are safe now. Your FBI showed up."

We found Kirian? Did I hear correctly? "Kirian?"

"Yes." Fara's voice sounded far away and controlled.

Hope blossomed in my chest for a moment. "My mother?" *Could she have been there too?*

Meridian shook her head. "Not yet. But we're not giving up."

I swung my legs over the side of the couch to sit up. "Where are we?"

"At the hospice. We wanted Delia to look at you," Meridian answered me.

"We think the condo is infested," Fara added.

I blanched, confused.

Meridian chuckled. "Bugged."

"Oh." Fara shrugged.

"Meridian, girls, come listen to this." Gus paused the report and turned up the volume. "There's been another racing accident."

"I thought they were canceling the race?" I asked.

"Lots of people objected, said the danger is what makes it exciting. Most years no one gets hurt; people said these were nasty coincidences," Gus answered me.

I rubbed my eyes and held my belly. How long had I slept?

Faye's chest rose and fell, but her body was even smaller than I remembered it. As if her soul would outsize her body, and soon.

Meridian nodded at Gus to press PLAY, and Jessica Martin began: *"First an accident on the track and now off. This team can't catch a break. This year's pole sitter has had to pull his name out of the running this year. His season is over after he was hit crossing Circle Street last night with friends. The hit-and-run accident had many eyewitnesses, but no suspects have been arrested yet. His femur was shattered. We're going to roll footage captured by people waiting to get into the club. They were race fans trying to get autographs, which is why we have any video at all. With a warning for sensitive viewers, this is graphic."*

It wasn't the picture of the black SUV hitting the crowd, but the sound of impact and the shattering of breaking bones, of traumatized flesh, that made me chalky. *Like butchering a carcass for parts.*

The reporter continued. *"Six others are also hospitalized for their injuries. Many considered this team and driver the favorites for this year's milk drink, so this development opens up the race to smaller teams."*

The in-studio newscaster couldn't keep the glee off his face. Carnage made for good ratings. *"Should make it fun to watch."*

"Yes indeedy."

"What do you make of that?" Gus asked.

A huge part of me desperately hoped they'd cancel

the event before anyone else got hurt. The other part knew the Nocti would just strike somewhere else when we weren't prepared.

Meridian answered what all of us were thinking. "I don't know."

"How is Faye?" I asked to fill the silence.

Flesh hung off Gus like a shell. This vigil was breaking him down. "She won't go. Every time Dolores shows up, Faye rallies, or at least her vitals increase again. Like she can't let go." He leaned down close to Faye's ear. "We'll be okay. Meridian and Juliet are here. Let them help you."

"Gus, why don't you go home, change your clothes, eat something. We'll call you if anything changes."

"I need to lie down for a while." He nodded.

"I promise we'll call."

"I'd just like her to let go now. I don't understand what she's waiting for." He kissed her cheek and left us alone in the room with Faye's shell.

"Gus?" I asked as he picked up his car keys.

"What, chickadee?"

"Does camping in the shade mean anything to you?"

He started to shake his head. "I usually pitch my tent under a tree for shade."

My face must have looked as crestfallen as I felt because he paused longer. "My parents always took me to Shades State Park as a kid. Gorgeous place to camp. Lost a little luster when I grew up and found out the history and real name."

"What's that?" My pulse galloped.

"It's called Shades of Death State Park officially."

Fara made an ick face and said, "Sounds like a great place to camp."

"Shade . . . where did I hear that?" Meridian started jotting notes down, but I couldn't bear to take my eyes off Gus.

I saw Gus struggling through exhaustion to connect the dots for us. "There are several stories. One is a woman killed her abusive husband and buried his body there. The town all knew but kept it secret because they knew what he'd done to her for years. Another is that there was a huge Native American slaughter. Some say it was an ancient place where a war was fought and many died. Now people call it Shades and don't know what the full name is."

Mini meowed and pranced out from under Faye's bed.

"Baba said the ancestors and Ahura Mazda, the Creators, used our texts to communicate with us. Juliet, when Tony asked his question at our Nowruz, what was the answer from the book?" Fara barely breathed.

I'd been trying to puzzle it out for days, so I knew it by heart. " 'The sun is relentless this week. For all I'd like is a tall glass of punch and a nap in the cool shade for all time.' "

"Child, what was his question?" Gus turned to Juliet.

"He said he wanted to know where my mother was."
Could she be at Shades?

"Oh, Lordy." Meridian paced. "Auntie gave me a message. She didn't understand it, but she said your mother was in shade."

Hope felt like a warm bowl of soup on a bitterly cold day. "Maybe my mother's body is somewhere at Shades?"

"It's a drive from here and it's a large park. I don't know how to find anything that hasn't already been stumbled over." Gus frowned.

"What are the chances the Nocti have moved Roshana or will follow you down there to hurt you?" Gus cautioned.

"I think toying with Juliet was solely on Ms. Asura. With her dead, I think they'll move on to bigger games," Meridian answered Gus.

She glanced at the television screen and whistled. Cells of severe-weather storm clouds were three states over and predicted to head straight here. They didn't seem to be diminishing in strength as they neared. Hail, tornadoes, powerful straight-line winds, and drenching, flooding rain were all over the radar. *Do we pray for bad weather?* "Do they cancel the race for rain?"

"Delay it anyway," Gus said.

"I hate to think tornadoes might be a pleasant alternative to the Nocti's plans, but . . ." I trailed off as Fara said, "Tony is on his way."

I wanted to start walking to the park that moment; instead I busied myself moistening Faye's mouth, squeezing her hand and brushing her hair out of her face. Her eyes were sunken more, and her pallor was yellow where it wasn't bruising. *We're here, Faye. You are not alone.*

The television brought up race graphics and Fara clicked off the mute. "Guys? Did you know there was a parade the day before the race?"

Rows of bleachers were being hauled in and the roads lined with black-and-white checkered flags.

"What?" Meridian turned the volume up.

CHAPTER 34

Dolores arrived to sit with Faye and kicked us out. So we headed back to the cottage. I wasn't sure how Juliet was handling Bales's death; I was shaky enough for both of us. I took out a mental box, stuffed the grief into it, and turned all my attention to the next few critical days. I would allow myself time to grieve later. *Way later.*

Fara finished stacking the paintings and photographs from the walls. With all the recovered Nocti documents, we needed all the space to figure out our next move. Tens added pages to the timeline until it covered the middle of two walls like a weird kind of ribbon on a gift. *Some gift.*

Rumi held a journal in his hands; he thumbed through

it without seeming to read any of it. The corners were blackened.

"Rumi?"

"We found this at the museum. It fell behind the fire. She was trying to burn it."

"That was in your nain's box, right?" I squatted down. Rumi's vitality was sapped and he finally appeared his age.

He nodded. "My uncle's." He opened his mouth and closed it, his gaze drifting off.

"And you asked your siblings about him, right?" If I remembered correctly, we'd found this journal in February and wondered at the time if Rumi's uncle was Fenestra or Nocti. I didn't like the expression in Rumi's eyes.

"Yes. No one remembered hearing of him. Knowing of him."

"And the Nocti stole it from your studio with the other papers?"

Rumi nodded. "I think he's of the Dark, lass. I think he left the Light behind."

"Why, Rumi?"

"That symbol she wanted is here. He talks of hurting animals to practice. Of drowning . . ." Rumi's voice trailed off.

I gripped his hand. "May I see that?"

His fingers relaxed and the little book fell into my hands. There were sketches and diagrams, notes, and seemingly endless fascinations with drowning and water.

Tony clicked off his phone. "Do you want the good news or the bad news?"

Fara shrugged. The rest of us simply waited.

"That was Timothy. The crusade to cancel the race this year because of the 'Centennial Curse' is proving the marketing miracle. More people are buying tickets simply to prove that Hoosiers don't believe in superstition. Rumor has it there are no tickets left for Sunday's race—they are sold out for the first time in decades."

"Which means how many people?"

"The owners don't release solid numbers, but estimates say record crowds are predicted to swell the festivities from a quarter million to nearly half a million people from all over the world."

"That's a lot of people in one place."

"Then we better get to work. The Woodsmen's clues were snakes, a driver, and artesian something." It's like a crossword from hell.

Juliet hummed her mother's song.

My heart hurt. I knew everything in her wanted to run to Shades and find her mother. And there she was, sitting here patiently, trying to do what we so desperately needed and help us figure out the Nocti strategies.

"The Woodsmen scoured the museum. They're going over everything. So far it sounds like the parade might be a dress rehearsal but not so big that the race is canceled."

"That's a fine line." *Too fine.*

Fara stared at Juliet, then glanced up at me with a sad smile. We had to be thinking the same thing.

"You need to go," I said, standing up. "Go to Shades, find Roshana. Go."

"But—" Tens tried to interrupt me.

"Can you try to be back for the race itself?" I asked Tony.

Juliet sat still as if she thought I might change my mind.

"We'll do our best." Tony nodded.

"We have the Woodsmen. We can cover the parade tonight."

"What about Faye?" Juliet asked.

"She'll understand." *If she dies while we're saving others, she'll forgive us for breaking our promise.*

"Nelli?"

"Is in the hospital and not leaving for a few days. Stop coming up with reasons not to go and GO!" I pulled her upright.

In a tiny voice, she asked, "What if she's not there?"

"If she's not there, we'll keep looking. But you won't be able to focus on the race until you've at least tried, right?"

She nodded.

"So go!" *Go, already.*

Fara and Tens quickly repacked a bag of survival gear, food, and water that he always kept handy in case we had to run without much notice.

"Are you sure?" Juliet glanced at the door longingly.

"Of course. You've done enough," I said, convinced this was the right course of action.

She wrenched me into her arms and clung so tight I was afraid a rib might snap. "Thank you. Thank you. Thank you."

I smiled for the first time in hours. "Go."

We are horribly outnumbered, have no idea how to stop the Nocti's plans, and might be dead ourselves before the weekend is over. Why not give Juliet a shot?

CHAPTER 35
Juliet

Mini lounged in the backseat when we opened the doors of the car. With no bandages to hide under, her new pink healing skin, scabs, and stitches gave her a nightmarish appearance. And with hair that seemed more like five o'clock shadow rather than the long downy fluff I was used to, she was a candidate for a blue ribbon in an ugly contest. The determined glint in her eyes and the twitch of her tail told me she was coming along no matter what I might think.

Please let us find my mommy. Please let us find her.

"I'll take the back." Fara didn't seem to acknowledge

Mini's attitude as she flipped through a book about state parks.

"They close at dusk." Tony gripped the steering wheel as we headed east on 32 toward Shades State Park. "It's three thousand acres."

"We have time, or we'll stay overnight; we have until tomorrow morning to get back for the race." Fara shrugged and said it like rules were made to be broken.

Nicole? If you can hear me, I need my guardian angel on this, okay? I know I didn't believe you before, so maybe you can't help, but if you can . . .

As we passed fields and small towns, I tasted buttered popcorn and root-beer floats. We turned down one state road after another.

Tony turned on the radio, probably to break the silence.

I was all but shedding my skin by the time we pulled into the main parking lot. I rubbed the photograph of my parents between my fingers for luck. We swung out onto a muddy, rocky path, taking it all in and then some. S'mores and artificial orange drink powder danced at the back of my tongue.

Tony grabbed the backpack out of the trunk with food and water, folding shovels, and a roll of plastic. Fara's knives were all sheathed and sharpened. Her chain necklaces hung at the ready. I knew they easily broke at one joint to become weapons in her hands.

While blooming and leafed out trees towered over us,

we stood at the entrance and studied the list of trails. *No arrows. No divine signs. No clues.*

"Any ideas?" Fara took a few steps in several directions as if testing the earth.

"What did your mother's book say?"

I opened the book to the same page Fara read from at Nowruz and repeated. "She wants a cold drink of punch in the shade." We scrutinized the options. *The wrong choice and we'll waste precious time.*

Fara pointed. "What about heading this way?"

"The Devil's Punchbowl?" Tony asked.

I nodded, tucking the book into the backpack. "That feels right."

"Keep your eyes peeled for spirits—they may be able to tell you something," Fara instructed like I was supposed to flag down anyone I saw and ask them if they were dead. *Sure. Excuse me, are you haunting the park? Can you tell me if you've seen any suspicious behavior?* I still didn't understand quite how it worked for me to recognize those lost in time. Meridian tried to explain the feelings she had or the clues she saw, but I was focused way too much on the logistics of being a window. *She makes it look easy.*

The trails followed creek beds and ravines, where glaciers cut through the earth on their move north. Rock walls the color of sesame seeds and horseradish rose around us. Under our feet, the foliage blended together in a green sea of kale, parsley, and limes.

We walked to a point where the path seemed to disappear. I think I must have gasped at the vastness of the wilderness around us. Fara's gaze sharpened and she said sternly to me, "You focus on the little bits; we'll find her. Remember, let your heart guide us."

I nodded. As they began to descend a ladder to where the trail picked up again, I heard a call. "Wait up! Hey, you!"

I saw no one, so I finished my descent. Then I saw a ranger running toward us.

Tony and Fara strode ahead in the opposite direction as I turned toward the voice.

I said, "Tony, Fara, the ranger—"

Tony frowned. "What ranger—"

My legs crumpled and I was at the window, sitting at the kitchen table. "You're not a ranger, are you?"

His uniform seemed slightly off, as if he was wearing one several generations old. He didn't mind my question and answered, "I was up until a few days ago. Do you know who won the World Series? Did the Mets beat Boston?"

I shook my head. "I'm sorry, but I don't know."

"Man, 1986 just hasn't been my year!" He tossed his hat down on the table. He seemed prepared to sit here with me forever.

"Um, maybe if you turn around and go through that window, it'll get better?" *I have to work on my conversation skills. What does Meridian say to her souls?*

"Might as well." He huffed and picked up his hat before smashing it back onto his head.

As he started to step over the sill, I stopped him. "Wait! You haven't seen anyone like me, have you?"

He squinted, nodding. "Blond, scars on her face?"

"Yeah." I licked my lips, trying to keep the excitement out of my voice.

"Not for a while. She walked trail seven a lot over by the Devil. Didn't talk, though, so I gave up chatting with her."

"Thanks." I motioned for him to keep going. His window smelled of hot dogs and yeasty beer in the baseball stadium behind him. I wondered if he'd be able to see the decades-old game from the front row. The fans started a wave with him at the center and I blinked back into my world.

"Welcome back." Tony tapped my nose with his finger.

My head was in Fara's lap and Tony wiped my face with a cool cloth.

"He used to see her by the Punchbowl on trail seven."

"So we're going the right way." Fara grinned.

"He said it had been a while."

"Anything else?"

"Yeah, he thought it was 1986 and during baseball season."

"So, take it with a grain of salt." Fara's optimism made it impossible to stay pensive. Then her expression darkened. "Don't react, but someone very alive is following us."

"Who?" *Nocti? Another soul? A hiker going our way?*

"What do we do?" I questioned.

"Nothing yet. Let's pretend we haven't noticed. Stay between me and Tony, okay?"

"Let's keep going." I stood up and forced my legs to move. Humming mom's Wildcat song with each step, we trekked deeper into the woods. Around us, late afternoon light glazed the world with honey.

We didn't talk much, simply persevered. I wanted to ask Fara if we were still being followed but I figured she'd give us the all-clear if that changed. And she wasn't speaking.

As twilight approached, we heard footsteps coming toward us.

"Hide." Fara tugged us both off the trail under an overhang and behind a fallen tree. We ducked, holding motionless, hoping if they weren't looking for us, they wouldn't see us. *We're invisible. We're invisible.* I pressed the photograph of my parents between my fingers.

The chatting pair who passed us wore official, seemingly up-to-date ranger gear. We listened to them discuss unruly campers and the need for better security after dark. We held our positions until they were long past.

Owls began hooting their "who-cooks-for-you" as bats skittered low around the trees, snacking on king-sized mosquitoes. The oak and maple trees seemed to grow taller around us as light slipped farther behind the horizon.

All around me were lichen- and moss-covered rocks and tree trunks in a fuzzy carpet. Chunks of limestone littered the ground like a handful of garnish on a platter of food.

Nettles grew as tall as us and the undergrowth was lush, full, and impossible to see through. I knew a recipe for nettle tea that belonged to one of the deceased at DG. I could see her face but not her name.

Blisters rubbed my heels raw. "Are we still being followed?" I let the question hang, hoping Fara knew what I meant.

"Yes." She didn't even pause, which meant I had to keep going or she'd run over me.

I deflated. "We're not going to find her, are we?" Between watching my feet and trying to spot any sign of my mother's bones, frustration ate at me. If her remains were lying in an easy-to-see area, they would have long since been carried away, or reported.

"We've only started looking. Don't give up now," Fara reassured me.

"Juliet, we'll be here every day, all summer season, if we have to. If she's here, we'll find her." Tony's voice was troubled; it was clear he thought we were chasing shadows too.

Don't give up. You've waited this long. They mean it; they'll search until we find her.

We came to a fork in the road that was unmarked. Dirt went to the right and more went to the left. Both directions appeared the same.

"Which way is the Punchbowl?" Tony passed out headlamps, which we all turned on to their lowest setting.

Already on edge, a rustle under a canopy of ferns spooked us. Fara leapt between us, snapping her chains between her fists.

"Meow."

"That's Mini!" I said as my cat poked her head out.

"Meow." She pranced to the middle of the right-hand path.

"We go right." Fara's decisiveness usually felt over-powering, but today I welcomed it.

I leaned down to stroke Mini's face and she nudged my hand. "She can't walk all the way." I picked her up and she laid her head on my shoulder with a grateful meow.

We continued on, turning the headlamps higher to see the path and a few feet around us.

The sound of moving water, rushing against rocks, came from our right. Steps carved out of rock led down to a pool and a stream.

"Break time?" Tony asked. "Anyone want food? I have cookies from Helios."

"You need to keep your energy up," Fara said to me when I wanted to keep going.

I placed Mini in my lap and nibbled on the chewy goodness. "Drink all of this." Tony handed me a bottle of juice.

I watched the water of the stream cascade, flying through the air. It reflected back all of our light, twisting over rounded rocks and smoothed walls.

"I wish I had that goop," Tony muttered, slathering another layer of cortisone cream over mosquito bites.

"What is goop?" Fara asked him.

"Josiah delivered a sticky lotion for Tens and Meridian when the Nocti spiked the poison ivy. It made them feel better."

"What about the ivy?" she asked.

I said, "Ms. Asura somehow controlled the ivy, made it move and made it hurt us." Kirian's face suspended before me. "She used it to kill Kirian." I whispered this last sentence.

"Ah, and you told the ivy to stop this, yes? She is not the only one who can ask energy to aid."

"What?" I swung my head so fast in her direction that the headlamp blinded her. *Huh? We can use this too?*

Tony asked calmly, "Fara, can you please tell us more about this ability?"

"All angels can call upon creation." She shrugged. "You didn't know this either?"

"No. No, we didn't." Tony shook his head.

Fara frowned. "I do not know how it works; my kind do not usually have this ability. My baba, he say I don't need to know yet."

"How do you think it works?" Tony tried a different angle.

"Anything of the Creators' has energy that can be"— Fara paused—"plugged into?"

"Tapped into?" Tony asked.

"Yes, tapped." She smiled. "But I do not know how."

Silently, I contemplated the sounds of the night coming alive around us. Scurrying and chirping. I thought really hard at a rock by my foot. *Please move. Please?*

"I should tell Tens. Maybe Meridian can try." Tony dialed Tens to tell him about Fara's statement. "Right. Okay." He hung up. "We definitely need to be back for the race tomorrow."

"Time to search, then." Fara nodded and squinted at me, at Mini. "Where now?" She shone her light both directions down the stream.

Sudden tears of uncertainty gathered in my eyes. *Mommy? Nicole? Kirian? Is anyone listening? Help us, please!*

A spark caught my attention. *A firefly? Come on, show us the way.* It blinked again.

"That way." I pointed toward the lone, tiny insect lantern. "We'll go that way."

CHAPTER 36

We knew the Nocti planned on striking at the race and not the parade. *At least we think we know.* But untangling a plot that covered land the size of a small city and trying to save the lives of innocents in a crowd of half a million, with only a few cryptic clues? That felt downright, appallingly impossible. So we were at the parade tonight hoping our presence would keep the Nocti in check and buy us the ability to stop them before tomorrow.

My thoughts kept straying to Juliet and her quest to find bones in the forest, which had a definite needle-in-a-haystack feel to it. *Creator, please let Juliet find what she needs.*

"Supergirl? They'll be okay. Fara's tough; she can handle it," Tens reassured me.

"Yeah, but can Juliet handle it if they don't find Roshana?"

"She has to. She'll find the strength."

I wish I had Tens's confidence. "Do you think Sergio is here somewhere?"

"I hope. I'd like to talk to him." Tens's voice was grim and controlled. He continued. "You gotta focus on the here and now, okay?"

"I know." I sighed.

The parade route was marked on the map Timothy gave us. Woodsmen from all over the nation were driving and flying into town—more arrived every hour. They'd sent out the battle cry, though how exactly that worked, I didn't ask. We just needed numbers on our side.

A Woodsman gave us green baseball caps that matched the ones they wore, except on the tree was the letter *F* instead of *WoW*. "Wear these. If asked, the password is *speed*, but you shouldn't need it. Hear anything, see anything, use these." He handed us walkie-talkies. "Try to look less like security and more like tourists, please!" He laughed at our serious expressions. "Our job is to alert police to anything suspicious, okay? That's it. We have hundreds of people in these stands on our side, and beat cops are likely to not ask too many questions."

I'd prayed for weather cancellations, but that was asking too much. And the macabre nature of the days leading up to the race only meant more gawkers and sensationalists had purchased tickets. *Like bringing a picnic to an execution.*

The route started on Pennsylvania Street, made a fishhook around Washington, and then back up Meridian. We'd taken positions on the corners where the parade turned onto my road. *Okay, so Meridian Street was Meridian before I was born, but I claim it.* Crowds dibbed the prime seats hours ago. Metal railings blocked off access and checkered flag runners created one lane down the center of the road.

At the intersection, a police car flipped on the sirens and flashers to get through a mass of people. *What if they turn on all the sirens again? Will people leave?*

Black-and-white race flags were stuck in the tops of overflowing multicolored flower baskets hanging from each lamppost. The rooftops and balconies of all the buildings along the route were chockablock full of spectators. *None of whom wore signs screaming, "I want to kill you all." Too bad. Too easy.*

Tens stuck an earbud in and listened to the radio coverage begin. "They're starting."

I closed my eyes. Willed my heart rate to stay normal even though I couldn't stop the surge of adrenaline shooting through my body.

Balloons in the race colors of green, white, yellow, and black were handed out before the race began, making those in the seats an integral part of the decorations.

Kids, from toddlers to ten-year-olds, were down along the railings to catch sight of their sports heroes and to collect the candy and race car toys clowns passed out as they walked by. Several of the clowns seemed to have odd contacts in their eyes—or black pits of void. *Nocti*.

"Tens?" I squeezed his forearm.

"The clowns?"

"You see them?" I asked.

"Yep, did they have to be so obvious? Clowns? No one likes clowns anyway. I'll call it in." He clicked on the walkie-talkie and I saw a few green hats move farther up the route. I turned my eyes back to the passing—

POP!

I ducked as a shot was fired.

"Easy. Just a balloon popping," Tens soothed me.

I watched the crowds, searching for more faces that held blackened eyes, blank from the void of Dark.

Slowly, a murmur of applause and chatter began to drift over us. It grew in intensity and volume as the first floats rolled closer. The sun ducked behind clouds as if ashamed to watch.

"They're coming toward us now," Tens informed me, his head two stories above mine. *Maybe that's a slight exaggeration.*

As lines of convertibles drove near, the announcer introduced city and track officials over the loudspeaker.

"Anything?" I asked.

"Nada," Tens answered.

I nudged my way closer as a giant balloon panda came barreling around the corner. It was clear the handlers had trouble controlling it in the quickening breeze.

I glanced up at the sky; gloomy storm clouds boiled on the horizon. I'd given up trying to predict the weather this month. *One minute sunny, the next hail. Probably too far away for anyone to worry? Maybe?* "What are they saying about the weather?" I spoke into the walkie-talkie.

Timothy's voice came back: "A chance of a thunder cell, maybe hail, but they think the parade will be over before it spins into the neighborhood."

As a marching band belted out a local fight song, the crowd surged to its feet singing along. I stared at the stands across the road. Then, up behind them, movement on a balcony caught my attention.

"Sergio?" Could it be him? Right size, but in the jacket and hat it was too hard to tell.

I watched him pop a balloon. Then another. Deliberately. Then text or type something on his handheld. He disappeared back inside. With the music, no one heard the popping this time. "Tens, up there. Brick building, third-floor balcony."

Tens turned and we saw Sergio reappear with another couple of balloons and a girl who was as preppy as she could be in a pink polo and plaid Bermudas. *I don't know why I keep expecting bad guys to wear black.* He let one balloon go. She let the second one drop next to his. They were heavier than they should have been, drifting down into the unsuspecting crowd below them.

I glanced away, checking to see if anyone noticed, and saw another woman drop a balloon from a building two blocks down. *What's in the balloons? Nothing good.*

"We have to get people out of here," I said into the walkie-talkie, hoping I could be heard above the fiddling and guitar of the oncoming music float.

A country singer blared his latest hit from a tall boot of a platform, obscuring my view of the balconies. Next in line, an assortment of gowned race princesses and princes drew lots of catcalls.

Tens grabbed me, leaned down, and shouted in my ear, "Timothy wants to know what makes those balloons different from all the rest? What do they report to the police?"

I swiveled, and everywhere I turned, helium-filled balloons bounced and twirled. "They look the same," I whispered. *Exactly the same.* "They sink?"

He nodded, then turned back to the walkie-talkie. "We can't go to the cops with this. There's no way they'll just clear it out because of suspicious balloons."

"What is inside them?"

Bombs? Germs? Chemicals? It doesn't matter. I watched Sergio reappear on the balcony with an entire bouquet of dozens. These weren't falling; they floated exactly like those around us.

"We're running out of time," Tens said.

"Think. Think. Think."

I glanced behind Tens at the building and my jaw dropped. "That's it. Come on!" I knew how to clear the parade. *Do we have enough time?*

CHAPTER 37
Juliet

Thunder rumbled so near it shook the ground beneath our feet. I snapped my teeth and bit my tongue. Salty blood filled my mouth.

Left. Right. Step up. Step down. Don't trip. Where's the firefly taking us?

We had walked so far, up ladders, down rocks, across wooden footbridges, and under the overhangs of limestone walls. We were no longer on a marked path. We'd seen no evidence of humans for an hour or more. I'd lost track of time keeping the firefly in sight, and if we were still being followed, I had no idea.

I tripped, unable to catch myself because I clutched Mini against my chest. My knee snapped against a rock and shot pains up through my hips and back. When I righted myself, the firefly was nowhere to be seen.

"Where did it go?" I twisted in all directions.

Thunder crashed, drowning out all other sounds.

"I don't know. Let's wait here a minute. See if it comes back." Tony handed me a water bottle. Night out among the trees of this forest, under the blanket of storm clouds, was so much blacker that any night I'd seen living at DG or in downtown Carmel.

I started to argue with them when I saw a naked man stand up from the underbrush and head toward us. *He's transparent!* I stifled a scream. "Fara," I said, sitting down quickly.

As he approached, the hair on my arms raised. I gazed into his eyes. Then I was in my kitchen watching as he nodded to me while jumping through.

"Juliet!" Auntie called to me. I leaned in and saw my mother standing straighter. Her scars seemed less severe. Sunny and bright beyond the window, animals roamed abundantly; the forest was thicker, loftier than anything I'd ever imagined.

"Auntie! Mom!" I waved back.

"Call the light to help you. You did it with the firefly, but you need more than that."

"How?" I yelled.

"Juliet?" Tony wiped my face. "Are you back?"

I blinked open my eyes. "Auntie said to call the light." I tasted dried fruit, venison, and walnuts.

Call the light? How?

The first drops of rain smacked the canopy above us, hitting leaves that acted like little umbrellas, until it poured. In seconds we were all sopping wet; the sheets of rain obscured even the bright beams of light from our headlamps.

Fara stood a few feet away with her back to us. She'd turned her headlamp off.

"If you're okay, I'll go scout that way?" Tony asked.

"Sure, go." I swallowed more water, grateful this was a warm rain and not chilling.

Tony set off and came back to us quickly. "We can't go any farther that way. It's a cliff above a ravine. In this weather, it's too risky. We'll wait it out."

He and Fara exchanged a glance. We needed to get back to the car and on the road before sunrise to make it to Indy in time for the race.

"I think we're still being followed," Fara said. "We might be running out of time."

"I don't know where to go from here." I dashed at my tears.

"You saw Auntie again at the window?" Tony sat down. Both he and Fara sandwiched me.

"Yes, a Native American used the window and she was there. With Mom."

"She said something?" Fara prodded.

"To call the light." I shook my head. "She said I'd called the firefly but needed more help." *There's no way I called the firefly.*

Lightning flickered, followed by the Creator's percussion.

"Why not try?" Tony demanded, excitement filling his voice. "They wouldn't ask you to do something you're incapable of. I don't believe that."

"How?" I asked.

"How did we dispatch that Nocti? We believed we could." Fara wrapped her arm around me.

"Fireflies don't come out in thunderstorms, do they?" I asked, trying to think of another light source.

"What does?" She smiled at me.

Lightning? Lightning!

Comprehension made Tony suck in his breath and I nodded. I cradled Mini against me, thinking over and over again, *Lightning, light the way to my mother. Show me how to love her. Lightning, light the way to my mother. Show me how to love her.*

Lightning flashed and thunder rolled.

Fara and Tony held still. Both probably praying.

I gave every possible part of myself to the words.

"It's getting closer," Fara whispered as the lightning seemed to change course and the thunder stalled over the top of us. "Keep going."

I didn't open my eyes but felt Tony stand and leave.

Another volley of light behind my lids and shaking rippled around us.

"Lightning, light the way—"

"It's working, Juliet, keep going!" Tony yelled back to us.

I bore down with all of my being.

Several sequential flashes and a loud crack sounded almost on top of us. The rain lifted abruptly, continuing east and away from us.

Mini squirmed from my arms and I opened my eyes. Tony was coming back toward me. "You need to see this."

I hobbled to my feet. Blood rushed to legs that had fallen asleep cramped in the tight space. I limped my way to the cliff face with Fara at my side.

Below us in the ravine, a giant tree was cleaved into halves by lightning. Still smoking, the charred outline was evident only because behind it, a low glow flickered like a candle.

CHAPTER 38

As I ran, Tens easily kept up with me, his legs eating up twice the amount of pavement as mine. We headed away from the parade route.

Right a block.

Left a block.

Tens simply met my pace. Two months ago, I wouldn't have been able to sprint like this without sputtering out, but the training he insisted on paid off. *Prepping.*

My legs took over and I pumped my arms.

Three more blocks.

"The drivers' convertibles are part of the parade now. They've entered the course," Tens said as we slid around a group of race fans spilling out from a bar. We knew the sequence of the parade floats by heart.

Please let us get there in time. Which building is it? I scanned the doors and addresses we passed.

Finally.

An eight-inch-wide metal sign marked the old, nondescript stone office building.

We'd set records with the number of tornadoes this spring, including the one that took out DG. A surprising number of them came out of nowhere, with no warning and no prediction. All the warning people had, rested on hearing the tornado sirens. I hoped the weekly drills and unusually active tornado season would pay off with antsy parade fans. *Maybe people are jittery enough to scatter.* I glanced up at the sky. The nasty, roiling clouds moved toward us from Juliet's direction. *I hope they're okay.*

To Tens I said, "We need to set off the tornado sirens." I grabbed the door handles and shook. *Locked.*

Tens looked through the glass panes and around the locks. "Stand back," he said, leaning away, then slamming his leg into the doors. *Once, twice.*

The wood around the locks splintered and caved. The locks held, but the door didn't.

"Come on." I stopped to find the office number at the bottom of the stairs. The old building was pre-elevator, and what little ambient light was left didn't reach the hallway. We had Tens's cell phone light and that was all.

The sirens were computerized across the state. Each monitoring location had an override system, though.

Thank the investigative news team at Channel 6 for my knowledge. Late-night news was detailed enough to put anyone but me back to sleep quickly.

We pounded up the stairs. INDIANAPOLIS WEATHER SERVICE. Locked. I unzipped my bag and held the gun Tens insisted I carry. *Don't make me use this.*

I stepped back without Tens asking and again he broke in the door.

"What the hell?" A guy threw down his magazine. The poor kid was probably a college intern and got stuck with the parade shift. They didn't expect problems. I was sure any real threatening weather increased office staff exponentially.

"Flip the tornado sirens on. Please," I asked nicely. *We don't have time to argue.*

"Yeah, sure. N-no problem," he sputtered, and reached for the computer.

"Don't touch it." Tens held out his handgun like it was an extension of his hand.

"It's a felony, you know." The kid held his hands up.

Tens didn't blink. "I'm pretty sure shooting you is too."

"You are so dead, man." The kid glanced at his computer screen.

"We're trying to keep people from dying. Please," I pleaded.

"Tell them we held a gun to your head," Tens added.

"You are," he pointed out.

"It's pointed at your package. Don't be melodramatic," Tens scoffed.

"Shit." He looked like he might throw up the greasy taco dinner the wrappings around him attested to.

We don't have time to wait. "Just do it. Please," I begged. "It's not on the computer. Dial the phone." I held out my gun and walked closer. "Please don't make me shoot you."

He blanched. "How do you know that?"

"Television." To Tens, I said, "Computers crash. Phone lines don't go down as easily because they've buried cables. It's a code." I looked down at the phone. "And it's right here." A list of codes, including the alarm.

I smiled and punched 1-4-3 into the phone. *Nice coincidence, Auntie.*

Less than a second later, the sirens blared.

Tens used plastic strips to cuff the kid's hands and feet together in his chair.

"You can't leave me like this," he said.

"We need the sirens to keep going," I answered.

We ran down the steps and into the street.

Already people moved in waves out of the stands, down side streets toward their cars, and ducked into buildings with storm shelters in the basements. The flood of humanity moved away from the Nocti threat. *Now we pray that this time we're ahead of them.*

CHAPTER 39

Tens and I stayed in the neighborhood, out of sight, until the intern freed himself or backup arrived and the sirens cut off. Tens used the walkie-talkie to let the Woodsmen know the siren was false and the Nocti might continue with their plan. WoW sent a car to grab us and get us out of this part of the city.

"I'm exhausted," I said to Tens as we climbed into a Woodsman's car.

One Timothy spoke into a cell phone and relayed, "They're shutting down the main roads looking for"—he paused—"you two."

"I guess he freed himself," I said.

"We're heading to the Westfield house. Sit tight." The driver took a hasty left and wound his way through residential streets.

"Don't worry, in ten minutes there will be three eyewitnesses who not only have photographs of different people exiting the building, but also he'll change his mind. It'll all go away."

"How?"

"It's what we do." The Woodsman shrugged and turned back to the road.

Could that be it? Was the parade the only thing they'd planned?

"We need to check on our friends," I said as we were hurried inside the Westfield house.

Tens dialed his phone. "Tony? Uh-huh . . . right . . . okay . . . we'll need you . . . Tony? Dammit, the phone disconnected."

"What did he say?"

"I only caught every third word but he mentioned the fireflies and moving energy—said your name and lightning. Does that mean anything to you?"

I shook my head in frustration. "Try again."

Every time Tens dialed, he got a busy signal or voice mail.

Timothy suggested, "Could be the weather coming from that direction."

Or something worse. Did voice mail mean they were merely out of the service area, or did we need to wonder what might have happened to them? I frowned.

"Don't worry yet," Tens said, planting a quick kiss on my forehead.

"If I could get to the window, I could check in with Auntie."

"Need me to kill someone?" an overzealous Woodsman asked.

"No!" I yelled.

"No!" Tens shouted.

The guy frowned. Turning red, he said, "Sorry, just a joke."

"Not funny." I shook my head.

Another Woodsman said, "The apartment above the garage has a ghost. Would that work?"

"The wiring is bad," another answered. "Not a ghost."

"Wiring doesn't turn the thermostat up to ninety degrees every freakin' day."

It might work. Auntie told me I should be able to manifest the window myself, even without a soul, but if there was a willing soul ready to go, that seemed easier given the time constraints. "Is it close?" I asked.

"Out there." He pointed toward the back of the house.

"Take me."

Tens grabbed my arm and opened his mouth. I knew he hated me taking risks.

I shook him off. "It can't hurt, right? You stay here, keep trying to get ahold of everyone."

Two Woodsmen escorted me outside, through the rain, to a garage apartment. One opened the door and checked to make sure it was empty before letting me in. I almost laughed. Souls don't jump out and say, "Boo." *At least, they haven't yet.*

Immediately, the room's temperature elevated twenty degrees. And I was at a window.

I found myself in a fire station. The window looked down the pole and into frenzy below. *That's an odd perspective. Can't say I've seen any windows in the floor before.*

"Hello," I said.

"I'm Hank. Pleased to meet you." A fully suited fireman, in boots and coat, introduced himself to me, even shaking my hand.

"Would you like to join them?" I pointed down.

"Sure would," he said, stepping to the pole and swinging a leg around. "Never was going to hurt anyone, you know."

"I know."

"Those boys were just so fun to play with." He laughed and slid down. I peered over, hoping Auntie was down there. And that I wouldn't see any of my friends. *No one I know.* Which was a good thing, because that gave me hope the rest of them were all alive.

I blinked and my body reacted with no lag time. I moved back toward the door; there wasn't time to be excited about reaching this milestone. "The wiring is fine and the thermostat should be okay too."

"Told you." They bonked each other on their heads.

Tens was huddled in conversation with two other Woodsmen when I returned.

I shook my head as he came over to me. "No luck finding Auntie, but no one else either," I said.

"Good. There are reports of a white powder on the sidewalks at the parade, but the rain is making it impossible to collect. They don't know if it was a substance or residue from the float decorations. It's washing away too fast." Tens grunted in frustration.

"Just in case, they've called all cops in for duty. Even from surrounding areas. They've locked down the track to be safe. No one in and no one out until the morning cannon."

"So was it an experiment or were they truly trying to hurt people?" I wanted to know.

"We don't know yet, but assume the worst and hope for the best."

I nodded. *Kinda hate not knowing.* "Then that's it until tomorrow, right?" I asked Timothy.

He answered, shaking his head, "No, odds are the Nocti won't do anything tonight with the elevated police presence, but the parties started at sundown and continue until the morning cannon, then keep going all day long."

"There are parties?" I asked. *All I want is sleep.*

"Yeah, people camp outside the track, drink themselves into a stupor, and do dumb shit. Excuse my French," Tim replied, a soft blush on his cheeks.

"Fact is, the Novelty doesn't have to do anything—there's plenty of mayhem and injury without their help," someone else added.

"So we're going to the track now?" I sighed.

"You need to check on your friends, right? We've got a team patrolling. Why don't we call you if anything seems amiss? Otherwise come when you can."

"Oh, but—" I hated the idea of someone else having to do my job.

"Rumi needs us," Tens said quietly. "He's asking for you."

It was clear the conversation between Tens and the Woodsmen while I was soul hunting was much more detailed and explicit than what I was hearing.

"You want anyone to go with you?" Timothy asked. "As backup eyes?"

"No." I was too tired to explain. "We'll be fine." I wanted a few uninterrupted minutes with Tens. I missed him. Even though we were spending every minute together, it seemed like we were very far apart.

Someone handed Tens the keys to their truck with a shrug. *I guess providing transportation is part of their job too.*

Huge, heavy drops fell so close together it was like the Creators merely turned on an industrial-sized faucet. The windshield wipers barely kept up with the downpour. Streets were flooded, the storm drains overflowing with so much water.

Tens headed toward Rumi's. We didn't speak. There wasn't anything to say. *Or maybe there's too much to say?*

Finally, at the outskirts of the town, the rain stopped as abruptly as it started.

All of the lights were on in Carmel's Art and Design District. The windows of each shop were filled with black-and-white clothing, jewelry, home décor. Even the statues now held race flags. The world doused in black and white seemed very apropos. Us versus them. Black versus white. Good versus evil. *Gotta love the irony.*

At the stop sign, I gripped Tens's arm. "That's Sergio." Sitting on the bench, next to the newest statue facing Tony and Juliet's condo.

I leaned forward, squinting.

"Is it?" The skepticism in Tens's voice was palpable.

The light from the streetlights was terrible. But I saw that Tony and Juliet's lights were all off; they weren't home yet. *Why is he checking their windows and messing with the statue?*

"What's he doing?" I asked.

"He's doing something on a tablet. Why does he keep adjusting the statue's head?" Tens leaned forward.

"I didn't know the statues could move."

"Me neither."

A car behind us honked and Tens quickly turned onto a side street. "Did he look up?"

No! "Crap, he jumped up—" I lost my view, twisting in my seat.

"He'll be long gone." Tens found the first street parking he could.

We leapt out of the truck and ran back toward the statue and Sergio.

"Yep, gone."

Gone. Tens swore. There was nothing to see. Nothing to tell us what Sergio had been doing.

What was he doing? Come on, come on!

"What's that?" Tens bent down and lifted something from the curb. "A screwdriver? What for?"

"Check the statue. Is there a plate or a screw?" I ran my fingers over the metal and fiberglass.

We felt all over it. Every crevice. Every cranny. "Bingo."

A tiny door on the back of its hand was caught on the race flag it held. Tens used a knife to pry it open. Wires and USB plugs ran up the hollow arm.

I leaned closer to the statue's head. "Tens?" A tiny green light blinked. "They're watching." I stood up, quaking and nauseous. Statues were positioned everywhere around town. All the streets, most of the corners, placed perfectly to see everyone and anything that happened here. *Perfect to spy on us. On everyone.* There probably wasn't a square foot that wasn't under surveillance.

"There are cameras in the eyes?" Tens looked up until I nodded, then used his knife to leverage all the wires until he could yank them lose. The green light faded.

"No wonder Ms. Asura knew when to corner Juliet." I shivered.

"He'll know we know. If they're not miced for sound, I'd be shocked."

"Hello, Sergio. Did you know Ms. Asura is dead? We lit her up. Not sorry." I leaned over a baby carriage and talked to the fake baby. I wanted a baseball bat to dismantle the surveillance art. *Soon enough.*

"Let's get to Rumi," Tens said.

We ran to the studio and found Rumi drinking whiskey. He looked so forlorn I blurted, "Did I miss it?"

"What, lass?"

"Faye?" I said, sitting down and hugging him.

"Ah, no, last I heard, she was unresponsive but clinging." He shook his head. "Trying to make sense of my uncle's childhood writing." He pointed down toward the table where he'd taken apart the little journal piece by piece.

"Anything?" Tens asked.

"He spent a lot of time at one of the artesian wells, but I don't know where it is yet, or which one."

"Is it the same one the Woodsman warned us about?"

"There are numerous ones in this state. I do not know, lassy. I saw the parade scatter because of the tornado sirens. You have anything to do with that?" he asked.

"Yeah, that's about the only part that's gone right," I said.

"There's more bad news," Tens said, holding up the wires.

CHAPTER 40

Juliet

"Are you sure?"

I knelt by the old, hollowed tree. The light we saw came from within. The closer I got, the brighter it glowed. I saw strands of hair like mine but could not force myself to look deeper into the rotting tree.

"We can try to carry her out?" Tony held up plastic sheets. "Or we can report the location and have the police come. Have you given any thought as to what you want to do?"

I leaned over and vomited. I didn't know what I

thought we'd find, but a skeleton to wrap in plastic and hike out of the forest wasn't it. *I want my mother to hug me and hold me and make me okay.* Finding my mother was all I'd thought about. Not what to do if we did.

Mini wound around the tree and us, leaving scent marks with her chin and purring.

We'd never make it back to the car carrying anything. My heart broke into dust. To leave her here again seemed unthinkable. To stay here forever with her put my friends and thousands of innocent people in danger. I shook my head. "We can't carry her." I wasn't sure I'd survive picking the pieces of her body up. *I'm not strong enough for that.*

"The police will investigate. Maybe catch any people involved," Tony tried to reassure me.

"We trust the police in this country?" Fara asked, handing me a paper napkin and a bottle of juice to rinse out my mouth.

"Usually," Tony answered. "In this case, I think we should."

"Call the police," I said, the words barely audible. "Will they tell me if she's my mother?" *I know it's my mom. I feel it.*

"We can clip a little hair and do a fancy test, right?" Fara asked. "Americans do them on TV all the time. Make sure on our own?"

"Yes, we can order a DNA test," Tony answered.

I felt as if my skin were burrowing into the earth, rooting down like carrots so I would never leave my mother again. *I can stay here with her. Crawl into the tree and wait until death opens my own window. Or just step through when someone else uses me. Everything Meridian taught me was to keep that from happening. But what if I willed it?*

"What if the Nocti come while we're gone? Are we still being followed?" I asked in a small voice.

Fara frowned. "I don't think so. It was hard to tell with the storm."

Tony sat next to me. "This is a long way out, Juliet. The Nocti can't possibly know where to look anymore, and Ms. Asura is dead."

Mini meowed.

I slicked back my wet hair with such frustration that Fara moved behind me and started to rebraid it. The tug and strokes reminded me of Nicole. Of Bodie, who'd liked to brush it and hide in the cascade of it. I'd struggled too long without any family to give up on the ones I had now. I stood, ready to decide to return and leave my mother's remains here.

"Hello?" a young voice called from the woods to our left. "I see lights, hurry! Hello?"

Two hikers stumbled toward us. Wet and muddy, they wore local university colors and held hands like they were out on a date. I think they might have been in their twenties, but the guy had a hat pulled low over his eyes, so it was hard to tell. Rain dripped off them like soaked sponges.

With a hiss, Mini dove into the brush around us.

"We are so happy to find you. Our flashlight died

and we got lost." The girl smiled. "I'm so hungry I could eat a bear. What are you doing all the way out here? Are you okay? Have you been crying?" She prattled on, and even if I'd wanted to talk, her exuberance quickly overwhelmed me.

Fara stepped between us. "She's fine."

"Oh." The girl took a step back. "Do you have a fire? What's that glow? Can I warm up and dry off too?" She tried to maneuver around Fara.

I swallowed over a lump in my throat. Every cell in my body shrank back. *Listen to your gut, Juliet.*

"We don't have a fire, just headlamps. Here, take mine. We can share." I started to reach out and hand mine over.

"That can't be what's making that light. Where's it coming from?" The girl again tried to step around Fara.

"Take the headlamp and leave," Fara suggested. "Juliet, toss it on the ground." I watched her wrap the chains around her hands and roll her weight forward on her feet.

"That's not going to happen," the guy said. "Thanks for finding the bitch for us." He grinned, showing too many teeth like a cheap toothpaste ad. "Made it pretty easy, all in all."

The girl giggled.

My mouth went dry.

"Isn't it interesting how it takes a bunch of magic light to get rid of a Nocti but a itsy-bitsy bullet can do in a Fenestra?" He pulled a gun from behind his back.

I sensed Tony freeze.

Fara didn't flinch as she asked, "Why is that?"

"Let me enlighten you—pun intended. We're stronger. Creators like us better." He shrugged.

"Or maybe Fenestra are more human; they haven't lost their senses."

"I like my answer better. Who needs love?"

"We all do," I said quietly.

"Oh, I've heard all about you. Kirian had lots to say. Wherefore art thou Juliet?"

The girl laughed harder.

"You followed us here?" Fara asked.

"Of course. 'Three hikers had a nasty accident when they went off trail and were hit by falling trees during a storm.' Has a nice ring to it, doesn't it?"

"Why are you doing this?"

"You were bait, Juliet. Your mother? She was too. And it didn't work, so now we don't need you anymore."

"Bait for who?" Tony asked.

"Argy Ambrose. Name ring a bell?" the Nocti asked. The wind around us picked up, going from a breeze to gusts that lifted our clothes and ripped leaves off branches.

"Daddy dearest?" the girl inserted.

I tried to speak, but my tongue was glued to the roof of my mouth.

"We have no idea who you're talking about," Fara said.

"I don't have all day to explain it to you. So come on, get close together." He waved us toward each other, but none of us moved. "How are you going to die with a tree falling on you if you're all standing so far apart? We have things to do today. Time is awastin'."

Above us, branches cracked and creaked violently. The morning sun backlit the silhouettes in menace. With every blink, a little more of the peach-blush first light reached through the forest.

"Say good night, Juliet."

I saw Fara shift. I knew she was prepared to launch herself. I gripped the headlamp in my fist, ready to throw it. I hoped my aim from skipping rocks along the creek held true. I tried to remember how we vanquished Ms. Asura. *Good thoughts, good deeds.*

Movement to my right startled me. *Mini? Custos?*

As the Nocti raised the gun, Fara moved. Her chains struck flesh as a gun cracked and the world exploded, blinding me.

CHAPTER 41

After throwing down food to refuel, we left Rumi in the company of a few Woodsmen to protect him and read the journal. I didn't like the threat I felt in my gut. I didn't know how to keep all the people in our family safe. *Bales's death is proof that safety is an illusion.*

Tens and I arrived at the intersection of Georgetown and Sixteenth Streets, the main gate of the track, and followed the thumping base, bonfires, and traffic. The gigantic party, comprised of many parties like a super organism, began before dusk. We were late. *Very, very late.*

"Rumi will call if they figure anything out, right? Should we have stayed to help?"

"I wouldn't count on him to think clearly, Meridian," Tens advised. "Grief makes people dumb. You and I can't wallow. There's no time."

Plastic signs splashed beverage brand names everywhere. Line after line of canopies and tents were erected next to campers and trucks. Quads zoomed through the crowds, their drivers shouting unintelligible excitement. Tiki torches flickered, and a few brainiacs used their headlights to illuminate their camping spaces. Of course they wouldn't be able to leave in the morning, but that would give them time to sober up.

I gripped Tens's hand as we tried to finagle our way between tents and RVs. Car-camping partiers weren't even trying to make it appear as if they planned to sleep tonight.

Earlier rains turned the fields to muddy pits. We sank with each step. But that didn't stop a group from setting up a full bar and living room—I gaped at couches, recliners, tables, and barstools. *In the middle of the mud?*

Garbage barrels were used as makeshift fire pits. Bottles, plastic cups, and aluminum cans lay wherever they were dropped. Bug zappers filled the air with blue lightning and the singed smell of moth wings. One guy dropped trou and took a leak into the drainage ditch.

"Good aim," Tens commented, making me laugh.

"I've never seen anything like this." I knew my eyes were wide, and my sixteen years of cloistered freakdom showed.

"Timothy said it's like this every year."

"Seriously?" I blinked as someone pet a monkey sitting on the shoulder of a fellow partier.

We walked around, continuously on guard for Nocti. *Nothing. Nada. Where are they all?*

The festivities deteriorated until it seemed as though they took on a life of their own. The music thumped bass, rocking the ground.

"Don't eat or drink anything," Tens said as a policeman arrested a man who was groping a passed out girl who was missing the important parts of her bikini.

Poison? There's a happy thought. "You think that's how they're going to do it?"

"Easy to get drunk people to down spiked drinks when you make 'em free and easy to get to."

We waited until EMTs loaded Ms. Topless Bikini into an ambulance and then moved on.

Garbage already littered the grass and the mud slopped up until it seemed as though people were actually trying to make an area devoted to mud wrestling. One man said he'd give me twenty bucks to strip and slide down a mud runway. Tens answered for me.

We checked in with the Woodsmen twice an hour and spent more time trying not to get covered in beer or puke than looking for Nocti. The temperature never dipped below seventy.

An artillery blast was greeted with cheers and whoops. The sky was navy with violet streaks as the sun began to rise.

"What was that?" I jumped.

"The gates are open. Time to wake up." Tens smiled down at me.

All around us, men, boys, were passed out in camp chairs, their heads lolled back, beer cans littering the ground. I pointed. "I don't think they're going to see the race."

"They've got a few hours." He snorted.

Camera crews were present in force, interviewing ticket holders who carried in coolers and backpacks. Local roads were bumper to bumper with traffic trying to get into the infield. Tailgating took on a whole new meaning when it started before sunrise. Long lines of tour buses stretched as far as I could see. *Where do all these people come from?*

We headed toward the gates around the track. I'd thought there were tons of people at qualifying, but that was nothing compared to this. Elbow to elbow, shoulder to shoulder, we invaded the personal space of people from all over the world. The outfits ranged from matching color-blocked shirts worn by entire families to black-and-white ensembles to tanks and shorts to festive sweaters. *Definitely international visitors.* Most of the jeans were utility and meant for farm work, and boots carried field scuffs or manure. The majority of male heads were covered in hats advertising companies that sold tractors.

Once inside, though, shirts and shoes seemed voluntary for those under the age of twenty-five. Tattoo conventions must show less skin.

We bought funnel cakes and elephant ears for breakfast and washed them down with lemonade as we watched people hurry in.

"Did we bring sunblock?" I asked, seeing an already sunburned, shirtless guy weaving his way toward the bathrooms. The sun wasn't quite awake yet. *He's going to layer the damage.*

"No, don't burn," Tens grunted.

"I do," I huffed.

We merged with the crowds trying to get a great seat in the infield. We'd broken the enormous track, bigger than most towns, into sections. Quite a few Woodsmen were heading to the inside of turn three because it was called the Snake Pit and we'd been warned by their dead brother it was part of the plot. Tens and I thought our best guess was to assume the Nocti plan involved balloons, because I'd seen Ms. Asura and others near the hot-air balloons, not to mention the white powder in the parade balloons. *Guesses are all we have.* A group of Woodsmen headed there as well.

If Juliet showed up, she was supposed to position herself near the start/finish line. *If she is okay. Big if.*

Not a cloud filled the sky and it was already seventy-five degrees before the sun even started to bake the aluminum stands and black asphalt. They predicted setting new heat records.

We jostled through crowds, intent on reaching the lake and trees around it. By the time we made it closer, there were six hot-air balloons filled and tethered.

And a giant inflated pink bunny selling batteries? So

enormous it made the traditional hot-air balloons seem like toys. The size of an aircraft carrier, the bunny wore sunglasses and held a drum. Its feet were the size of trucks, and I watched people continually scramble to keep it attached to the ground. *The bunny has a mind of its own.*

I didn't spot the same balloon I'd seen Ms. Asura riding in. Ryder and U-Haul trucks parked next to each other in a nice line that blocked the view behind them. No telling what lurked inside those bad boys.

"Dammit," Tens said under his breath as we rounded a corner.

A flimsy plastic fence cut the masses off from getting near the balloons. Yellow-shirted guards asked for credentials.

"Now what?" I asked.

"Ah, we find a place to sit and watch. There's time."

How Tens could be so serene and Zen, I didn't know. *He's never ruffled.* "What's with you?" I griped.

"What? I have a good feeling about today," he answered, sounding as calm as he appeared.

"Nothing's going to happen?" I asked hopefully.

"No, something's up, but I think good may come too." The fortune-cookie answer did nothing for my attitude.

"Have you seen Custos recently?"

"Not since last night."

"Mini?"

"I think she's probably with Juliet. What's with the roll call?" Tens stopped me.

"I just want to make sure we're prepared." I felt itchy with anticipation.

"Supergirl"—Tens tugged me into his lap and nuzzled my neck—"haven't you figured out that preparation means acknowledging we're never in control? Best we can do is the best we can do. So we sit and watch." His hand slid over my hip.

"And make out?" I asked with an unrepressed giggle.

"It makes us less conspicuous." His lips curved against my ear. "It's important work."

"In that case." I saw a woman and a black cat striding purposefully toward me. "Uh, Tens? Soul, two o'clock."

"I gotcha," he said as I flowed to the window.

CHAPTER 42

Juliet

I had to shield my eyes against the glare.

"What did you do? What did you do?" the girl kept screaming.

"Shut up!" Fara smacked her on the head with the chain and she collapsed.

Where moments ago the Nocti stood, nothing but singed earth remained.

What just happened?

"Fara? Tony?" I called out tentatively, almost afraid to

move. Blinking my eyes back to normal. *Like Ms. Asura.*

"I'm here." Tony's voice sounded funny.

"What's wrong?" I turned around and my headlamp shined on a growing red splotch on his arm. "You got shot!" I sprang into action.

"Just a flesh wound. Just my shoulder." Tony was pallid and his tone weak.

Fara stripped off one of her many black layers of clothing and wound it around his shoulder. "You'll be okay. But you're shocked."

"In shock?" Tony laughed weakly. "I've seen combat. I'll be fine. Are you girls okay?"

"Yes." Fara reached into the backpack and yanked out a roll of duct tape. She wrapped the girl's wrists and ankles and put a small piece over her mouth. "She's not Nocti, but she's not a nice person," was the only explanation Fara gave.

"Juliet? Are you okay?" Tony asked again.

"I think so. I don't know how I did that, though. It took all of us with Ms. Asura and I'd barely even started thinking about it . . ." I trailed off as Fara stilled.

"Maybe you didn't do it by yourself," Fara said, looking behind me. Her eyes narrowed and her breathing slowed as if she wasn't sure what to make of what she saw.

Tony's eyes widened too.

I twisted and gasped. "You?"

The man I'd seen outside my windows, looking up,

disappearing, then reappearing hesitantly approached. His arms were full of Mini, purring so loud I could hear her ten feet away. She flexed her paws as if kneading dough.

"Hello, Juliet."

And I knew, in that instant, I knew this man. "Dad?"

CHAPTER 43

In a long, faded cotton gown, like something out of *Little House on the Prairie*, I stood at the window with an ancient crone and her black cat. With her white hair braided up into a crown, her fingers were gnarled and bent like Auntie's used to be. The sunbaked folds of her skin almost covered her eyes, and her bare feet were filthy hooves from walking shoeless for years.

"Polly Barnett?" I asked. *Can this really be her? All these years waiting at her farm for release? Relief? To right a wrong done to her family?*

"How'd ya know?" she said without looking at me. She stared past the window at the scene unfolding behind it.

"Lucky guess."

Across the panes in the next world, the track faded in and out, like a clock being rewound. *As if she isn't sure which time is hers.*

"They be back here. The devils. This time they not git the chil'ren." Her hands fisted and her face scrunched. "You can' let 'em git 'em."

"Do you know how we can stop them?" I asked. *Please know.*

She shook her head and nodded consecutively as if she kept changing her mind. "Follow the stream home. They like the water; it's got magic."

I hadn't seen every inch of the racetrack grounds, but a stream? *I haven't seen a stream.*

She hummed a tune I vaguely recognized as Juliet and Rumi's song while she picked up the black cat and stroked it.

"Where's the stream today?" I asked. "In my time. Where do I look for the devils?"

The cabin I saw with the Woodsman came into my view. I heard laughter come from inside the house.

"Find the well. Find the shadows." Polly handed me the cat, which immediately relaxed into my arms like a bag of flour. He was heavier than he appeared. His golden eyes blinked up at me. "I'm tired. I can't fight no more," Polly said apologetically. "I thought with many people they would leave this place, but they keep coming back. I need my love, my child."

"It's okay, go on." I nodded. "We'll take over."

She nodded and climbed through. I stayed as long as I could. Each step easier than the last, her elderly form sloughed away like so much dirt until her previous youth unfolded fully. Once again straight and clean, she moved to the side of the house, and I saw the water gurgling up from the ground. It bubbled up and ran down a stone trough toward the woods.

"Is that the stream?" I asked.

"Is what the stream?" Tens asked me as I opened my eyes.

"I saw Polly. There's water coming up out of the ground, like the hot springs we went to with Auntie? Remember?"

"Yeah?"

I paced in a tight circle. "She said we'd find the devils at the water, at the well. Where's running water here?"

Tens pulled out his walkie-talkie to ask the Woodsmen. His phone rang, and he handed the phone to me.

"Rumi? Are you okay?"

"Ay, lass, we've cracked the code. There's an artesian well on the grounds."

"What's that exactly?"

"Deep water pushed to the surface by tectonic pressures and energy. People say it has special minerals and healing properties. Have them all over this state—there's even one in Carmel folks come from miles around to fill up jugs at."

"So the water bubbles up on its own?"

"That's right. My uncle's journal, all the water, all the

notes are about an artesian well at the Barnett farm. It's the track now."

"Where is it?" The stream I saw at Polly's window. Her well. I tried to see around the crowds of people.

Rumi sighed. "None of us know. There's a tiny map here we can't figure out. Tim is at the computer trying to find more."

"Can you call Gus? See if he knows?" I knew we were grasping at straws, but we had to try anything.

"We already tried that. I'm sorry, lass." Rumi sounded crushed.

"Just call us if you think of a clue, okay?"

"Course," Rumi said.

Tens grabbed my hand and started walking. "Woodsmen don't know. Best guess is to look by the lakes. Maybe at the golf course—they've sent a team over there."

"The lake is near the hot-air balloons; it's the only water here. We've got to get closer," I said. The sun grew hotter and higher. Planes circled overhead, towing banners for restaurants and team sponsors; even an engagement proposal fluttered above us.

As marching bands played a lap around the two and a half miles, their brass and drums gave a lively soundtrack to all the humanity around us. Scattered applause erupted for hometown favorites. I knew Woodsmen mingled in the crowds. Though I couldn't help but feel as though we were severely outnumbered.

The viewing screens jumped to life and the thirty-three drivers began to walk out toward the pits from the cement block garages. Surrounded by their families, they wore stony and resolute expressions. They all wore the same type of jumpsuits, covered with patches, symbols, and words.

Pickup trucks with members of every military branch sped around the track to thunderous applause and salutes from a very patriotic crowd. After all, service and sacrifice were the reason for the weekend. *Fitting.* I wished they had an inkling of what was coming. My dad used to threaten to call the National Guard if I misbehaved. *I wish he could do that right now.*

The screens filled with shots of the stands. What started out as empty gray benches became speckled with colorful hats and clothing. Then the camera panned the photographers set up every few feet all around the inside of the track. A group of sunglassed yellow shirts huddled together and the camera zoomed in as they argued with a photographer.

"Tens, wait. Look up," I said as the screen filled.

"What are they doing?"

"They're taking him away?"

Tens and I stared transfixed as one photographer was replaced by another, and an upset shouting man was physically carried off to a security vehicle.

Abruptly, the camera shot shifted back to the main stage by the Pagoda.

"They had the tattoos." *Nocti aides or Nocti themselves?* I easily recognized the skull, wings, and snuffed candle.

"They're not bothering to cover them up anymore," Tens said grimly.

Not a good sign.

"Where was that? Turn three?" I asked.

"Turn two?" Tens swiveled his head, trying to place the few landmarks. The crowd was in front of the skyline. The camera panned down. "Gotta be three. Over there."

I gripped his hand and we tried to weave between people.

The announcer said, "Please stand for the National Anthem."

The crowd surged to its feet and whipped off their hats, leaving us unable to see where we needed to go.

"We have to stop," Tens said to me under his breath. "Try moving something with your mind. Fara says you can invite energy to change direction."

"Like the telepathy I'm so good at?" I complained, but concentrated on a blade of grass. *No go.*

I heard a clock ticking behind my eyes. *Every second counts.* That was the longest song in my life, until they began playing "Taps." Faces of soldiers and marines I'd helped transition came to mind. I'd begun writing bits of stories down in March, but now I was convinced that words were my thing. Auntie's were quilts. Juliet's were recipes. Mine were stories. Life stories.

The race itself was starting. Tens plugged in earbuds to listen to the radio and the Woodsmen. I smashed in earplugs. My job was to watch for souls. For Nocti. I didn't need distractions.

We wrestled our way closer to the barrier, keeping spectators away from the photographers and the track.

Eyes set on the replacement photographer. *Trigger man? Spotter?*

"Do you think he knows when and what they're planning?"

"Don't you think?" Tens handed me the binoculars .and radioed to the Woodsmen.

A moment of silence was held for all the drivers injured and killed this month. Then the drivers were introduced. Eddie Smith, the replacement driver, received by far the loudest cheers; people loved to root for an underdog. *If only they knew.*

"Merry, check out the patch on Smith's jumpsuit." Tens nodded.

I swallowed back bile. Above his heart, next to the black armband he sported, was the same artwork as the tattoo. Wings around a skull and a smoking, snuffed out candle. It could have been interpreted as an artistic expression of grief, but we knew it for what it was.

Tens's expression was grim. "Let's move." At least we had confirmation who drove for the Nocti today.

We headed toward the lake around the perimeter of people. A woman's voice came over the loudspeakers. "Ladies and gentlemen, start your engines."

The crowd surged to its feet in a deafening roar and a wave of energy. My heart picked up its rhythm.

Here we go.

CHAPTER 44
Juliet

"You have your mother's eyes," he said, stepping a little bit closer. The headlamps fell unneeded at our feet with early morning light.

I paused, unable to trust my eyes. "Are you real? Fara, can you see him too?"

"I can see him." Fara shifted as if uncertain.

"I'm real." He hesitated. "I've thought about this for months. I'm not sure what to say. May I hug you?" His voice cracked.

I felt bound and stiff. *My dad is here. He's right here.*

A foot taller than me, muscular as if he used his body for manual labor. The tan of his face told me he spent a lot of time outdoors. His wheat-colored hair curled around his neck and ears, falling across one brow.

"Mini likes him." Tony wobbled, breaking the silence. "You took out the Nocti, didn't you?"

"I tracked them. I couldn't risk moving earlier; I needed to know what they had planned." He nodded. "I'm Argy."

My dad. "Tony. I knew Roshana when she was pregnant." The sadness in Tony's voice cut me.

My father's eye filled with tears. "Someday maybe you'll tell me about that time, please?"

"Of course." Tony looked at me with love in his eyes. "Thank you for coming. Juliet needs you."

I blinked, breaking eye contact with Tony, and turned to my father. "You were watching me," I said, finding my voice. All these weeks glancing outside and seeing a shadow across the street. It was him. Maybe his eyes were the only ones I felt? Maybe the statues were art and not evil.

"Yes." He nodded. "You're her Protector?" he asked Fara.

"I am Fara Vishi." Fara shook his hand.

"I've seen your work. You would make your trainer proud." His grin flashed white teeth and a dimple in his chin.

"My father, my baba." Fara's voice hinted at a smile.

Around us the light of the day glowed; the first day

dwellers chirped and sang each other into motion. *Speak up. Ask questions. He's here.*

"There's so much to say—I know you'll have questions. I didn't know you existed, Juliet. Not until months ago when DG was on the news. I thought my Ana died in the crash. I would have come for you sooner, I swear it." His voice roughened with emotion; he fell to his knees. "I never would have let them touch her, or you, never again."

It was as if I'd been released from a spell. I tripped over my feet, over sticks and rocks, sliding into his embrace.

CHAPTER 45

Everyone wore sunglasses. *So much for knowing who around here is Nocti.* All my little hairs and spine shivers started the moment we arrived—my body was a vibration of Nocti alerts. *Not helpful.* The first laps went by without incident and I began to feel the rhythm of the race. *Straights are speed and turns technique.*

The sun tightened the skin across my nose and at the back of my neck. I didn't need to pee no matter how much I drank, which meant I was sweating it out quicker than I consumed. The temperature hit ninety-two degrees in the shade.

Is that Sergio? "Tens, that group of volunteers—is that

Sergio?" *What are they doing? Moving crates? Unpacking what? Drinks? Food?*

Tens glanced down at me. "What?" he yelled over the cacophony of noise.

"Sergio!" I mouthed.

When he still didn't understand me and started to take out his earbuds, I grabbed his hand and pulled him.

I hate being so short! As the crowd around us undulated and shifted, I couldn't see Sergio's group anymore but kept my eyes peeled for volunteer vests.

A gasp waved over the spectators followed by moans that made us stop and look up at the JumboTrons.

"Ouch!" I said, watching the replay of a car hitting the outside wall. Debris flew in all directions and two cars barely missed smacking the wounded car as it slid down the track toward the infield.

Immediately, the green flag changed to yellow and all the cars slowed down. Emergency personnel sped onto the track in red trucks with flashing lights. The crowd held its breath until the driver got out safely and waved to the crowd.

"They're saying he's a rookie driver," Tens said loudly against my ear. "Where are we going? I thought we needed to get to the lake."

"I think I saw Sergio unloading crates over there."

Tens's face closed and fearsome he said, "He did say he volunteered here. Maybe we can convince him to talk? Tell us what's going on? Where is he?"

I knew Tens wouldn't pour Sergio tea and have a delicate conversation, but any clues, however we got them, might help. "I lost him." I shook my head. "Maybe it wasn't him. They were still doing something odd, though."

"Here, jump up." Tens leaned down and hoisted me onto his shoulders, my thighs around his head. All of a sudden, not only was I taller than everyone, I could see exactly why threading through this crowd was so difficult—the sheer numbers of people standing shoulder to shoulder and lounging on roofs of cars and in truck beds. I was overwhelmed.

"See anything?" Tens said as he began walking in the direction I pointed.

No, no, Sergio. No Nocti. Only broken crates? Wood planks ripped apart in haste or carelessness.

As I opened my mouth, I heard screaming. Horrified. Terrified. Screams.

Footsteps like a herd of wildebeests pounded.

Thundering, panicked running.

Then, all I saw was a tsunami of humanity, wild-eyed and frightened. *Coming toward us.*

"Put me down. Put me down!" No way could Tens run with me perched up here. I scrambled lower, thinking I'd run next to him, but he had different plans.

"Piggyback, now!" Tens held on to my thighs and I wrapped my arms around his.

It wasn't pretty and it wasn't the cute piggyback rides of little kids, but it kept us from being separated. He didn't know which way to go, as the mob kept scattering and changing directions.

"Snakes!" someone screamed.

I heard an ominous rattle as Tens leapt onto the hood of a car and I saw a pile of snakes untangling below us. They put live, poisonous snakes in the Snake Pit. Only Nocti would think that made it a party.

CHAPTER 46

Juliet

I never wanted to let go. I felt safe. *My daddy.*

"You need to get them to the track," Tony interrupted our reunion.

"But . . . Mom's remains are here," I said, pulling away from my dad's strong arms.

"She's not, though." Argy held on to my arms. "She's not here. You have to let her move on."

I nodded. *Can I? I just found her.*

"Meridian is counting on you," Tony said weakly. "Can you take them?" he asked Argy.

"I can."

"Before you go . . . They said Juliet was bait for you?" Tony pressed.

"After the accident, I studied them and became a hunter." Argy's expression dimmed.

"Of Nocti?" Tony asked, surprised.

"Yes. I can sense them, see the darkness around them before they know who I am. I shine Creator's light upon them. They fear me now, even more than they did then."

"So, you can help Juliet and Fara? Make sure they're safe?"

"Yes, you have my word. But you come too." Argy tried to help Tony to his feet.

"I've lost too much blood. I will wait here for the police."

"I can carry you." Argy bent as if to try.

"No, I'll keep Roshana company so Juliet can focus on defeating the Nocti with you."

"Tony, come with us." Fara shook her head. "Roshana isn't going anywhere."

Pointing at the girl who lay on the ground, unmoving, Tony said, "We don't know that those two didn't have friends out here somewhere."

"All the more reason for you to stay with us." Fara almost stomped her feet.

Argy reached into one of his cargo pockets and withdrew a palm-sized screen. "I brought two." He handed one to me and pressed a sequence of buttons. "Use this to get out, then call for help. Give them the coordinates. They'll know exactly where to come find us."

"You're not coming?" I asked. *What are you saying?*

"You'll worry less if I stay with your mother and Tony. Just in case." His eyes overflowed with warmth and understanding.

I realized he was right. "You're right, but if you can defeat the Nocti, we need you with us."

Tears filled his eyes as he gazed at the tree trunk. The glow disappeared.

I gasped. "You made them glow? It's not because they're Fenestra?"

"Bones are bones, Juliet. I asked for Light's help to recognize those we sought. Especially after I realized you and your friends were searching for souls touched by the Nocti." He knelt by Tony and they clasped hands. "If I leave you here to wait, you will take care of my girl?" Argy asked, his voice rough and cracking.

"With my life. I failed her once; I will not fail her again," Tony answered with a conviction I'd never heard before.

Is this how he sounded in the middle of a war? How he prayed with men who no longer knew what they fought for?

Fara took the GPS unit from me. "We have to go." She tugged my braid.

I know. I hugged Tony carefully around his wound. "I'm sorry. I love you. I do." I let the tears I'd been holding back fall.

"Oh, Juliet." Tony cradled my face in one hand. "Go make all of your family proud of you. Kick some Nocti ass."

I choked on a laugh that dried my tears instantly. *Tony doesn't swear. Doesn't show a temper.* I nodded, slipping my hand into my father's.

"Call on the Creators to guard Tony and your mom," Argy instructed me before we turned to go. "Remember no creature is inherently evil, just given hard choices to survive. It's part of your gift."

I glanced at Fara, who smiled. "You can do it."

Life energy around us, will you please come? Watch over my mother? Tony? I didn't know what else to say.

I closed my eyes and even though I felt insanely silly, I called out silently to the woods around us for help.

The bushes rattled. Branches of the trees rustled. I opened my eyes to see birds flying in and settling in a circle around us. On the ground, they came too.

"Custos will keep watch, right, girl?" Tony said as the wolf sidled up to him and sat down.

Mini, too, rubbed her head on Custos's chest and forelegs. She meowed when Custos barked. Coyotes took up the howl. Raccoons hissed and chattered. Possum climbed the tree.

"That's very Disney," Tony remarked.

"Where do you think they got their best ideas?" Argy smiled. "That's my girl."

CHAPTER 47

"It's snakes!" I saw a thick, black-scaled body slither under the bed of a pickup truck, trying to get away from the stamping feet and hot sun. Near every crate, every box, a pile of multihued snakes uncoiled and slithered, scared as much as the people around them.

I heard the announcer vaguely in the background but couldn't understand his words. All around us, snakes coiled and struck defensively. People fell either from bites or from being trampled by others. Wounds wept, leaving blood streaks down bare legs. *Who knows what the Nocti did to rile them before releasing?*

The Snake Pit was party central for the duration of the race. It came to life in the most macabre way.

"We have to find the well," I yelled. *We're running out of time.*

Tens started for the fencing that separated us from the hot-air balloons around the lake.

Around us, chaos waved as people ran mindlessly. A girl not much older than me was carried by with a bleeding bite wound on her leg. A child lay motionless near a car. Tens kept us moving, but I found myself at the window with the first casualties of the day.

CHAPTER 48

Juliet

Argy drove toward Speedway and the track as if the Nocti chased us.

"We did the right thing leaving them there?" I asked again.

"Don't second-guess yourself," Fara admonished.

All I ever do is second-guess myself.

I didn't have to look in the mirror to see the mess we presented; I could smell us too. "Do I look as bad as you two do?"

"Like bathing is overrated? Yes, you do," Argy answered.

We have the same sense of humor.

"Oh, good." We used wet wipes to get the worst of the dirt and grime off.

We made it to the track as the race started. Argy—Dad—bought a ticket from a scalper as we picked up ours at will call. *Thank God, Fara knows about the world. I would have wandered around the outside fence.*

I saw a Woodsman in a yellow shirt and black pants, his insignia tattooed on his forearm. "Where's the finish line?" I asked him.

"Head two entrances over and use those stairs. Careful, girls." He frowned as if he wanted to say more, but a family who was lost demanded his attention.

The scents of fried food, roasted turkey legs, and egg rolls coaxed me from the edge of exhaustion. Fara tugged me to a stop. "You need to eat. What do you want?"

There were so many recipes floating at the back of my throat I was sure I would cook for a month when this was over. *One way or another.*

Sleek military jets swept across the sky above us with a roar, and helium-filled balloons in red, white, and blue rose behind them.

"They told us to be at the pole for the duration of the race. Just in case. We have to go." I yanked on Fara's hand.

"Juliet, they know where our seats are. I'm sure if they need us, they'll find us." Dad hugged my shoulders, double-teaming me with Fara.

Fara stood her ground. "You have to eat. You can chew and walk at the same time, can't you?" She bought us fifty bucks' worth of grease and starch.

I smiled. "I don't know. It's been a long day." *Week. Month. Life.* I swallowed without tasting much of it.

Any normal day, the sheer volume of people and the throbbing energy of the track would have overwhelmed me to paralysis. But I kept moving. *Where is Meridian? Tens? Are they making progress?*

"Girls? I see a group of Nocti." Dad slowed us down.

"Where?" Fara asked, reaching for her chains.

"Eh, stop!" Argy hissed. "Selling T-shirts. Go on, find your seats. I'll catch up with you. I need to take out as many as I can. Remember"—he paused and looked at me—"you can shine light through them, Anyone can, You just have to believe."

"But—" I protested as he left us. *Believe?*

"Yeah, I think he makes that sound too easy," Fara said with a glance at my stunned expression. "He forgets he's been doing this for a long time. Like my baba, who could talk anyone into anything. They forget."

I smiled. "Thanks." Fara didn't always say what I wanted to hear, but she often said what I needed.

Fara tried dialing Tens's cell but got weird static. Up two flights of rusty metal steps, Fara held my braid behind me. Our seats were empty but flanked by Woodsmen in green ball caps. *Friends.*

Sparks flew off the bottoms of the cars as they zigzagged past us on the track. I knew nothing about what I saw, and nothing prepared me for the sounds and feelings humming through me as the cars roared past.

The green flag dropped and the crowds erupted into cheers. Around and around the cars zoomed. With each turn, my anxiety heightened. I glanced at the people across from us, below us. *Who is Nocti? Who is working with them? How many people will die today?*

When the leaders of the race zoomed past at full speed, it was all I could do to focus my eyes. Everyone around us lurched to their feet, cheering like one mass with many arms.

On lap twenty-five, the crowd gasped.

I leapt to my feet, watching the screen with everyone else.

A car bumped into the wall. Blew a tire. Nothing else. *Too much pepper in the recipe, but not arsenic.*

"The lead driver, but she'll be fine," a Woodsman declared. "Want binoculars?" He handed me a pair.

"Will she race more?" I asked, trying to see.

"Nah, these cars are so finely tuned, a spider can throw them off. No more racing after a hit like that. Here comes the pace car to slow 'em all down."

The yellow flag waved caution and the pace car drove back out as crews cleaned up the track.

Is that it?

I loosened my grip on the chair rails as waves of screaming rushed toward us across the infield. *Now what?*

CHAPTER 49

I focused on breathing past the souls, on making my body move, and on staying present while also transitioning the dead. I wanted to stop everything and announce I finally understood how Auntie worked in both places, but we didn't have time.

The green flag waved again; the cars picked up speed as Tens tossed me over a five-foot fence. "Get safe! Get above the snakes!" He yanked a knife from his boot and slashed at one particularly brutal-looking snake as it slid by.

"What about you?" I called.

A yellow-shirted security guard began yelling at us and running. "You can't be in there. Get out! Get out!"

Evidently he's not one of our WoW.

"Go toward the water. I'll find you." Tens disappeared back into the melee and I took off in a sprint toward the trees, nearer to the few hot-air balloons left tethered to the ground. I swung myself up into the branches of an oak to catch my breath. I listened to the announcer try to calm people down. They evacuated the Snake Pit, moving people toward the other side of the infield.

Think, Meridian. Think.

A tainted driver who's driving oddly and releasing snakes? What's the end goal? Where's the well? Eddie Smith's car drove around again, completely off pace, so slow I easily read the Nocti insignia on the tail of the car.

Each time crashes occurred, the cars bunched back together, lined up two by two in turn three, before they accelerated around to the pole and the flag.

This whole day felt like a giant cat playing with a tiny mouse until it died. *I hate being the mouse.* The Nocti, and Smith, must be angling for a disaster to happen at turn three. Why else would they use snakes to move people closer together in a panic?

I glanced up into the sky at the hot-air balloons hovering above us. What if the balloons weren't the actual plan at all? What if they simply needed a vantage point to spot the well and see the track to make final arrangements? *They were scouting. It's a leap, Meridian. You need proof!*

Restarts were the only time in the race where all the cars were bunched together. A crash amid all of them would throw debris and spread carnage everywhere. I tried the walkie-talkie and got static. I turned the dial, changed frequencies. *No, no, no, no!* We'd already seen the havoc fuel fires caused.

Drivers and teams depended on radio communications to avoid driving right into wrecks. Jammed radio signals meant no one would have any idea how to avoid the pileup. *Brilliant.*

A pack of cars raced by through turn three. Eddie didn't dip low on the track to let them pass like I'd watched slower drivers do all day. Instead, he kept his ground and two cars went hurtling into each other, and the wall, to avoid hitting him.

"Did you see that?" I yelled. I might not be anywhere near an expert, but it seemed like he'd deliberately been in the way and made them crash.

Green became yellow again.

I looked down at the earth below me. Bunches of official-looking people milled around in trailers and tents, huddled over computers and electrical equipment. I surveyed them, looking for Nocti, even for Sergio, for answers.

Well. Water. Water. Lake. Think, think, think.

One hundred and fifty laps from the start until the white flag of victory. We had seventy left and already yellow was the color of the day.

I needed to stop the race entirely before we found out exactly what worst-case scenario looked like.

Where's Tens?

The announcer said, "Just a few more laps, folks,

while our safety teams make sure all the debris is off the track. I'm being told fans need to stay away from turn three. Please follow signs to the overflow area between two and three. Again, if your tickets are for the Snake Pit, please head toward the overflow. Now officials are saying they're going to wave Eddie Smith around befo—"

A wave around meant Smith would get to catch up to the pack and be right in the middle of all the action. And people sent to a specific predetermined area? *This can't be good.*

I needed to stop Eddie Smith from driving into the pack of cars.

I needed to stop the race completely.

I needed to find the well and finish this. Now.

CHAPTER 50
Juliet

I felt drawn to my feet, toward the railing, my eyes focused on the hot-air balloons. Meridian was out there somewhere. I felt her. I knew that was the direction they'd planned to go. Are they still there?

Where are you, Meridian?

The announcer's voice cut off mid-word. People around us were pulling off their headsets and earbuds, complaining loudly about screeching static. No one heard the radio calls. None of us could communicate.

The Woodsman next to me frowned and shook his head. "We've got nothing."

A breeze kicked up and blew tendrils of my hair into my eyes. I quickly dragged them behind my ears, out of my way. *Radios not working means we're all isolated.*

"Tell us what you know," Fara demanded.

He dropped his voice low. "Eddie Smith is working with the Nocti. We think he's the trigger man for explosives, but we don't know where they are hidden."

"In his car?" Fara frowned.

"No, not possible. He's running slow and heavy, though, so every time there's a crash and the yellow comes out, he is waved around to the back of the pack. If he doesn't slow down once he gets around behind them . . ." He let his thought trail off.

"You think there's a bomb somewhere near the track?" Fara asked.

"We don't know anything for sure."

"When did you last hear from Meridian?" I chewed my cheek.

"Tens radioed in that they were heading for the lake. Something about finding a well? The signals have been bad all day. We're trying to figure out how to stop the race and clear the stands."

The screens switched from showing the cars on the track to panning a running, chaotic crowd moving like a tidal wave away from the third turn. "What's happening?" I asked.

The announcer's voice sounded garbled and impossible to understand.

"Is that—" *That can't be a snake, can it?*

"Are those snakes?" Fara asked loudly.

Meridian's in trouble. I felt it. *How do I help them?* I looked above me. The roof. If I could get up there, I might see the infield better.

"Fara?" I said.

"Yep?" She didn't take her eyes from the crowd stampeding randomly. I felt her tension radiate toward me, taking my own anxiety up a level. Her hand hovered over her boot knife.

"We need to get up there." I pointed at the roof. *If I can see over the Pagoda, maybe I can see the lake.*

"All righty, then." Fara nudged Timothy. "We are going up that emergency ladder and you gotta make a big distraction so no one sees, okay?"

"Now? You got it." Without asking questions, the Woodsman glanced around and picked a drunk spectator who was several rows down to the right. He started yelling while advancing toward the bystander menacingly.

The drunk man began shouting back. We moved quickly, so by the time Timothy took a swing, security guards and yellow shirts rushed past us as we headed under the caution tape. We took the rungs two at a time to the metal roof.

It was like stepping out onto a hot cookie sheet. The

wind plastered my clothes to me and swallowed up every drop of sweat.

"What's that?" I asked, pointing at an inflated pink bunny that rivaled a skyscraper for size.

A possessed pink bunny.

It's moving.

Walking toward the track.

CHAPTER 51

If I can free the immense inflatable and get it onto the track, they have to stop the race. At least until they can remove it. I can buy us time. The bunny's size made the trucks and trailers parked around it look like itsy-bitsy toys my brother Sammy collected. *That's a lot of mass to try to control.*

I needed Tens's help, but he'd disappeared into the rioting crowd. Without much preamble, I simply started calling out to him in my mind. As much just wishful thinking as hoping our telepathy might finally work. *"Tens, where are you? Where are you?"*

"Merry?"

I blinked, glanced around. I heard him. But I couldn't see him.

"Tens? Where are you? We have to untie the bunny. Get him onto the track."

"I found Sergio. I'm behind him. See the U-Haul by the left foot? They're working on computers. A countdown."

We didn't have time to free the bunny and investigate Sergio. I ran, my feet flying across soggy grass and between vehicles. I leaned against a van, trying to see Tens in the melee. *"Tens? Tens?"*

"Quit shouting. I can hear you fine."

"Are we? Actually telepathically talking? Crazy!"

"Be excited later—focus now. Your bag has an extra knife underneath the bottom cardboard. Use that to protect yourself."

I fumbled through the messenger bag as the wind picked up, whipping my hair. I ripped the material up and snagged the handle of the knife. *"Got it."* Although protecting myself wasn't quite what I had in mind. *"If I get the bunny onto the track, they'll have to stop the race."*

"What's your plan?"

"I'll take care of the bunny. You get Sergio."

"You sure?"

"Go!"

Plan B was running onto the track myself. But even if I did, nothing guaranteed Smith would stop rather than hit me. The bunny was our only option.

"I'm right behind you. Go."

"Be safe," Tens replied.

"You too. Please let this work," I said as wind gusted from the west. The flags whipped and flapped around the perimeter of the stands. People's hats and umbrellas went flying. The other hot-air balloons ripped from their grounding pegs. People ran to grab the tether lines and deflate the balloons as quickly as possible.

To my left, I saw a Nocti grin and stand over a girl with a snake coiled around her. *They are winning.*

"Auntie, I need your help. I need our ancestors," I whispered, kneeling by the first peg, but instead of cutting the cords, I pried the hooks from the earth. There were twenty-plus pegs.

One down.

I ran as fast as I could to the next. Sweat made my hands slippery and stung the sunburn on my cheeks and arms.

Two yellow shirts ran toward me.

I worked faster. Popped loose pegs two and three.

I kept moving, waiting for the yellow shirts to stop me, yell, or tackle me to the ground.

Instead, they joined me, yanking other pegs out of the ground. When I glanced over, one gave me the Woodsmen hand sign Timothy taught us two days ago. *Has it only been two days?*

They might have been security but they were Woodsmen first.

The wind aided us as if it knew exactly what I needed even before I knew. Answering every fervent prayer with each gust and squall. As fewer pegged lines were loaded with more weight, the wind heaved the bunny, making it pitch toward the track as if it were alive.

Every minute or so, the announcer would try to come onto the loudspeakers, but only high-pitched screeching came out.

State patrol officers arrived on scene, but my Woodsmen ran interference. *Faster, Meridian. Faster.*

Seventeen

Eighteen

"Go! Go! Go!" I shouted as the last peg broke free.

Groups of bystanders, Nocti or officials—who knew at this point who was who—finally noticed the bunny heading toward the track. They frantically began leaping to grab at the ropes dragging twenty feet above the ground. Just high enough to be out of reach but too low to make it over the top branches of the trees.

I glanced up at the screen. The track was okayed to race. The race could restart any moment.

The bunny's going to hit the trees and snag. It was too heavy, too close to the ground.

The main grouping of drivers lined up in their restart positions.

I saw Eddie Smith start around to the back of the pack.

We had about ten seconds to go and the trees were firmly planted between the track and the bunny.

CHAPTER 52
Juliet

I heard nothing over the roaring thunder of the race cars spinning their tires around the track.

The frantic commotion in the infield drew almost everyone's attention.

"That's Meridian." Fara handed me binoculars. "You see?"

"What is she doing?" *Is that it? The bunny?* "Is she trying to get the bunny onto the track?"

"If not, it's okay. There are trees in the way," Fara said, seeing me point.

"They'd know that." I shook my head. "That's not Nocti; that's Meridian. Us."

I closed my eyes and saw my mother's eyes in my mind. My father's smile as he said he loved me hours ago.

The wind caressed my face like my mother's hands.

I did it with lightning. *I'll ask the trees to bend.*

Bend, please bend.

I focused on one tree. Its branches all spun and bowed as if in silent applause.

Help us. Bend.

I opened my eyes and watched as the tops of the tree's branches moved. It was like watching a butterfly relax its wings. I kept my thoughts focused and waited. Adding another and another until the whole line of them bent.

It's working. It's working.

"Here comes a car!" Fara shouted. "It's Smith!"

The bunny seemed to stomp everything in its path toward the track. Across the sandpit. The wind aggressively moved the pink inflatable over pine trees.

Did I do the right thing? Does she want the bunny on the track?

Time slowed down. The car accelerated as the pack of drivers seemed to decelerate.

I saw the bunny cross the first fence.

The second.

Onto the track.

The pack went past. *Safe.*

Eddie Smith seemed to speed up, trying to avoid a head-on collision with the bunny foo-foo.

Then the pink cloud of bunny material swallowed the racing car from our view.

CHAPTER 53

I ran to the lake's edge. Was I right? Was the answer out in the open all this time? I heard the sirens of emergency vehicles and the crowd of spectators roar. The chatter of so many people talking at the same time created waves of sound, coming toward me from all directions. I found myself vaguely disoriented.

"Tens, where are you?"

"I'm watching Sergio and another kid about his age work on computer tablets. They're walking toward the black trailer."

"Like the one he used with the statues?"

"Maybe the same, I don't know. Move fast, they're waiting for someone to arrive. We've got less than four minutes."

I glanced around. The black trailer was parked near the edge of the lake. I watched as activity, like an ant hive, grew in ferocity. I ran, forcing myself to take silent, shallow breaths. To my right, bright light exploded like the flash of the Creator's camera. *Like when we took out Ms. Asura? "Tens, did you see that?"*

"Supergirl, hide!"

I turned back and ducked behind a truck. I peeked my head around and saw an entourage of old men coming from the other direction, driving golf carts. I swallowed back a gasp as I focused on the evident leader. *"He looks like Rumi in fifty years."*

"I'm thinking the same thing."

They stopped near the back of the truck. I was close enough to hear, "You're right, sir. We don't know what happened."

"Find out! Call up to the Pagoda—one of our people should know. He was paid to run into all those cars. Can no one do what they're asked anymore?"

"Yes, sir."

"What are you waiting for—open the doors!"

"Sir, I can't call up to the boxes; we jammed the communications."

"Don't scream—I'm about to slide out next to you."

As Tens's thoughts registered, his hand brushed mine. He leveraged himself out from under the truck.

The old man spit and launched himself at the computer geeks, Sergio in particular. "You said we could stop them from talking, but not us."

"I d-don't know why it's not . . . um . . . I'm trying to fix it." Sergio's voice shook with fear.

Kinda hard to feel bad for him.

"Do you see what I see?" I pointed at the tiny pipe flowing between bricks along the waterline. If I hadn't been up in the tree, I never would have seen the movement of the water. *"The lake is fed by the artesian well."*

Tens answered me, *"How'd you see that, Supergirl?"*

"Luck."

"You see the bags lined up in that truck over there?"

I followed Tens's head nod and saw bags with pretty pictures of healthy, flourishing corn and wheat. *"No one's farming this land."*

"Nah, but done right, fertilizer makes for a big boom."

Horrifying memories of the train derailment and inferno rushed to the forefront of my thoughts. *"If we get the computers and disable them, will that stop the explosion?"*

"Possible. Lots of their electrical equipment is parked too close to the water. Not smart."

"Why did I ever let you all talk me into using this ridiculous technology?" the old man mumbled. "We don't have much time. Has my successor arrived? He's late."

"Sir, last we heard, he was on his way."

Two of the Nocti conferred with heads lowered, whispering.

"*Tens? They look scared.*"

"*Yep.*"

"*But why? I wish I could talk to Auntie.*"

"*You can, Supergirl. Call your window.*"

"*What?*"

"*You've done it before.*"

"*Not on purpose.*"

He raised his eyebrows. I didn't need to read his mind. I focused, closing my eyes, not because I needed to at this point, but because it still felt odd to be in both worlds.

.

CHAPTER 54
Juliet

"You did it!" Fara shouted as we watched the bunny capture Smith's car in an obliterating embrace. The impact threw bits of car and pink material in every direction. Flames danced up the bunny's face. *The fuel from the car must have leaked.*

"It's not over." I didn't feel right. *Not yet.*

The tow trucks and fire trucks, ambulances, and a fleet of other vehicles raced toward the crash, spraying white foam on the invisible fuel.

Someone in a jumpsuit ran across the low cement wall

from the pits to the main track and frantically motioned cars to drive to their respective spots. I wondered if this was a team member or a Woodsman. It didn't matter; the sight of a person on the track was so alien that all but one car pulled into the pit lane. As the drivers turned off their engines, people held their breath, their eyes turned to the screens and the fiery mess in turn three. The silence was oppressive.

Like a flash mob, people peeled out of the infield crowd and headed toward the lake. It looked choreographed and planned. *Nocti?*

"Where's my father?" I asked Fara.

"I don't know," she answered.

CHAPTER 55

"Auntie?"

I stood at my window and saw the living room of Auntie and Charles's house in Revelation. I recognized the piles of quilts and crazy knickknacks from all over the world. *This isn't here anymore; it burned.* But Auntie's scents of apple blossoms and fresh grass told my heart this was real.

"It's still here on this side because I remember it. Everything changes, sweet one, but nothing disappears, not completely."

"Auntie!" I wanted to fling myself through the window

and hug her. Eat her chocolate cake. Talk about everything that had happened to me since Tens and I said goodbye to her and this place.

"We don't have time for all of that. You know what you must do."

"I don't!" I disagreed.

"You do. Just as Juliet can call energy, so can you." She nodded her head like I was being stubborn. "The world and its elements are yours for the calling. They move through your Light. Perimo wanted to kill you before you took over for our family. When he couldn't do that, he wanted you to join them, right?"

"Yes."

"You can call the window yourself to help souls over who have lost their faith in light and love. That's a gift. I almost didn't recognize it when your window changed with the soul's desire. You can visit this between without needing to be in a place where the line is thin."

"What does that do for me?"

"You'll see in the years to come. It'll allow you to aid the dying and the living both. It's why the Sangre, Josiah, helped you. You're special, more than a Fenestra. More than a lovely young woman."

"But—"

"It's time for me to go to the Light." She gave me a gentle nod.

"What about your bones? They're not buried. They're not marked—"

"A Fenestra who goes through a Fenestra is never lost. Did you forget? I do not need to be buried. We move on when we're ready; now you're ready for me to go. It's not the physical a soul is trapped by; it's the emotion. You weren't ready for me to leave you, so I didn't."

"Roshana's wounds?" I asked, confused.

"Guilt, fear, terror. She'll be healed of them when Juliet frees her. That's why they say forgiveness is the ultimate gift, why karma is so important to our friends."

"The Woodsmen?"

"We didn't have them in Revelation. Too small a town, too quiet a life in my later years maybe. They'll continue to aid you. Help you find more Fenestra, teach your gifts and your truths."

I nodded. "But how do I stop the Nocti today?"

I heard a man's voice call down the hallway. *Charles?*

"It's time for me to go. You've learned all I can teach you. And you've taught me."

"What? How?"

"You've reminded me of what love that's just starting out can promise to the world. Cherish Tens, let him treat you like the precious gift you are. Be strong for each other. The battle is only beginning. You can live on the tangible plane and still help souls, without skipping a beat. You are on your way.

"But, Auntie—"

"1-4-3."

I blinked and found myself staring at the water of the lake. "I love you too."

"*Tens? You know how to swim, right?*"

"*Sergio is coming right at us.*"

"*What?*" I lifted my eyes and met Sergio's fearful, troubled gaze.

CHAPTER 56
Juliet

I saw flashes of light moving toward the infield. I wondered if my dad was dispatching Nocti as he came across them or if there was lightning on the ground. *The words my dad have such a delicious sound.*

"What now?" Fara asked.

The wind yanked at our clothes and I felt the heat from the roof through the soles of my shoes. I tasted cranberry sauce, Yorkshire pudding, pho, and rocky road fudge on my tongue. *There are victims already today.*

I reached out and took her hand. "We can't make it to the infield to help Meridian, can we?"

"Not unless you can fly now too?" Fara joked. "But we don't have to be down there, you know."

I turned to her. "You're right." I'd called the firefly, the lightning. I'd asked the tree to bend. She needed energy and I could call it.

Fara faced across the track, her body positioned toward the straightaway of turns two and three, the far side of the complex. She started chanting. I recognized the words from confronting Ms. Asura.

I tasted the soul dust of generations who visited this place, from corn cakes to catfish to short ribs to peanuts.

I let my eyes unfocus and relax; I saw with my heart, the way Faye saw our light. I saw my mother's smile, felt her arms, tasted her joys and heard her voice singing to me:

"When I die, hallelujahs hand in hand,
I'll fly away
Home to family evermore,
You'll fly away
Set your heart free,
Leave the pain behind,
We'll fly away
Down the creek we will float
When we're Light
Hallelujahs fly away."

I began humming the tune as I remembered Kirian bringing me rosewater pastels he stole from one of the DG nurses because he knew I hungered for new flavors, of him giving me pretty fossils he collected, of crowning my head with daisy rings and planning a fantastic future with me. I let the pain of his betrayal go. I let the wind carry it away.

I thought of Mistress's anger and the beatings I took, but stood taller instead of hunching in, because I survived and I was fiercer for it. I opened the fist of those memories, shoving them away into the wind.

I heard Bodie's giggle as he tried to swing from the branches of my tree into the deep glen of the Wildcat creek last summer. I knew he and Sema both were healing, making s'mores by wood fire and running after fireflies, seeking their secrets. I had no words of gratitude to Joi for taking them in and giving them the family and future I hoped for.

I thought of the last patients at DG, Enid and her sister Glee, whose frailty was only of body and not of soul. I smiled in memory of their bond and squeezed Fara's hand because I knew that feeling now. I knew what to accept and what to give.

I smiled, seeing Tony run toward me after the tornado, his embrace of all my wounds, his acceptance of the little I was able to give him in return. His anxious interior decorating that gave me a home and a bedroom like the ones I dreamed about in my early days of Dunklebarger, of pink and sparkles and cotton candy. Who stayed with my mother's remains because he knew without asking I couldn't leave her again, not alone, not there. He taught me that faith was tangible and touchable.

Meridian, who was out there among the worst of darkness, battling for people she would never know and who, if she succeeded, would never know exactly what could have happened. She who searched for me and never gave up, even when I most wanted her to.

Bales, whose devotion to Nelli cost him his life. Who gave me lavender and his grandmother's recipe for short-bread because he heard I liked food. The way he gazed at Nelli when she wasn't looking was the expression I hoped someday was turned in my direction by a man even half as steady and good.

I felt Fara's hand in mine and glanced over at her. With eyes closed, fervently calling for Light and Good, she looked like the heroines in action films Tens made me watch as part of my education about the real world. With her funky hair, metal, leather, and affinity for black anything, I knew the heart under that kick-ass shell would always have my back, whether I liked it or not.

I thought of Faye and Gus, who gave love, before and after life, faces to see and hands to hold. *How much love can two people share in one lifetime, in a single exchange of powerful words?* Immeasurable.

I turned back to the stands, thinking only of the joy of life and love and light. I sang my mother's song low and under my breath, but I watched the crowds of people stand. As if with the engines shutting down, the noises dropping away, the solemnity of the day changed. Black, yellow, and red flags were flown from the tower over the finish line.

I felt them begin to pray, to who or what I didn't know, didn't care. I knew they wished for hope that Smith would walk out of the fire alive and well.

I kept singing and calling for Light, along with Fara, as a geyser rocketed into the sky.

CHAPTER 57

Behind us, the Nocti leader shouted, "Where is my successor? We're running out of time! He should be here by now."

Tens grabbed Sergio and knocked his feet out from under him. For a second I almost felt sorry for the little boy behind his eyes.

"Get out of here," Sergio gasped.

Tens dragged him back between truck tires. "Keep focused, Merry."

I could hear them struggle behind me.

My attention was completely fixated on the stream of water flowing out of the pipe. I knew if Rumi was right, then there was pressure forcing the water to the surface, lots of untapped energy. *If I can call it, maybe it'll short out the electrical system, the generators.*

"They're emptying the stands and evacuating people. It's too late," Tens said.

"You don't have time to beat me up. Get out of here," Sergio pleaded. "I can't stop it. I'm dead anyway."

I saw yellow shirts and uniformed policemen moving among the crowds, which slowly began to disperse. *Are there Woodsmen up there holding vigil too?*

The water's steady trickle flowed like an open faucet. The brick wall around the pipe cracked, water finding weaknesses and flowing through.

Call the elements and the energy. I repeated Auntie's declaration over and over again.

I asked the water to surface. The level of the lake rose dramatically, as if filling from underneath as well.

Tens swore, but I didn't break my concentration. "What's the plan?" Tens growled.

"I don't know. I swear. I think that dude is retiring," Sergio muttered.

"You don't know much, do you?"

Sergio sniveled, "I just wanted to find my brother, I swear. Not kill people. Here, take my computer. There's a backup, but take it."

I saw a knife flash in the sunlight and worried until I realized Tens wielded it.

I asked the water to keep coming.

A golf cart sped toward us. The man driving seemed possessed and determined. I froze for a moment before I recognized Timothy in the seat next to him, holding on as they bumped and swerved as fast as they could.

I shivered. The heat of the sun seemed to turn on inside me. My fingertips burned and itched.

The driver strode off the cart before it was even stopped. He didn't say anything but waded into Tens and Sergio, backhanding the younger man with the strength of ten men. I heard the reverberation and the smack. He kept walking toward the Nocti in the trailer.

"You!" the leader called to him.

Tens grabbed the computer, tossed it into the lake, then scooted back to me. "Who's that?"

"No idea," I muttered as the water pushed over the banks. It lapped at the computer and the tires of the trucks parked at the edge, waving over the cords and reels of wire along the ground connecting the trailers.

Sergio slunk away out of my sight. "Tens—"

"Let him go. I'll find him later," Tens answered me. "What do you want me to do?"

Timothy motioned to us. I squinted at the well. I pictured a great gush of water surfacing. Carrying the Nocti away, shorting out their equipment, washing this place free of their poison.

"Enough!" the driver shouted, raising his hands, light already flowing from his fingertips.

"He's one of us," Tens said. "Don't stop." He picked me up and carried me to the golf cart.

Water, pour forth, out of the dark and into the light.

"That's our friend Argy," Timothy informed us.

"Juliet's father?" Tens put the pieces together immediately.

I swallowed back questions, my eyes never leaving the lake, which was now twice its size and growing fast.

I saw the brick wall crumble completely, the pipe became a projectile, and an explosion of water filled the air as a blinding light told me Argy enlightened the Nocti near him. Saturated, Tens drove near Argy, who jumped onto the side of the cart and we dodged fleeing spectators and sympathizers ahead of the massive wave.

Behind us water poured up, pushed up hundreds of feet into the air; it fell like a heavy rain. Trucks began to float; circuits shorted out. The electricity everywhere at the track blacked out. The screams we heard weren't of fear but of frustration, of thwarted evil.

We drove onto the track, through turn four and toward the tunnel that would lead us to the outside. I saw the finish line, the line of bricks the winners kiss, and knew that today we'd won. The war wasn't over, but this victory belonged to us.

CHAPTER 58
Juliet

It seemed as if the water was the last bit of excitement officials needed before they hurried to get people away from the track. People threw around the words *terrorism* and *terrorist* as they joined the throngs. They passed along pieces of gossip in loud voices, faster than the speed of light.

"We have to find my dad," I urged Fara as we were swallowed into the hordes of exiting people.

"He knows where to find you. He's fine. I'm sure of it." Fara tugged me along, and even though I knew she was right, I hated leaving before we knew everyone was safe.

"I don't remember where we parked," I said.

"Doesn't matter. Argy has the keys. We'll hitch."

"We'll what?" I asked as she started to jog. We dodged around people, who stumbled, shocked and shaken, into the neighborhoods around the track, as we headed toward the massive parking lots in the distance.

I stopped questioning Fara as she got us from place to place and finally into a cab that could take us home. "Wait." I didn't want to go back to the condo. "Let's go see Faye."

"You sure?"

"Yes, Gus'll know what's going on and I think it's time."

Fara changed her instructions and chatted with the cabbie, who'd listened to everything until the radio signals failed. She acted like this was a normal day.

I hope this isn't our normal. I don't have the stamina for it. I yawned, closing my eyes in the sway of the car and adrenaline crash.

"Juliet? Wake up." Fara shook me.

"I slept?" I asked. *No nightmares? No tornadoes? No Kirian pleading with me?* I felt rested for the first time in, well, ever.

"Yes, can you handle souls or should we wait?" she asked.

"I'm okay." I meant it.

We walked into the hospice, and several nurses smiled

at us, but it was Delia who exclaimed and ran over. "You two look terrible. Are you okay?"

I smiled. "We're good."

She lowered her voice. "The track still standing? Gus told me to pray all day and I have been. My whole prayer chain."

"Thanks. The track is there but we don't know how many casualties there are yet."

Her face closed. "I'm sure there are less than there would have been. You did your best, right? We haven't had any deaths here today, so no souls to worry about." She opened a door. "This is the staff locker room. Clean scrubs are in the cabinets—use anything in my cubby and get cleaned up. Faye and Gus need you."

I cleared my throat. "Thank you, Delia."

She nodded and left. It wasn't until I saw our skin scrubbed clean that I realized how filthy we were.

By the time we walked into Faye's room, Gus and Rumi were there, as were Meridian and Tens.

I hugged Meridian as if I hadn't seen her in lifetimes. It felt as if we hugged for the first time. I finally understood so many of the conversations she'd tried to have with me, so many opportunities she presented that I shied away from. "Were you behind the geyser?" I asked.

She nodded. "You helped, though. If you hadn't figured out how to move energy through you, I never would have even known to try."

I grinned.

"Your dad showed up and killed the Nocti leader."

She turned to Rumi. "I'm sorry, Rumi. I don't know how to tell you this, but you were right about your uncle."

Even though Meridian's tone was soft and apologetic, I watched Rumi crumble under her words.

She continued. "But without your help, we never would have known to look for the well or how to use it. And the Woodsmen used the Spirit Stones to spot the Nocti." She embraced him. "You have nothing to be ashamed about."

"Ah, lass, you're kind, but my heart aches nonetheless."

Gus reached out and touched Rumi's back. To me he said, "Tony called from the hospital in Crawfordsville. He's going to be fine and they've recovered the remains as well. A friend was headed over to pick him up; he'll be here soon."

"You found your mom?" Meridian asked. "You have to tell us everything. Your father is debriefing the Woodsmen and coming to your condo as soon as he can."

Fara collapsed onto the couch and said, "Is anyone else hungry?"

Tens high-fived her, while Meridian and I shook our heads in laughter. Over pizza and warm cookies, we traded stories.

It wasn't until Meridian began talking about what they saw when leaving the track and the amount of water flooding the area that I realized Faye and I sat listening to Meridian at my kitchen table.

On the other side of the window was a working farm

at the height of summer. Corn grew taller than Rumi. Animals fragrantly and loudly lived near the big farmhouse. Out in front was a picnic table covered with a whole roast pig, piles of sweet white corn, green tomatoes, and hunks of watermelon.

"Hello, Juliet," Faye said. "You've had quite the full week, haven't you?"

Among the guests gathering were my mother and Kirian. They waved to us. I barely recognized my mother; she was young, beautiful, and voluptuous like a healthy girl my age should be.

"It's a lot," I said, waving back to them.

In a role reversal, Faye bent down and kissed my cheek, much like the many times I'd kissed hers these last weeks of her illness. "What shall I tell your mother? Anything?"

I stuttered. So many things sped through my mind. "Please tell her she'll be buried soon. As soon as I can, so she can move on." I paused. "And I love her."

"Let me tell you something from a mother's perspective." Faye stepped closer to the window. "We always watch over the children we love. Buried or not, we never leave them. Never worry that she wants to be anywhere else."

I nodded.

"And you, tell Gus to live long and happily and that his wife will greet him?" Faye asked me.

"Yes, of course."

She slipped into the cornfield and ran toward her

home, the screen door banging open as crowds flew down the porch steps, running toward her.

My mother waved again, took Kirian's hand, and they headed toward a glorious sunset on the horizon. Their forms faded until all I saw were the myriad colors of perfect light.

I closed my eyes.

CHAPTER 59

As hard as it was to admit, Faye's transition to the Light was a relief for everyone. *Her most of all.* Gus kicked us out late, told us to go home and sleep for a week. I didn't have the energy to argue with him. Too much.

Freshly showered, with aloe caking my blistered sunburn, I lay in our bed pestering Tens telepathically.

"Say something else. Say something else."

"Can we stop now?" Tens answered me.

"Are you annoyed?"

Speaking out loud, he said, "How can you tell?" He groaned, rolling toward me. He pulled me close, snuggling a thigh between my legs and my head onto his chest.

I sighed. *I love this man more each day. How is that possible?*

"Because it's true," Tens answered.

I gasped. "That wasn't for you to hear."

"Then don't say it." He chuckled. "It's not like I listen in on purpose."

"What? So now we have to practice not hearing each other?"

"Tomorrow. Please tomorrow. Or the next day, or next year." Tens rubbed my arms with his palms.

"What if it goes away?" I asked.

"It's not going to."

The clock flipped to three a.m. but I was too jazzed to sleep. *We did it. Spanked Nocti ass.*

Eddie Smith died in the crash with the bunny. There were rumors of bribes, pills, and gambling, but I guessed we'd never really know why he'd agreed. Race officials vowed to have all the water damage cleaned up in time for the next race. The race results were frozen with the last yellow flag. People grumbled about it ending under caution, but it was the best-case scenario I knew.

Tens and I hadn't yet talked about the other sidelight of our telepathy. I hadn't told him yet—was waiting for the right time, if ever there was one to tell him—that while we were able to communicate without words, I also saw his whole life as if it were my own. The parts he didn't want me to know—the ugly pieces of surviving and living on the streets—until he got to Revelation. I knew he'd rather those memories stayed hidden for all time. "I know about your life," I said.

He nodded. "I know. I've remembered more about my mother and what happened because of you."

I nodded and touched his cheek. "I love you. All of you." I lifted his chin and made eye contact. "I mean it. I love you even more now, knowing everything about you. All those experiences made you who you are. Let me love you the way you love me, okay?"

He nodded. "It all came back to me too. I remember the mounds, the trip, my mother. My father. I don't know what it all means, though."

"We'll figure it out together." Because that's what we did. "We don't have to talk about it until you're ready."

"Good, because I'm very tired. But we'll talk; we have time." Tens kissed me lightly on the lips, shifting against me. "You're thinking too hard."

"I am not hard." I giggled. *He is.* "I thought you were sleepy."

"I am, but you smell good."

We'd promised each other to wait until we were both ready, until there would be no regrets, no rethinks, no wishes for do-overs. "Can you read my mind now?" *"I want to make love with you."*

"Are you sure?"

"More than anything."

His touch lost the hesitation, the holdback, that I'd sensed he had difficulty maintaining. As I pushed his shirt up off his shoulders and neck, he lifted my tank top. His mouth trailed kisses down my chest until his lips locked on my nipple. I lost track of where his hands caressed, where mine explored.

I loved touching him, feeling the textures, the roughness of his body hair over dense muscle and velvety soft skin. I loved listening to him catch his breath, to his involuntary moans of pleasure. I loved the freedom he touched me with, as if he could explore me all day and never tire or grow bored.

I felt an urgency, a pull toward the unknown, beyond the line we'd drawn in the sand months ago. When he slipped on the condom and settled back on top of me, there was a moment of the unknown that scared me.

"Okay?"

I nodded. Feeling him press inside, I lifted my hips and wrapped my legs around him. After the initial discomfort, I smiled. *"You're in me. I like you inside me."*

He laughed against my lips. *"Good thing, cuz I like being here."*

As we learned our rhythm, it was just us, just a girl and a boy in love. Just Meridian and Tens.

"I would have come looking for you, you know," he whispered against my ear. "If you weren't on that bus, or a plane, or in a cab, I would have found you."

"I know. You're my home."

As we fell asleep tucked around each other, fingers

entwined, sweat sticking our bodies together, I heard Custos pad into the cottage living room and take her place on the couch instead of on the bed with us. *"Maybe she likes me now?"*

"Nah, she's just too tired to fight you for your side of the bed tonight," Tens answered me.

MEMORIAL DAY
ONE YEAR LATER

Cars lined the pathways of Riverside Cemetery. I'd learned from Rumi Memorial Day in Indiana meant gathering with the departed. Around us, families dug holes to plant fresh peony plants or laid vases of cut flowers.

Row upon row of American flags marked the fallen, from the Civil War to present day. Sparkling white rectangles and crosses perched starkly against the green of the freshly sheared grass. Today there were no violets. Only red, white, and blue. Bunting swagged over monuments and mausoleums.

Peony bushes fell to the ground, their arms unable to hold up the fragrant bounty of their heads. Tulip trees offered golden cups toward the heavens. The buzz of bees, call of birds, and lazy dips of yellow swallowtail butterflies reminded us this wasn't a place of death but of celebrating life.

We spread blankets on the earth and unpacked a picnic lunch from Shapiro's deli. Thick, juicy Reuben sandwiches, potato and macaroni salads, veggies and chips. I opened a grape soda and leaned my back against a walnut tree. We were all accounted for: Tens, Juliet, Fara, Rumi, Tony, Argy, Gus, Nelli, Joi, and Robert. Bodie and Sema were taller with gap-toothed smiles and new interests.

Rumi recited verses from James Whitcomb Riley's "Silent Victors" as he cleaned and tended the gravestones.

"And gild with brighter glory every tomb
We decorate to-day."

All around us, people scrubbed headstones and laid flowers in the arms of stone angels and at the feet of lambs. Several Woodsmen and their families joined us, laying rosemary at the Fenestra and Protector graves. We loved extra attention on those of our fallen family. Kirian and Roshana were laid to rest side by side. Neither stone was changed to that of a Fenestra or Protector, though Rumi's Spirit Stones hung from each grave marker.

Bales and Faye were also together with a spot next to Faye for Gus when the time came. Gus and Nelli talked quietly; they were no longer just uncle and niece but the living halves of couples. They planted gardens of summer flowers and scrubbed the stones, pink granite for Faye and moonstone for Bales. I didn't know when Nelli would ever move on and let that kind of love into her life again, but the baby she held gave us all hope that Bales's last gift would bring her a lifetime of joy.

After dessert with Juliet's fruit tarts decorated like flags, Rumi passed out bottles of bubble juice and wands. Bodie and Sema started up a game of tag, involving a lot of squealing and fewer rules.

Auntie's grave was marked but empty. I didn't need to bury her to let her go. Since the race, we hadn't seen any of our loved ones at the window. I hoped it was because we didn't need them as we used to.

An official remembrance program with military bands and speeches started over the hill at the Gothic Chapel. We stayed nearer our loved ones but listened, leaning against each other in all the ways that mattered. I looked around the family we'd cobbled together and couldn't help but feel as if everything worked out as it needed to. Even the horrid, painful parts served a purpose.

Juliet watched her father with shining eyes. I saw Argy sketching Roshana as he tried to explain a funny story about the first time they snuck out to see a movie called *Ghost*. It was their first date. Juliet confided last winter she was drawn inexplicably to water; Argy planned to take her to see the Pacific Ocean next month.

Death changes things.

Tens and I were moving forward in our studies and teaching Woodsmen what we knew about Fenestra and Protectors. I spent time each week at the hospice with Delia, having a cup of tea and greeting the newly deceased as they departed.

Rumi's business boomed like his voice and he'd taken to selling Tens's wood carvings, including little cars and wolf-dogs.

Word reached us last week that an elder Fenestra in Rhode Island wanted us to visit to help her transition. I finally looked ahead, not in fear but in love and life. I opened a blank book and picked up my pen,

Dear Future Fenestra,

    I'm going to do things differently. While I don't mind sounding like a fortune cookie, you won't think I'm very useful as a guide. So I'm going to start at the beginning of my story and someday I'll get Juliet to share hers. Just know this is possible. You can do this and we've got your back. Ready?

    The first creatures to seek me were the insects; my parents cleaned the bassinet free of dead ants the morning after they brought me home from the hospital. My first word was "dead."

"Supergirl, look up!" Tens yelled, and I put down my pen. Above our heads, a giant, vivid rainbow appeared, stretching from one side of the sky to the other. We stood and clustered together to get a better look. The bright sunny day left no indication as to how or why a rainbow appeared. As we watched, pink petals fluttered from the sky, covering us all. A light breeze danced them around us happily.

No trees around us were blooming. None were pink.

Rumi raised astonished eyes, and even Bodie and Sema stopped running around to stand in the swirl of petals. *Faye? Auntie?* I smiled and blew a kiss to heaven.

In the distance, the rainbow doubled, then tripled, each color level brighter than the last.

faye's red velvet cake with cream cheese frosting

Ingredients

Cake:
1/2 cup unsalted butter, softened
1-1/2 cups sugar
2 large eggs
1 teaspoon vanilla
4 oz. bittersweet chocolate, melted
2 tablespoons liquid red food coloring
2/3 cup buttermilk
1/3 cup Coco López cream of coconut (use the solids; reserve liquid for frosting)
2-1/2 cups cake flour, sifted
1/4 cup Dutch-process cocoa powder
1/2 teaspoon salt
1 teaspoon white vinegar
1 teaspoon baking soda

Frosting:
2 8-oz. blocks of cream cheese
1 teaspoon vanilla
2 cups powdered sugar
1 cup cold heavy whipping cream
1/2 cup Coco López cream of coconut liquid

Preheat the oven to 350°F and place a rack in the center of the oven. Grease two 9-inch cake pans and line with parchment paper.

Cream the butter with an electric mixer; add the sugar and beat until fluffy. Add the eggs one at a time, beating well after each addition. Add the vanilla and the melted chocolate and beat well.

In a small cup mix the red food coloring with the buttermilk and the cream of coconut. Use only the solids in the cream of coconut can (they look like bacon fat) if possible, saving the liquid for the frosting.

In a separate bowl, combine the flour, the cocoa powder, and the salt. Add the dry ingredients gradually to the butter mixture, alternating with the buttermilk mixture.

In a small cup mix the vinegar and the baking soda—it will fizz. Quickly fold into the batter.

Divide the batter between the prepared pans. Bake for 20 to 25 minutes, or until a toothpick inserted in the center comes out clean. The cakes will pull away from the sides of the pan, and if touched gently should spring back.

Once the cakes have completely cooled in the pans, refrigerate them for an hour or more. This makes frosting the cake easier.

For the frosting, beat the cream cheese until smooth. Add the vanilla and the powdered sugar and beat until smooth. Gradually add the whipping cream and the cream of coconut liquid until the frosting is thick enough to spread. It should be the consistency of sour cream.

Add more sugar, about a teaspoon at a time, if needed for consistency.

To assemble the cake, spoon frosting onto the bottom layer and spread evenly. Top with the second layer and cover the top and sides of the cake with the remaining frosting. Garnish with toasted coconut flakes if desired.

Refrigerate if not serving immediately.

acknowledgments

My health proves complicated and challenging even in the best of times, but I'm blessed to have the most compassionate old-school physician in Dr. Heidi Rendall in my corner. Dr. Jean Dydell, who was ready to do whatever it took to help last December. And Dr. Michael Towbin, who removed my appendix and gave me my life back. I owe my ability to write this book to you all.

Marty and Tom Davis of Crown Hill Cemetery and Crown Hill Heritage Foundation proved invaluable. Their knowledge and willingness to answer my many questions about the cemetery are much appreciated. If you are in Indianapolis be sure to stop by and take part in one of the many events and public tours. Crown Hill is truly one of the most beautiful cemeteries in the country. Visit CrownHill.org for information.

This isn't a world in which projects can keep moving at the right speed without technology, so special thanks must go out to Gail LaForest and Bruce Alexander for keeping my tech happy.

To my beta readers, who fielded "what do you think about's" and helped work out plot points and other questions—thank you, especially to Trudi Trueit, Jen Greyson, Lisa Bjork, and Sarah Diers.

I have to give special thanks to my fans—many of whom share with me music recommendations for my writing sound tracks. I've found perfect songs because of you. Thank you for reading, for sharing, and for spreading the word. I couldn't do this without your support!

Picking Meridian's favorite grape soda was no easy feat, and I must acknowledge my panel of experts: the LaMars, the Wicks, Steve and Laura Cooper, Rachel Kizer.

Michael of Historic Indiana Ghost Tours at UnseenPress .com provided a fantastic tour of Westfield, Indiana, with tidbits that proved inspirational for this book. I give a hearty recommendation for a tour if you're in Indiana. Many thanks as well to Amy Kraft and Tiffany Obrecht for joining me in this ghostly research trip.

I adore the Indianapolis 500. It's a family tradition that goes back generations. Many thanks to Kate, Mark, and Tim LaMar for joining me at Qualifying/Pole Day. Sarah Lamar continues to be a much-loved contributor to my career—love you, girl!

Memorial Day is only one day, but the sacrifices made by our men and women in uniform are made 365/24/7. They serve our nation while I exercise my freedom of speech—you make my life possible and I am forever grateful. A special acknowledgment must be given to the children of those who've died, especially Pilot Bryan Nichols's son and the thirty-two children left behind when the helicopter went down in Afghanistan. Know that your parents are as proud of you as we are of them. I will never forget.

Barney and Beth Wick were wonderful hosts for my May research trip. They were patient and loving with my odd requests, the window-ruining plot board, and my hail damage panic. This book's authenticity was possible because of you.

Finally, to my mother, who passed down our family's traditions as both Indy 500 race spectators and Memorial Day grave tenders. Cemeteries will forever be places where I hear stories in the silence because our family doesn't fear death. I am grateful for that lesson and so many others. Mom, I thank you for your unyielding love and support, and for having a new favorite book every time I ask.

FIND OUT HOW IT ALL BEGAN
WITH *MERIDIAN*!
CONTINUE WITH *WILDCAT FIREFLIES*,
THE SECOND MERIDIAN NOVEL.

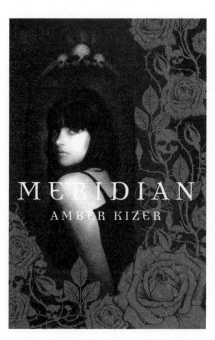
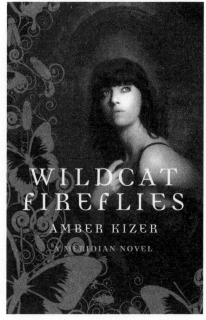

Amber Kizer believes in living every day as if it's her last. She eats dessert first, buys flowers for no reason, and says I love you (1-4-3) loudly and often. Her health challenges have taught her to take nothing for granted and to live in the moment. Amber's passions include baking, quilting, gardening, music, reading, playing Wii, and scented candles—and she feels no shame in admitting that she enjoys reality TV. Insatiable curiosity and intense motivation keep her on her toes, as does a true love of story. With an ever-changing eclectic mix of two- and four-legged family and friends, Amber lives north of Seattle on an island. Her books have been translated into several languages and have won acclaim for their complexity and authenticity. She loves to hear from readers and can be found at AmberKizer.com, MeridianSozu.com, and OneButtCheek.com.